A SWORD IN THE SUN

Book 2 of the Nightcraft Quartet

Shannon Page

A SWORD IN THE SUN:
BOOK TWO OF THE NIGHTCRAFT QUARTET

Published by Outland Entertainment LLC
3119 Gillham Road
Kansas City, MO 64109

Founder/Creative Director: Jeremy D. Mohler
Editor-in-Chief: Alana Joli Abbott
Senior Editor: Gwendolyn Nix

ISBN: 978-0-9963997-5-3
Worldwide Rights
Created in the United States of America

Editor: Alana Joli Abbott
Cover Illustration: Matthew Warlick
Cover Design: Jeremy D. Mohler
Interior Layout: Mikael Brodu

Printed and bound in the United States of America.

PRAISE FOR SHANNON PAGE'S THE QUEEN AND THE TOWER

"Witches and warlocks and covens... Oh, my. An absolute page-turner filled with mystery, spells, and romance. Not to be missed!"

-Barb Hendee, *New York Times* best-selling
co-author of the Noble Dead Saga

"Witchcraft and science, friendship and heartache, love and deceit: Shannon Page takes the essential threads of urban fantasy and weaves something totally new, and totally delightful."

-Chaz Brenchley, award-winning author of *Bitter Waters*

"Page conjures contemporary San Francisco witches and their nightcraft with a deliciously sexy plot--new, unsettling, delightful."

-Karen G. Berry, author of *The Iris Files:*
Notes from a Desperate Housewife

"Page's relatable characters invite readers into a fully-fleshed world of witches, warlocks, and the science of magic. A must read for lovers of Ilona Andrews's *Innkeeper Chronicles*."

-Alana Joli Abbott, co-editor of *Where the Veil Is Thin*

For Karen
Who has always believed in Callie
And in me.

— CHAPTER ONE —

When one's world has been torn apart, it is natural to reel a bit, unsteady. To search for meaning.

To try to figure out who—if anyone—one can trust.

I stood over my kitchen stove, brewing a low-grade strength potion. Nothing much more than vitamins, really, except formulated for my witchly constitution. And safe for the daughter growing inside me...no matter that her father was human.

Petrana, my rebuilt golem, stood beside me. Watching. Learning.

"Bring me the mortar, would you?" I asked her.

My golem stepped lightly over to the far end of the counter, picked up the heavy stone bowl, and carried it back to the stove. "Here you are, Mistress Callie."

"Thanks." The scent of fresh ground rosemary wafted from the bowl. Petrana had done a good job with it. I reached in and picked out a pinch of the herb, scattering it over the bubbling potion. Its fragrance melded with the lemon balm, verbena, and goat's milk already brewing.

The cursed ring on my right hand glowed almost imperceptibly. It was thanks to that, in a roundabout way, that my golem was so much improved from her former huge, shambling presence. We had tried to remove this ring that Gregorio Andromedus, my mentor, had tricked me into putting on. The resultant magical rebound had blown Petrana half apart, and my whole hand had stung and ached for days.

But I'd put her body back together, reshaping her in the process, with new-sanctified mud from my backyard. Then I'd reanimated her spirit with my magic—taking care to keep any influence from the ring out of the effort.

I hoped that was what I'd done, anyway.

Petrana was lithe now, more woman-shaped, her limbs much better articulated. You would never mistake her for a human, not without a glamour over her, but it pleased me to watch her function. It even seemed that her mind was sharper. Of course, that had been happening anyway, as she lived with me and did tasks for me, as I taught her and trained her. It was just more obvious now.

"What does the rosemary do?" she asked. Even her voice had a bit of inflection.

Taking the initiative to ask a question was another improvement.

I turned to her and smiled, brushing a strand of hair out of my eyes. I had spelled it to keep it tame and tidy and out of the way, but it was behaving worse and worse as my pregnancy progressed. As if it knew I didn't dare use strong magic on myself. "It's an antioxidant and strengthens the energetic channels of magic," I explained. "But I can take only small amounts: since my child has human parentage as well as witchkind, it can be toxic to her in larger doses."

"I see." Petrana nodded. "It might improve the flavor as well?"

"Sure," I said, stirring, "but that's a secondary concern. I'll be taking only a few swallows of this at a time."

"I see."

After I'd stirred the potion fifteen times clockwise and seventeen times counterclockwise, I handed the wooden spoon to Petrana. "You take over for a bit," I said, stepping back from the stove and rubbing my aching lower back. "No need to count, now. And I need to sit down."

"Do you need me to get you anything, Mistress Callie?"

"No, no. Just work on the potion, thanks." I pulled out a kitchen chair and eased myself down into it, grateful to be off my feet. I wasn't *that* pregnant, but I was far enough along to feel the changes in my body. And my energy.

Of course, grief and betrayal played a role in my energy level as well…

I pushed the thought aside. Wallowing in my emotions wasn't solving anything.

The trouble was, I didn't know what *would* solve anything. I had been so jazzed when I'd thought of quietly searching for Gregorio's "two other instances," which could refer to two other witches who'd had children by humans, or the witch-human hybrid children themselves. But my initial excitement had quickly worn off as my research turned up nothing.

I had a good-sized supply of witchkind DNA samples (well, blood) upstairs in my lab from my experiments to find the "infectious agent" that had killed my best friend Logan and sickened several other witches. Of course, the culprit had turned out not to be an infection at all, but essence thievery by a rogue warlock. Nevertheless, I hadn't disposed of the samples, so I'd gone through them carefully over the last week, searching for any traces of human DNA.

And found nothing.

It was entirely possible the instances were not in our community. The trouble was, I couldn't ask Gregorio about it. I couldn't begin to let him suspect that I was doing anything other than complying with his orders to be a good, well-behaved witch, keeping my astonishing secret from all of witchkind.

It rankled me. I'd never been good at being well-behaved.

I didn't see any way out of it, though—except for finding others in my position. Even then, it was a long shot. Gregorio Andromedus was the leader of our Elders, an ancient and insanely powerful warlock. I, on the other hand, was a young witch, barely forty-five—the equivalent of early twenties by human reckoning. Not only that, I was the junior-most member of my coven. A coven I'd alienated even before I'd decided to move out of the communal house to live on my own for a while—so I could breathe, live more freely...and see more of the human man I'd been dating.

No, I had to work quietly if I was to have any hope of learning what I sought to know, of finding allies to recruit. And I had to keep pretending to be meek and compliant all the while, even as my mind was reeling with the revelation of my daughter's parentage.

Witches aren't supposed to be fertile with humans. We're barely fertile with each other; our kind has been so winnowed—you might even say inbred—over the millennia as our ancestors selected for magical strength and longevity. In the process, the natural fertility of our humankind forebears was heavily compromised. But if we could in fact make babies with humans...as this daughter in my belly made plain...well, it would be game-changing.

"I believe it is quickening," Petrana said from the stove.

I looked up, momentarily startled, then realized she was talking about the potion. Not my daughter. "Good," I said, and flicked my fingers toward her, turning the fire under the cauldron to its lowest setting. "We'll let it hang on the edge there for another twenty-two minutes, and then turn it off. In an hour, we can bottle it."

"Yes, Mistress Callie."

"You can stop stirring, too," I added.

She set the spoon down and stepped away from the stove, moving to take her usual position standing near the wall at the back of the kitchen. I'd tried to get her to act more like a human when she wasn't at some task, but had eventually given up. Now I just pretended she was the magical equivalent of those little round household robots humans buy to vacuum their floors. The ones that freak out cats.

As if I had summoned her with my thought, black-and-white Elnor prowled into the room, whiskers and nose twitching inquisitively. "It's just potion," I told her, though I knew the brew wasn't likely to smell like food to her. "To get me through this evening."

My familiar blinked her yellow eyes at me. Her nose was still working as she finished determining for herself whether the concoction was of interest. Who knew, maybe it would be. She did like goat's milk.

"Would you like me to open her a can of tuna?" Petrana asked.

I heaved myself to my feet. "No thank you, I'll get it." I needed to keep doing things for myself, even if I just felt tired all the time, just wanted to curl up and take a nap. This was only going to get worse and worse as the baby's time came nearer. Indulging myself now was no way to keep me strong.

Elnor twined around my ankles as I walked to the cabinet over the sink. "Careful, milknose," I said to her. "If you knock me down, there will be..." I left my usual faux-threat unspoken. As Petrana had just made clear, there *would* be someone to feed the greedy cat.

Why didn't this make me feel less alone?

Fortified with my new potion and dressed in comfortable, loose-fitting clothes, I headed to the coven house a little before five o'clock, Elnor under my arm. The front gate was ajar, which was strange. I closed it behind me and set the binding spell before standing quietly in the front yard, searching for any signs of intruders. Elnor twitched to be let down, so I set her on the ground. She paced around the yard, sniffing. When she came back to me with the cat equivalent of a shrug, I said, "Huh. All right, then."

I walked up the front steps and let us inside. A few cats, familiars of my coven sisters, sniffed at my heels, then at Elnor. I greeted them and reset the door spell before taking a deep breath and heading farther in.

I was glad to find only Sirianna in the kitchen. She, at least, didn't resent me, disapprove of me, or find me inscrutably weird. "Hey," I said as I dropped my bag on the window seat.

She stood at the stove, stirring something that didn't seem like dinner. "Callie, hi!" She pulled me into a side hug and gave me a quick kiss on the cheek before her hair could embrace me, then returned to the kettle.

"Is Leonora here?" I asked, once I'd gotten free.

"I don't think so, but I've been here all afternoon. I'm not sure."

Even as she was answering, I peered through the kitchen wall to the small converted sunporch that was our coven mother's study. It was empty—well, except for Logan's body. I widened my vision, searching the house for Leonora's essence. Nothing but traces, the residue any living creature leaves in their dwelling. I pulled my sight back to the kitchen. "Nope."

"I don't know, then." Sirianna frowned, her face flushed. "Sorry."

I looked at my coven sister more carefully. "What's the matter?"

She sighed. "I just want to get this right for tonight! I've had to start it three times already. It keeps discomposing just when it's about to set."

My heart clutched with a pang of guilt. I forced my voice to be cheerful, light. *Everything is fine. Nothing is weird.* "Oh, you sweetheart! Is that for the naming?" I leaned over to sniff at the cauldron. It was a special tea, chock-full of divination herbs. It smelled nasty and would probably taste like pond slime, but that wasn't the issue. I took a deep breath, scanning the brew for anything that would harm a hybrid child. Fortunately, it seemed clear.

I needed a better way to take care of myself—and her—through this process. Blessed Mother, I wished I was not holding this ugly secret…

"Yes," Sirianna said, wrinkling her nose, "and it's driving me bats. But *you* shouldn't worry about it! Go on, relax, join the others. Leonora will be here soon, I'm sure. A few sisters have gotten started in the sitting room."

Of course they had. Pre-dinner cocktails were as obligatory to coven life as our midnight Circles. And yet another minefield.

"Okay," I chirped at her, trying for a genuine smile and managing something pretty close to it. I loved Sirianna, and I knew she loved me back. Though I'd have much rather hung out in the kitchen with her, my presence was probably distracting her as she tried to get the tricky brew to set. Her magic was far more tenuous than mine; her strengths lay in her grasp of history, her teaching skills, and her pure, kind heart.

So I hugged her and headed for the sitting room, where Flora and Peony were tatting doilies, their doddering cats stretched across their laps. "Hi, sisters," I said, finding a chair.

"Greetings," they both said, and scanned me from head to toe. Peony particularly scrutinized me for any signs of exhaustion, ill health, or low essence.

One thing I had learned right away: being a pregnant coven witch meant having twelve anxious mothers, no matter how else they felt about me.

Niad looked up from a leather easy chair by the window. Her ice-blond hair was pulled back into its usual tight bun; not a strand dared escape. "Oh, there you are." Well, eleven, anyway. Niad was never going to pretend to care about anything I did.

I gave her a weak smile anyway. Given our history, I didn't have to be faux-bubbly with her, which at least made things easier. "It's lovely to see you, Niad." I gave my words a measured amount of politeness.

"Likewise," she said, returning my tone exactly.

Flora returned to her tatting; Peony frowned at both of us before asking me, "What have you eaten today, Calendula Isadora? You look peaked."

"I feel fine," I said, too quickly. Flora's head rose again, and now both elder sisters were scrutinizing me once more. "I even took some strength potion just before I got here."

Peony's eyebrows arched. "What strength potion? Where did it come from?"

"I brewed it myself."

"Calendula!" Flora chided, setting her tatting down and starting to get up, annoying her cat.

I waved her back to her seat. "It was simple, easy, and I had help—" I blurted that last part out before I could stop myself. *Not helpful.*

"Help from whom?" Peony demanded.

I shook my head. "Just…Petrana."

Both witches sighed, and I was pretty sure I heard Niad stifling a snicker. "You know she uses your magic—" Flora started.

"Yes and no," I said, echoing their sigh as I resigned myself to having the battle after all. "She is animated via my magic, but she has a life force of her own, which regenerates without any input from me."

Peony shook her head and bit her lip; Flora continued to gaze sternly at me.

"Besides," I added, "it was the simplest potion ever, I promise. It wasn't any more strenuous than making soup."

"Goat's milk soup," Niad said with a laugh.

Our elder sisters both glanced at her and then turned their faces back to me. It was eerie how they did this. Even after all this time, I couldn't get used to it. They weren't twins, or even blood-related, but they had been coven sisters for nearly a hundred and fifty years. They were thick as thieves, rarely seen apart, voting in lock step on any item that required the counsel of the entire sisterhood. They even looked more alike every year, with their thin, beaky noses, upswept blue-black hair, and shapeless black dresses trimmed in the lace they were endlessly tatting.

"Pregnancy is the most sacred, and the most perilous, time in a witch's life," said Peony. A witch who had never been pregnant herself.

I nodded, so not wanting to have this argument yet again. "I understand." I tried to make my voice meek. *They really do care,* I told myself.

The front door opened just then, thank the Blessed Mother. I heard Leonora come in as the strong presence of her magical essence filled the house—the house of which she was lady and mistress. Elnor's ears perked up as she sensed the presence of Grieka, Leonora's familiar. Our coven mother must be returning from her regular Tuesday visits to other San Francisco covens.

Our conversation stopped as she swept through the first floor of the house, ensuring that everything was as it should be. Then she joined us in the sitting room, her ermine-rimmed robes brushing cats and doilies as she made her way to her usual chair. Today, her steel-gray hair was arranged in a multitude of small braids, which were then woven together in a complicated pattern pulled to the nape of her neck. I wondered who had done it for her, or if she'd just used magic; it was precise and beautiful. "Greetings, sisters," she said as Grieka settled on her ample lap. "Shall we have a libation before dinner?"

Though Leonora hadn't addressed anyone directly, Niad slowly rose to her feet and went to the tray of brilliantly colored bottles on the sideboard. She poured Leonora's Framboise, two glasses of Bénédictine for Flora and Peony, and an absinthe over cracked ice for herself. She turned to me. "A sherry for you, Callie?" The bottle was already in her hand, poised over a cordial glass.

"No thanks, not right now."

She gave me a theatrically aghast look. "Really? You know that a growing witchlet needs wine to grow her power."

"I'm fine. I've taken all I need at home." It was the best I could do without outright lying.

"Oh, how very sociable of you," she said with a sniff. She poured a measure of sherry into the glass anyway, downing it before returning to her chair with her absinthe.

I smiled at her and placed a hand on my belly. "I'm afraid all my appetites are just so hard to predict these days. So when I find I have a craving for something, I go ahead and satisfy it, without worrying about whether the timing will suit others."

Peony and Flora both nodded at this, though Peony frowned slightly. Looking for the barb? Leonora said, "That is most wise, my daughter. So long as you are listening to the needs of both your body and that of your witchlet, I expect all shall be well." Her gaze turned toward Niad. "Niadine Laurette, perhaps Calendula would care for a glass of water or a cup of chamomile tea."

As enjoyable as it was to see Niad try to control the horror and disdain that threatened to take over her face at the thought of having to *go to the kitchen* to wait on me, I really didn't want water or tea either. "I'm fine, Leonora, Niad," I said. "Really. Maybe I'm even a little nervous about tonight." I patted my belly gently, nudging Elnor as I did; she shifted and settled more comfortably. "I'll have something with dinner."

"Very good," Leonora said, sipping her Framboise before setting the tiny jeweled glass on the side table by her chair.

The three older witches conversed among themselves as I let myself relax. Niad finished her drink and poured another. By now Elnor was on the floor trying to lure Grieka into a tail-batting game. Fletcher, Niad's familiar, strode into the room. I hadn't seen him in a while. He was a scrawny all-black tom who didn't seem as closely bonded with his witch as most of our cats were.

Can't imagine why.

Niad returned to her chair and gazed at me across the room. "Heard from Jeremy lately?"

"Not for a little while. Have you?"

"Why should I have?" she asked, all innocence.

I shrugged. "You were acquainted with him before I was. You're old friends, aren't you?"

A crafty smile slunk across her face. I should have known better than to bait her. I *did* know better; sometimes I just couldn't help myself. "As may be, but not such…intimate friends as you and he are."

I stifled a sigh and tried to sound bored as I forced down the memory of the last *intimate* thing Jeremy and I had done together: performed a cautery on Flavius Winterheart, the warlock who had been convicted of stealing witch essence. That had been sickening enough. Now, I had my doubts about his guilt, which made it potentially ten times worse. And I could not think about this—not here, not now. "You know how difficult ætheric communication is from such a distance."

"They don't have the internet in the Old Country?" she asked, her eyes widening in mock surprise.

"Not that I am aware of."

Jeremy had checked in a few times, but his ætheric messages had been stilted and awkward, above and beyond the rigors and uncertainties of their transmission. He still believed he was the father of this child, and I supposed he still entertained the notion that I would agree to sign a contract with him. That we would become witchkind's equivalent of husband and wife, at least during the years of raising her.

I hated lying—to anyone—but as his father Gregorio had made utterly, painfully clear, I didn't have any choice in the matter. I had to go along with this terrible charade.

I wished I knew a way out of it.

"Hm," Niad said, taking another sip of her drink and glancing down at her cat. Fletcher was trying to join the game between Grieka and Elnor, but they were having none of it.

Like familiar, like witch.

"I'm not sure why the Old Country's rulers would have allowed anything like the internet in," I said, stupidly continuing the conversation when I wanted nothing more than to be out of it. At least, that's what I thought I wanted. Apparently my traitorous mouth felt otherwise. "Why would they want to open mechanical portals to a system created by humans?"

"You're right, I suppose," Niad said, still smirking. "I guess none of the fancy warlocks and witches there have lovers over here in the new world."

"Or if they do," I said, "they don't mind waiting for handwritten letters to come in the mail."

"Oh!" Niad cried, sitting up with a bright smile, the very picture of interested delight. "You've gotten letters from him, then?"

"Here, kitty kitty," I said, leaning forward and wiggling my fingers for Elnor. After a final bat at Grieka's tail, she came. I scooped her up into my arms and got to my feet. "If you'll all excuse me," I said to the room in general. "It's astonishing what a growing fetus does for one's bladder capacity."

After the formal dinner in the coven house's elegant dining room, we forwent our traditional Tuesday midnight Circle with our ancestress Nementhe in favor of a more unusual ritual, one I had never participated in. I stifled my nerves as the entire coven gathered in the back garden, obscured from the street by the house. Here, among the magical herbs, potent stones, and small creatures of the night, was where we performed rites that were bound with soil, or darker things.

Creeping Jenny had grown over the disturbed patch of dirt out of which I had initially created Petrana, though the ground still bore the indentation of her body.

A few feet to the side of that, under the cold light of the full moon, we sat in lotus position in a Circle on the ground. As ever, we arranged ourselves by age, from Leonora at the head all the way around to me, the youngest, at her left hand. The force of the Circle never failed to move me. All this concentrated female power, all our petty differences set aside.

Usually the senior witch begins any ritual, but since we were naming my daughter, I was tonight's leader. I cleared my throat and tried to clear my mind. I opened the phial of my preserved menstrual blood, dabbed three drops onto the ground, and began the chant. My sisters joined in; Elnor settled on my lap, though it seemed like there was less room for her there all the time. Had I eaten *that* much stew? Maybe I shouldn't have had that second dinner roll. It had seemed like a good idea at the time...I put a hand on my cat's soft fur and tried once more to clear my mind as I continued chanting, my voice melding with the others.

A silver light began to glow, enveloping us as the earth answered our call. The droplets of blood vanished into the soil, and I recapped the phial. I would lock it back in the menstrual closet with all the others later. I continued the chant, seeking for my daughter's name among the many possibilities. Her second name would be Leonora, following general coven tradition. Her first name should be a botanical, as were all the witches in my mother's line. Within those bounds, there was much to choose from.

I felt a chill as the moonlight seeped into my bones, bringing the silver earth-light with it, joining the blood in my veins, probing my womb, seeking to know my daughter. I stifled the urge to shake off the uncomfortable, invasive magic. I closed my eyes and clutched Leonora's hand, feeling her send silent reassurance. Long before she had created our coven, I knew that she had borne several daughters, and that they had all been named in this manner. The tradition was cold comfort. I did not understand why this particular magic could not be gentler. After all, as Peony had pointed out, "Pregnancy is the most sacred, and the most perilous, time in a witch's life."

But I continued the chant, not breaking the rhythm, though my teeth chattered and my knees and hips ached from sitting so long in lotus. If the old sisters didn't even twitch, I certainly wouldn't. After a numbingly long while, my throat raw from the repetition, I suddenly smelled the distinct aroma of rosemary. My eyes snapped open as I broke off the chant. A large sprig of the dark green herb sat inside the circle. The plant grew on the other side of the yard, near the fence. None of us had moved.

Leonora gazed at the rosemary. "So it is done!" she cried. "The first daughter of Calendula Isadora shall be called Rosemary Leonora."

"Rosemary...Rose, for short," I whispered.

Leonora turned to me, raising an eyebrow. "Rose? The barkeep?"

Someone—Niad, no doubt—snickered softly. Rose's Bar was a favorite hangout of the younger witchkind crowd.

"It's a perfectly nice name," I said, my voice stronger. "And perfectly common. Ordinary." I hated being called Calendula Isadora. It always made me feel like I was in trouble. Or that I should be wearing a long, elegant gown over a corset. And a snood.

"As you wish," my coven mother said after a slight pause. "Rosemary Leonora is now named, and our Circle doth ratify this choice. Amanū essūlå!"

"Amanū essūlå," echoed Honor, our next oldest sister after Leonora. This bound the naming. The rest of us joined in, sealing the spell with the salt of our joyous tears.

— CHAPTER TWO —

"Here," Sebastian Fallon said.

I looked up from the lab bench to see my friend holding a syringe. "What's that?"

He grinned. "Just vitamins. Mostly."

I was at the witchkind clinic. Yes, the same one that the warlock Gregorio Andromedus had built—Gregorio, who I was not entirely convinced was working for the good of all witchkind...though I couldn't prove anything. This was part of why I was here. I had brought in a new batch of my research homunculi from my home lab to test. My quieter purpose was to see if I could surreptitiously increase my sample size of witches' blood to test back at home.

"Thanks, but I've already eaten."

"Ha, ha." He waved the syringe at me. "Come on, Callie. I brewed it just for you. It can't hurt."

I shook my head. "No, really, I'm good."

"Trust me. I'm a healer."

Technically, he wasn't yet, he was just a doctor. But that wasn't the reason for my hesitation. I set down my pipette and put a hand on his arm. "Sebastian, you're so sweet, but seriously. I don't need anything more. I'm keeping real careful track of my nutrition, I'm taking a strength potion regularly, and everything's going great.

I'm fully nourished and I feel terrific." Before he could argue further, I added, "You can examine me—and her—if you like."

He frowned a moment before setting the syringe on the bench beside the pipette. "Sure, I'd appreciate that."

I turned to face him so he could more easily reach the swell of my belly. It was a small price to pay to assuage the guilt I felt about deceiving my friend. He knew there was something I wasn't telling him, and I could tell he was hurt about that, though we had never spoken about it directly. I hated it, too, because he *was*, in fact, my friend. Even though we'd only really gotten to know each other a few months ago, I trusted him all the way down. He had my best interests at heart, and he had no idea what was really going on. It killed me to keep him in the dark. But I had no choice. *Because* I cared about him, I could never tell him. He was Gregorio's freakin' postdoc, after all.

He was endlessly curious about the process of witchkind pregnancy, of which I was our community's only current example. As a healer-in-training, of course he would focus on every aspect of the process.

Too bad anything he was learning from me would be...only halfway useful to him in the future.

He put both hands gently on my belly, as he'd done so many times already, and closed his eyes, sending his magic carefully into my system. It always surprised me that he didn't detect what was unusual about my baby. (About *Rose*; she had a name now. I had to keep reminding myself.) Then again, I had barely been able to detect her mixed parentage when I searched for it myself, and I had known what I was looking for.

Sebastian finished his probe and, as ever, gave me an apologetic smile. It lit up his gawky features, making him much better-looking. "She seems great. Growing and thriving."

"Yep," I said. "But you're always welcome to check."

"I just wish I could *do* more." He huffed out a small, frustrated sigh.

I unsuccessfully tried to stifle a grin. "Typical warlock. You-all just hate letting witches be in charge of anything, don't you?"

Now he laughed. "Touché."

"You're already taking such good care of me," I assured him. "You're a fussier mother-hen than even my coven sisters."

"Yeah, I'm sure Niad dotes on you day and night."

I rolled my eyes. "Most of them, I mean. With her, I consider it a win that she's not actively trying to poison me."

He held up the syringe. "You're absolutely sure about the vitamins?"

I patted my swelling belly. "One hundred percent. Sorry."

"No need to apologize." He tucked it in the pocket of his lab coat, but then stood there a beat or two longer. He seemed to have more to say but was unable to broach it.

Trying to nudge him along, I turned back to the lab bench and picked up my pipette, leaning over the tray of samples and pretending to focus on them.

"Dr. Andromedus, um, is excited about the baby?"

Wow, Sebastian, way to fish, I thought. I turned back to him with a careful smile. "I think everyone in the community is."

He had the grace to look uncomfortable, even though he pressed on, undeterred. "Well, I mean, he is her grandfather." I could see his face reddening. "I know he's not a very cuddly guy, but he seems pretty stoked about this."

He was practically begging me to confide in him, but given that he was already too close to the truth, that was the very last thing I could do. I let my smile linger, bland and polite. "Yes, he is very pleased."

Sebastian cleared his throat. "Even though, well, with Jeremy still in the Old Country…"

Hmm. "I'm sure his research there is very complicated," I said, "though I haven't heard any details about it."

"You don't get regular updates from him, I imagine?"

This was safer territory, at least. Niad had asked much the same question, but for very different reasons. "You know how things are between us," I said. "He still can't believe I didn't want to sign a contract with him the minute I learned about the baby."

"Yeah. He is a traditionalist."

I nodded. "And there's the technical challenge as well, with communication being so hard at that distance. Plus, even if things were great between us, it's not like I can just pop over there to say hi." Witches and warlocks can, if we must, fly in airplanes, but the speed and elevation required *really* mess with our equilibrium, our connection to the threads of the world. There was more than one documented example of a witch losing her magic altogether after a lengthy flight, and plenty of occurrences of access to magic never being quite the same again. Ley line travel is far easier on our magical systems, except for the fact that it only exchanges one set of issues for another—the incredible distances involved, the disruptive effect of large bodies of saltwater, and the energy expended to make it work. There had actually been more overseas travel by witchkind back in the days of steamships.

In many ways, we weren't built for this modern world.

"Right." Sebastian glanced at the bench behind me. "Well, I should let you get back to work, I guess."

"It's all right," I said, though I was grateful that this latest gentle interrogation was finally over.

He turned to go, then suddenly turned back and blurted, "Did you ever wonder why such an old, esteemed warlock came to live all the way out here in San Francisco?"

I blinked, startled. "Who? Gregorio?"

"Yeah. He was in the Old Country for centuries. He even left his son to be raised there. And then he came to live here? Why?"

I shrugged, unsure what he was trying to get at, and not bothering to correct his timeline. Gregorio had been long established here when his mate died and he sent young Jeremy off to be fostered. "I don't know. I never really wondered about it. Maybe it was so he could be a bigger fish in a faraway pond. Maybe he had an argument with someone there. Maybe he liked the climate here."

Sebastian raised an eyebrow as if wondering if I was kidding, then shook his head. "From what I hear, there are some pretty toxic fish in the Old Country pond. So maybe you're right." He bit his lip. "Still, it seems out of character. He doesn't seem like a San Franciscan."

I thought a moment. "Sebastian, remember when we talked after my dinner party?"

"Of course. When I told you that I'm gay. And you pretended not to be astonished." He smiled.

"Yes, that too," I said, grinning back at him. "But the rest of the conversation—about independence, about not just blindly following all the rules of our elders. About making our own way in the world. Making our own decisions." I was warming up to my own narrative, trying hard to put recent events out of my mind and remember the Gregorio I'd known all my life. To remember who I'd always thought he'd been, and how much that had impressed me. "I think Dr. Andromedus must have done that. He could have had a comfortable life in the Old Country forever, but he chose to make a new life here. To bring his experience and wisdom and power to this fledgling community." I stopped, suddenly feeling a little uncertain at my own words. Had I laid it on too thick? Yet it was only what I had believed. Until recently, I had no reason to question any of it.

Now my life was full of questions...and I was on my own in finding the answers. Gregorio Andromedus might truly be working for the good of witchkind, or he might have everyone fooled. If my daughter and I were to remain safe, I had to keep mum about my doubts—at least until I knew more. Much more.

Sebastian was nodding. "Yeah, that makes sense." I could see he wasn't entirely convinced but was thinking about it. He admired Dr. Andromedus as much as...well, as I once had. And maybe could again.

"Anyway," I said pointedly, glancing yet again at the lab bench before me.

"Right." Sebastian gave me an apologetic smile. "I'll let you get back to work."

"Thanks. And hey—let's get coffee some time, okay?"

He grinned. "I'd like that."

I had barely managed to find my focus once again when I felt the telltale tingle of an ætheric message. *Callie?*

Hi, Mom, I answered her. *How are you feeling?*

She had been one of the victims of the sickness supposedly inflicted by Flavius Winterheart, but she was relatively young and in good health, so she was recovering.

Great! Almost a hundred percent.

I'm glad to hear that. What's up?

There was a brief pause. I knew better than to try to get back to what I was doing. I leaned against the bench, letting my hand rest on my belly. Did I feel the baby moving? Probably not.

It's been too long since I gave a luncheon party, Mom finally answered. *Are you free tomorrow?*

Yes, I said at once. Whether I was actually free or not, I would make myself free. *What time?*

One-thirty. See you then!

I worked another two hours, but never really found my stride. Whether it was pregnancy-brain, regular distraction, or some problem with the homunculi, I couldn't tell.

I didn't even manage to sneak any extra samples home.

Oh well. I'd try again another time.

I showed up at my parents' grand Pacific Heights home a few minutes early. Elnor followed me on the ley line. She had grown increasingly independent with this as my pregnancy progressed. Time was when she'd refuse to use her own magic for ley travel at all, forcing me to carry her. Now she hopped on the line as if it were nothing, though she still sneezed five or six times when we emerged on the street corner.

Familiar cats are to regular cats as witchkind is to humankind: superficially similar, yet essentially different. Their lines are bred from normal, mundane cats, reinforced for any magical tendencies and abilities—just like witchkind had been at the outset. I'm not sure why the cat strains haven't become more pure and attenuated like ours have. As far as I know, witches have been breeding cats this way as long as they've been breeding themselves. And yet even today, two regular magic-less felines could easily birth a litter with magical powers, while more than half of familiar-crossed litters come out magically null.

Cats are just more stubborn than us, I guess.

We walked up the tidy brick pathway to the front door. Mom had left the house wards down, something she only did if she was having a large enough group to make the ask-and-enter ritual cumbersome. (Not to mention that a group that large could join forces to protect the house from anything the world was likely to throw at it.)

Even so, I rang the doorbell and waited to be invited in.

Mom herself came to the door, and drew me into a warm hug. "Callie! You look marvelous. I've never seen you glow so much."

"I always thought that was a figure of speech," I said as I disengaged and shrugged out of my sweater.

Mom hung it on the elegant hall tree, then turned and took my arm. "But you can see it yourself, can't you?"

I let her lead me down the hall. I could hear a party full of voices in the dining room, but couldn't pick out who was there, exactly. More guests than I'd expected, to be sure. "I can, yes. My magic has gotten…fizzy, maybe. Strong, but also more granular."

"Exactly!" She beamed at me.

Of course, much of the new strength of my magic was coming from Gregorio's obnoxious golden ring. But Mom didn't need to know that; it would just make her fret.

"Here we are!" she sang out to the gathered crowd as we turned and stepped into the dining room.

The big table was pushed to the wall, with a sumptuous buffet set out on it. This left room for the probably two dozen witches and handful of warlocks who were gathered. Most of the witches were friends of my mom's, while the warlocks were Elders and colleagues of my father's.

I know my parents thought they were terribly progressive, staying together for love and all, but they sure hewed to the old gender-based divisions.

Most everyone turned and at least nodded politely at me before resuming their conversations. My dad smiled warmly and stepped toward me, setting an empty glass on the buffet table to free his arms for a hug.

"Lucas, please," my mom murmured at him as she picked up the glass, wiped the ring it left, and handed it to a maid whose name I didn't know. We never had household help when I was a witchlet living at home. Mom had begun hiring them ten or fifteen years ago. She'd said she wanted more time and energy to work on her tarot studies. Mostly, it seemed to me, she'd enjoyed a life of leisure.

I'd challenged her about this recently, just as she'd challenged me to take the tarot more seriously. I couldn't see that either of these challenges had ended well for us: with Mom in the hospital, and me…still without my best friend, or any satisfying answers about her demise.

The maid moved unobtrusively around the room, collecting empty glasses and plates, replenishing the buffet. I wondered where Mom kept finding new ones. And why they kept quitting.

My thoughts were interrupted before they could even get started. "Calendula," my father said, still beaming down at me. "You are looking so well."

"Thanks, Dad." I smiled back at him. It was rare to find him at home on a workday, but this was clearly a work function. At least three-quarters of the Council of Elders were present.

Including, I saw with dismay, Gregorio Andromedus.

The ancient warlock caught my eye from across the room, nodded courteously, and returned to his conversation.

Well, I couldn't avoid him forever, though I'd certainly been trying to. I took a deep breath and turned my attention to the buffet table. "Mom!" I said, with only partially feigned enthusiasm. "This is an amazing spread."

"I wanted to make sure I made something for everyone—including you." She snaked a hand around my widening waist as she turned toward the food that she almost certainly had *not* made herself. Dad patted my arm and stepped away to greet another newcomer. "I remember being pregnant. One's appetites get a little strange."

"I'm mostly past that now," I assured her. "Instead, the baby is starting to squish my stomach. I feel starving and then three bites later, I'm stuffed."

Mom laughed. "I remember that too." She filled a plate with delicacies and handed it to me. "Here—your favorites."

It was true, these were things I particularly enjoyed—meatballs, strong cheese, dark seedless grapes—but at the moment, nothing appealed to me. "Thanks," I said, taking the plate with a grateful smile. "I think I'll find a chair."

"Don't forget to stop at the bar. I've made a fresh batch of elderflower wine."

Ironically, I knew that Mom had indeed brewed the wine with her own hands, her own magic. Using flowers grown in her own garden, either fresh or preserved. Part of me wished I could have some, but the rest of me thought it sounded awful.

Thank goodness for the wisdom of the body.

"Oh, that's great," I said as I stepped away from her, pretending to head for the bar set up in the far corner (staffed by another maid I didn't know) but really just looking for a quiet place to sit down for a moment.

There was a pass-through room off the dining room, not really a formal butler's pantry, more just a large space between this room and the kitchen to provide distance from the kitchen's noises and odors. During parties, it usually filled up with people, but I was grateful to see that no one had wandered into it yet.

I sat down on the little divan under a high stained-glass window and began nibbling at my food. It was the honest truth, what I'd told Mom: I couldn't remember the last time I'd eaten a big meal.

And I still had months more of this to go…months during which things would only get worse, not better.

I took another deep breath, sending a silent wish to my baby that she should let me take in some sustenance. *It's for your good as well as mine,* I thought.

Elnor turned up, nose twitching pointedly as she gazed up at my plate, appearing from wherever she'd eeled off to when we arrived. Not to visit Mom's familiar; Mom had never replaced Pixel when the old cat had moved on to the Beyond decades ago. Witches aren't required to keep familiars, of course, but this was yet more evidence that Mom didn't intend to spend any of her time doing serious magic.

Oh well. It was her life. She got to make her own choices in how to spend it.

I had a mouth full of meatball when a shadow fell over my plate. Even Elnor, happily munching her own little bite, hadn't heard the warlock step into the room.

"Gregorio," I said, after I'd managed to swallow.

He gave a polite nod and took a seat on the other side of the small room. "You are looking well, Calendula Isadora." It was a statement, but it held a hint of a question.

I nodded, wishing my heart rate would settle back down, keeping my face calm. "Yes. Everything is just fine."

A smile ghosted across his face, gone almost before it appeared. "I am glad to hear that." Then he gazed at me. By the intensity in his ancient eyes, I knew he was scanning me magically. I sat still, not fighting it, not reacting in any way. After a minute, his eyes softened as his focus relaxed. "Yes, all appears to be proceeding as it should."

I took a careful breath. "I am doing everything that has been… recommended," I said. Still struggling to keep all emotion out of my voice.

Not that I was fooling him. That little flicker of a smile touched his eyes this time. He was far too suave and self-controlled to openly sneer at me, but he was enjoying his power over me.

I hadn't thought it was possible to feel any more uncomfortable than I already did. Surprise, surprise.

"I am glad to hear that," he repeated, and nodded sagely.

Elnor sat very still under my feet, but I could feel her energy. She was picking up on my emotions, though she understood that, while this man was making me unhappy, he was not a threat that she should attack with her claws and teeth.

At least, I hoped that's where her fuzzy brain was going. My mom's luncheon party did not need a catfight, even a one-sided one.

I smiled politely at Gregorio, waiting for him to say what he'd really come back here to say, or to leave. The silence stretched on. If it made him uncomfortable, he didn't show it.

Well, he was eight hundred years old. His time sense was clearly on a different scale than mine.

Finally, he cleared his throat and his eyes sharpened a bit. "Calendula, I notice that you have continued your biological research. And that you were at the clinic's laboratory yesterday."

I nodded, not at all surprised that he would know this. "Yes, I see no reason to give up my work." I said the words blandly, but we both knew what was behind them. "My daughter is not due for some months yet, and I am in full possession of my strength and faculties."

Gregorio gave a well-practiced chuckle. "Oh, of course you are, that is plain to see."

More silence reigned for another minute or two. This time, I caved. "And I wouldn't want to get bored, just sitting around the house."

"No." He leaned forward slightly. Coming to the point, at last?

I blinked at him, waiting.

He said, "I regret that I did not have the opportunity to look over your work while you were there. Perhaps I could have been of assistance."

"It was just a few assays, using blood samples Dr. Fallon provided for me. With, I assume, your permission and knowledge."

His eyes narrowed at the word *blood*, but I ignored that. I wasn't doing blood magic. I wouldn't be so reckless, not in a lab established and run by Gregorio.

Not *anywhere*, for that matter, and certainly not when I was pregnant. But, despite what he so clearly wanted me to believe, this man was not the boss of me. I would make him spell it out, if he truly wanted to accuse me of working forbidden magic.

"Of course," he said, nodding. "It's only—"

Our tense but polite standoff was cut short by Jacobus, one of my father's colleagues, a middle-aged warlock—only two or three hundred years old—who stepped into the passageway where Gregorio and I sat. "Oh!" Jacobus exclaimed. "Dr. Andromedus, I am so sorry, I did not mean to interrupt." He nodded deeply to Gregorio, almost bowing, as he shuffled a few steps backward. As if not daring to turn his back on royalty.

Gregorio waved his hand dismissively and favored Jacobus with a kindly smile. "Please, young sir, you are not interrupting anything. My protégé and I were merely chatting. You are most welcome to join us."

I took the opportunity to get to my feet, holding up my empty plate as an excuse, and when had I eaten all that food? I cast a suspicious glance down at Elnor, who kept near my ankles. "If you'll excuse me," I said to Gregorio.

He nodded, barely frowning as Jacobus took my seat. I had almost escaped when I heard Gregorio's voice behind me. "Oh, Calendula, I almost forgot. Jeremiah will be calling on you soon."

I froze in my tracks. Calling *on* me? I turned around. "Jeremy? Is he back from the Old Country?"

"He is expected any day. Friday at the latest." Gregorio gave a half-smile to the other warlock before returning his gaze to me. "You know how travel goes."

"Yes," Jacobus said, nodding eagerly.

I just stood there, my mind racing. What was Gregorio trying to tell me? I was very, very clear about the fact that I was expected to pretend that I believed my child had been sired by Jeremy. But surely nobody in the community was supposed to think that Jeremy and I were madly in love, headed for a union or anything. He'd been gone for months, and we'd been stilted and awkward together before that.

Everyone knew we had collaborated on the cautery, the ugly punishment that removed Flavius Winterheart's magic forever. Nobody could imagine we were giddy, carefree lovers.

Finally, I settled on a stiff smile. "Well, I will be happy to see him," I said, letting my hand drift to my swollen belly. I was surprised to realize, even as I said it, that this was actually true. "It has been far too long," I added, more confidently. Then I gave my empty plate another meaningful waggle and left the passageway.

Back in the dining room, the party had settled into several small conversation circles. The buffet table was as well-stocked as ever. The maid had clearly been busy. I wasn't at all hungry, but I put a few more things on my plate just in case Gregorio was peering through the walls to watch me.

Mom detached herself from a gaggle of her pals and came to my side. "Did Dr. Andromedus find you? He mentioned he needed to tell you something."

"Yes, he did. Jeremy's coming back soon."

"He did say that!" She looked genuinely happy at the prospect. "Such a fine warlock."

"Mom," I started, but she patted my arm.

"I know, I know," she said. "But why not give him another chance? There's no need to rush into anything. I mean, beyond what's already, um, rushed into." Her gaze darted to my belly.

I laughed out loud. Oh, Mom. "I never said I wouldn't. I just—you know how it is. We talked about this."

"You're not still seeing the human, are you?"

"His name is Raymond, and no, I'm not." I narrowed my eyes and looked more closely at Mom. "But seriously, we've been over this. What's going on?"

Her eyes darted toward the passageway where Gregorio presumably still sat, then back to me. "Oh, well, it's just…it was just something about the way Dr. Andromedus was mentioning Jeremy's return. He seemed so…hopeful. I thought maybe absence had made the heart grow fonder." She gave me a perky little smile that was very nearly convincing.

Except that, well, this was Mom. Though she was many things, perky was not one of them.

I drew her further into the corner, glancing around to make sure we weren't being overheard. I could of course throw a zone of privacy around us, but that would attract far more attention than just keeping my voice low. "Mom, what is it about Gregorio?"

She looked at me blankly. "What do you mean?"

I stifled a sigh. "I know he's Dad's friend from forever ago. From the Old Country."

"Friend and *colleague*," Mom corrected me.

"Right." She knew I knew this. I had grown up in this very house, with Dr. Gregorio Andromedus coming for dinner at least once a month, when my parents would give the formal dinner parties that elder witchkind seems to love so much. It had been Dad's idea that I train with Gregorio when I came of age and hadn't lost my youthful interest in biological research. Why was she explaining to me things I knew perfectly well? "But, do *you* like him?"

Her blank look grew, if anything, even blanker. "Callie. What a question. Of course I do." Then she focused on me, as if I had suddenly appeared in front of her and we were just starting our conversation. "Are you sure you're feeling all right, dear? Pregnancy can be very exhausting. Come, let's get you a chair."

She tugged on my arm but I pulled back, resisting gently. "I was just sitting down a minute ago. I'm fine, Mom. But I do want to know: how do you really feel about Gregorio? Do you just invite him to these things because he's important to Dad, or do you enjoy having him around?"

Mom was shaking her head even as I asked the questions, and she kept tugging on my sleeve. "Callie, really, what's gotten into you? Please, let me get you a glass of wine or something."

I relented and let her put me in a chair. It was the only way I could get her to not push the wine on me. Wine is apparently as bad for developing human babies as it is good for developing witchlets. (I didn't bother wondering about my half-and-half baby; any alcohol just sounded so unappetizing these days, I figured I had my answer right there. Again, the wisdom of the body.)

By the time she finished fussing over me, convincing me to at least take a glass of lemonade and another couple meatballs, something was happening in the kitchen that needed her attention, and our conversation was over. And then the party itself was over not long after that, as first the few Elders in attendance and then some of the younger set began gathering their coats and wraps and kissing my mother goodbye, thanking her for a lovely afternoon.

I briefly considered sticking around to see if I could try again, but I started feeling as tired as everyone had been insisting I was, so I took Elnor and went home.

— CHAPTER THREE —

Jeremy clearly thought his message to me the next day would come as a surprise, but since his dad had already spilled the beans, I said, *When did you get back?*

There was a pause. *Er, this morning, actually. I had been trying to return in time for your parents' gathering, but there were occlusions on more ley lines than usual, and the journey took quite a while.*

I stretched my feet out, arranging them more comfortably on the ottoman, and set my teacup on the side table. After a productive (though inconclusive) morning in my lab upstairs, I'd been enjoying a peaceful afternoon alone in my house. Well, for the value of alone that includes a cat in one's lap, a golem cleaning up dishes in the kitchen, and a baby in one's belly. *I'm sorry to hear your travel was such a trial.*

His pause was longer this time. The trouble with ætheric communication is how hard it is to send tone, expression, and emotion along with the words. I hadn't been trying to be snippy or passive-aggressive, but it was entirely possible he was interpreting it that way. *I am happy to be back,* he eventually offered.

I imagine you must be, I said, then quickly added, *I'm happy you're back too.*

May I come visit you—at your convenience, of course?

I smiled at his carefulness. *Yes, whenever you're rested up, just let me know.*

I'm rested now.

"Eager, is he?" I said aloud to Elnor. "Interesting." *Then by all means, come on over.*

I'll be right there.

I swallowed the last of my tea and eased Elnor off my lap before getting to my feet. It seemed like every day, my balance shifted as the baby grew. And there was no getting used to it—just constant change.

My cat followed me back to the kitchen, where I put the kettle on for more tea. Jeremy, of course, would want something stronger, even though it wasn't technically cocktail hour yet. Who knew what time zone his body was in, anyway? I didn't even know how long his trip had been. Well, he could drink all the brandy he wanted, it wouldn't bother me. I was going to have tea. I could have more mint, that would be good…

I stopped in the middle of the floor and laughed at myself. "Overthinking it much, witch?" Yes, I could admit it. I was nervous to see Jeremy again.

Fortunately, I didn't have long to wait. He let his presence be known through the æther a few seconds before he knocked on the front door.

Petrana started down the hallway to answer it. "That's all right," I told her. "I'll get it."

"Yes, Mistress Callie." She paused as if a thought had just occurred to her. "Did you want me to stay out of sight, then?"

"No need, Jeremy knows what you are." Could she not sense who was on the other side of the door? Her magical abilities were still something of a mystery to me, though I had been trying to nail down just what she could and could not do.

That might have been easier if she would just stop developing new abilities.

I didn't have time to laugh at myself again before I opened the door.

Jeremy, I had to admit, still looked pretty good. He might have been jetlagged (as it were—leylagged?) and exhausted from his travel, plus whatever he'd been up to in the Old Country. But his green eyes were as luminous as ever, and his long, sleek dark hair hung neatly down his back, tied today in a casual ponytail. He even smelled good.

He always smelled good to me.

No matter how inconvenient that might be. Because I really had no idea if I wanted him back in my life or not...or in my bed... though we had to pretend to be a couple...and here I was overthinking it again.

I shook my thoughts away once more and pulled the door wide. "Greetings, Jeremiah Andromedus, and welcome to my home. Please come in."

He nodded and gave me a relieved smile. Technically, just the act of opening the door to him was invitation enough, but I knew he really did prefer the old-fashioned formalities.

You can take the warlock out of the Old Country...

"Thank you, Calendula Isadora." He stepped over the threshold and paused as I shut the door. When I turned back to him, his eyes widened as he took in my enhanced figure. "Oh, my. Have I been gone so long?"

I couldn't help it, I snorted with laughter. "And here I thought you were a diplomat."

A horrified look crossed his face. "Callie! I didn't—"

Still laughing, I put a hand on his arm. "Stop. You're fine. It's all fine. Yes, you've been gone quite a while, and babies do grow."

"You look magnificent," he said, clearly trying to recover himself.

"Thank you, and you don't have to say that, truly." Somehow, his discomfort put me entirely at ease. "Come on, sit down."

"Thank you." He followed me into the front parlor.

Down the long hall to the kitchen at the back of my Victorian house, the tea kettle whistled. "Petrana," I called to her, "please bring me a cup of mint tea." Then I turned to Jeremy. "Sit anywhere you like. Can I get you something to drink?"

"Not right now, thank you," he said, sitting in the overstuffed chair. "Are you feeling well? I did mean it, that you look wonderful."

I settled on the couch. "Well, thank you. Yes, I'm feeling very good."

"I am glad."

"We named her recently."

He raised an eyebrow. "We?"

I felt my face flush. He did think this was his daughter. But didn't he know the customs around such things? Or were they different in the Old Country where he'd been raised? Did he think he should have had a say in the matter? "Yes, my coven. We held the midnight ritual and discovered her name: Rosemary Leonora."

"That is lovely." He nodded, but he still looked confused, and at a bit of a loss.

"Are you sure you don't want anything to drink?" I blurted. "I have Bulgarian frog brandy."

He flashed me his bright smile again, relaxing slightly. "Perhaps later. It's just..." He shook his head.

"What?"

Before he could answer, Petrana walked in with a full cup of tea. Jeremy watched her openly. "Where would you like it, Mistress Callie?" she asked. "On the coffee table?"

"No, just here, thank you." I took the cup from her.

She gave a tiny nod and then waited, politely but expectantly.

"That's all for now, Petrana," I added.

"Yes, Mistress Callie." She nodded again and left the room.

"Astonishing," Jeremy said. "She's—what have you done with her? She's nothing like the clumsy, lumbering golem she once was."

It was hard to not gloat. But, dang it, I was proud of myself. "I had to rebuild her for, ah, reasons. I worked on the shape a bit, and I figured out how to get her to tap into my own magic more smoothly, but mostly, it's just been practice. She's been working really hard."

He shook his head, looking impressed. "Wow. I'll want to hear more about all that."

"I'll be happy to tell you."

I smiled at him, only then realizing he'd called Petrana "her" and not "it," like most everyone else in the witchkind world did. Giving her some personhood.

Interesting. Was he trying to butter me up, or did he really think Petrana was more than just an animated thing?

He glanced away a moment, looking suddenly uncomfortable once more, before turning back to me with a determined look on his face. "But before we get too far afield, I do want to... Callie, we are long overdue for a talk."

I blinked at him. "Well, you've been a little hard to get hold of recently."

"The fault is entirely mine!" he blurted. Then he swallowed, calming himself again. "I've been away for so long, far longer than I had imagined being, and for that I am truly sorry. I had no intention of letting things get to this point without...honest words between us."

"What *did* keep you over there so long?" I asked.

He shook his head. "I will share all that with you, but I believe we should speak of us first."

"All right." I reached down and scritched Elnor, who was lurking by my feet. The golden ring glinted in the late afternoon sunlight peeking through the front window. I could see Jeremy notice it; a struggle passed across his face.

How much did he know about what had transpired while he was gone? Probably not much, but I was tired of playing guessing games. I would lay as many cards on the table as I was permitted to. "Your father gave me this," I told him, holding my hand out so he could see.

"Hmm, that's interesting." Jeremy frowned, and didn't reach out to take my hand or look more closely. "What…did he say about it?"

"That it's an old family heirloom. That he had hoped you would give it to me." I watched his face.

"Oh." Now he looked very, very sad.

"It's strange, though," I went on, keeping my tone neutral, "it clearly holds a lot of power, power that I can wield, yet that can also be wielded against me. It seems to be something of a leash." I laughed without humor. "Because you see, I cannot take it off." I tugged at it gently, to demonstrate.

He shook his head. "I am so sorry, Callie."

"Did you know he was going to do this? Had *you* planned to do this?"

His eyes widened. "No, you must believe me—I had no idea, and no intention myself—when I proposed a contract between us—well, you turned me down before I had even had a chance to think about jewelry."

I snorted softly. "This isn't jewelry."

"I would *never* leash you, Callie. You have to know that." He was leaning forward now, his emerald eyes seeking mine. "This is part of why we need to talk. I still think we could be good together, despite…well…" He trailed off, looking as helpless as a diplomat could.

I sighed. "Oh, Jeremy. It's not that I can't imagine a future with you, or wearing a ring that *you* chose and gave me. I could see being very happy with you—someday. But this, this feels too much like being railroaded into something—the whole thing, all the way through. And this ring," I waved my hand in the air, "stuck to my finger. I'm sorry, but this is just obnoxious. You know?"

He gave an answering sigh. "Callie, believe me, I know all too well. For my entire life, my father has either been nowhere in evidence or he has been managing every detail for me." He shook his head and gazed at the side table next to his chair. I could almost see him wishing he had agreed to that brandy after all. He turned his green eyes back to me. "Encouraging my relationship with you was only the latest of his campaigns to run my life. As I told you before, it was a happy bonus that I happened to like you very much of my own accord. In fact, I had hoped that this might represent a turning point, of sorts; that if you and I signed a contract, I would have someone else I was legally bound to." His brave smile was painful to see. "Perhaps the two of us could stand up to him, I thought. Silly of me, I know."

"Oh, Jeremy." If he had been sitting closer, I almost would have wanted to reach out and take his hand, he looked that vulnerable. I could see the fragile young man he must have once been, desperate to measure up to his powerful father, to be seen as worthy by him. To be respected by him. It broke my heart. Jeremy couldn't know how duplicitous Gregorio truly was, how...conniving. He clearly did not know it now—he would have never been able to disguise it with me, now or previously—and so I could never, ever tell him. I would have to walk this line carefully. "You must know a different side of Gregorio than I do. It's that way with every child and every parent. I like your father—I've always found him an inspiration. A mentor." I smiled, even as the words felt like ashes in my mouth. That they had been true once only made their flavor all the more bitter now. "Yes, a little old-fashioned in his thinking sometimes, but he *is* pretty old."

"Yes," Jeremy said, nodding eagerly. So glad that I understood. "He moves through the modern world smoothly enough, but never forget, there are some very dated notions deeply rooted within him, including that parents own their children—until a witch joins a coven or a warlock apprentices in his trade. No one owns themselves until they are hundreds of years old—if they do at all."

"And a union?" I asked, with a wry smile.

"Yes, in his mind, the warlock leads and the witch follows." He leaned forward, catching my gaze earnestly. "You must believe me, I in no way share those beliefs."

"I never got the impression that you did. But thank you for making it clear."

He gazed at my hand, and the ring, again. "It looks lovely on you. You are, ah, well suited to strong jewelry."

"Thank you." I peered back at him, absorbing the odd compliment as I decided not to protest his calling it jewelry again. This man wasn't an idiot, and our connection had been powerful. Yet the complications between us… "I'd like it better if I could take it off, I have to say."

"Of course." He averted his eyes again.

We were silent for a minute, while I sipped my tea. "Are you sure I can't get you something?"

"How would you feel about dinner?"

I started to protest before realizing that I was, indeed, hungry. And a change of scene might do me some good; I hadn't been outside at all today. "Sure."

We went to a little hole-in-the-wall in North Beach so trendy that we had to spell a table into existence. Which made the place even more crowded, but the noisy, cheerful humans gathered around the tiny tables hardly seemed to notice.

"May I?" Jeremy asked, holding both menus. It took me a moment to understand what he was asking.

I stifled a laugh. "Sure, go ahead."

He did a good job ordering, though I told him he was going to have to eat all the mussels. I've never liked bivalves, and now it made my stomach ache to even think of them. Rose might not be communicating to me in any usual witchkind sense, but it seemed pretty clear that she liked them even less than I did.

My only alteration to Jeremy's choices was when he got to the wine list. "None for me, thank you," I told the waiter. "I'd love to try one of these shrub drinks instead."

Jeremy raised an eyebrow but didn't question me until the waiter left. "Shrub?"

"Sipping vinegar," I told him, "and soda. It's all the rage these days. I've been meaning to give it a try."

He still looked confused, and then suddenly his face cleared. "Ah! Oh, Callie, I'm sorry. I shouldn't have suggested a human place. Of course it would be awkward to drink alcohol in front of them in your condition."

I smiled back at him. "It's really all right. I've been wanting to eat here. And don't worry, I'm being very careful to get exactly the nutrients I need."

He nodded. The waiter brought our drinks—lemon-lavender shrub for me and a glass of cognac for Jeremy. We'd barely sipped them before he returned with a basket of bread, and then antipasti plates.

"This is nice," Jeremy said, as we shared both dishes. "Just enjoying a meal together. Thank you for coming out with me."

"My pleasure," I said. "In fact, this is the kind of thing I was talking about months ago when I said I wanted to get to know you better before rushing into becoming your consort."

He gave me a grateful smile. "I'm sorry that…all that got interrupted by circumstances."

"Me too."

We were both quiet a moment. I thought about how quickly things had changed…from the giddy rush of falling into bed with an exciting new lover, to the shock of discovering I was pregnant, to the horrible cautery magic we had performed together, followed immediately by Jeremy leaving the country and being incommunicado for so long.

"I'm glad you don't hate me," he said at last, so quietly I almost didn't hear him.

"I absolutely do not hate you," I assured him.

He leaned back, studying my face for a long moment before taking a sip of cognac. "Tell me about your childhood."

I blinked, surprised by the sudden conversational turn. "What?"

"I mean it. I didn't grow up here. I don't know much about you, and that feels like quite the oversight."

"Huh." I took another bite of carpaccio to cover my confusion. "What do you want to know?"

"Anything you like. Everything. Start at the beginning."

"All right." I sipped my shrub, thinking. "Well, you know both my parents."

"Yes, though I am better acquainted with your father than with your mother."

I nodded. "She's quite a bit younger than he is. It's her first union; she was only in her coven a few years before she met and fell in love with my dad."

"Theirs appears to be a good union."

"It is. They were good parents. They enjoyed me a lot." I smiled at the thought of them, the small, quiet ways they showed how much they loved one another, even as the daily rhythms of their lives did not overlap all that much. I pushed aside the odd moments from their luncheon yesterday afternoon and Mom's strange reluctance to talk about Gregorio. Jeremy had asked about my childhood, after all. "They renewed their contract for another term ten or so years ago. I know they're very happy together.

Though I sometimes wonder about my father's unions before her," I admitted. "Or, more generally, I wonder what it's like to be head-over-heels in love with someone who's had so much more life than you have. Not just loves, but friends and communities and work and, well, everything." I smiled at Jeremy. "I know you're a bit older than me, but basically we're contemporaries. Dad is like six times Mom's age."

"Oh, I did not realize the difference was so vast. She must have been quite young when she had you."

"Mid-thirties." Younger than I was now. A different server, a waitress this time, brought our entrees. I took a bite of ricotta gnocchi, pausing to let the flavors bloom in my mouth before I said, "I had a happy childhood, for the most part. Not much to tell, really. Mom spent more time with me than Dad did. I think that's why I followed him into research." I grinned a little self-consciously. "Always trying to get his attention. You know."

"I do know. As we have discussed."

As we ate, I told him about studying in Leonora's coven as a youngster (as did nearly every young San Francisco witch, along with many witchlets from the surrounding area), and then the exciting, nerve-racking time of choosing which coven to join when I turned twenty. Nementhe had announced her intention of moving Beyond several years earlier, but had changed the date several times. It was unclear whether or not there would be an opening for me. I'd visited an East Bay coven that also focused on education, and one in Marin County that was situated in a lovely house overlooking the ocean, but my heart was in San Francisco. Finally, Nementhe did travel to the next plane, and Leonora made me a formal offer.

I found myself relaxing as we talked—well, as I talked and he asked the occasional question. I knew we weren't on a date; I didn't know what our relationship was going to be, from here on out. But we were going to have to be on comfortable and familiar terms, whatever it was.

Over tiramisu, I said, "All right, enough about me. I still want to know what happened in the Old Country. Did you find out anything about the larger conspiracy? About Dr. Winterheart's confederates?" I'd rehearsed this question before I asked it and was pleased that it came out sounding entirely natural.

He frowned slightly. "Not as much as I had hoped. Nothing conclusive."

"You must have learned *something* in all that time." As his frown deepened, I hastened to add, "I'm not criticizing, I'm just very interested to know. The whole community is, in fact. This kind of thing is a big deal for us here."

"Oh, I understand that, and I'm not reluctant to tell you. It's just…well, you've never been to the Old Country. I am trying to find the best way to explain my experience there so that it will make sense to you."

"Is it really so much different than here?" I scraped my spoon across my empty plate. I'd eaten appetizers, a big plate of pasta, and my entire dessert—a bigger meal than I'd had in forever. How was there suddenly room for it? Well, it had been pretty tasty. It was nice to have an appetite.

Jeremy smiled softly. "Yes and no. Do you remember the night we met, when you and Logandina asked about it?"

"Of course." A small pang of sorrow went through me at the thought of my best friend. She had had such a crush on Jeremy. I still missed her so.

He nodded, acknowledging my frown. "A community where everyone wields magic, where it does not have to be hidden, is so fundamentally different from how things are handled here—and most everywhere else in the world—you would almost have to see it to begin to grasp it."

"I do hope I get to travel there someday," I said, and I meant it.

"I hope so too. Not now, of course." His eyes darted downward, though he couldn't really see my belly through the table.

"No."

He took a last bite of his own dessert, seeming to gather his thoughts. "It's not just that magic is used openly there, though it is certainly that. It is more that...the human forms of communication and interaction, the forms that we rely on out here, are downplayed so thoroughly, they are almost not used at all."

"What does that mean? Nobody talks to each other?"

He smiled. "Much less than we do here. There is also far less going out into the world—here, for example," he gestured, indicating the little restaurant. "This would be unthinkable there. There is very little in the way of even walking about on the streets, shopping, or socializing."

"Really?" I thought about it. "That sounds pretty lonely."

"Again, yes and no." His smile grew apologetic. "I am sorry. I truly am not trying to be evasive. You would have to experience it to really understand what I mean, but in a sense, you are always so much more *with* others, even if your physical form is alone in a house."

"Because you're always talking to each other ætherically," I suggested.

"It isn't even always speech, per se. Our minds...those who are close to you, both in physical proximity and in emotional trust and fondness, it's as though they are always gently in your mind, and you in theirs." He shrugged, watching my expression. "It's not mind-reading or anything so crude or invasive as that, not at all. Perhaps you can think of it more like..." He paused, his lovely green eyes going vague as he considered. "Like a telephone line, connected, but you set the receiver down and go about your business, and so does your friend. But you could raise your voice and call out to him at any point, and he would hear you."

"Huh," I said, trying to visualize it. Did that sound nice, or not? I couldn't quite decide. Both, sort of. "It must feel strange to you to be here, then," I said. He'd grown up there, after all, only coming to San Francisco in the last year.

He tilted his head. "A bit. I find it refreshing here, and I actually do love going out in the world. To bars and restaurants and gatherings. And I like…well, the privacy of being alone in my mind."

"I like that too," I admitted. "I'm not sure I would do very well in the Old Country. Does everyone who makes a pilgrimage there have to do this?"

"No, of course not. Tourists rarely do, in fact, and they almost never travel beyond Balszt, the capital. Balszt is a little more like what you're familiar with, people do go out there, some. But that is a large part of why so many tourists and pilgrims report experiencing such a coldness from the locals. A sense of many things being said and understood that they have no access to; a hostility, almost. It's not—well, usually not—that the locals are deliberately shutting visitors out of their social lives."

"But why invite someone in who is only going to leave in a few weeks?" I finished, nodding. "I get that."

The waitress came to clear our plates and ask if we wanted anything else. Jeremy looked at me; I shook my head and put a hand on my belly. Yes, I was pretty full. She set the check down near the center of the table. Jeremy snagged it at once.

I let him. He'd invited me out, after all.

"Okay," I said, after he'd put a pile of cash on the bill, "so given all that, what did you find out about the conspiracy?"

"On the face of it, nothing," he said. Before I could say anything, he went on. "And that's what leads me to be almost entirely certain that there is something to be found there. I only managed to see a few old friends and acquaintances in person. There were an astonishing number of people who were not available for one reason or another. Travel to foreign lands, for work or on holiday, pilgrimages to mountain shrines. One warlock, whom I was sure would be able to illuminate me, had the temerity to tell me that he was in the middle of a three-month silent meditation retreat in his own home and could utter not one word, under any circumstances."

I gaped at him. "He told you this silently."

"No. He let his housekeeper do so; he had blocked me out of even ætheric communication." Jeremy was a master of his emotions, but I could almost feel his irritation, prickly on my own skin. "The shut-out was so complete that I am convinced that there is much to be known."

"That...must have been frustrating," I said.

"It was," he bit out. Then he shook his head and managed another smile. "Yet my time there was not entirely wasted. I did manage to spend a good deal of time with my foster family, with whom I remain close. And, once I realized how stymied I was in my search for Winterheart's co-conspirators, I spent some time inquiring about Logan's parents."

"Oh, you did?" I leaned forward. "Did you find anything?"

"A bit. They were indeed seen in Zchellenin, at least for some months after they got there. No one I spoke with was able to identify the 'friend in trouble' who had been the ostensible reason for their going there, though, and it was a relatively quiet moment in the ongoing Iron Rose struggles, which leads me to wonder whether their 'friend' was a cover story."

"A cover story for what?"

He frowned. "I do not know, and no one I spoke with had any ideas. Augustus and Lorenna arrived, paid six months' rent in advance for a small cottage at the edge of the village, then kept largely to themselves. Just like everyone does. No one knows exactly when they vanished. By the time their landlady came by to see if they wanted to renew the lease, the house had clearly been abandoned for some time. Perhaps even months, judging by the spoiled food in the cupboards. Villagers remembered seeing

Lorenna in the market a few times but could not remember just when the last time had been. And of course, everyone's memory is now blurry, so many years later."

"Huh." I sipped my water as I tried to swallow my deep disappointment. He had never promised he would be able to find any leads, after all. "That's basically what everyone here found out when they investigated. What gets me is that—well, it was a small village, in a tight-knit community of only witchkind, no humans. Even if people don't get out and about much, folks can just vanish like that, and no one notices? No one goes to check on them, ever?"

"Remember, they were probably considered outsiders, at least to a degree. Yes, they were originally from Zchellenin, but they had moved away so many years before. And they clearly demonstrated that they valued their privacy."

I shook my head. "It still seems like someone must know something."

"Yes. I was hoping I could do better than I did. I still might be able to, but it would take a lot of time, and probably some divination work. Not to mention luck. In any event, by the time my father contacted me, I was ready to return to San Francisco." He smiled at me across the table, candlelight picking up sparkling highlights in his eyes.

"He contacted you?" Gregorio hadn't mentioned that part. He'd made it sound as though Jeremy had told his father he was coming back.

"Yes." Jeremy looked a little confused. "He told me that your pregnancy was progressing, and that my prolonged absence was liable to cause increasing talk in the community. And since I wasn't making any headway, I might as well return, and we would work out some other way of getting to the bottom of this mystery." He frowned slightly. "I was under the impression that he had spoken with you about this."

"No. He only told me that you were on your way back, and that I'd be hearing from you soon."

Now his small smile returned. "Well, wonder of wonders; has he finally decided to let me manage my own personal affairs?"

I smiled back, shaking my head. "Don't go overboard. Maybe he was just busy." *Or maybe he's testing both of us, wondering how far he can trust me to keep these secrets, and how oblivious Jeremy will be to the fact that there are secrets being kept.* "Well, I'm glad you're back," I added, feeling more and more confident that I truly meant it.

"I am as well."

He escorted me home—in a taxi, out in the world on the dark city streets, not on the ley lines. He saw me to my front door and kissed my hand. I did not invite him to stay the night, though a small part of me was tempted—and I wasn't quite sure why. I was in no way ready to let that warlock back into my heart. Or my bed. Even if our dinner had been quite pleasant.

He was hardly to blame, after all, for the sins of his father. And for the terrible magical working that we'd done together. He was as much a pawn in this game as I had been.

Anyway, there would be plenty of time for resuming an intimate relationship, if I ever decided I wanted to. If he was amenable to our getting to know one another at a reasonable pace, then that was all to the good.

— CHAPTER FOUR —

The evening out with Jeremy left me energized and unsettled. I kept running the conversation over in my mind, marveling at the strangeness of the Old Country. Really, nobody talked to each other? What would that even be like? Surely he was exaggerating. I mean, it was almost too convenient, wasn't it? Why even live in community if folks hid out in their own dwellings?

Why did Logan's parents rush back there, only to disappear forever?

Finally, to distract myself, I climbed to my lab in the attic and put in a few good hours of work at the bench. Elnor was sacked out in the corner, and I was carefully pipetting a droplet of blood into a Petri dish when there was a sudden shriek in my head. *Callie!!!*

I dropped the pipette and jumped in alarm, startling Elnor awake. It took me a moment to realize that it was my student Gracie, and that the cry was coming through the æther. Gracie was a smart, accomplished witchlet...but she was also fifteen, and occasionally prone to dramatics.

What is it? I asked, putting my hand over my pounding heart.

Can I come over and see you RIGHT NOW?? PLEASE!!

Are you in danger?

There was a slight pause, then, *You haven't been here for dinner in AGES! I thought you were going to be here and you're not!*

I sighed, letting myself relax the rest of the way. *Gracie. I come to every Tuesday dinner, and many others as well. You know that.*

But I need to see you now! I've been waiting to talk to you for days!

I would have been well within my rights to close the connection until she could be more civil. But she was clearly distressed about something. Still, it was five in the morning, and I was, I suddenly realized, finally exhausted.

Is it something we can talk about this evening? I asked her. *I promise I will be there for dinner tonight. I can even come an hour earlier and we can have a cup of tea or go for a walk or whatever you want. But I need to sleep now, and you probably should as well.*

Another pause, then, *Okay. Fine.* I felt the connection snap shut.

I sighed again, so loud that Elnor woke up again and glanced over at me. "Teenage hormones, sweetpea," I said, walking across the room and ruffling her ears. "Come on. Bedtime."

I intended to nap for a few hours. Instead, I slept most of the day. Pregnancy will do that to you. Apparently Rosemary decided she needed the downtime, and I, as her mere vessel, her crucible, had no choice but to comply.

Or maybe we were both just busy incorporating all the calories from that giant Italian meal.

I did, however, remember my promise to Gracie. Elnor and I showed up at the coven house nearly two hours before dinner. My young student met us at the front door, her kitten at her heels. "Finally!"

"Gracie, what in the world is the matter?" I tried to pull her in for a hug, but she dodged it.

"You said we could go for a walk." She pushed past me, hurrying out of the front garden and down the sidewalk without waiting for my response. Her dark hair fretted wildly about her head, and Minky (or Mynquie or however Gracie was spelling it today) darted along behind her. Elnor gave me an inquisitive glance.

I shrugged and started walking fast enough to catch up with the witchlet and her cat. We walked for a block in silence. I absently admired the fancy homes up here as I delicately probed Gracie's magical output, hoping to get a sense of what could be on her mind. But she just marched along, fuming.

We turned a corner, bringing the Castro and Church neighborhoods into view, with downtown behind them. At last I could sense Gracie calming down—just a smidge, but enough that I felt I could begin to reach her. "We'll need to head back for dinner before too long, so if you want to talk in private, we should probably get started," I said.

She stopped on the sidewalk and turned to face me. "You're leaving us!"

What? "I moved out months ago, dear. We've been over this. I'm not going anywhere."

"You said you were going to raise the baby here and I was going to babysit! But Dr. Andromedus's son offered you a big long contract! You're going to quit the coven and leave us and move in with him!"

"Who told you such a thing? Was it Niad?"

"No! Mina and Kat said they heard it…somewhere. Everyone knows, all the coven sisters are talking about it."

I shook my head. "Gracie, that is just not true. He did offer—"

"See! I knew it! Why are you—"

"But I told him no. Ages ago, before…everything."

"What? Why?" Doubt was strong in her voice and painted all over her pretty face.

"Because I don't actually *want* to leave the coven, and my life. Everything I told you before is still true." I patted my swelling belly. "This doesn't change what I fundamentally want out of life. And that is to keep doing my research, and to keep teaching science to you witchlets." I smiled at her. "We need *more* genetics researchers, not fewer." *Now more than ever,* I thought sourly. "Have you given any more thought to the direction of your life's work?"

"No!" She tossed her dark curls, sending them twitching and shivering, and started walking again, her kitten darting between her feet. Gracie didn't even seem to notice her; they were settling into one another's energies well. "I don't have to decide on anything yet. My mom says it's way too early."

"She's not wrong," I said. "I was just wondering."

"Did you know you wanted to do biology research when you were my age?"

"Yes, I did. But then, I had the example of my father and... Dr. Andromedus." I hurried on, hoping she wouldn't notice my discomfort. "I've always been fascinated by what makes us tick. But I was unusual; most of my friends weren't like this. Many witchlets choose their life path quite a bit later than fifteen. And you can always shift gears after the first fifty or a hundred years, if you decide you've gotten into the wrong field."

"Yeah." She kicked at a small stone, sending it skittering down the sidewalk. Minky darted after it. "I'm thinking maybe I want to act."

"Act?" I blinked. Elnor strolled after Minky, pretending to supervise the kitten, but I noted her poorly suppressed interest in the bouncing pebble too. Speaking of acting.

"Yeah. Think how cool it would be to have magic in movies! I wouldn't need a makeup artist or special effects or anything." She reached up a finger, pulling a small thread of shadows around herself. Suddenly she looked ten years older.

"Gracie, that's scary. You're not serious, are you?"

"Why doesn't anybody believe me! I thought you of all people would understand!" Now she was almost wailing once more.

"Stop shrieking!" I said, more sternly than I'd intended. Both cats turned and stared at me. I lowered my voice, and softened it. "If you want to act, I'm sure you can find a way to make it so." Actually, the more I thought about it, bringing magic to the movies could be really interesting. Certainly many members of witchkind had successful careers on the stage. And Gracie did have a flair for the dramatic, to put it mildly. "In fact, I think you're a natural for it."

"You don't have to humor me," she said, sulking.

I laughed. "You're proving my point. But I'm not humoring you at all. I was just surprised. You've never mentioned an interest in acting. You've never even mentioned movies."

She shrugged, feigning boredom, but she was watching my face carefully. "I hadn't really thought about it before, but I saw a documentary on actor kids, and it got me thinking…"

"I think it's a perfectly fine thing to explore." Who could I send her to, to mentor under? I had no idea. None of the local covens had anything to do with entertainment careers. "Let me talk to a few people and think about this a bit. For now, though, we should head back."

She glanced in the direction of the coven house, not letting go of any of the sulk. "Do we have to? Can't we just go out to a restaurant?"

"Why? Isn't Sirianna making roast chickens with sage stuffing? I thought that was your favorite."

"It's not the food! I just…I hate it there. I always did, and I still do. Why do I have to go to school there? Can't I learn witchcraft in a different coven?"

"Well, perhaps, but this is the main teaching coven for the Bay Area. You know that. If you transferred somewhere else, it would be to begin your internship." I gave her another wry smile. "And like I said, I'm going to ask around, but off the top of my head, I don't know of any acting covens."

"Nobody understands me." She kicked at another pebble. This time the cats ignored it. Minky stayed close to her mistress's feet, ready to provide comfort when Gracie was ready to receive it.

I bit my tongue. Because she really was in no mood to hear, *Yes, actually, everyone understands you way better than you wish they did.*

Was it wrong of me to feel such a sense of guilty relief every time I talked to Gracie? My life was a baffling disaster, but at least I wasn't fifteen.

The evening ran long. Dinner was served late—nobody really explained why, and Sirianna looked so flustered, I didn't want to ask—and Leonora had a good deal to say to the assembled witches and witchlets in the grand dining room. Most of it was about the coven's finances—or, rather, its investments; our day-to-day finances were nothing any of us needed to worry about.

Frankly, neither were the investments. It wasn't like we got to vote on any of this stuff: Leonora made all the money-related decisions, and did a spectacular job at it, as far as I could tell. Our holdings grew every year; we could have established a small country. Apparently, tonight she just wanted to talk about it. At great length.

At any rate, by the time dinner and cleanup were over, I was too exhausted to want to take a ley line home. I couldn't quite believe that I needed sleep again, after sleeping most of the day before, but again, being pregnant made everything about my body out of whack. I decided to crash in my old bedroom here. Maybe Gracie would be reassured when she saw me at breakfast.

I didn't see her the next morning, though; by the time I woke up, classes were already in session. So I just went downstairs to get some breakfast. It was a rare sunny morning (rare for San Francisco, that is; no fog) so after I prepared my tea, toast, and scrambled egg, I carried it out to the back yard.

We rarely sat out here. The back of the house faced northeast, so by the time the fog burned off in the afternoon, it would be in shade. I brushed the dust and dead leaves off a wicker chair and settled in, setting my plate and cup on an equally dusty table before me. My unbound hair fluttered around my head, enjoying the sunlight. Elnor seemed to be enjoying it as well, pausing in the middle of the yard before going off to sniff around at the base of the fence.

I took a sip of my peppermint tea. Ah, so peaceful.

So of course the next sound I heard was the back door opening.

Niad's familiar, Fletcher, prowled down the back stairs and over to my table. He gave me a dark look before continuing on to the edge of the yard, a good distance from Elnor. He started pawing through the underbrush, making a ruckus on some dry foliage.

"Is he looking for a place to pee?" I asked Niad, without turning to look at her.

She stepped lightly down the stairs and over to the table, pulling out a second chair and giving it a disdainful glance before sitting down. "I'm surprised to see you here this morning, Callie."

I nodded and took a bite of my eggs. Any snarky reply would only give her ammunition.

After a pause, she added, "This is the part of the conversation where you ask me why I'm surprised."

"Oh, I'm sorry, were we having a conversation? I thought I was enjoying a quiet breakfast alone in the morning sun." Oh well. I managed to avoid snarkiness for ten whole seconds.

I could see the satisfaction shimmer across her face, though she didn't overtly smile. "As you know, Leonora, our coven mother, prefers us to be polite to one another, dear sister."

I gave her a weak smile. "Was I impolite? Should I have invited you to break your fast with me? When I came downstairs, it was so late I figured everyone had already eaten."

"I meant about the conversation." She gave a tiny sigh, just a little huff out of her delicate nostrils, and glanced across the lawn to her familiar, who was still doing whatever he was doing over there. "Fletcher," she called, in a tone devoid of warmth. "Come back here, please."

He ignored her. He was a punky cat at the best of times, and they clearly had no bond whatsoever. I wondered why she didn't return him to the cattery and try again with a warmer, better-behaved kitten. Not that it was any of my business.

Elnor, however, took the opportunity to come back across the yard and jump into my lap. I petted her as she settled in, purring.

Niad returned her gaze to me.

"Okay, I'll bite," I said. "Why are you surprised to see me here?"

"Because Jeremiah Andromedus is back in town." She leaned forward, watching me carefully. "I thought you and he might take some time together."

"Niad, although we had a nice dinner out together the other night, I'm not signing a contract with him. Are you responsible for this rumor that all the students are passing around?"

Her eyes widened. "Me? Of course not. I don't speak to the students about our personal affairs."

A contract, even a romantic one between a witch and a warlock, was hardly personal—or at least, hardly private. It involved terms and conditions, money and housing arrangements, and a witch's coven had to be part of the negotiations. I didn't argue the point with her, though. She was just trying to distract me. "Well, I'm glad to hear that. But I do wonder why they're so exercised about it all of a sudden."

"Children." She sniffed and tossed her hair, which was pulled back in a ponytail, pouring down her back in loose waves emanating from the braided band she'd held it with. "Who knows why they become concerned about things? Next week it will be something else entirely."

"I'm sure you're right." I sipped my tea. It was starting to get cold. "Were you wondering something more about Jeremy, or was that all?"

"Fletcher!" she called again, more sharply this time. Ignoring my question. "Fletcher, get out of that catnip."

Elnor, curled on my lap, purred a little louder, as if to say, *Look what a good familiar I am.* I scratched her ears. She didn't need to convince me.

I took the last bite of my eggs and set my fork down. "Well," I started.

"I suppose we're all curious to learn what answers the warlock came up with, after all this time in the Old Country," Niad suddenly blurted out.

I gave her a winning smile. "Oh, I know. I've been just as curious as everyone else. Alas, it seems to have been a huge waste of his time. He hardly learned anything."

"How unfortunate," she said flatly, staring back at me.

I shrugged. "You don't have to pretend to believe me," I told her. "You are welcome to talk to him yourself. Who knows? Maybe you'll get more out of him than I did. If there's anything there to tell, that is."

"It wouldn't bother you if I talked to him?" she asked, eyes narrowing in suspicion.

"Not in the least," I said. "I don't own him. And, at the risk of repeating myself, I have no plans to sign a contract with him."

"But you have made a daughter with him."

Not true, though I had to pretend it was. "How observant of you."

She gave an uncomfortable laugh. "How *modern* of you." Then she sniffed. "But you always were a bit of an iconoclast."

I finished the last cold swallow of my tea and picked up my plate, setting Elnor on the ground before getting to my feet. "Well, this has been just as much of a delight as ever, Niad, but I have things I need to be getting on with."

She rose as well. "Fletcher!"

I left her with her obstreperous cat and the morning sun.

A week or so later, I stood in the nursery at my house. I'd been in and out of here all afternoon, experimenting with furniture and trying to decide whether I should paint the walls or leave them the quiet blue they were. It was a good color for the house, but was it a good color for a baby? Especially a baby girl? Not that such things should make a difference—I mean, I was an *iconoclast,* after all—but for crying out loud, the girl's name was Rosemary.

But I didn't really like pink.

Though Rose didn't have to mean pink—roses came in all sorts of colors. Yellow might be nice. I narrowed my eyes and gazed at the wall, letting my magical sight overlay a buttery yellow.

No. Too garish.

I softened it, making it more lemony. But that just looked insipid. The blue was better than that.

And would the smell of fresh paint bother her? Newborns had such sensitive constitutions. The last thing I needed was to fill my house—the very room she *slept* in—with toxins or unpleasant odors.

Of course, that was even assuming she'd sleep in here, and not just with me. Did I even really need a nursery, or was that just another human concern I'd taken on? Traditionally, witch mothers slept with their babies, holding them safe in their magic.

Well, she'd need her own room eventually, and the color question would remain.

I felt a prickle at the back of my neck as my coven mother's intention found me, forcefully.

Yes, Mother? I responded.

Calendula Isadora, come to the coven house. At once.

I dropped the magical color filter and let reality fall back into place. "Elnor!" I called. "Elnor?" The cat didn't appear, so I left without her, arriving at the coven house a few moments later.

Leonora was at the front door as I stepped through the gate.

"Yes, Mother? What is it?"

"Is young Graciela at your house?"

I took a surprised breath. "No, why?"

Leonora frowned and shook her head. "I thought not. Come inside."

In the front parlor, most of the active teaching staff was gathered—Niad, Flora, Sirianna, and Maela—along with several of the students. Niad glanced up at me sharply. "Well?"

"Well, what?" I asked. "What's going on?"

"Graciela did not show up at history class this afternoon," Leonora said. "Katerina here said that she has been upset recently, but would not tell her why."

I looked at the glum student. "Kat? Do you know anything?"

"No!" she wailed. "I swear, she didn't say a word to any of us! She's just…gone!"

Leonora said, "Since you are the only teacher in whom she confides, we naturally thought she might have sought you out."

"She did not—well, not since a week or so ago. We went for a walk and talked about potential career paths for her. She told me she might be interested in studying acting." I took a chair. "Did you ask her parents? Maybe she went home."

Niad rolled her eyes.

"Of course," Leonora said. "It was the first place we looked."

I ran my memory over our recent conversation even as I was casting my senses about, searching the house, the neighborhood, the city… my power and perception diminishing the farther out I sent it.

"She is not in the area at all," Leonora said, watching my search but not stopping me. She knew I would insist on trying myself. "We have all searched. She is not within magical reach."

Oh, Gracie, I thought. I knew she was struggling, but I'd had no idea she was on the verge of running away. Had I missed some important cue? "Maybe she went to Los Angeles."

"Excuse me?" Niad asked.

"Where do you go to study acting? We don't have any covens teaching dramatic arts around here. Maybe she ran off to Hollywood. Who do we know there?"

Leonora nodded. "I'll send word to Prima at once," she said. "I don't know what they teach in her coven, but she will know whom I should ask, if it is not her." She closed her eyes briefly. After she'd sent her message, she leaned back in her chair. "In the future, Calendula, please report any important conversations to the rest of us."

"I didn't know she would run away!" I said. "She was frustrated and felt stifled here. That wasn't new. She did mention acting, but she always had some new idea she was passionate about. This didn't seem any different."

"What did you tell her?" Leonora asked.

"I didn't discourage her, but I didn't encourage her either. I told her I would ask around, but I confess I haven't remembered to. I mostly just listened to her—that's usually what she's really looking for. I counseled her to stick with her studies, to trust the process, and be patient." I looked pointedly at Niad. "As I always do."

"Yet your example..." Leonora started and then paused as she paid attention to something we did not hear. "Prima has not seen her, but she will have her searched for," she said. "She's calling her sister covens now."

Oh, Gracie, I thought again. I sent a message of my own. Since I had no idea where she was, I just sent it out generally. She would find it only if she went looking for it. *Come home! We love you and miss you. You can talk to me any time, night or day. Just return to us!*

— CHAPTER FIVE —

On Thursday, I returned from a visit to my birth mother's earlier than usual. She was having company later, and I wasn't invited this time. That was fine with me, as I was exhausted and ready to spend some time alone. I wondered at times if my growing fatigue and introversion was a result of keeping a horrible secret, or if this was just what happened during pregnancy.

Too bad I couldn't ask anyone about it.

Leaving Mom's early had meant that we hadn't had a chance to work with Logan's cards, as we generally did when we got together. I was surprised to find I sort of missed it.

I was trying to visit Mom more regularly, and not just because I still wanted to worm information about Gregorio out of her. Her illness had made me realize how much I had taken her for granted. She was always happy to see me, even if she took every opportunity to instruct me further in the tarot. I would never be a convert, but I was beginning to see what people saw in it. It exercised my brain in different ways to open up my intuitive side and do a reading. Mostly, though, it was just a nice way for us to spend time together.

I sat in my study on the second floor, playing idly with the cards, feeling Logan's energy on them still, though it had been many months since she left us. Her body lay in Leonora's study at the coven house, still unchanged. If it ever began to decompose, would her energy leave this world more fully?

And where was her spirit? It must be still tethered to her body, though no one could find the connection. But these mysteries had to be connected.

Her familiar, Willson, had never turned up anywhere. I'd checked her apartment a few more times, but other than that one glimpse of his essence, he didn't show up there, or the cattery, or anywhere. I hoped he had been adopted by some human family by now; he was unlikely to have been hit by a car or suffered some other tragedy, with his extra abilities. But it was baffling.

Could I use the thread of Logan's energy here to search for him?

But what would I do if I found him? It wasn't like I needed another cat, though I'd be happy to take care of him, of course. Elnor liked him. I could always return him to the cattery, if he didn't want to live with us. It just felt...wrong...for a witch's cat not to live with witchkind.

That wasn't really the most pressing issue here, I realized. I would much rather find Gracie. And *her* cat, who of course had vanished right along with her witch.

I had been shuffling as I mused; now I cleared some space on the coffee table and began laying out a tarot divination. I used a simple Question and Answer spread, rather than the more traditional full Celtic Cross.

"Where is Gracie?" I asked aloud, then placed the cards in front of me.

In the first position—"You"—was the Two of Cups. A lovely, peaceful image of two people facing one another, holding golden cups. Mom had told me it symbolized, quite appropriately, a relationship between two people. Sometimes romantic love, but also just any close connection. Gracie's and my friendship, very likely, since it was the "me" card.

It was a card that implied that everything was under control. Which was...somewhat less than encouraging, I thought, given the circumstances.

Below the single first card, I laid out a second row of two cards: "The Background." The first one was Strength, and next to it was The Chariot. "Interesting," I muttered. Elnor wandered into the room, perhaps drawn by my poking at the threads of magic that surrounded us. She sniffed at the cards and then jumped up onto the couch next to me, settling against my side. I rubbed her ears as I stared at the cards.

Strength is the card that comes just *after* The Chariot in the major arcana, but here it appeared before it. What, if anything, did the switch mean? The picture on Strength is a woman with her hands on the head of a lion—shoving his mouth closed, or trying to pry it open? The symbol of eternity floats over her head, symbolizing (or so I'd been told) emotional fortitude, courage and patience. The message of this card was to stop trying too hard to force something if it's not working; to be patient, perhaps even withdraw for a while. And then there was the symbolism of the lion—a big cat if ever there was one. What did this mean, in relation to any of my questions?

The Chariot's message was more forceful, direct. A quasi-military fellow, staring straight ahead in a chariot pulled by two mirror-image sphinxes. It was also a card of emotional control, of putting aside grief in order to take action and move forward.

Grief. My sorrow over Logan no longer ruled my days, as it had at first; but it was never far from the surface. Working with her cards brought her even more keenly to mind. Was I supposed to put that aside?

What I felt about Gracie was not grief. It was worry and anxiety and even maybe guilt, but not grief.

At least, I didn't think so. But no. I had to believe that she was all right. That this was some sort of extended tantrum; or even that she had gotten caught up in something too exciting and new for her to feel safe letting us know where she was. Leonora would absolutely demand her return to the coven, no matter what Gracie—or her new companions, whoever they might be—had to say about it.

But this was all the background to my current questions. So what did that mean? Did it mean I *had* put my friendship with Logan aside too much? Not appreciated her?

Guilt is not helping here, I told myself. *I cannot do anything about the past.* Moving forward: I would focus on that.

I laid out the third row—three cards, signifying "The Solution." Another one of the major arcana, in The Star; followed by the Ten of Wands, then the Page of Cups. The Star was an amazingly positive card. I smiled when I saw it, and could almost see my mom's face light up when she had talked about it last week: "When all hope seems to be lost, The Star will be there to light your way. But it will do so quietly. You must pay attention, watch for it, listen for it."

"Listen?" I had asked.

She had nodded. "It is a very spiritual card—and thus all the more relevant to witchkind. It speaks to our essence. The Star's energy is the spark of divinity within us all."

Okay, that was encouraging. Unfortunately, right next to it was the Ten of Wands: a poor fellow heavily burdened by ten heavy sticks, his back bending painfully under their weight. This was a card about power being blocked, and usually (as you might imagine) rather negative in a reading. It could, of course, be a spur to action, but it was pretty dismal. It was a message to stop butting your head against something that wasn't working, to try another path.

Not much different than Strength, I thought. Both the Background and the Solution seemed to be telling me that I was heading down the wrong path. So, should I *not* be looking for Gracie? Or not today? Or not this way?

My mini-reading's message turned back to the positive with the cheerful Page of Cups, however—a happy fool in a fancy outfit, holding a cup at a jaunty angle. (Though I'm not sure I'd be quite so cheerful if I had a live fish in my wine.) The card signified one's own childlike qualities—romantic and impractical, but also spiritual, nonrational. Kind of a poster child for tarot itself: a message to believe in your intuition, to trust your dreams. It was a card of emotional beginnings. Very fitting for a fifteen-year-old.

What a jumble, I thought, as I laid out the last card, on a row of its own: "The Final Outcome." It was the Ace of Swords: a glowing hand, emerging from some stormy clouds, holding a gleaming sword pointed straight up. A king's crown floats near the sword's tip.

"Huh," I muttered. A sword cuts both ways, I remembered: the wielding of power and justice, but also an instrument of death and injury. Being the Ace, it symbolized the beginning of a situation—it was interesting, and a little puzzling, to find it here as the Final Outcome. Was it hopeful, or was it a warning? (I could almost hear Mom's answer: "Both!" *Not helping, Mom.*) It could also mean a breakthrough or insight into the spirit world, which we generally took to mean the Beyond and the realms beyond that.

I sat staring at the spread for a long time, letting all the messages and images tumble through my mind, trying hard to not control it, not overthink it. I'd been getting better at this, but it was still a challenge for me. Not my natural way of solving a problem.

It was an interesting mix of "advice." Nothing specific to the issue of finding Gracie, of course; I told myself that I hadn't really expected that, though I felt disappointed all the same.

But what had I found out? The thing that kept resonating was the *wrong path* message. The *let go, try another way.* Gracie might be only fifteen, but she was a witch—and a strong one, at that. I'd been fretting about her like she was a helpless child. Was that the piece I was supposed to let go?

There were also lots of pointers to the spiritual realm. Should I be calling to Nementhe and our other ancestresses more often? Taking more action here in the real world?

Change course, I told myself.

But it was days before I took action.

When I did, it was to focus elsewhere entirely—taking the tarot's advice for all it was worth, though I didn't realize it at the time.

What I did realize was that I had let myself become so completely isolated in the last few months. I'd moved out of the coven house, ostensibly to live alone and do my work with less distraction and interference, and with better space. Of course my more immediate reasons had been to pursue my relationship with my sexy human boyfriend Raymond, and to live my life with less supervision—not that I would have admitted any of that to Leonora or any of witchkind's powers-that-be.

What is it about making plans? Even about having intentions? Because of course none of what I'd envisioned had come to pass. Raymond had turned out to be a completely different kind of boyfriend than I'd imagined he would be. It was almost like he'd wanted to move in, or something crazy like that. And the burden of my not being able to tell him who I was or what I could do...the very fundamentals of my identity...had created a strain between us where our relationship could just not survive.

I hadn't formally broken up with him, coward that I was. But we were through, and he and I both knew it very well.

He wasn't the only part of my life that the coven had stifled, though. I'd enjoyed not just fraternizing with humans, but also mingling with the younger set of witchkind. Witches my age, who were *not* in my coven. With whom I might actually have a thing in common.

I suddenly realized that I hadn't even been back to Rose's Bar since the night of Logan's birthday…when we had met Jeremy.

I patted my belly, sending warm thoughts to my own little growing Rose as I let myself feel the sadness all over again. Logan had been so happy that night. She'd sparked up an altogether uncharacteristic crush on Jeremy the moment she'd laid eyes on him. Not that I could blame her: he was charming and attractive, and more to the point, he was a complete unknown. The field of eligible warlocks is small in any community. We'd known our local dweebs all our lives.

Even though I still didn't want to drink any alcohol, I found myself missing the social scene at Rose's, and wondering why I hadn't even thought about it in months. Had the associations with Logan been just too strong—was I avoiding it, like a painful bruise?

No matter. Now that I'd thought about it, the next step was to get myself there.

I changed into a sort of shapeless black dress, one that still fit over my growing belly. It didn't hide the pregnancy exactly, but it didn't accentuate it. Then I walked out my front door and locked the house with the physical key before walking to the end of the block, where there was a more major ley line. Magical transit would be easier to take from there, with less twisting and turning, all of which drained my energy, already busy with baby-nourishing.

I supposed I could have taken a taxi, but I wasn't feeling in the mood for interacting with humans. Not right now, at least.

The moment I stepped inside the back room of the bar, I wondered again why I'd let this part of my life fall so completely off my radar. "Callie!" came a happy voice from the far side of the room.

I made my way through the crowd, following the inviting sound, and found Shella and Gentian at a tiny table.

"There's room for one more!" Shella cried, reaching around to steal a chair from the next table.

Gentian smiled up at me as well. She and Shella were the two junior members of Jasmine's coven, which focused on botanical magic, though in a more grounded sense (if you'll excuse the pun) than my mom's old coven, led by Isadora. I had been tempted to apply there when I turned twenty, but my love of teaching had kept me at Leonora's.

Paths not taken.

I sat down as Gentian raised her arm for the waitress. "We're doing Smol's," she said, unnecessarily; I could plainly see, and smell, the Smoldering Dragonflies in front of them. They smelled both great and awful. "Want one?"

"No thanks—just a soda for me," I said, as Glenna arrived, positioning her hands as though holding an invisible order pad. "Do you have lavender, or mint?"

"We have a basil-mint," she said.

"Perfect!"

Both young witches turned back to look at me, puzzled, as Glenna slipped back to the bar. "Those herbs are great, of course, but—" Shella started, pointing at my belly.

This time, at least, I'd thought ahead. "Healer's orders: Nora is carefully monitoring all my nutrition, including my alcohol intake; I'm not allowed to have anything fermented that she hasn't prepared with her own hands." I patted my belly and gave them both what I hoped was a sad smile. "She's being *very forceful* about it. Apparently I've been under unusual stress lately, and she wants to be sure everything is perfectly balanced."

"Wow," Gentian said, giving me a sympathetic look.

Shella shook her head. "Wow indeed. But she's right: Callie, we haven't seen you in months. We knew about the pregnancy, of course—"

"Who doesn't?" Gentian interrupted. "Story of the year!"

Shella gave her a little swat on the arm. "Gen! Be nice. Callie has been through a lot." She turned back to me. "How *are* you doing? We all miss Logan so, but I know you and she were particularly close."

We spent the next fifteen minutes getting caught up, as I sipped the herbal soda and realized that it was actually pretty nice to have friends. It was true that Logan had been my absolute bestie, and I missed her to pieces, but our community had been much larger than just the two of us.

Somehow, grief and loss—and my whirlwind romance with Jeremy—had eclipsed so much. I hadn't even realized it.

Even so, I couldn't tell them everything. It was hard to decide whether this felt better or worse, unloading at least some of my troubles to sympathetic witches.

Better, I told myself, leaning back and watching the two of them order more Smol's and giggle at some shared joke. A joke I'd missed by being so out of touch.

"So," Shella said, leaning forward and taking a big draught of her fresh drink, "what's it like, being pregnant?"

I smiled, resisting the urge to put my hand on my belly again. "It's marvelous, and weird, and energizing, and exhausting. I love it. I've never experienced anything like it."

"Is she communicating with you yet?" Gentian asked.

I shook my head. "No, that comes a bit later, I'm told. I mean—stuff about what I'm hungry or thirsty for, yeah, but that's not really communication."

"No," Gentian said, laughing, "everyone's stomach does that!"

"Is it true that it was a surprise?" Shella asked, lowering her voice.

Fortunately, I'd thought about this question too, though I wasn't sure anyone would have been so bold as to ask it. Oh, I did like my friends. "It was, though everyone seems to think that I must have somehow wished myself into conception without being fully conscious of the fact."

"Amazing. You're so lucky."

I smiled at them both again. "Our family is really fertile. My mom has two siblings, you know."

"But you don't have any, do you?" Gentian asked.

"No. I could, maybe, someday. My parents are still together." Though they'd always been vague about any intentions along these lines.

"Wow."

"It's almost like being human!" Shella put in. "Imagine, being able to just...make babies, whenever you want to."

"Oh, but then they wouldn't be special," Gentian said.

Shella rolled her eyes. "Have you ever *met* a human? They totally dote on their babies. They think they're the most special things ever."

"As if any planning or foresight went into them!" Gentian huffed, still smiling. "They just frolic in bed and pop out babies."

"And then act like they've done something amazing!"

"Are you going to sign a contract with Jeremy?" Gentian asked me.

"Oh, so you guys *are* going to let me back into the conversation?" I joked.

Shella laughed, pretending to rear back and swat Gentian again. "Only to ask you rude questions," she said to me.

"Well, *are* you? Will there be a huge party?"

"He offered a contract, but I'm still thinking about it," I told them. "There's just been too many changes in too short a time for me. I couldn't add something else on top of it. Not right now anyway."

The two witches shared a glance, and maybe even some silent communication. I could guess what they were thinking: *But what about the baby? Won't she need a father in her life? Is this really a good idea?* As young and hip and progressive as my friends might be, they were as steeped in our society's old-fashioned rules as I'd been.

"Plus, Jeremy's been gone so long," I added. "Now that he's back from the Old Country, we're going to be spending more time together. I'm sure we'll talk about it more."

"Sure, that's good," Shella said.

Yet I could almost feel the quiet discomfort that had settled over our table. I wished they could just be happy for me, and for baby Rosemary...but they just couldn't get their heads around there being any alternative way to do things.

Shella turned the conversation to gossip about some witches I barely knew. I tried to keep up, but soon just finished my drink and stood to go.

"You just got here!" Gentian cried, getting up to give me a hug.

I pulled her into a strong embrace. Despite the awkwardness, it had been really nice to get back out into the social swing of things. "It's like what I said earlier—my energy is unpredictable. But let's do this more often. Let me know when you guys are coming out next, and I'll try and join you."

"We will!" they both promised.

I left Rose's back room, waving at acquaintances at a half-dozen tables on my way out. The front room was, as ever, half-full of humans who had no idea what was in the room behind the shabby bar they saw. I hardly gave them a glance. I was too busy thinking about the conversation. What had been said, and what had not been said.

Out on the street, I hailed a taxi after all, not feeling up to the ley lines. As the city passed by outside the windows, I remembered what Leonora had told me about Niad's upbringing. How her mother had been covenless, and the father was out of the picture, and how this had helped shape Niad's entire personality and value system.

Niad was an uptight, judgmental rule-follower who drove me nuts even when she wasn't overtly insulting me or trying to boss me around. It felt downright pathological at times...because it probably was. She'd had such a painful, uncertain childhood, no doubt shunned and bullied by witches and warlocks from stable, traditional homes. She'd risen above this, joining San Francisco's oldest and arguably most prominent coven, and—despite her youth and lack of seniority—taking on a leadership position in it.

As if she were determined to put her past behind her.

And as if she were determined that no other witch should go through what she had suffered.

Niad always maintained that she was bossing me around because she cared about me. It was probably true, in a twisted-up way.

Didn't make me like it any better.

The taxi turned onto my street; the driver slowed down, peering at the house numbers. "Here is fine," I told her.

She pulled over in a driveway. I paid her and got out, happy to walk an entire half-block. That was about all the energy I had.

I let myself into my house, went through the feeding-scritching-settling down ritual with Elnor, and sat on the couch in my front room.

Was I making a mistake here? Just out of stubbornness and contrariness? I never liked being told what to do—who does, honestly?—but could generations of witchkind be entirely wrong?

Yes, said a little voice inside me. *They can be entirely wrong.*

They could also be entirely dishonest, couldn't they? Come to think about it. Hiding such an enormous secret—that we are *not* necessarily infertile with humans—didn't make me any more inclined to trust anything my elders told me.

I'd gotten through my life until this point largely on the strength of trusting my gut. Listening to my inner wisdom. Yes, listening to my parents and elders and teachers too—I would never pretend that I was some sort of self-made miracle paragon of wisdom and specialness—but it was when I questioned stuff and went my own way that I often learned the most. Made the breakthroughs. Got things done.

If I was going to raise this daughter alone, I would do it proudly. She would never feel the sort of shame and humiliation that Niad must have. She would know that I had had options, and that I had chosen the one that was best for the both of us.

I sighed, scratching Elnor's ears absently. If only I knew what that was…

Well, there was only one way to find out, at least about this part of it. I sent a message through the æther to Jeremy. *Would you like to come to my house for dinner tomorrow night?*

There was an unusually long pause. He hadn't left the area again, had he? It had been a few weeks since our dinner. We'd left it vague, but it had been a nice time. At least, I'd thought so.

I had almost decided that he was not going to answer when I got, *Calendula! What a delight to hear from you. I would be honored to dine at your lovely home.*

Come at eight?

Perfect. May I bring anything?

Just yourself.

I look forward to it. Then I felt the connection close.

— CHAPTER SIX —

Though my favorite food was takeout, I decided to cook for Jeremy. If I was going to raise a child, we couldn't spend twenty years eating out of Chinese cartons.

Just another way coven life had ill-prepared me for anything other than…well, coven life. I could teach biology to witchlets all the livelong day, but my cooking skills were basic at best.

Nevertheless, a few hours before Jeremy's arrival, I went into my kitchen, pondered the contents of the cupboards and fridge, and ultimately decided on carrot soup and grilled chicken sausages. Simple, but it should be tasty. How much could go wrong with soup?

Weirdly, as I got into it, I found I was rather enjoying myself. I didn't even let Petrana help. It was true, what Logan had said all those months ago. Cooking wasn't a whole lot different than brewing potions.

The warlock arrived at eight on the dot, carrying a paper bag in which I heard the clink of bottles. After I invited him in, he handed me the bag.

I pulled out a bottle of Zinfandel, and then another bottle with a label so fancy I could barely read it. Eventually, I figured out that it was a handmade shrub—lemon-rosemary. "I hope this is all right?" he said.

I looked up at him and smiled, surprised and pleased. "Yes, this looks amazing."

"I knew that the healers are measuring your intake of fermented beverages, but you seemed to enjoy shrub when we last dined, so I took a chance."

And how did you know that? I wondered, but I probably shouldn't have. Nora and Manka worked with his father at the clinic, after all. And who's to say what Shella and Gentian might have passed along? It wasn't as though it was a secret. It might even make things easier for me, come to think of it. Not having to make weird excuses or half-true explanations every time I hung out with anyone. "It's all perfect," I told him. "It'll go great with the meal."

"The wine is for me—though you are of course welcome to have some should you like," he added. "I'm not as big a fan of the vinegar drinks as you are."

"No, this is great. Come on back to the kitchen—it's almost ready."

He followed me down the long hall. I handed him a corkscrew and two wine glasses. "Don't think I won't put you to work," I said. "Wine for you and shrub for me, to start. There's soda to add to it in the fridge."

"I am delighted to help in any way I can."

Soon we were sitting at the kitchen table with fragrant bowls of soup before us. "This is delicious," he said, savoring a spoonful, wiping the corner of his mouth. He was unbelievably attractive. That, at least, had not changed.

"I'm glad you like it." I took a bite of my sausage and chased it with soup. "I don't have a lot of practice cooking."

"No, I imagine not. I like what you've done with the seasonings."

"Thanks."

Then we ate for another few minutes. Blessed Mother, did we truly have not a dang thing to say to one another? I tried to remember how suddenly and fiercely we'd connected, in the wake of Logan's demise. How he seemed to be the only person on the planet who understood what I was going through...who might even have shared the loss, though in a smaller way.

Was there truly none of that connection left?

"So—you've been busy lately?" I tried. *Ooh, not awkward at all!* I cringed inwardly.

His green eyes rose to meet mine. "Indeed, I have. As have you, I understand."

"Oh?"

"My father tells me you've been by the research lab at the clinic a few times."

"Huh." I shook my head. "I actually haven't seen your father in...some time. I didn't realize he knew I'd been by. I'm working with Dr. Fallon, mostly—if I work with anyone there."

Though of course, Gregorio was certainly monitoring me with this blessed ring.

"I spoke with him this afternoon," Jeremy said. "He sends his regards, by the way. He was delighted to learn that we are dining together this evening."

I'll bet he's delighted, I thought, then caught myself and gave Jeremy a smile. *He doesn't know anything,* I reminded myself. *He doesn't know how badly he's been manipulated—and by his own father. And you're trying to like him. To repair things. They were good once. Before...* "Please tell him hello for me," I said. I took a sip of the shrub (it was scrumptious, by the way) and went on. "Jeremy, everything is so...sideways these days." I put my hand briefly on my big belly before picking up my soup spoon again. "It feels like ten different lives are trying to be crammed into the space for one. We never even got to talk about...what we did to Flavius Winterheart...before you had to go to the Old Country. Can we...I don't know, start again? Maybe have regular meals together like this—no expectations, just getting to know each other once more?"

He reached out across the table, taking my right hand in his. "Oh, Callie. Of course we can." He squeezed my hand, his finger brushing against the family ring. "There is absolutely no trouble between us."

I looked back at him, feeling both relieved and sour at his words. "I am happy to hear that," I said, almost automatically. Yet anger flashed through me as I spoke; I felt my cheeks flush. Blessed Mother, I couldn't do this. Dishonesty would never work. I dropped his hand. "No, that's actually not true. Nothing about this is normal—we were pushed together by your father from the start, to the point where I don't even know what's real between us or not." I stared at him, frustrated, stymied by how much I couldn't say. "Then we had to basically commit murder together—and then you left for months, and we couldn't even communicate." I huffed out a breath and leaned back in my chair.

He started to say something, paused, and then started again. "I… confess I have not known what to do. I am glad you are speaking of it. You are entirely right—this is a very peculiar, very awkward situation." He swallowed and glanced away before looking back up at me with a small, endearing smile. "I am a diplomat, and I do not know how to talk to the woman I love."

My heart softened. "Maybe *diplomacy* is the problem here." He was trying, I knew he was. It was me who had the secrets. But I couldn't even let him guess that. No wonder he was confused. And for someone with greater than average emotional intuition… "Just, I don't know, let's get to know each other again. Like we did before."

"I would like that."

We smiled at each other across the table. Okay, still awkward, but with a little more comfort now. It felt more like we had a common problem we were trying to figure out together, rather than that we were at odds.

"Well, what shall we talk about?" he said, after a minute.

"I don't know, anything," I said, shrugging. "I do still want to hear more about the Old Country—what it's like there, what it's even like to travel there. What you did there. Anything."

It was like a shutter fell over his eyes as I spoke. "I have told you, the last time we dined. I looked into things and got nowhere. I also did a few errands to help my father with his research."

"That's not what I meant," I said, my irritation rising once more. "I know you can't tell me his precious secrets. I just wanted you to tell me about, I don't know, the markets and the architecture and stuff. I know the people don't talk to each other, but I don't even have a sense of what it *looks* like." His gaze stayed closed. I shook my head. "Never mind. Forget I asked."

He glanced away again, then took a deep breath. "Calendula, please, can we not quarrel?" He reached a tentative hand across the table again; I took it. "I would very much like to start over with you, as you say. I miss you...I miss your touch, your smile, your wit and energy. I want to raise our daughter together, in any way that is acceptable to you. I feel that we have the potential to form an amazing partnership, romantically and magically. I have no secrets from you." He emphasized the "I" just a bit, just enough.

Oh, how I wished I could say the same. For the millionth time, I wanted to slap Gregorio Andromedus, scream myself silly at him. I sighed, still holding Jeremy's hand, feeling worse by the moment. Wondering what to do with this—this whole thing. "I'm sorry. Pregnancy is making me weird. Emotional." I felt bad using the baby as an excuse, but it was certainly the easy way out of so many impossible situations.

"I understand," he said. And maybe he did, who knew? "The Old Country has a bit of a, well, old-fashioned look, I suppose. I'm not sure if you would like it or not—it's a bit rustic, without a lot of the modern conveniences of San Francisco—but there's a quiet comfort there. An ease in not having to hide our basic natures."

"That must be nice," I said, thinking about it. It would be like coven life, I decided, except everywhere.

"Despite the coolness and reserve I spoke of before," he said, "there's a feeling of welcome. At least," he added with a shrug, "I feel it. But then I was raised there. I don't know what it would be like for an American visitor. I do know that tourists—"

"Yes, you mentioned that," I said. "I still want to go there."

He glanced at my belly, looking mildly alarmed. "Do you realize—"

"Yes, yes," I said. "Not now, I know that. After she's born."

"Then we shall do that." He smiled at me. "We will go there together, after you recover, when you and the child both are strong enough to travel. Perhaps in a year or two. I will be happy to take you, to show you the ropes. To help you with the travel."

"Do you really mean it?"

His smile grew warmer. "I do, Callie. I very much do."

"All right." I took a sip of my shrub. "Thank you." I wasn't sure if I believed him or not, but arguing wasn't going to get us anywhere.

"You are most welcome." He glanced down at his bowl. "I fear my soup has gone cold. Would you…mind?" He held his finger at the ready.

I laughed. "By all means. You don't need my permission to work magic in my house."

He focused a small heat spell at his fingertip and pointed; steam rose from the bowl. "How is yours?"

"I could use a warm-up too, thanks."

Our time together passed more comfortably after that, at least for a while. We veered away from sensitive topics and tried our darnedest to do what we'd agreed to do: start over, get to know one another. I told him about going back to Rose's Bar, how nice it was to reconnect with some of the younger witches in the community.

Then I found myself telling him about Gracie running off, likely to Los Angeles, and that I was worried about her. I'd sort of blurted it out without thinking...Leonora hadn't said anything about not telling the community at large—in fact, she'd immediately contacted her coven-mother friend in L.A.—but I had this guilty sense of airing dirty laundry. Oh well, too late now.

"She's fifteen?" Jeremy asked, frowning.

"Yeah."

"Only five years from her majority. When I was fifteen..." He trailed off, his face darkening a moment. "But then, as I was just saying, this world is not that world. She is a magical practitioner: she will not have to fear the ill designs of mortal men."

"That's true." I'd had that thought myself. Not that it provided a whole lot of comfort. "I just wish she would let someone know where she is, that she's okay."

"I don't mean to minimize your concern, but she is almost certainly all right. You've mentioned that she's willful, strong-headed? Not happy with the old ways?" His eyes twinkled.

"Yes, that's our Gracie."

"And powerful?"

"She is. She's one of our strongest students."

His smile was kind, gentle. "She does sound like a certain witch I know, and for whom I care a great deal."

"Yeah, yeah." I sighed, smiling back at him. "I guess I'm just practicing to be a mom."

"You will make a marvelous mother," he said, his tone turning entirely serious. But still kind.

"You think so?" I wasn't fishing for compliments. Well, not entirely.

He nodded. "I do."

We gazed at one another over our empty dishes for a minute. Then, "Well," I said, as he said, "I thank you—" We both laughed.

Jeremy recovered first. "I thank you for the delicious dinner."

"You are most welcome."

Another pause. "I am happy to be seeing you again," he said. "Shall we dine together again soon?"

"Yes, I'd like that," I said. "It's…a good idea." There was so much more to say, but that was a good place to start.

"I won't impose on your hospitality any longer," he said, getting to his feet. "But may I return the favor soon? There's a lovely little Persian restaurant in Pacific Heights I've been wanting to try."

"Sure."

He leaned over and kissed me on the cheek, completely chastely. "I can see myself out."

"Don't even think of it," I said, getting up and walking him to the front door. There, we smiled at one another again.

"I'll be in touch, about dinner. Thank you again."

And he left.

That was nice, I thought. Very nice. The fact that he hadn't assumed I'd ask him to stay—hadn't even acted like it was a thing that could happen—perversely made me think about it more.

But this was a good way to go about it, I told myself. If we were to find our way back together, it should be natural. Not forced.

Like the way we came together in the first place—after working a complex, *good* bit of magic together, in warding my house. And that only after weeks and weeks of friendly, emotionally important conversations, during which we were most expressly not courting one another. Our connection had grown organically…before the outside world had busted in and knocked everything over.

If there was any hope for us, that was how it would have to work again.

I was getting my life in order. What I could control of it, anyway. It felt important to at least do that.

So, a few nights after that second dinner with Jeremy, I pulled my dusty cell phone off its charger and called Raymond.

Naturally, I got his voicemail. "Hi," I said to the machine. "It's Callie. I'm sorry about how we left things, and I'd like to get together to talk, if you're willing." *What else?* I thought. "I…have some news, which is probably best conveyed in person." There, that ought to get his attention. "Call me." I hung up and stood in the kitchen, a little stunned at myself.

Petrana was at the sink, washing my dinner dishes. Her movements were so natural, they were frankly starting to get a little Uncanny Valley. She still didn't look like a human, exactly. But she was darn close.

See, you can do good work, I told myself.

An hour later, I was upstairs on my way to bed. I'd stopped to gaze into the nursery, still unsure about a wall color, when the cell phone rang.

I pulled the phone out of my dress pocket. "Hi, Raymond."

"Callie." He sounded wary. And who could blame him? "What's up?"

"I was hoping maybe I could, um, see you?"

A pause. "Sure, I guess." Then another pause. "Right now?"

"Whenever works for you. But soon, I hope."

"Sure, okay. You wanna come here?"

That seemed only fair. "It's not too late?"

He laughed. "Dude. I just got in from a gig. Won't be able to sleep for hours yet."

"All right. I'll be right over."

"Cool." Another brief pause, then he added, "Hey, I got a thing to tell you too."

"Okay." I detected something in his tone…excitement? Happiness? Though still very guarded. "In person?"

"You bet."

I dawdled a bit getting ready, wondering if I should change clothes. None of my jeans fit anymore, of course, not even with magical assistance. I was wearing a shapeless long-sleeved cotton dress, basic San Francisco black (i.e., faded), and stretchy leggings. I finally decided that that would do fine. I pulled on a pair of boots, rebraided my hair, and headed downstairs, thinking to call a taxi. I decided at the last minute to try this new Lyft thing I'd been hearing about for the last few years…yes, I know, even young witches live on a different timeline.

I stood on my front porch and pulled out the cell phone again, trying to figure out the Lyft thing. It was hopelessly complicated. What even was an "app"? Why did humans have to change things all the time? I'd just gotten this new-fangled phone when I was dating Raymond. Last year.

Finally, I gave up and sent a burst of magic into the phone. Moments later, a gray sedan pulled up in front of my house and a slightly addled young man drove me to Raymond's apartment.

I magically added money directly to the driver's bank account before hopping out of the car. Well, not hopping, exactly, in my condition; more like levering myself out. In any event, I made it to the apartment door and rang Raymond's bell. He buzzed me up, and then I was at his apartment door.

"Hi." He stood in the doorway, looking good enough to eat. His red-blond hair tumbled down loose over his shoulders, a little damp and smelling freshly of his shampoo. I smiled at him, genuinely glad to see him. Remembering very well what I'd seen in him in the first place.

He looked me in the eye a moment, then, with a small shrug, opened his strong arms for a hug.

I went for it. As I got there, my belly pushed against him. He tensed and pulled back, looking down. "Oh. *Oh.*"

"Yeah." An awkward blush colonized my face. No matter how much I'd anticipated this moment, nothing could prepare one for actually being there. "I've got lots to tell you."

"I guess so." He lifted his gaze to mine. His face was a cascade of emotions—surprise, fear, curiosity—happiness? We stood there a moment longer, then he collected himself and said, "Uh, come on in."

I followed him into his cluttered studio apartment. He'd clearly made some attempt to tidy up since our call—most of the laundry was in a pile in the corner rather than strewn everywhere, and I saw a few dripping dishes in the drainer—but it was mostly how I remembered it.

He closed and bolted the door behind me before stepping back and looking me over. "How far along?"

I lowered myself to sit on the futon and tried to ignore my conscience. I knew what he was really asking. "Almost seven months."

I watched him do the math. "So it's…?"

The moment of truth. Except I had to lie. Gregorio had made that perfectly clear. I had to lie even to humans…and most particularly to this one. Did I imagine I felt the ring heating up on my finger, just the tiniest bit? It had to be my imagination. The magic didn't work that way.

Unless Gregorio wanted it to, of course.

No matter. "No. You are not the father."

"Oh." He sat down at the other end of the futon, a good distance from me. "Um. Congratulations?"

I gave him a sad smile. "Thank you. I'm really excited, actually. And I'm sorry I didn't tell you sooner."

"Yeah. Okay. Wow." He glanced at my belly again. "So…you wanna tell me about…the father?"

I nodded. "His name is Jeremy. You met him once, actually." He looked confused, which was when I remembered that I'd blanked his memory of that whole terrible evening. Rats. "I mean, I think you did," I backtracked. "It was right when everything was so crazy. When Logan died—my friend, who I told you about." That was true, at least.

"Yeah. Oh." He relaxed a bit, his natural sympathy bubbling up. Making me feel even worse for the lie.

But I pressed on. "He's the son of one of the important leaders of our intentional community. But our relationship..." I'd thought all this through, I'd been thinking it through for days now, but telling it to Raymond's face was not the same as rehearsing it alone at home. "It's not...I'm not sure where it's going, exactly. This wasn't something I planned, or chose. There's a lot up in the air."

"Ah." *An arranged marriage,* I could almost see him thinking. *And she's not happy with it.* Oh, why did I have to do this? Why couldn't he be furious with me? Why did he have to be so kind, so understanding?

Why couldn't I just have made it work with him?

Yes, I know, I know. But it still didn't make any of this any easier.

"I still live alone," I blurted out. "But I'm—you know, concentrating on this right now." I patted my belly.

"Right, sure." He looked like he wanted to say more, but didn't.

"Anyway, I wanted you to know." I gave him a gentle smile. "It was hard to think of how to tell you, which is why it took so long. I know that doesn't make it better." *Big old coward that I am.* "I can go now, if you like."

"No, no, stay," he said quickly. "I...I guess I just need a minute to get used to it. I knew you said you had something to tell me, but... that's kinda not what I expected."

"I bet not!" I laughed, nervously, but also relieved. He shifted awkwardly on the futon. "Well, it's good to see you."

"I always like to see you, Callie." He was smiling, but his voice was sad. "You look good. You look really good."

"Um. Thanks." More silence ensued, until I remembered what else he'd said on the phone. "So, what's *your* news?"

He suddenly brightened. "You're not gonna believe this!"

"Try me."

"Okay, so, remember my band?"

"Of course." I laughed. "How could I forget? The Warm Nuggets will always have a place in my heart."

He snickered. "Yeah, sure. Well anyway, we got asked to open for Demonhead on a big tour! All the way through So-Cal and then the Southwest after that."

"That's amazing! When do you go?"

"We got back two weeks ago."

"Oh!" Right. We had been very thoroughly out of touch. "So... how did it go?"

"It was awesome, major awesome." He relaxed against the back of the futon, his face filling with delight. "Everything went right—Demonhead was awesome, the crowds were awesome, the cities were awesome, the reviews were awesome, the money was awesome—"

"Yes, that all sounds very awesome." I tried not to giggle.

"Oh, sorry—I'm doing it again. Peter says that's why I can't write the lyrics. Okay—it was incredible, amazing, extraordinary, super-duper. How's that?" He cocked his head at me. Oh Blessed Mother, he was adorable.

"Much better," I said, forcing down inconvenient warm and tender feelings. "But don't let Peter boss you around. He's no poet himself."

"True that. But hey, I don't care. 'Cause you know why?"

"No, why?"

"It's the best part of all! Just before the end of the tour, this dude comes to meet with us, and guess what! We signed a recording deal with TCA! They want three albums, and they're giving us *huge* piles of money! We already dropped a single on SoundCloud, and they've made a YouTube channel for us. I'm gonna be a rock star!"

"Oh my god that's amazing!" I said. "You guys totally deserve that!" I'd always thought they were pretty good, but when did that ever make a difference? Any big city had a wealth of talented musicians, and San Francisco was no exception. "So you get to quit construction?"

He laughed. "I kinda already did, by not coming home when I said I would."

"Your own father fired you?"

"Well...we agreed to go our own ways in this, is kinda what he said." Now he looked sheepish, but still very happy.

"Raymond, this is fantastic. Congratulations."

"Thanks! So of course we're gonna have a huge mad party! Everyone's coming, everyone. We're renting out the Rat's Nest Bar for the night, my sister's springing for the food—cuz, well, we haven't actually got the first check yet."

"Ah." *Oh, no,* I thought. *I hope this is real...*

"But on SoundCloud, a little bit of cash has started to come in," he went on, still excited.

I nodded, though I had no idea what he was talking about. "Great."

"So the band's gonna play a set, and the audience will all vote on what tracks we should put on the first album." He looked at me earnestly. "Will you come?"

"Yes, that sounds like fun. When?"

"The 17th."

A week and a half from now. "I'll be there."

His excitement was infectious. It was such good news, such a one-in-a-million shot—at something he'd always dreamed about. It was probably real. He'd said they'd signed a contract, at least, and that money was coming in from some cloud thing. Still smiling, I leaned toward him, almost without thinking. He pulled me into his arms again, side-hugging me around all this baby.

And I tried to ignore that familiar, comforting scent.

After a minute, I drew back. "So—"

"Yeah, I know, I know." He looked sadly at my belly, then into my eyes. "Jeez, I didn't even offer you anything to drink! Except, um..." He looked at my middle again.

"Raymond, it's all right, I don't need anything. And I really can't stay very long; it's late, and, you know, I need more sleep than I used to..."

He snorted. "That's a change! Can you stand it?"

"Yes, I might almost need as much sleep as you now."

What a dumb thing to say. Now we were both remembering being in bed together, and feeling even more sad.

If I didn't know I was forty-five years old, I'd think I was fourteen.

I hugged him again and took my leave before the awkwardness could bloom further.

— CHAPTER SEVEN —

I probably shouldn't have even tried sleeping the night after I went to see Raymond; I was too stirred up, with emotions and memories, second-guessing myself up one side and down the other. Usually when I can't sleep, I head up to the lab to poke around with my Petri dishes, or go harvest things at the secret night garden, or read a book. But my belly felt heavy and my legs were tired; I knew my body needed sleep.

I just couldn't convince it to fall there.

So I tossed and turned, and rolled onto my side and eased a pillow under my bulge, and then shifted around and redid the whole arrangement on the other side.

Eventually, I did fall asleep, and then I *really* wished I hadn't.

The dream started innocuously enough. I was walking through some sort of retail space, clothing maybe, looking for something but not finding what I wanted. I came across two small white cats. They were lying on one of the shop's shelves and started that cute rolling-over-and-gazing-at-you thing that cats do when they want you to pay attention to them. They were adorable, and identical; I walked up and petted them both. They squirmed with delight under my hand. "Nice kitties," I said. "Pretty kitties."

I suddenly became aware of a human woman standing behind me and just a little off to the side, as if she wanted to talk to me but was hanging back. Shy, or polite; reluctant for some reason. I turned to look at her, but I was also still looking at and petting both cats, in the impossible-is-also-normal way of dreams.

"You have to adopt them," she said.

"Oh, no, I can't, I have a cat at home."

The human woman moved closer, almost menacingly close. Though in my waking life, such a thing wouldn't frighten me at all—I could zap any human unconscious with a flick of my fingers—I grew scared in the dream, unable to move away or to do anything to stop her. "You must take them home," she said.

"I told you, I can't. I'm sure someone will take them. They're very nice cats." All this while, the cats were still rolling around, being adorable, enjoying my petting. Ignoring the strange human woman.

"They came from an abusive home," she said. "I rescued them. The man was hitting my sister, and he was going to kill the cats."

"I'm really sorry to hear that. I'm glad they're safe now."

She leaned even closer to me. I could see the pores on her face, smell the cured meat she'd had for dinner, plus a whiff of stale wine. It turned my stomach, but I still could not move or do anything besides pet the cats. "You have to adopt them."

"I can't," I protested yet again. Weak. Ineffective. She was not hearing me. I wished someone could come help me...I tried to think about calling out, about reaching for my magic, reaching through the æther, but it was like I was in a magical straitjacket.

And part of me *wanted* to help! They were adorable cats; I didn't want them to suffer. I certainly didn't want them to go back to an abusive home. (And dream-me didn't even think about the weird woman's sister, wonder why she was only concerned about the cats...) But I couldn't. It was simply impossible. But I could not make her understand that.

Callie? It was a familiar voice, pushing through the fog. I couldn't place it, though.

"You *have* to take the cats."

I struggled as hard as I could to pull away from the entire situation, to get even the tiniest bit of movement out of my limbs…I managed to take one step. It was as though I was drowned in syrup.

Then I felt a sharp pain in my hand. I wheeled around, suddenly able to move very well. Both cats were biting me, sinking their sharp fangs into my hand, drawing blood. Neither of them looked so sweet or cute anymore. "Hey!" I cried out, trying to take my hand back. But the cats hung on tenaciously. The pain grew.

Callie!

"Who's there?" I called out, and now I was aware I was in a dream. I was not usually a lucid dreamer, but it had happened before. Usually when I went into a dream state intentionally—but it seemed like a good development now. "Who is it?"

"Callie!"

It was Sebastian! Now I could hear his voice in the real world, but I was still being attacked by the cats, and it really, really hurt.

"Sebastian!" I tried to yell. It came out as a sort of weird warble; I heard it both in the dream and in my physical-world ears.

Needle-teeth sank into my hand, into my fingers…into one finger particularly. I cried out again, without making a sound this time.

Then both cats suddenly let go of my hand. They stared me in the face, opened their mouths, and in unison said, *"You have to listen to the cats."*

I stared back at them—none of this made any sense—and I lost all my words. I didn't even know how the cats had spoken to me; it wasn't in language, but they did speak, and those were their words. I felt myself running out of air, no longer just struggling to speak but even to breathe—my body started to shake—

My shoulders were shaking. I had no control over my movements. Just as I was about to go under, I sprang awake—and Sebastian was here, leaning over me, shaking my shoulders. "Callie! Oh, thank the Father."

"Oh Blessed Mother," I gasped, trying to catch my breath. "Oh, oh."

"Callie!" he cried again, putting his face close to mine, still shaking me.

"You can stop pummeling me now, I'm out of it," I finally managed.

Sebastian let go of me and sat down on the side of the bed. He was still looking hard at me, obviously very worried. "What in the world was going on there?" he asked.

"I don't know. Just an awful dream, I think." I picked up my right hand with my left, as if the right had no strength. Maybe it didn't, for all I knew. I didn't trust it; I expected to see blood dripping from it. Of course there was no blood, but it still hurt.

Right where that horrid gold ring sat.

Sebastian took my hand and peered at it. "What's this red mark?"

I looked too. "Um, I tried to magic the ring off a while back…it didn't work. I guess this must be from that."

He frowned, but didn't say anything, just keep inspecting the area.

"How did you get in here?" I finally had the presence of mind to ask. "And, *why*?"

The young warlock looked up at me. "Your wards are down. Don't you set them when you go to sleep, at least?"

I shrugged. My heart rate was slowly returning to normal. "Not usually. The, uh, reason for making them isn't really a thing these days."

He gave me a puzzled look. I didn't elaborate, just reiterated, "Why are you here? I mean, I'm always happy to see you, but…"

"I felt—something, I couldn't define or explain it, but I knew you needed help. I tried to call to you, but you didn't answer. So I came over and knocked, but again, nothing." He glanced around my bedroom and looked sheepish. "Sorry, but—"

"Don't apologize," I said. "I'm glad you did. That was awful."

"Just…a bad dream?"

"No, it was probably more than that." I shivered, remembering it. Still feeling the pain in my hand, though it was starting to fade. "It was sort of a lucid dream, but I didn't have any control." I told him about the human woman, the cats, and what the cats had said. "I don't know what to make of it."

Elnor walked into my bedroom, gave Sebastian a look, and jumped up on the bed.

"Where have you been?" I asked her, suddenly freaked out all over again.

She just looked up at me, in her silent way of asking for a scritching.

"She usually sleeps with you, doesn't she?" Sebastian asked.

"Of course. And even if she didn't, she should have known I was distressed."

Now, at least, she was sending her calm feline energy into me, letting me pet her while she purred and nudged her head against me. But it was as though nothing was out of the ordinary. As if she'd had no idea anything had been wrong; as if she'd simply heard voices and wandered in for some attention.

"Too weird," Sebastian said.

I took a deep breath and swung my legs over the bed, setting Elnor aside. There would be no more sleeping for me tonight. "Can I make you some tea?"

"Sure thing."

Downstairs, we talked over every detail of the dream, but neither of us could make much sense of it. "There's a human," Sebastian mused, "but a woman, not a man, so it can't be your human ex."

"Could be," I said. "I just saw him yesterday. Maybe I had humans on the mind."

"You did? Saw him…how?"

I chuckled. "Not like that. I wanted to see how he was doing, and tell him about the baby."

"Ah."

"Don't worry," I said. "He's not going to be back in my life—"

"I'm not the one worried about that!" Sebastian said, putting his hands up in a warding-off motion.

And that made me laugh. "Okay, I know, I know. Anyway, it was good to see him. His band is doing well; I'm going to a party for them in a week or so."

Sebastian frowned. "So it's probably not him, then. That leaves the cats."

"I know. 'Listen to the cats.' When do I *not* listen to the cats?"

"Do you think it has anything to do with Logan's cat? He never turned up, did he?"

"Not yet."

We sipped our tea in silence for a while. Moonlight came through the back window, puddling on the kitchen floor in interesting ways as it filtered through the breeze-blown leaves outside.

"Well," Sebastian said, setting his empty cup on the table. "Speaking of cats, if you're fine here…"

"Yeah, entirely fine. Thank you for coming over and pulling me out."

He got up; I did too, and he drew me into a gentle hug. "Of course. What are friends for?"

Life got quiet again in the following days. No more strange dreams; nothing strange at all, in fact. It almost made me uncomfortable, but mostly I was just relieved to have a bit of a break.

Pregnancy, as I may have mentioned, takes a lot out of one.

I was just beginning to think about whether I should reach out to Jeremy again when he called to me. *May I return the favor of dinner, and have you to my house?*

Your house? I hadn't known he had a house. *Aren't you staying with your father?* Blessed Mother no, I wasn't going to Gregorio's. Not if there was any way in the world I could avoid it.

I am not. I've lucked into a place of my own. In the Marina.

I suspected luck had little to do with it, but polite fictions must be maintained. *That's awesome,* I said, inwardly cringing at my Raymond-ism. *When?*

If it's not too desperately impolite to assume that you might have no plans this evening, what about…this evening?

I chuckled. *Well, I have been maintaining a* very *busy schedule of puttering around with research that's going nowhere, interspersed with sudden attack naps at the least convenient moments. But I think I could squeeze in a dinner cooked by someone else this evening.*

Marvelous, he sent back. *I'll expect you around seven thirty?*

That works.

I showed up at the appointed time and we passed a lovely, quiet evening: cocktails (and mocktails) in the gracious front room, whose bowed front windows overlooked the Marina Green and the bay beyond; followed by a delicious chicken dinner that I was pretty sure the warlock cooked himself. He served dessert in the small sunroom at the back of the house.

After dessert, he gave me a tour of the rest of the place, including his bedroom, which was extremely gracious as well. I made polite noises and returned to the front room to admire the view once more before heading home.

Other than showing me his bedroom, Jeremy made not the slightest suggestion that we revisit our former intimacy. He was obviously leaving any further moves to me—at least for now.

Which suited me just fine. I liked this comfortable balance we'd found. The future…would unfold as it would, when it would.

The Rat's Nest was a classic dive bar, on the cusp between the inner Mission and South of Market, under a freeway overpass. Nevertheless, I decided to dress up. It was a celebration, after all.

I found a great dress in a thrift store in the Haight. After I made a few modifications for my pregnancy, it fit perfectly. The skirt was black, and very full; the fabric just skimmed the floor, the hem ending in tiny blood-red roses, leaving just the toes of my favorite 'vogs to peek out. The dress's long sleeves were sheer black, almost net, and lace-tipped at the wrists. The bodice was also black, with a corset-like design of bright red laces which expanded over my breasts, nipped in a little, then expanded again to frame my belly.

I was taking these odd new ride-share cars all the time lately, and only occasionally needing to spell them to me; once I'd finally figured out the app thing, I found that it worked pretty well. I told myself that I'd teach my daughter ley travel once she was out here with me. For now, conserving my energy felt right.

I pushed open the dingy door to the bar and stood just inside, blinking to help my eyes adjust to the dimness. Wow, this place was even shabbier than the front room at Rose's. There was a small, empty stage near the back, an assortment of tables on the main floor, and a long wooden bar, scarred and stained from years of serious drinking.

Raymond and his band and various hangers-on had pushed a couple of tables together in the center of the room. Seeing me, he grinned and waved an arm, calling me over. "Callie!" He made room between himself and a redheaded woman, pushing aside beer bottles. "This is Christine."

"Nice to meet you." I shook her hand, blanking for just a moment on who she could be—surely he didn't have a new girlfriend he'd failed to mention?—before remembering that this was his sister. I gave her a big smile. Right, now I could see the family resemblance. The red hair *should* have been a clue.

Christine was dressed as casually as the rest of the group, but on her it looked respectable and mature. Her jeans were clean, her T-shirt white and unadorned by any rude words or gory pictures. A silver pentacle on a chain rested at her collarbone, and she wore a fabulous pair of black boots. Her long red hair sparkled with life; it almost looked like witch's hair.

She smiled back at me warmly. "It's a pleasure to meet you too. Can I get you something to drink?" Her eyes flickered to my belly; I remembered that Raymond had said she was a midwife. And a Wiccan.

"Not right now, thanks," I said. "Sorry I'm late," I added, to Raymond.

"It's cool," he said. "We were kind of waiting for the guy from the studio to show up before we started, but he's not here yet. Maybe..."

"Dude, let's give him another ten minutes," Dave the drummer said.

Oh no, I thought. *It's falling apart already...* The music industry and its notorious flakiness.

But then Raymond said, "Here he is!"

The whole band and several girlfriends (or tambourine players) sprang to their feet and rushed over to greet the TCA rep and offer him a beer, a sandwich, a shot, a young virgin, whatever he wanted. Christine and I were suddenly alone at the table. Her eyes filled with amusement as she said, "God, I'm so relieved, I thought he was making the whole thing up!"

"Who, Raymond?" I said, with exaggerated seriousness.

After we'd collected ourselves, she said, "That's an amazing dress, by the way."

"Thanks. Secondhand special."

"I never thought of actually emphasizing pregnancy like that, but it's gorgeous. It really works."

"Yeah, thank goodness for modern society," I said. "I'd never have been allowed out of the house in earlier times, much less dressed up—in any way."

"So true." She paused a moment. "It's nice of you to come tonight. I know it means a lot to Raymond, even though you're not with him anymore."

"I'm hoping he and I can still be friends," I said. "Things got a little chaotic in my life for a while there, and we lost touch…but he seems like he's doing well."

She sipped from a beer bottle, thinking. "He's okay," she said after a minute. "He puts a good face on it." Now she smiled. "The record deal helps."

"I'll bet!"

"Especially since it seems to be actually real."

We both laughed. I was really liking her.

"Are these seats taken?"

We both looked up to see a group of four guys standing over our table. Young insurance salesmen or realtors trying to seem hip, by the look of it. "Yes," we both said in unison.

A minute later, we chased away another group of strangers, but then we realized that the band was now setting up onstage and wouldn't be needing their seats back. "Just as well," Christine said with a wicked grin, "none of those guys were nearly cute enough. Ooh—maybe that one wants to come sit. Riiight here." She patted her lap as she frankly appraised a guy standing at the door, but he didn't notice.

Barely moving my be-ringed right hand (I might as well get *some* good use out of the awful thing), I sent the guy a nudge. He was by Christine's side in moments, offering to buy her another beer. They began an animated conversation while I studied him. Blond, and somewhat cute, I supposed. Not my type.

By doing Christine that favor, though, I had just deprived myself of her company. So I watched the band warm up. I did love to see Raymond with his bass guitar...he handled it lovingly, appreciatively, rather like...hmm, no, that wasn't such a good idea either. Yes, there were definitely things I missed about him.

I turned back to Christine and whatever-his-name-was, and now saw that she didn't like the guy after all. Which didn't take magic; her body language said it all. With another flick of my finger under the table, I put the idea in his head that he needed to be on the opposite side of the room from her for the rest of the evening—and the rest of his life. He fled.

"My god," Christine said. "Incel special. He was so much better from a distance."

"Well, he's at a distance now."

"Good thing." She swigged her beer and grinned. "I'm sorry. This is selfish—you can't drink."

"Oh, that's fine, I don't even like beer. But it makes me happy to watch you enjoy it." And that was true.

She gave me a thoughtful look. "I see what Raymond likes about you. You're a good person. I'm sensitive to people's auras and energy."

"Yes," I said. "I can see that."

"You're sensitive too," she went on. "I could tell you noticed that Steve was an asshole, even though you weren't talking to us. And as soon as you noticed, he was out of here."

Interesting, I thought. Christine was pretty sharp. Maybe too sharp. "It wasn't a huge challenge," I said. "You were practically squirming and rolling your eyes at the ceiling. I was hoping you weren't packing a knife in one of those boots."

She snorted with laughter, then shook her head. "Callie, I'm so sorry we didn't get to meet earlier."

"Me too," I said. Raymond had mentioned his sister to me a few times, but I'd had no idea she was so cool. Though I should have known. She was related to him, after all.

"We should get lunch or something together. Do you work in the city?"

"Yes—at home, actually."

"What do you do again?"

Before I had to come up with an answer (because I didn't know of many molecular biologists who had labs at home), the band launched into a screamingly loud opening number. Christine and I laughed and pointed at our ears. I shrugged, she mouthed "LATER," and we sat back to enjoy the music.

The concert was great. The band had really matured since the last time I'd seen them—apparently their time on the road had sharpened them considerably. There were several very tuneful new numbers, intermixed with revved-up versions of songs I already knew. They also covered some perennial rock favorites.

Most importantly, the TCA rep sat right up front, smiling and tapping his feet for the whole set.

"I don't know which songs to vote for," I said to Christine when the last number was still echoing in my ears. "They were all great."

"But they can't put out a CD with twenty-five songs on it."

"People still make CDs?"

She grinned. "Retro bands do. They're even talking about vinyl, if you can believe it."

The band in question was still onstage, breaking down; one of the hangers-on had passed out pens and little slips of paper. Instead of ranking songs, I wrote down my name and cell phone number and gave it to Christine. "Here. I gotta run—tell Raymond bye for me. And call me, if you're serious about that lunch date."

She dug a business card out of her jeans pocket. "I am, and I will. Here's mine, if I flake."

"I don't imagine you flake much," I said.

"Hmm." She smiled. "No, not often."

— CHAPTER EIGHT —

Time passed. My belly grew. I slept a lot, and didn't get much work done.

On a Tuesday a few weeks after Raymond's band party, I stepped into the coven house for the regular dinner and Circle, then stopped, just inside the door. What was different? Was Gracie back? No—I could tell that at once. But something was off.

Elnor, in my arms, sensed my alertness and began sniffing the air, then turned her golden eyes to mine.

"What do you see, kitten?" I asked. She just blinked, so I set her down.

I could hear several of my sisters moving about—in the kitchen, the schoolroom, bedrooms upstairs—but I didn't detect Leonora's presence. Not all that unusual.

I walked through and into the kitchen, and that's when I figured it out. Leonora's study, just behind it, was missing something.

Organza was chopping zucchini on the big kitchen island. "Where's Logan's body?" I asked her.

She looked up. "Hello, Callie."

"Sorry. Hi. Where's Logan's body?"

"Gregorio Andromedus was here, meeting with Leonora. They've agreed to take it to his clinic for further study."

At the mention of the warlock's name, I went rigid with alarm, even as I tried to hide my reaction. "Oh," I managed, striving for casual. Yes, now I could tell—it wasn't just the absence of her body, but it was also the odd essence of warlock still in the air. Warlocks only entered the house on special occasions. Gregorio came here even less frequently. "Did she say why?"

Organza shrugged. "Well, I guess it's easier for him to study it there than to ask us to let the wards down again."

"Has he been here before today?"

My coven sister glanced up at me. "A few times. Just in the last week or so." She scraped the zucchini into a mixing bowl and started peeling garlic.

I stifled any further questions. "You want some help with that?"

"Sure." She passed over a head of garlic and a knife.

"What else has been going on around here?" I asked, as I smashed cloves with the flat of the knife, breaking the papery skin.

"Oh, the usual," Organza said. "You know."

I supposed I did, but I was also squirming with curiosity. I wondered if Leonora would tell me anything. If I dared to ask her. No, I shouldn't ask; she would just shut me down. Maybe I should spend more time at the coven house. "Yeah," I said, after probably too long a pause. But Organza didn't seem to notice; she was concentrating on her own garlic. "Nothing…else unusual, I mean?" I tried.

Now she put her garlic bulb down and turned to me. "You'd have to ask Leonora." Her tone was kind, but she went on: "Perhaps you've forgotten what it's like living here. Our coven mother has not begun consulting the rest of the house about her business."

"Of course not." I smiled at her. "I must have lost my mind there for a moment." I smashed another clove. "Can I plead pregnancy brain?"

"That seems reasonable." She smiled and turned back to her work. "Though what do I know? I am two hundred years older than you, but I have never borne a daughter."

Was that sadness in her voice? She still looked relaxed and gentle, even kindly disposed toward me. She'd been my coven sister for twenty-five years. I'd have said I knew her well—as I knew all my sisters—but the truth was, I so rarely interacted with the older set in anything but rituals and other formal events. It wasn't like we'd ever had a heart-to-heart. "Did you want a daughter?" I asked.

"We are all looking forward to Rosemary Leonora's arrival," Organza said. Then she went to the stove and stirred a pot, not meeting my eyes.

At dinner, Leonora was testy and short. I tried to find a way to sort of casually ask about Logan's body, or even to bring Gregorio into the conversation, but there was just no way. She asked the table at large if anyone had heard anything from Gracie—even though if anyone had, certainly they would have told her, and everyone, at once.

"Calendula, please give a report on your current research findings," she said, once she'd exhausted the topic of Gracie.

"Um," I said, stumbling for an answer that didn't involve *I'm still fruitlessly searching blood samples for evidence of hybrid human-witches.* "I'm still not seeing the methodology that Flavius Winterheart used for essence extraction, but I'm sure I'll find it eventually."

"What makes you so sure of that?"

I glanced down the table. Everyone was paying really close attention to their meals, even the witchlets, who usually giggled and made faces at one another when they thought their elders weren't watching. "Because I won't stop looking until I find something," I said, trying to keep my tone humble and earnest. "There has to be something."

"Perhaps you are going about it the wrong way. Or better still, perhaps it is time to begin your maternity leave; your energies would undoubtedly be better focused entirely toward Rosemary Leonora now."

I opened my mouth to protest—I was already listening very carefully to my body and my baby, and did not enjoy being scolded about this—but she abruptly turned to another sister. "Liza, have you and Peony found those books yet?"

"No, Mother," Liza said, "we, um, we're trying to..." She stammered to a halt.

Peony, sitting next to her, at least managed to show calm poise—no matter what she might actually be feeling. "We have a lead on a bookseller in New York," she said. "He only accepts handwritten and hand-delivered correspondence, however, so we are in the process of arranging for that."

"Hmph," Leonora muttered. "Very well."

The younger students fidgeted, while clearly trying not to. The rest of the meal passed in silence.

At last, after cleanup, post-dinner digestives and canasta in the second parlor, and the witchlets fleeing upstairs to let their hair down, it was time to formally gather. The front parlor was big enough that not much rearranging was needed; the red, black, and gold Persian rug had to be rolled up and moved aside, and some couches and chairs were repositioned in order to reveal the dark pentagram inlaid into the hardwood floor. Our familiars drifted to the corners of the room as we dimmed the lights, spread the salt, lit the candles and incense, and settled in, seated on the floor in our traditional order.

As the ornate grandmother clock in the front hallway chimed midnight, Leonora began the incantation. Her murmuring voice lulled us all, soothing everyone and bringing us into light trances. After a time, I felt Nementhe join us, floating in the center of the pentagram. Calm and rightness settled over me at last.

Leonora finished chanting, and Nementhe gave the ritual response: *Thank you for welcoming me into your midst, Mother.*

"We thank you for returning to this plane to guide us, Ancestress." Leonora reached forward with her right index and middle fingers and closed the small gap in the line of salt before her, and we were in Circle. A glowing light rose from the pentagram. The line of salt also glowed, drawing power from the intersection of ley lines beneath the house.

Nementhe communed with us for a time without words; I felt her regard brush over me, seeking Rose's energy.

When Nementhe was done with her gentle scrutiny, Leonora spoke once more. She reported to our ancestress what important collaborative spells the coven had cast this week, what communications were made with other covens, the status of our financial investments, and the like. She mentioned nothing about Logan's body, or about Gregorio being in the coven house. Had she told Nementhe these things silently? I wanted to squirm almost as badly as the witchlets had.

I hated secrets.

After Leonora, each sister was invited to share. Honor spoke of the winds and the rushes and the reeds and the journey ahead. She made very little sense to me, but my older sisters nodded solemnly. Many sisters had not much to say that was new. Despite my impatience and curiosity, I felt myself once again relaxing into the comfortable, well-worn rhythm of the ritual, and stopped attending very closely to their words. When it came Niad's turn, though, I perked up; but she only reported an unusual dream.

Should I mention my dream? About the cats? I wasn't sure.

When it was finally my turn, I began with, "Nementhe, can you share with me any insight about when my daughter will be born?"

There was a pause. *Rosemary Luna walks many paths,* she finally answered.

"What? That's not her name—she's Rosemary Leonora," I blurted. My coven mother squeezed my hand in warning. "I am so sorry, Ancestress; but I'm not quite sure what you mean?" I added, as politely as I could.

It is not for me to tell her story.

"I'm sure Nementhe has larger things to worry about than the precise date the child is born," Leonora muttered, her testiness from earlier surging once more. "She hardly even shares our notion of time any longer."

Luna, Nementhe said. *Luna.*

What was she *talking* about? I had not known Nementhe well while she was on this side of the veil; she had long since retired from teaching by the time I was a student here, spending much of her time in her room, speaking mostly to the oldest sisters. She was rumored to be slightly mad. Because her going to the Beyond had created the vacancy which I filled by joining the coven, we were supposed to have a special connection. If we did, it was largely symbolic.

Our dealings with her in Circle over the last twenty-five years had never revealed any signs of confusion or madness, though. This was unsettling.

After another pause, she said, *Do you have more to share, my daughter?*

"No, thank you, Nementhe," I said. Now I was a little frightened to mention my sort-of lucid dream of a few weeks ago, and how Elnor hadn't felt it at all. "That's all."

"We all thank you for your love and wisdom, for your guidance in our mortal lives, and for your continued intercession from your much greater place," Leonora said, reaching for her athame to break the Circle. "Until next week, Ancestress."

The gathered sisters murmured their ritual farewells.

Light filtered back into the room as candles were extinguished and lamps relit themselves. The cats rejoined their mistresses as we put the room back in order.

"Calendula, I am not sure why you felt the need to bother our ancestress with such trivialities," Leonora said, as I scooted an easy chair back into position.

"I hardly think a baby is trivial," I said.

"You are being deliberately obtuse, and I do not appreciate it," she said. "Of course the *baby* is not trivial. The exact moment of her arrival, however, is."

I shivered slightly. It was never fun when Leonora was in this mood. But it would pass. It always did. "What was wrong with Nementhe?" I asked her. "She wasn't making any sense. What was all that about 'Luna'?" Several other sisters gathered around, looking worried. Even Niad frowned.

"She may well have been referring to the full moon of the twenty-ninth of October," Leonora said. "Two days before Samhain. Your daughter will surely make her appearance by then."

I looked back at her, stifling the urge to argue as my brain began to re-engage. What if Nementhe had been trying to send me some subtle message? She, at least, would not be confused about who Rose's father was: denizens of the Beyond saw and understood vastly more than we did on this plane. She had never spoken to us in code before...at least, not that I had ever been aware. "I'm sure you're right. Thank you." I smiled and turned to help Sirianna with one of the loveseats.

Leonora nodded, then said to the gathered coven, "Are there any other urgent matters that need tending to before we retire?"

Twelve witches shook their heads in unison.

I was tempted to flee to my house, but it had been my practice to spend at least Tuesday nights here, if not more; I didn't want to trip Leonora's temper yet again today. I climbed the stairs, then tried to arrange myself, a bellyful of baby, and a cat into a single bed.

That went about as well as one might expect.

As much as I would have loved to continue avoiding Gregorio, I needed to know what was going on.

Sebastian Fallon greeted me at the clinic's front door. "I thought I felt your presence nearby," he said, pulling me into a sideways hug.

"It's good to see you. Thanks for the other night."

"How are you doing?" He drew back and looked at me.

"I'm all right. No more weird dreams." I patted my belly. "This is pretty much the biggest thing going on in my life. No pun intended."

He snickered, appraising my bulge. "It is getting hard to miss. When do you think—next week?"

"Or the week after. Leonora thinks just before Samhain."

He lifted his hands. "May I?"

"Sure, but…inside?" I glanced down the street. Though it wasn't very busy, there were still humans passing by.

"Oh! Of course."

I followed him into the building and then to one of the small exam rooms in the first hallway, sat in the padded examination chair, and leaned back. Sebastian put his hands on my clothed belly and sent his senses into me, doing his usual gentle probe into Rosemary's health, essence, development, and anything else a healer-in-training would want to look for.

After a few minutes, he removed his hands and looked up at me. "She seems great—very strong, robust. Ready, I'd even say."

"*I'm* ready," I agreed, hefting myself up out of the chair. "Whew."

He smiled to watch my struggle. "It must be hard to get used to, with it changing all the time."

"You have no idea."

"So, did you just come in for an exam, or—"

"Not at all," I said. "I hear Gregorio brought Logan's body here for further study?"

"Ah." He frowned. "Yes."

"Have you guys learned anything?"

Sebastian stepped over to the exam room's door, opened it, and peered down the hallway. Then he came back in and shut the door. "Gosh, I could use a coffee. Want to join me?"

I raised an eyebrow, then nodded. This again, eh? "Coffee sounds *fantastic*."

Five minutes later, we were squeezed into a noisy café South of Market. "Something isn't right," he murmured over a double cappuccino.

I leaned over my wretched cup of chamomile tea. I should have gone for mint. "I've had similar thoughts myself. What's going on there?"

Sebastian shook his head. "Dr. A. won't let me, or anyone else, even see the body. It's not here, anyway—he took it to his Berkeley lab, and he's spending a whole lot more time there. He's recruited a bunch of 'volunteers' and isn't telling anyone what for. He insists he's perfecting something and needs to be able to concentrate on it fully…but that's no reason not to let any of us *look* at whatever he's doing."

"Volunteers? What do you mean?"

"Unaffiliated witches and a few young warlocks. I don't like it."

I felt a coldness in my belly. "That sounds like…"

"Yeah. Like what Flavius did."

Or supposedly did. "Are they—where are they—" I couldn't quite put the question together. "Is he doing, whatever he's doing, with the volunteers in Berkeley too?"

"You mean are they going to the lab there? Yes, though some of them check in here. I don't know what to make of it."

"Is there any way of telling if they're still…around?" The implications of my question were awful, but I didn't know how else to put it.

He sipped his coffee. "So far as I know. But it's hard to check, without…" His hand trembled slightly as he set the cup back in the saucer. "Callie, I just don't know what to think. He's my mentor, and he's taught me so much; I trust him implicitly." It hurt to hear his words—I'd felt that way myself, not all that long ago—and it hurt even worse to keep this to myself. "But I don't even know the full extent of his powers," Sebastian went on. "I've never known anyone so old! If he's just gotten stronger over the centuries…" He bit his lip and glanced nervously around the café.

"He is powerful, but he can't hear us here—we're blocks away," I assured him, though I didn't say the warlock's name out loud either.

"How do you know?"

I shrugged. "No one is that strong. And if he was using that much power, we'd feel it. Wouldn't we?"

Sebastian frowned. "Yeah, you're probably right. Unless he knew how to mask it."

"But, I have been thinking…" I paused, wondering just how to say this. "I haven't ever known anyone that old either."

"You've known him a long time."

"All my life. He's a good friend of my father's. He taught me most of what I know about biogenetics."

"Has he always been like this?"

"Like how, exactly?" I thought I knew what he meant, but I wanted him to say it.

"Well, you know—paranoid."

I sighed. "No, not overtly so. But he was always…polished? Guarded?" I thought for another moment. "What I mean is, it's always been really important to him to be in control."

"It's a fine line between control and paranoia, don't you think?"

"Indeed." I stirred my tea. I wouldn't be so foolish as to add more sugar, but wow, I wished there was *something* I could do to make it even slightly palatable. "Why do you think he's still here?"

"You mean, why hasn't he decided to go Beyond?"

"Yeah."

"Because he likes it here?" Sebastian tried for a teasing smile, but it came out somewhat sickly.

I leaned forward, speaking even more softly. "Are we sure he's…still entirely in his right mind?" That was about as far as I was willing to test the waters. In fact, probably too far. But surely Gregorio had better things to do than monitor my conversations all day, didn't he?

And I wasn't giving away any precious secrets. Nothing wrong with asking questions. Even leading questions.

Sebastian's eyes widened. "I've seen no evidence of mental decay. Just this odd possessiveness."

"Okay. Forget I asked." I shrugged, as if none of this mattered.

"I mean, a change in behavior *could* signal the onset of senility. But, Callie, I doubt it. He did find out who was behind the essence-stealing, after all, and set up the trap to snare him. That's not the work of someone who's losing his marbles."

"True," I had to concede. I couldn't push the idea any farther. Though the point still stood: if Gregorio had committed the entire crime and set up a fall guy to take the blame for it, that too would hardly be the work of a senile old warlock. I took another sip of my tepid nasty tea.

"And even if he was losing it," Sebastian went on, "what could we do about it?"

I kind of wished I hadn't brought it up, though I was also relieved. Sebastian wasn't going to let this go. I'd wanted an ally, some company, someone to confide in…too bad for me. But also good! I hoped. "Nothing. Everyone gets to decide when they want to go Beyond." *Unless some horrible criminal decides for them,* I thought. "But usually they do it long before eight hundred years."

"He does enjoy being unusual," Sebastian said, shaking his head.

"Indeed he does. So, are you able to accomplish anything else in the lab these days, or are you all just standing around waiting for Dr. A. to let you in on his secrets?"

Sebastian brightened. "Oh! Actually, one of the healers showed me something really interesting..."

Thus diverted, he filled me in as he finished his coffee. I supposed it was interesting, if you actually wanted to be a healer. When we stood to go, I left my tea half-finished; it was disgusting, and my belly left very little room for food and drink anyway. I sort of felt hungry all the time, and mostly couldn't eat much. I would be very glad when Rose decided to join us out here. Pregnancy was all very nice, but it was pretty all-consuming.

When I got home, I found Petrana tidying up, as she did most days when I hadn't asked her to do something specific. Today she was working in the front room on the second floor—the room I'd decided was the library/reading room, though I didn't spend a lot of time lounging there reading.

"Are you using magical power to do that?" I asked her, trying to recover from the enormous task of climbing the stairs to get here.

"No, Mistress Callie. Would you like me to?"

"No, no," I said. "You're doing great just as you are." I turned to head for my bedroom. Maybe a little nap would perk me up.

If Petrana wasn't directly draining my power by using magic, was she still a drain just by the fact of existing—or because of the potential power resting within her? She was supposed to be self-powering, self-propelling, as it were.

Yes, it would probably have been smart to have researched *this* part of golem-lore before I'd made her. I'd focused so hard on her creation, I hadn't really given much thought to what happened afterwards.

You're supposed to unmake them long before this, I could almost hear Leonora lecturing me.

But why? She was so very useful.

Besides…she didn't seem like a machine, despite what the lore said. She felt like a living, sentient creature. I was just supposed to *kill* her, when I didn't need her anymore?

No, thanks.

My ringing cell phone woke me from my nap. How nice to hear from Raymond, I thought, reaching for it with a smile. It was good to be on speaking terms with him again.

I just barely noticed in time that it was an unfamiliar number. "Hello?"

"Callie? It's Christine."

"Oh, hi! You called!"

She chuckled. "I told you I would. Sorry to take so long, and I only have a minute right now, but I wanted to get on your calendar for lunch. How's next Thursday?"

I thought a moment. That was two days before the coven house's big annual Samhain party. Even more importantly, that was the day of Rosemary's arrival—if Leonora's assumption was correct. "Hmm, that's not the best; I might be having the baby that day. Can you do any earlier?"

"Oh! Are you inducing? Where are you having it?"

"No, I'm not inducing, I just…I have a feeling. It's my due date."

She laughed. "Callie, you know those dates are estimates at best. We usually don't even know the exact time of conception."

You humans don't, I thought, though probably they could narrow it down in most cases. Unless humans were even more bunny-like than I'd previously understood. "Oh, I know. But I'd like to leave the day free anyway—call me superstitious. Can you do any time this week? Or earlier next week?"

"Can't—I'm out of town all this week, and next week is slammed—Thursday is all I had. What about the following Tuesday?"

"That should be fine."

"Assuming you're not in the middle of having a baby then," she said with a chuckle. "Though if you are, at least I'll know what to do about it."

"Right, you will."

"And if you have a newborn by then, we'll just reschedule."

"Or I can bring her along."

I heard a brief pause on her end. That's right; human women needed more time to recover post-partum, didn't they? "Well, let's just check in with each other," she said. "I'll call when I get back, on the weekend. And if you can't answer or can't call me back right away, I'll know what's going on. You just take care of yourself, okay?"

"Don't worry. I will."

"Good luck!"

Nice as it might be to have an extra midwife around, if for some reason Rose hadn't arrived by the time of our lunch date, she certainly wouldn't come then. Not during the waning moon; we would be safe. I'd be happy to bring a newborn to lunch, though I wouldn't want to freak Christine out. Well, as she said, we'd play it by ear.

I really looked forward to getting to know Christine better. Why the heck hadn't Raymond ever introduced us before?

Jeremy came to my house for our next date night. He'd offered to take me out, but I couldn't get the image of potentially going into labor in public out of my mind, so I suggested my place.

I let Petrana help me cook this time. Again, we kept it simple—a small pork roast, with potatoes and carrots in the pan with it.

Jeremy was gracious as ever, and we had a polite, even comfortable conversation. Yet it was clear that we both knew that whatever spark we'd once had was just gone. I liked him, and he was sophisticated, intelligent, and easy on the eyes, but…had the terrible thing we'd done together killed our passion forever? Or was I just having a hard time trusting Gregorio's son?

Maybe I just wasn't feeling passion for *anyone*, being this pregnant? But of course, Raymond had stirred thoughts in me…

I was quite sure that Jeremy had no idea of his father's—well, machinations. Jeremy truly believed this was his child I was carrying, and that his father was delighted by it, and eager to see us in a formal union. It was all the more credit to the warlock that he didn't pressure me about the situation at all. I could, and did, appreciate that.

What if we never reconnected at a more passionate level? How long would we go on like this—polite, friendly strangers, trying to raise a daughter together? I mean, of course I—and my coven—would have the greatest part of the raising of Rosemary. But I wanted her to have a father figure, even if he shared no biology with her.

After he left that evening, I sat in the front parlor for a long while, thinking. Could I see being domestic with this warlock? Setting up a household here with him, so that Rose wouldn't have to travel around so much? My house was plenty large enough; Jeremy and I could each have our own spaces, to live and work and sleep and entertain; we wouldn't have to interact any more than we chose to. It seemed clear that he would have no objections to my leading my own life, within certain reasonable parameters. Why was I being so stubborn?

I sighed, leaning back against the couch cushions as I thought. I knew that unions generally had very little to do with true love, with passion and romance. And yet…I looked at my parents' union. They so clearly adored one another; they brought each other joy and delight, even though their lives were separate most of the time. And they'd renewed their union, which was far less ordinary.

I guessed I'd always sort of hoped to find that kind of love for myself. Even though a union contract was for a specific period of time, I imagined that at least my first one might be a purely emotional decision.

That is, if I'd thought about it at all, which I realized I hadn't, not really. I hadn't been looking for any of this, when first Jeremy and then Rosemary had tumbled into my life. I'd been working on growing my magic, and I'd been straining at the bounds of coven life. I'd wanted *more* freedom, *more* independence…not less.

Not a daughter and what amounted to a husband.

I rubbed my belly, absently, and then with more attention. Gentian's question from weeks and weeks ago came back to me. If this baby was coming as soon as it seemed she was, shouldn't she have communicated with me by now? I knew she was strong and healthy, growing robustly—not just because I could sense that myself easily, but all my checkups with Nora and Manka, and Sebastian's probes, had shown her to be in excellent condition.

Perhaps I should ask them, at my next appointment.

Assuming the baby didn't come first.

I heaved a sigh as I heaved myself to my feet and began the slow waddle upstairs. Petrana was still rattling around in the kitchen, washing pots and pans, when I went to bed.

— CHAPTER NINE —

As my due date drew closer, I essentially moved back into the coven house, making camp in my old room. I wanted to be there for the delivery and thought maybe I'd even be allowed to help with the preparations for our annual Samhain party.

Well, that's what I'd imagined; what happened was some of the most profound sleep of my life. Night after night, sometimes lasting well into the following day, I lay down and tumbled into deep unconsciousness. I slept and slept, waking briefly for small meals and a bit of conversation with my coven sisters, only to plunge into sleep again. Sebastian and the healers came to see me and pronounced everything to be just fine, so nobody worried much about it. My tiny, crowded bed became the center of the universe, the most comfortable place I'd ever been, and I barely stirred out of it. Elnor greatly approved of this development; she curled against my body, while Rosemary curled inside it.

I dreamed much during this time, though I never saw the pair of white cats again. Instead, I visited complicated worlds, far beyond the planes I knew. Fiery demons and silver wolves floated past me, harmlessly. I dreamed of this world too, of my house, of my sturdy golem, of the terrible secret I held, and my search for answers, for other half-human witchkind. I dreamed of my mother, who had been ill and had recovered and yet still seemed somehow…remote, and as though she too held a secret. I dreamed of Raymond, kind and loving and sexy, and entirely inappropriate for me. I dreamed of dear Logan, returned to life, smiling and happy before me.

I dreamed of my body, slender and babyless once more, and the sensual pleasures I'd taken from it: my pleasure in Jeremy's body, and in Raymond's, and other lovers before them; eating and drinking my fill; filling my lungs with fresh air and working strong magic. I sighed and dreamed of other things, cold winter afternoons lazing by a fire, my body flying through space over an unknown realm, battles and heroes from books I'd read, dangerous children who knew too much. What was real and what was not melded in my dreams, tangled together in a smooth braid. Time passed, and I slept.

At last, the day arrived. I slept late as usual, but woke feeling refreshed and almost energetic. I knew the excessive sleeping was finished: perhaps I'd been preparing myself to have a newborn; my body had been stockpiling rest. I stretched and yawned, pulled on a silk robe, and went to wash my face before making my way downstairs.

It was long past breakfast, but Sirianna, Peony, and Organza were in the kitchen, cooking up a huge batch of moonberries for the fermentation of Witch's Mead. Our Mead was famous. It blew Gregorio's "safe for pregnancy" stuff out of the water; even his regular stuff couldn't touch ours.

Too bad I wouldn't get to drink any.

Not that I cared, honestly. I didn't want any; alcohol had never started sounding any better to me.

"Good morning," I said to my coven sisters, going over to the window seat and arranging myself gingerly down onto it.

"Good *afternoon*," Sirianna said with a chuckle, though it was barely ten a.m. She handed her spoon to Peony, who took over stirring. "I'll make you something to eat."

"Thanks." I leaned against the window frame. "It feels funny in here."

Organza said, "Well, it is a full moon. Plus, Leonora has begun loosening the house-wards for the party."

"Oh, that must be it." I'd liked it when my own house was ward-free (before Jeremy and I had built my own personal ones), but it felt really peculiar here. Like a missing step.

Sirianna lit a burner and suspended a piece of bread in mid-air, toasting it. "How are you feeling?"

"Pretty good. Awake, finally." I put a hand on my belly. "Full moon. Today's the day," I added, completely unnecessarily.

"Such a blessing on our house!" Sirianna said, smiling as she buttered the toast and brought it to me on a china plate. "Tea?"

I took a bite. "No thanks. I shouldn't fill my stomach, right?"

"True."

After the toast, I felt entirely stuffed. As usual. And I would be hungry again in an hour. "What can I do to help?" I asked them.

"Nothing. We're good here," Peony said.

"Are you sure? Leonora has hardly let me do anything."

"You're pregnant!" Sirianna said.

I gaped at her. "I *am*?! Why didn't anyone tell me!"

"Oh, hush." She gave me a gentle swat on my arm. "You just relax and keep us company."

"Want me to stir that?" I asked Peony.

"No, thank you."

We chatted a while, but it became clear that they needed to concentrate on what they were doing. I drifted out of the kitchen, looking for something to do. But though all my sisters were frantically getting the house ready for the party, nobody else would let me help with anything either.

I should have had lunch with Christine after all, I thought. And then, *Come on, Rose.*

With a sigh, I sank onto the couch. Elnor jumped up, gave my bulging non-lap a disdainful glance, and settled on my legs.

Lunchtime came. I nibbled a little and didn't have a baby.

The afternoon passed. I didn't have a baby.

Just before dinner, I felt a little something. Was it a contraction? No, it was just my meager lunch shifting. I didn't have a baby.

The evening wore on. I didn't have a baby.

I stayed up almost until midnight, quite sure that things would start any minute.

But they didn't.

I finally went to bed. *Now it will be at least another two weeks.* Until the moon waxed again. Ah well. These things were never all that predictable; Leonora had said this to me several times throughout the day.

But wow, I was tired of being pregnant.

Samhain morning, the house was crazed with the final preparations, and still no one would let me do a thing. I might as well work on my costume. I hadn't given it any thought; I had expected to have a newborn, and to be relaxing with her, enjoying my recovery.

Upstairs in my tiny room, I leafed through my closet, then studied my stout physique in the mirror, frowning. Dressing as any kind of animal was out; I had no intention of showing up as a hippo or a hedgehog or a roly-poly bug. I could magic myself to appear smaller, but the illusions involved with that were more than I felt up to at the moment.

Gracie should be here. She loved dress-up. I realized that, without consciously thinking about it, I'd been holding out hope that she'd return by Samhain.

"I should just put a sheet over myself and be a great big ghost," I grumbled to Elnor.

But that gave me an idea: I'd be an ifrit. Ethereal, insubstantial, and my size wouldn't matter. All I needed was a few yards of magical fabric.

I searched through the æther, looking in several stores before I found what I needed. The coven even had an account there. Within minutes, I had armloads of shimmery fabric in several shades of white, from opaque to a ghostly mist, which I draped around myself strategically. It would have gone more smoothly if Elnor hadn't taken a fancy to the cloth. She batted at pieces of it as they slipped by her nose, getting her claws stuck in the netting. "Out!" I finally commanded. She slunk away.

When I was done, I looked in the mirror. I was pretty much see-through, except I wasn't, except I was. I spun slowly. Or maybe I was invisible. It was a weird, cool effect. I even felt lighter.

Unfortunately, I hadn't managed to use up much time.

Well, that's what naps were for.

Apparently, I had a little more sleep left in me after all.

I awoke—and the party had started. I levered myself out of bed, smoothed my rumpled costume, and headed downstairs.

I hardly recognized my staid coven house. The furniture was shunted away and the rooms were stretched to their full supernatural capacity, but even so, the throngs of guests threatened to burst the house's edges. Witches and warlocks mingled, flirting and chatting as they dipped into the smoking vats of Witch's Mead and sampled from plates of delicious munchies my sisters had spent days slaving over. It seemed like there were even more guests here than at Gregorio's party, though that was probably just because our house was smaller.

Everyone was in costume. There were the usual vampires, fangs dripping with real human blood, and the faithful old fallback looks of sexy-witch or scary-witch—cleavage or warts, respectively. A horse, a mynah bird, and a griffin were in conversation in a corner of the living room, monopolizing the Mead-vat they stood over. A knight in full armor stood in another corner—he must have been roasting in all that metal. I saw a mermaid with a real fish-tail, and looked to see what the sloppy thing was doing to Leonora's precious parlor rug—but of course, the rugs had all gone the way of the furniture. Our inlaid pentagram gleamed from the polished wood floor; a magical sheen protected the finish.

I was nearly invisible in my costume. Which was great. The gauzy fabric even covered my head, leaving only my eyes exposed through a Salome-like veil.

I moved into the room, taking in the mood, the laughter, seeing if there was anyone I didn't know—or couldn't recognize. Sirianna found me. She sipped from a smoking cup of Witch's Mead, and wore a catsuit, complete with furry tail and tufted ears. "Oh, look at you!" she said, grinning through her whiskers.

"You look great too. How did the Mead turn out?"

"Pretty good." She frowned. "Last year's was better, but this is all right. Oh—we made punch too." She pointed to a pitcher on the sideboard.

"Ah, thanks," I said, and got myself a cup as she disappeared into the crowd.

I stood at the edge of the room, enjoying the punch before putting the empty glass down. My belly was full again. The punch was not an intoxicant, but it had been brewed with health and well-being in mind. It rolled lovingly through my veins, relaxing me.

After a few minutes, I worked my way through the living room and into the kitchen, also jam-packed. The door to Leonora's office stood open. All the furniture was gone, leaving only the window seat and its comfy pillows. Three witches from Purslaine's coven were in there, making goo-goo eyes at the old fellow who watched the university portal in Berkeley.

Which made me think yet again of Logan's body, and Gregorio, and everything else. Was Gregorio here? He must be; it would be politically awkward to avoid our party.

Which didn't mean I wanted to see him.

"How are you feeling, Calendula?"

I turned. Leonora was at my shoulder, wearing one of her Elizabethan gowns, complete with diadem. "I'm good—I got a nap."

She smiled faintly, focusing most of her attention on reading my energy. Then she nodded. "Yes, all seems well. But take it easy this evening."

"I will." I glanced around the kitchen. "Is Dr. Andromedus here?" Better to be prepared than blindsided, I figured.

"Yes. He and several Elders are in the dining room. Along with your warlock."

Jeremy. Though we were on more comfortable terms, it was still all pretty surface-level. And I hadn't seen him in a week or more, not since I'd been spending the nights here, since I'd fallen down the sleep-well. "Good, thanks."

Leonora smiled, then moved off to greet more arriving guests. I made my way toward the dining room, stopping every few feet to catch up with folks. There were witches I hadn't seen since last year's party—witches I liked. It made me realize yet again how different this past year of my life had been. How distracted and isolated I'd become. I looked around for Shella and Gentian, but the crowd was so thick (and in disguise), I couldn't spot them even if they were here.

"Callie!" Mina's happy burble stopped me again. "Look!" The young witchlet stood before me and twirled. Her costume changed with every inch of her turn. She was a cat, then a dog, then a princess, then a warrior, then flowing water, then—

"That's awesome," I said, closing my eyes a moment. It was dizzying. "Stop—hold still a minute! I can't focus on you."

She laughed but stopped. Now I saw that she was drinking Mead. I raised an eyebrow, looking around for Leonora.

"Coven Mother said I could!" Mina blurted, before I could say anything. "She said we all could."

"All right, if she says so," I laughed. "I guess Samhain is a night to be naughty."

"Tragic that it's only one night of the year," Sebastian Fallon said, joining us. "Where are the rest of the witchlets?" he asked Mina.

"In there." She waved vaguely toward the front parlor. "Bye!" She dashed off.

"You're almost invisible," Sebastian said to me. "Great costume."

"Thanks." I looked him over. "Are you…Peter Pan?"

He laughed. "I'm supposed to be a wood elf, but I guess that's close enough." He took a sip of a dark blue cocktail. "Have you seen Dr. Andromedus?"

"No, not yet. Leonora said he's in the dining room?"

"I don't know. I just meant his costume."

"*Gregorio* dressed up?" I gaped at Sebastian.

"Yeah."

"As what?"

"An eminent warlock scientist," he said, with a perfectly straight face.

"Jerk." I snickered. "You had me going there."

He bowed, doffing his little green cap. "My work here is done." With a raise of his glass, he sauntered back into the crowd.

I stood in the kitchen a few minutes longer, working up the energy to walk all the way to the dining room. The very next room. Goodness, I'd be glad when this pregnancy was done… Two. More. *Weeks*. I put my second empty punch glass down, steeled myself, and headed in.

The dining room looked strange without our huge table. It was just as crowded as the rest of the house, but the mood in here was far less festive. In fact it was almost gloomy, I realized, as my eyes adjusted to the dim light. My father stood in one corner, talking very seriously to Gregorio. Neither was in costume. *Dad does like to take his cues from Gregorio,* I thought, with an inward eye-roll. I looked around for Mom, not seeing her. She, at least, would totally be in costume; she loved dress-up parties.

I watched my father and his old friend, who hadn't noticed me. What could be so dire? I wished I could hear them.

Only then did I see Jeremy. He was also part of the conversation, behind them, partly in shadows, seeming to be mostly listening. I walked across the room to join them.

"Hi."

Gregorio stiffened almost imperceptibly, then gave me a gracious smile. "Calendula Isadora. What a lovely party. Your coven has outdone itself."

"Hello, dear," my father said, leaning to kiss my hair, but getting only a faceful of gauze for his efforts. I brushed the headpiece back a bit and smiled at him.

"I hope I'm not interrupting anything?" I asked, trying for a look of convincing innocence.

"Of course not," Gregorio said. "We were just remarking on the delicious petit fours."

I caught Jeremy's eye. He gazed back at me with practiced charm. "Indeed, the salmon triangles are some of the best I've ever had. Did you make them?"

"No, my sisters haven't let me help with anything. Apparently I'm pregnant, and therefore incapable of lifting a finger."

My father patted my arm. "You do not want to do anything to tax yourself when your time is so close. It's good you have such caring sisters."

Gregorio nodded. "With younglings being so rare among us, we must protect each one very carefully." After a nearly imperceptible pause, he added, "As well as their mothers."

Ugh. Well, at least I could cross this social nicety off my list now. Surely I'd been the polite co-hostess long enough now. "I'm so happy to see you all, and glad you're having fun."

Jeremy said, "I am happy to see you too. Shall we go sit somewhere?"

"Yes, please." I glanced around the extremely crowded room. Sitting down sounded great. Where had all the chairs gone, anyway?

He gave me his brilliant smile and reached for my hand. "Somewhere...more quiet, perhaps?"

My father gave us an indulgent, affectionate smile, as Gregorio chuckled. "Yes, you two run along. We are fine here."

"Out back?" Jeremy asked. "I think the porch is less crowded."

I started to answer, then froze as Rosemary gave a violent shift. An entirely novel pain sprang to life inside me. I gasped, clutching my stomach.

Another pain, harder than the first, as my water broke and my baby decided that now, *now*, she was ready to come into this world.

I wailed, sinking to the floor.

The room was suddenly a flurry of activity. Jeremy bent down over me, looking shocked. "What's wrong?"

"I..." I started to say, then paused, catching my breath. "No—there was...it's stopped." I looked at the floor around me. "I made a mess."

He stared at the floor, then at me. "Oh...my. The baby is coming...now?"

"Yes," I gasped. "Oh Blessed Mother. Now!"

"I've got this," he said, motioning to the floor, making the water disappear. "Let's get you upstairs."

Everyone in the world was standing over me. My father looked pale, Gregorio looked stern. "The clinic," Gregorio said.

I started to protest, but my father cut in. "No time—Jeremiah is correct, we will take her upstairs." He bent down to take my other arm and help lift me up.

"Where's Mom?" I asked.

"The back way is less crowded," Jeremy said to my dad, glancing into the packed kitchen, ignoring my question.

Other witches, and a few warlocks, were noticing and coming to the dining room. "Should we call a healer?" someone asked.

"Not just yet," my father said.

"Sebastian's here," I put in. "Somewhere."

My dad and Jeremy led me through a seldom-used passageway, once a servants' hall. The sharp pain had ceased, but now I felt a downward pressure building. It was only a matter of time before the contractions would start up in earnest.

We moved up the back stairs, passing a startled couple clinched in an amorous embrace. Elnor was already in my room, pacing the floorboards, meowing. My father and Jeremy laid me on my bed.

"Find my mom, and Sebastian," I murmured, as the pressure increased a notch. "And Leonora."

"I'm right here," my coven mother said from the doorway. "Everyone out, who doesn't belong. Out!" The room had filled with curious onlookers, offering help or just gawking. They all fled the room at Leonora's command, leaving only my father and Jeremy. Leonora bent over me.

"Get this costume off her," she said. "I can't see anything."

My father nodded, and the magical fabric fell away, leaving me suddenly naked, and very grateful that everyone had been evicted. Then a new force of pain swept away all modesty. "Ohhhhhhhh!" I gasped, the breath turning into a scream at the end.

"That's it, that's a good girl," Leonora crooned, wiping my forehead with a soft cloth. "Ease up a little here—that's right." She placed pillows behind me, propping me up in the bed, when all I wanted to do was lie down and curl up around my agonized mid-section. "Gravity will help us."

The contraction lasted about a hundred and fifty years—and then it was gone. Leonora, sitting on the edge of my bed, gave me an unworried smile. How could she look so relaxed? Hadn't I just almost *died*? Stunned, I looked around the room. Jeremy was on the other side of the bed, still close. He looked serious, and a bit frightened, but I saw the light of happiness in his eyes. He believed his first daughter was about to be born. I gave him a weak smile. My father stood just inside the doorway, seemingly not sure if he should be there.

There was a soft knock; my dad opened the door to let Sebastian in. The young warlock looked pale but excited. "How can I help?"

"Just attend, for now," Leonora said. "Mostly, this is Calendula's work."

"I will find Belladonna Isis," my dad said.

Then another contraction hit, and my mind fled. All the universe was the pain, the tearing, rending, blinding pain. I howled and thrashed about. When my rational mind began to return, my first thought was, *Never again, I will NEVER again do this to myself...*

"You're doing great," Leonora said, again wiping away sweat, from my face and arms and chest now. She spread my legs further and examined me. "Dilating wonderfully! Just hang in there, you're doing so well."

"Why does it hurt so much!" I gasped. "Can't you *do* something?"

"Yes, but not yet," she said. "You need to breathe with me here—remember our lessons. Help us out—we need you alert. Pain potion now will just make it harder for you to focus."

"Oh, Blessed Mother," I moaned. Yes, she had told me this before, and it did make sense. Leonora had done this many times before. Between contractions, I felt all right. Except for the pressure, and for dreading the next one...

Soon they came fast and hard. I lost count. It happened twenty times, or twenty thousand. During them, Leonora's voice rose. She commanded me to breathe, breathe with her, stay up, stay with her, push, hold, relax… I tried to follow her commands, but I felt swept away by the force of the pain, astonished with it, helpless in its face, in its teeth. Between contractions, she mopped me up, Jeremy stroked my hair, Sebastian tried to make me laugh, and they all murmured encouragement.

Time came unhinged. The pains ebbed and flowed. I was exhausted. I could hear the party downstairs. Surely the guests knew what was happening, but as they'd all been evicted from the room, apparently they decided to keep celebrating. I became less and less able to respond to Leonora's coaxing. I howled with pain. I wailed for relief.

Finally, she and Jeremy had a whispered conversation. She frowned as he rose from the bed and stepped away. "What… where?" I managed.

"I will be right back, my dear," he whispered.

"Where is Mom?" I muttered. She should be here; why wasn't she? Dad had never come back.

"I am here, Calendula," said Leonora.

"No—my birth mother, Belladonna! Where is she?"

"I'm sure she'll be along," Sebastian said.

Then Jeremy was beside me again, holding a glass of amber liquid. He leaned down and brought it to my lips. "Here, for the pain," Leonora said as he did. "We're close enough now."

I drank, gratefully. The taste was foul, but the pain eased, and I left my mind and body, just enough. Now I floated over the scene, still somewhat aware, but blissfully vacant as well. I could no longer speak or react, and I didn't care. It was out of my hands.

More time passed. I don't know how much. My mind drifted. My body labored. My mouth screamed and hollered. Leonora, Jeremy, and Sebastian attended. My mother…didn't appear.

And then, something shifted. Rosemary broke free, slipping from my body into Leonora's waiting arms. So easily, after all that. *Why not earlier? Why so long?*

Leonora held my daughter, looking her over. She frowned, looking worn and confused. What was she seeing? I tried to reach out to take my baby, but my arms would not obey. My mouth would not open to speak. "She appears healthy, and..." Leonora said at last. There was something off in her voice. Doubt. Fear? Did she see, did she know? She knew. She saw the human blood; I didn't know how, but she did.

But of course she would. Leonora didn't miss much.

My coven mother reached down and severed the umbilical cord, using magic rather than a blade. I didn't feel anything physically, of course—the cord has no nerves—but I sensed the magical separation between me and my daughter. We were now distinct people. Distinct witches.

"Here," Leonora said, but I couldn't see what she was doing, who she was handing the cord to. Probably Sebastian. I knew it would be preserved, just as our menstrual blood was.

Rose gave a tiny sigh, taking her first real breath out here in the world. My heart twanged in response. *My baby!* Again I tried to move my arms, to take her, to hold her.

Leonora leaned down and set the baby into my arms, giving me an exhausted smile. I was weak as a kitten; she held Rosemary with my arms, helping me hold my daughter. Rose lay on my chest, breathing, blinking. "Will she nurse?" I said, barely able to raise my voice above a whisper.

"Not yet. Just hold her. Let her know you," Leonora murmured.

Then my coven mother looked up, and her eyes met Jeremy's. Something passed between them, there and gone in a moment. "My father asked—" he started, but she interrupted him.

"I know," she said, and her stern voice brooked no argument. "But whatever his urgency may be, it can wait until a witchlet has bonded with her mother."

Jeremy nodded, seemingly abashed, though he wouldn't meet my eye.

Slowly, a tiny bit of strength came back to me. My arms found their purpose and cradled my baby. Leonora loosened her own supportive hold, gently, slowly, making sure I had Rosemary before she let go entirely. I smiled up at her. "Thank you." My voice was hoarse, but at least I had voice. I leaned my head down a fraction, smelling the top of Rose's head, suddenly understanding why people did that. She was clean and dry—had some magic been done to make her so? This wasn't what I'd expected. Maybe Leonora had wiped her off when I'd been confused with the pain potion? Probably I just hadn't noticed.

Mostly I just held her. I wasn't in any pain, not anymore. Just bliss. And exhaustion.

I know I didn't sleep, but my universe shrank for a while, until it contained only me and my baby. I held her. She lay against me, alive and breathing calmly. I knew she had gone through at least as much of an ordeal as I had…but she seemed content, and at ease.

I slowly began to wonder about our witchkind bond. Babes in the womb often exchange rudimentary communications with their mothers. Not always, but I knew it was more common than not. Rosemary never had. Would she now?

I opened my eyes and focused again on Leonora. She had lowered herself into the small chair in my room, obscuring it entirely. Sebastian watched us both, wide-eyed, awed. Jeremy still stood by the door, waiting for…something. Oh right. Gregorio wanted to see the babe.

Not if I could help it.

"Mother," I asked Leonora. "Should she be talking to me?"

My coven mother smiled. She knew what I meant—that I wasn't asking if a newborn was going to open her mouth and speak words. "Most likely, in time. Is she not?"

"Not yet."

"You cannot sense anything? Not hunger, or gratitude, or discomfort of any kind?"

I thought about it. "I think she's happy. Relaxed."

"Then that is good." She glanced back at Jeremy, behind her. "The sooner you let your warlock take her to her grandfather, the sooner she will be brought back to you." She said this gently, but I heard the implacable insistence. I was not going to be allowed to refuse this. "She will grow hungry, anon," Leonora added.

I gave a heavy sigh. I could admit to no good reason why Gregorio shouldn't be allowed to see Rosemary. To continue to resist it would just look weird. I was pretending that the old warlock wasn't my mortal enemy, after all. That he was the child's loving grandfather. "All right," I said, forcing myself to smile. "I had no idea how hard it would be to let go of her." *Poor addled new mother, awash in hormones and sentiment, oh everyone should be so gentle with me.*

Jeremy stepped up to the bed.

"Can't he just come here?" I asked, still clinging to Rose.

"Calendula," Leonora said, a warning in her voice.

Defeated, I handed my baby to Jeremy. He took her gently, both love and a bit of confusion shining in his eyes as he peered at her. "Such red hair," he murmured.

Oh, Blessed Mother, he knew too. Well, it might as well all come out; then I could stop pretending. Of course I had no idea what Gregorio would do with this once everyone knew, how I would be punished…my mind started racing, even as my arms ached to hold my baby once more.

"Well, she is a child of the waning moon," Leonora said to Jeremy. "Both conceived and born. That is always a wild card."

Jeremy frowned. "And her energy..." He shook his head. "I will take her to my father."

Leonora nodded. "Bring her back quickly, please. She will need to take her first meal."

"I'll be as quick as I can," Jeremy promised. "He's just upstairs."

I frowned, confused, but then remembered the Samhain party still raging on the first floor. "Where...?"

"I have told Dr. Andromedus he may view the child in the third floor meeting room," Leonora told me. "The healers are there with him, and they will take the opportunity to look her over." Now she gave me a warm smile. "I know you want to keep her entirely to yourself, but you must remember how important your daughter is to our whole community."

"I know." The first baby born in years; the first baby born since we lost Logan, since witchkind was threatened with greater loss to our numbers. "I know."

"I will be as quick as I can," Jeremy said to me. He leaned down and brushed my forehead with a soft kiss. I could smell his scent, and that of my daughter. They were nothing alike.

I nodded, and kept my mouth shut. It was all out of my hands—literally, at the moment.

"I'll go up with you," Sebastian said.

The warlocks left, closing the door softly as they went.

— CHAPTER TEN —

After Jeremy and Sebastian left, Leonora turned back to me. "Let's get you cleaned up in the meantime. I believe fresh sheets are called for." She whisked away the mess magically and replaced the bedding underneath me. She wasn't wrong about that: it did feel good.

I felt like I should have more questions, now that everyone else was out of the room...wait a minute, my father had never come back. He'd gone to look for my birth mother, hadn't he? "Where is my mom?"

Leonora frowned. "Belladonna was not feeling herself. At least, that is what she told Maela. She felt that being here for the birth would be...difficult for her."

"Difficult?" I echoed, dumbly. "Why?"

My coven mother put a gentle hand on my forehead, just where Jeremy had planted his kiss. "I do not know for certain, but I am given to understand that she has long wanted another child herself."

I stared back at her. "But, I've asked her about that. She made it sound like..." I tried to think back. What had she said, exactly? Had she just deflected the question? I'd certainly gotten the impression that she and Dad were still deciding if they wanted to try again. Yes, fertility was low for all of witchkind, but they had already succeeded once…

I felt myself filling with grief and sorrow—and guilt. Could this be true? Why had she never let on about this to me? How insensitive had I been these last months, being all pregnant around her?

Leonora clearly read my expression. She brushed my hair out of my face and whispered, "Do not torture yourself with this, Calendula. I know that Belladonna is so very happy to have a granddaughter." She glanced at the floor. "For right now, I believe your familiar would like to join you up here on the bed. Would that be comfortable for you?"

I had a hard time believing that Elnor was sitting politely on the floor waiting for an invitation, but I appreciated Leonora's attempt at deflection. "Of course. Here, kitty," I said, patting the covers beside me.

Elnor jumped up, purring loudly and sniffing around, exploring all the new, familiar-but-not scents. And maybe even looking for the baby, who knew? "She'll be right back," I told her.

Just then, there was a soft knock on the door.

"Enter," Leonora called.

Jeremy opened the door and walked in, my daughter in his arms. He gave me an uncertain smile. My arms were totally behaving me by now; I reached for the baby, and he handed her over.

I drew Rosemary back to my breast. She reached for it, her intentions clear.

"Now, there's a bit of a learning curve involved for both mother and child," Leonora began, but even as she spoke, Rose latched on and began nursing.

Words cannot describe the sensation. I felt my milk coming in—that had to be what that was; it was a sense of ease and release, and I could almost feel Rose's delight in it, in her taking nutrition from my body. My body that had been *our* body just a short time ago.

Both Leonora and Jeremy watched us, Jeremy looking shy and wary, my coven mother looking confused. "That's…not usual," she murmured.

I smiled up at her, holding my daughter. She sucked gently, with none of the biting or struggling that the healers had warned me about. "I guess instinct is strong," I said.

"There's…something else a bit odd," Jeremy said to Leonora.

I knew what it was, and I just didn't care anymore. I had my baby, and I was feeding her. Everything else could go hang. I closed my eyes and gave myself over to enjoying the sensation.

"What is it?" Leonora asked him, quietly.

"The child is quiet now, even happy," he said. Which was obvious enough. "But when I took her to my father, she would not let him hold her."

"What do you mean, would not let him?" Leonora asked. "She's a newborn."

I opened my eyes, now intrigued.

Jeremy went on. "She struggled and cried out, and I…I couldn't hand her over. Nora, Manka, and Sebastian all held her briefly, but she would not abide my father. It was so clear that she didn't want him to touch her." He looked at me. "It was as though I was physically prevented from doing so. It is strange, don't you think?"

Clearly my daughter had absorbed my feelings for Gregorio, even if she wasn't communicating with me about them—or anything. Well, not in mind-messages, anyway. "I guess," I said, trying to look innocent and as confused as they were. "Maybe she was just hungry and knew he wasn't the one to feed her." I glanced down at her, happily suckling away. "Why did he need to see her so soon anyway?"

Of course, I knew the answer to *that* too, but as long as I was playing dumb…

"He was concerned about her health," Jeremy said. I could see that he believed it. "With the weird things going on with essence in the community, he's always been worried that, even though the healers have said she was developing just fine, they might have missed something." He gave me a small, proud smile. "She is a very important child. He wanted to make sure everything was perfect."

I smiled back at him. I could see how happy he was to have a daughter...and I could see that he still believed she was his daughter. Even though he'd noted her red hair—he'd clearly dismissed it. Which was a relief. "I think she is perfect, even if she didn't want to be held by an old warlock."

Her suckling was winding down; I could feel her drifting off to sleep. It reminded me how exhausted I was too. We could both doze off like this, joined so intimately, cradled together...

"We should leave her now," Leonora whispered to Jeremy. "Let them both sleep."

Sounded like a great idea to me.

All three of us slept, in fact: me, my baby, and my cat.

We awoke sometime later. It was starting to get light outside. The party downstairs, which some part of me knew had raged through the night, was over; perhaps it was the silence that woke me.

Baby Rose stirred in my arms and gave a soft little coo. I gazed at her. She was the most adorable thing I'd ever seen in my entire life. Tiny, yet perfectly formed. Rosebud lips. Dark eyes, that already seemed to focus on what she was looking at. Little shell ears, under coppery red hair. And her fingers! Oh, newborn fingers, I could not believe how precious...

I took her little hand in my index finger. She held on, wrapping her tiny, tiny hand around my finger. "Look at you!" I whispered, unable to keep from grinning. "Such a strong girl!"

She blinked up at me and unpeeled her fingers before wrapping them around my middle finger. The one with Gregorio's golden ring.

The moment her finger touched the ring, she opened her mouth and drooled a little, lolling her eyes up at me. "Maaa," she might have said. She made a sound, anyway.

The ring grew heavy, loosened, and fell off my hand.

"Maaaaaaaa," Rosemary said again, adding more drool as she did. She might have pointed at the ring on the sheets, or maybe she was pointing at Elnor? In any event, my cat was up and sniffing at the ring.

And I was frozen with shock. "What...did you know...how did you..." I stammered. As if she was going to answer me.

Did my daughter just use magic to take Gregorio's terrible leash off me? Something I'd tried so hard to do myself that I basically blew my own golem apart?

No. It couldn't be. As a half-human, she would be *less* powerful than me, not more. No, it was far more likely that whatever spell or dark magic he'd used to attach it to me was set to release after Rose was born. For whatever reason—I knew he'd wanted to keep tabs on me while I was pregnant.

Of course, he undoubtedly wanted to keep tabs on me now too. I wondered what new indignity he would come up with.

My heart pounded as my magic explored the boundaries of my own body. Yes: my magic was entirely my own now, roaming pure and free through my system. Blessed Mother, it was good to be free of the cursed thing.

Between that and having the baby outside me instead of inside me, I was freer than I'd been in many months.

Elnor stopped sniffing at the ring and batted it with her paw, knocking it to the floor. It made a surprisingly loud clunk as it hit the hardwood and rolled off into a corner.

"Good job, kitty," I said, reaching down and petting her.

She purred and rubbed against my side.

Rosemary was reaching for my breast again, so I helped her latch on, showing her to the other one this time. Her nursing soothed me as it had last night, and I slowly calmed down. Yes, it had to have been a coincidence that she'd touched the ring just before it released.

I touched her soft hair as she nursed. It was a dark copper-red, a mixture of my own dark brown and Raymond's ruddy blond. I knew baby hair often fell out, but for now, it was gorgeous. It sat quietly on her head, not yet showing any witchly movement. My daughter and I passed another delightful few minutes nursing before I realized she'd fallen asleep again.

Once again, an excellent idea.

The next time I woke up, it was full daylight, strong autumn sun slanting in through my window.

Someone was approaching. I felt the brush of magical intention, of polite query.

"Leonora?" I called out, softly. "Is that you?"

She opened the door and stepped into my room. "I thought I felt you awaken. Have you rested well?"

"We all have," I told her. "I'm finally thinking I might want something to eat."

She chuckled. "Yes, you must replenish your stores. That was not the easiest birth, Calendula, and at an unexpected moment."

"Actually, I feel pretty good."

"Have you left your bed yet?"

"No," I admitted.

She smiled at me. "As I thought. I'll have some food brought up, and then you should sleep again, if you can." She put a gentle hand on my forehead once more, testing my essence. I relaxed under her touch, willing my system to open to her inquiry. "You are doing surprisingly well," she said as she took her hand away.

I wanted to say something like *Well of course, I am mighty and powerful*, but, on second thought, I was pretty wiped out.

She left, and a few minutes later, Sirianna came up with a plate of scrambled eggs mixed with bits of sausage, and a steaming-hot biscuit beside it.

"Ooh, you are the best witch on the entire planet," I said to her, scooting over to make room for her to sit on the small bed beside me.

She set the plate on my nightstand; I took a big forkful. It was delicious.

"You're looking marvelous," Siri said, then gazed shyly down at Rosemary. "And so is she."

My baby was awake, just looking around the room. Her gaze landed on Sirianna; her eyes seemed to follow my coven sister's wild hair as it fluttered about.

"Do you want to hold her?" I asked.

"Oh! Could I?"

"Of course." I handed Rose over, wondering if she would object as she apparently had to Gregorio. But she let Sirianna take her without complaint, even maybe reached for her hair.

"Such a sweetling," Siri cooed, rocking Rosemary slightly and grinning at me. "The sweetest baby ever in the whole wide world!"

"That is correct."

"And I am the sister who got to hold her first!" Sirianna giggled, giving me a mischievous grin.

"Anyone can come in, if they want," I told her. "Has Leonora been keeping the house away?"

She rolled her eyes. "What do you think? 'Calendula needs her rest. You will have years in which to hold the baby.'"

"Oh, honestly," I said. "I mean, it's nice to be taken care of, but I'm just fine." I took another bite of the eggs, followed by some of the biscuit. "This is amazing, by the way."

"Thanks." She rocked the baby. "Protein and carbs, and strengthening herbs from the garden. Including rosemary, of course."

I nodded. "Of course."

"Do you want some tea?" she asked.

I started to say no, but then realized I didn't have to. "Hey, I can have pennyroyal again, can't I?"

Sirianna frowned. "I don't know. Is it safe if you're nursing?"

My heart, so elated for such a brief moment, sank again. "I don't know either. I'm going to ask Manka." I paused and sent a silent inquiry to the healer. "Because I am one thousand percent sick of chamomile tea, I tell you what."

Siri gave me a sympathetic look. "I don't blame you." She glanced at my rapidly emptying plate. "Do you want some more food?"

"Not just yet," I said, around a mouthful. "Let's see how this settles." I swallowed and set the fork down. "It's weird to have so much more room in my stomach again all of a sudden."

My sister gave me a mock-serious look. "You do understand why you have the room now, right?"

I just smiled back at her, suddenly too exhausted to go through our usual bantering game. "Yeah. You're holding her."

Then we sat there for a few minutes just giving goofy grins to my daughter.

Manka's voice floated into my head. *Yes, you can reintroduce pennyroyal to your diet, as long as you don't overdo it.*

What's overdoing? I asked.

Two cups a day should be fine.

"Manka says I can have pennyroyal tea!" I blurted out, startling Sirianna.

But not Rosemary. What a calm, peaceful baby. I was the luckiest mother in the world.

The first full day of my baby's life in the world outside my body passed peacefully, happily. All my coven sisters, followed by all the witchlet students, came by to see us, in ones and twos so as to avoid crowding my tiny room and overwhelming us. (Well, almost all the witchlet students…my heart panged to think how Gracie would have loved holding the baby.) My visitors brought me things to eat, and (yes!) exactly two cups of pennyroyal tea.

Wow did that tea taste good.

In between visits, we all dozed, or I nursed Rosemary.

"Let's have a tutorial about diapers," Leonora said in the late morning, when she was the only visitor in the room.

"Oh, goody," I said. But even that, I found interesting, and not yucky at all. Every single thing about my daughter was charming, and precious, and perfect.

No, of *course* I wasn't biased. What mother is?

After I'd successfully changed my daughter, I asked my coven mother, "Is Jeremy around?" During what little alone time I'd had, I'd realized I needed to act like I believed he was Rose's father and might want to see her more than once.

"No, he left when we reestablished the house wards after last night's gathering. It's less comfortable for warlocks here with them active, you know."

"Oh." I hadn't realized they'd been reset, but now that I opened my awareness to it, it was obvious. Goodness, I had been rather out of it, hadn't I?

Leonora chuckled at the look on my face. "And this is why we have wards: to protect those of us whose vigilance is compromised, for whatever reason."

"Right." Something in the tone of her voice made me look up at her more closely, though. "I do have wards at my house, you know."

"I know you do, and that you built them with Jeremiah Andromedus," she said mildly. "But I hope you don't think you're in any condition to return to solitary living at the moment."

"No, not right now." *I'm saying nothing about tomorrow,* I added, to myself.

I didn't feel any particular urgency about it, though. I had what I needed right here. Well, almost.

"I suppose my dad isn't around either, then," I asked her. "Or my mom?"

She relaxed a little. "No, no one is here but those who live here. Would you like me to invite your birth parents to come see the baby?"

I yawned, settling Rosemary more comfortably in my arms. For such a small thing, she could get kind of heavy after a while. "Not right now. Maybe I'll nap a little more. I'll call to them later."

"Very well."

I didn't ask where Gregorio was. He could sit and spin for all I cared. And I hadn't even looked for the ring that Elnor had knocked onto the floor. Good riddance.

It's funny that she doesn't cry, I thought, late that first day. Jeremy had told me that she'd cried when he'd tried to hand her to his father. Or had he said that, exactly? Maybe he'd said "cried out"? But she was nearly twenty-four hours old now, and she hadn't squalled or complained or fussed or done *anything* negative yet.

She just seemed so content and relaxed. Maybe she had nothing to cry about. All her needs were being met—I fed her when she was hungry and changed her when she was wet or messy (not that the messes were much of anything, at least so far; just a little tar-like). We slept when we were tired. There was no need to alert me to anything, when I was right here with her.

By now I'd managed to get out of bed, though I hadn't felt up to leaving the room yet. We spent some time standing before my little window, looking out into the front garden. My room would have had a view of the street, if not for the heavy growth of trees and vines. I'd never spent much time looking out this window. It was very pretty, I realized.

Still didn't make me want to move back here, though. I did miss my grand and gracious house, with its three floors of space…and its privacy.

All in good time.

I finally sent a message through the æther to my birth parents… well, to my dad. I was still feeling awkward and confused about my mom's feelings. Maybe I'd get a chance to feel him out, see if he could tell me any more clearly what was going on with her.

Hey, do you guys want to meet your granddaughter? I asked him.

Of course we do, my dear, he answered at once. *Leonora has told us you are both resting, however. We don't want to tire you out.*

I'm feeling pretty good, I said. But it was already getting dark again. It was All Saint's Day: not an important witchkind holiday, to put it mildly; more a day when most folks were getting over whatever they had done on Samhain the night before. *Maybe you guys can come visit tomorrow?* I asked.

We would like that very much. Shall we send word in the morning, to make sure you are feeling up to it?

Sounds like a plan. And then, before I could chicken out, I added, *How's Mom doing? I heard she left the coven house party early.*

Was there a slight pause? *She is quite well,* Dad answered, *and she very much looks forward to seeing you, and the child.*

Okay good.

He dropped the link, after sending a little fillip of love down the channel.

Was it true, what Leonora had said? Was Mom just feeling wistful about babies?

I settled back into the bed. Rose made little happy sounds.

My daughter was all right, wasn't she? I mean, there was nothing *wrong* with her. Right? Just as some babies were colicky and cried all the time, there had to be other babies who were just mild and content.

Right?

I told myself not to worry about it. I told myself that I could ask my elders about it, if she didn't start fussing sometime soon. I told myself I was lucky to have such an easy, happy baby.

Right?

My birth parents declined to visit the next morning. *We are still very much looking forward to seeing you both,* Dad sent me, *but your mother and I have realized that we both would rather visit you in your home. I understand you will be returning there in a day or two?*

That's my plan, yes, I answered, trying to stifle my disappointment. I guessed I understood it—the same reason all warlocks didn't want to come over—but seriously? Their first grandchild, and he couldn't bring himself to fortify with a little charm or something? Or I'd bet Leonora would be willing to take down the wards for their visit, if I asked.

No matter.

I'll let you know when I get home, I added.

Please do. We both send our love.

My feelings got a little more bruised an hour later when Sebastian Fallon knocked on my door. "Hey, you look great!" he said, when I invited him in.

"Thanks. Grab a chair, any chair," I joked, pointing at the only one.

He sat beside the bed, grinning at me—the wards were clearly giving him no trouble—and the little one in my arms. I handed her over, since he so obviously wanted to hold her.

She snuggled into his arms. He held her like she was a fragile piece of Ming china. "Wow. She's so tiny, and so perfect."

"I know, right?" My heart filled with pride and joy, yet again.

I watched as Sebastian looked carefully at her, clearly using his magical vision to check out her inner health, her system. Was he going to notice what was strange about her? If he did, he didn't let on; he just smiled and looked up at me. "So perfectly healthy too. Thank you so much for letting me be here for the birth, even though I didn't help much."

"There wasn't much for anyone but me to do," I said. "Well, and her."

"True." He couldn't stop grinning. "It was amazing to be here, though." He rocked Rosemary gently, humming under his breath at her. She seemed to be gazing up at him, almost as if she was focusing, as if she was seeing him. What a precious thing she was. She blew a little bubble and made a tiny sound, and reached a fist up, as if wondering where his hair was—unlike some warlocks, he kept it closely trimmed.

"You look good with a baby," I said, teasing gently.

He looked up at me. "You think so?" Then his grin widened. "Do you think I should specialize in pediatrics?"

I snorted a laugh. "Not if you want to make a living in medicine."

"Ha!" Sebastian leaned forward, handing Rose back to me. "I think she might be hungry. She keeps grabbing at my chest."

"Good luck with that, girl," I told her, and pulled her close to suckle again.

Sebastian watched the ease with which we managed this. "You're an old pro, apparently," he said, after a minute.

"She makes it easy. She came out knowing just what to do."

We sat there another few minutes, till Rose fell asleep on my breast.

"She seems like a happy baby," Sebastian said.

I nodded. "She really is. I'm hoping that's not—weird, you know."

"Weird?"

I told him how she'd been, and what I'd been thinking about. "The only time she expressed any dismay at all was when Jeremy tried to hand her to Gregorio."

"It's true." Sebastian frowned.

"What happened, exactly?" I asked.

He gave a small sigh, glancing around the room.

"If there's any safe place in the universe to talk about the warlock, it's here, behind the coven house wards," I added. "My own dad doesn't want to come visit here."

Sebastian nodded. "Yeah, I'm gonna need a huge meal when I get home, and maybe even a nap. But it's worth it, to see her—and you."

"Thanks." I said it casually, but I meant it. It said a lot that he would come see me here, and now.

His eyes narrowed as he leaned in closer to me. "It was truly weird. She was totally calm, until Jeremy tried to hand her to Dr. A. Then she just gave this...*shriek*. I'm surprised you didn't hear it down here."

"Huh." Yes, that was weird, and also not weird.

Sebastian clearly had something more he wanted to say. I watched him chew on it for a minute, before he came to some decision. "I didn't want to bother you with this till you're up to it, but...there's something else odd going on with Gregorio."

When isn't there? I wondered. "What is it?"

He sighed again. "Remember those 'volunteers' he was treating at his lab in Berkeley?"

"Yeah..."

"They're all missing. Every last one of them."

I stared back at him. Against my breast, Rose stirred, giving a small whimper, before falling back to sleep. "Missing?" I echoed, because apparently my brain hadn't come fully back.

He nodded. "I got to thinking, after we last talked about Dr. A. in the café a few weeks ago. And I got to wondering. So I... well, followed up, on my own, as discreetly as I could. It was hard to do without alerting him, so it took a while, but none of those volunteers have been seen since."

My heart started pounding as I thought about it. What could it mean? "He doesn't have them sequestered somewhere, does he? While he treats them?"

"Maybe?" Sebastian shook his head. "But if so, why hide the fact? It only made me wonder, made me ask around about them."

"I hope they're all right," I whispered, as dread continued to fill me. But dread of what? I knew Gregorio was sneaky, and that he wasn't the man he pretended to be. That he knew truths about witchkind that he deliberately kept from us, for reasons of his own.

And I knew that he was no longer monitoring me with an enchanted golden ring.

"Sebastian," I said, suddenly leaning forward. Rose murmured again, but didn't shift. "Do me a big favor."

"Of course."

I gave a half-smile. "Don't say yes till you've heard it."

"Callie." He held my gaze, his eyes as serious as mine. "I have a feeling I know where this is going."

"Maybe." I leaned in closer, whispering for no other reason than because it just felt like we should.

He left a few minutes later, with a spell-disguised gold ring in his pocket. I sincerely hoped I hadn't just made a terrible mistake.

I didn't want to lose another friend before their time.

— CHAPTER ELEVEN —

I spent one more night in my room at the coven house, letting my sisters bring me meals, coddle me, and coo over my baby. Then I spent another day making sure I had the strength to be on my own—walking up and down the stairs carrying the baby, cooking myself small meals, sitting out on the back veranda. The day after that, I returned to my house.

"It is customary to take one to two weeks for recovery," Leonora said.

I smiled at her. "I'm sure that's the tradition, but honestly, I'm feeling just fine." We stood in the front parlor as I held Rosemary, jiggling her slightly, though she had still not yet cried. "And besides, I have Petrana to take care of me if I need household help."

To her credit, Leonora refrained from letting out a dismissive snort. "And besides *that*," she said instead, "you have a coven full of sisters who are more than happy to take shifts at your house, since you insist upon living there. Every single one of them has asked me about it."

"Have they indeed?" I asked, unable to stifle a smile. "Asked to come and help me there, or asked you why you're letting me leave so soon?"

Now she did smile back. "A mix."

I shook my head. "I understand, but I really do want to get back to my own home. Also, Jeremy won't come see me or the baby here, and neither will my parents. They need to see her, and she needs to get to know them. *All* of them."

Leonora nodded. "Allow me to bid farewell to the child, then, before you depart."

"Of course." I handed her to my coven mother, who rocked her and made all manner of extremely undignified noises at her. Rosemary appeared delighted by the old witch. I swear she actually laughed, though maybe that was just more drooling and random sounds.

Leonora's face was soft and relaxed when she handed the baby back. "I will come and visit once you are settled."

"Yes, you are always welcome."

"You are not taking the ley lines, are you?"

"No, no." I shifted Rose to one arm so I could dig my cell phone out of my pocket. "I'm going to call a car."

"A taxi?"

I smiled at her. "Something like that."

The phone, however, was entirely dead. I so did not understand the poor, feeble magic of these devices. How could they run out of power when they were turned off and not being used?

Fortunately, the coven house had a few electrical plugs. We even used them from time to time, so some clever human at PG&E wouldn't notice that such a big house had a zero-balance bill every month, and wonder why.

I plugged it in and left it to do its thing while I packed. When I went back for it, I saw I had a couple of voicemails.

"Crap," I whispered. They were both from Christine—Raymond's sister. Today was the day we were supposed to have lunch. I'd forgotten all about her—about everything in my life except this baby, it seemed.

I called her back, only to get her voicemail in turn. "Hey, it's Callie," I said after the beep. "I'm so sorry I blew off our lunch, but as you probably guessed, I have the world's best excuse! I'm holding a sweet baby girl in my arms right now. Anyway, let me know when you want to reschedule. Talk to you soon!"

My phone buzzed with a text a few minutes later. *No worries! I figured that's what must have happened. Just call when you're up to it—and congrats!*

Thanks! I typed back, happy she wasn't mad at me.

I turned off the phone and tucked it into my pocket.

Then I remembered why I'd charged the phone in the first place, and pulled it back out again, so I could open the app and call for the car.

Apparently, pregnancy brain didn't just evaporate when you had the baby.

The Lyft dropped me, Rose, and Elnor off in front of my house. I could tell that the driver was dying to ask something—anything—about what I was up to, but I wasn't sure what exactly seemed weird to him.

Only later did I figure it out: most cats don't like to ride in cars. Not only that, but most women with infants travel with a great deal of equipment. I didn't have a baby carrier or diaper bag or anything.

Well, whatever. If I was going to worry about confusing humans, I'd do nothing else all day.

I felt the wards of my house brush across me, acknowledging my presence, and that of Elnor, then pausing when they got to Rose. They let her pass, of course; she had been in this house plenty—in fact she had been conceived here—but she had never been her own, self-contained person before. Ward magic is fairly mechanical, though, and my wards let us in after a moment.

My house felt stale and unoccupied. "Petrana!" I called out. "We're home!

My golem came walking down the long hallway from the kitchen, where she waited when I wasn't having her do anything else. "Welcome home, Mistress Callie, and Mistress Rosemary."

I smiled. "You *really* don't need to call *her* mistress," I said. "She's a baby."

"She is a very attractive baby."

"Thank you." Was Petrana developing more of a personality all the time? And was this an independent action on her part, or was she just mirroring me? I wished I understood golems better.

Elnor was marching around the whole first floor of the house, nose active, re-securing the space that we'd been away from for such a time. As usual, she paused at the closet under the front staircase. Petrana glanced at me, as though for permission. I nodded, and she opened the door. Elnor shot inside.

I shrugged and headed down the hallway. "Petrana, I am going to have some people over, probably several times over the next few days," I told her. "I think it would be a good idea to get some food prepared, stuff that we can just eat without a lot of fuss."

I got to the kitchen and glanced around. It was all well and good that I'd prepared a nursery, but I could already see that I was woefully unprepared for what it really meant to have a baby. It wasn't like I could just plunk Rose down on a wooden chair and go about my business.

I shifted her to a hip so I could use at least one hand to open cabinets.

"Would you like me to hold her for you?" Petrana asked, stepping into the kitchen behind me.

I started to say *No*, but then thought about it. "Are you... equipped for holding a baby?"

"I am not sure what you mean by that."

"She's the most precious thing in the world to me." I watched my golem, still wishing her face could display some sort of emotion. "She must be held gently, but firmly. She cannot, under any circumstances, be dropped. She is very fragile."

"I am equipped to hold the baby without dropping her. I have never dropped any of the fragile dishes."

"Dishes don't wriggle about unexpectedly," I told her.

"Begging your pardon, Mistress Callie, but sometimes they do," my golem returned. "Particularly when they have soap on them."

I stared at her. Was she…being funny? No, surely not. "Well, let's give it a try. I'll stand very close, in case…anything goes awry." In case Rose objected to being held by a mud-creature animated by my own magic.

She'd objected to an eight-hundred-year-old warlock, after all.

Petrana stepped up to me, and I handed her the baby, holding my breath.

She took Rosemary gently and held her to her breast, just as she'd seen me do. Rose lolled her eyes up at the golem, then at me. Then—this can't be literally true, but I know what I saw—she *nodded*, and settled in against Petrana's chest.

Petrana stood entirely still, all her attention focused on holding the baby. I could almost see her thoughts: *gently, but firmly.*

"Okay," I said, after a long moment. "I guess you can hold the baby." I took a step back.

The baby seemed happy in Petrana's arms.

It felt really strange to turn away from them and look through the cupboards—I kept sneaking looks back, making sure everything was all right—but I finally had to admit that, even though it practically gave me vertigo, it was going to be all right.

I still needed to get some real baby furniture, though. Highchairs and strollers and, what-do-you-call-them, those little net cages with the soft floors. Something to pack her into cars in so I didn't freak out any more Lyft drivers. Why hadn't anybody prepared me for *this* part of the experience?

Maybe it would have been easier if I'd actually ever known anyone who'd had a baby. By the time witchlets got to the coven house, they were school age.

Maybe I should have let some of my coven sisters come over, take shifts helping me out.

But then I thought about Niad prancing around trying to tell me how to be a mother.... Nope.

Rose rested happily in Petrana's arms until she got hungry again, an hour or so later. Petrana didn't even need to sit down. I coached her on walking around a bit, since Rose seemed to like the movement.

Only I could feed her, though.

I was sitting at the dining table doing just that when Elnor wandered in. "Where have you been, kitty?" I asked. I didn't think I'd seen her since we'd gotten back home. Usually she'd be bugging me for tuna by now. "Is the house all secure now?"

She looked up at me and started washing her whiskers.

On the stove, a dozen eggs were boiling, so Petrana could make deviled eggs for all the company I was planning. I'd deal with getting groceries later; I had enough stuff here to keep us all going for a few days.

I just needed to decide who to invite first.

When I thought about it that way, the answer was obvious. I sent a message to Jeremy: *We're home, and Rosemary and I would be delighted to see you whenever it's convenient.*

May I come now? he answered a moment later.

Please.

He must have already shopped, because he knocked at the door within minutes, and was holding a large, beautifully wrapped box.

"Do come in," I said, grinning at the present and then up at him.

"It's for her, not for you," he teased, following me inside.

We sat in the second, more casual parlor, and he cooed over the baby, still clearly delighted by her. Still clearly in the dark about her parentage, despite his earlier hesitation. I pushed my worries aside and enjoyed his smile, enjoyed how silly babies made everyone. "Who's the pretty child?" he crooned at her. "Who's the special powerful witchlet?"

Hmm, I hoped she'd be powerful. I hoped Gregorio was wrong about that. I kept my mouth shut.

"Who's my smart girl?"

"Smart as she is, I'm not sure she can open that box," I finally said.

Jeremy looked up at me with a foolish grin. "No, you'll probably have to help her. Be my guest."

I snagged the present off the coffee table, pulled off the elaborate ribbons, and tore away the paper. Inside was a box holding a lovely quilt, folded neatly. It was clearly handmade, and obviously not new, though clean and very well preserved.

I looked up at Jeremy. He was watching me carefully. "It was mine," he said softly. "My mother made it for me, before she… It is one of the few things I have from her hand."

My eyes filled with tears as I drew the blanket to my face, breathing in the warm scent of Jeremy, the emotional traces of his long-dead mother, the love and sorrow and pain and warmth and generosity of this amazing gift. "Oh…" My throat threatened to stop up with emotion. "Jeremy, this is…too much." He looked worried, so I put the quilt in my lap and pulled him into an embrace. He was still holding Rose; we were both careful not to squish her. "I don't mean it's too much. I mean—I don't know what to say. It's an astonishing gift."

He held me close—held both of us close—and whispered, "I have always intended to give it to my firstborn."

Even though none of this is how I imagined it would be went unsaid between us. I just kept holding him, holding her between us, as I grieved for a warlock who had lost his mother far, far too young. He'd hardly known her, but he must have felt her absence every day of his life.

Rose would never know that feeling, I vowed. She would know the love of her mother…

When an image of Gracie's face sprang into my mind—the young witchlet out on her own, bereft of any parent, any elders—I stopped the entire train of thought before I could blurt out something ill-considered. Instead, when I finally pulled away, I wiped a stray tear and said, "Thank you. Thank you so very, very much."

"You, and she, are most welcome."

Rosemary reached out and pulled on a strand of his long hair. He had it in his usual simple ponytail down his back, but our embrace had brought it to her attention. Jeremy smiled as he gently extracted his hair from her hand. "I wasn't wrong about her being powerful. Strong, too." He looked up at me. "She seems…quite alert, interactive even, for being so very young."

I shrugged, smiling down at my baby. "I don't really know what to expect."

"Neither do I, I confess."

Rose blew more bubbles and lolled her head about, or at least as much as she could with Jeremy holding it steady. We both knew *that* much about infants, anyway.

Sitting here with them forced me to think about his contract offer…still on the table, I supposed. At least, he hadn't retracted it. Nor had he pressed it. He was clearly fond of Rosemary, and I knew how he felt about me.

But would he still feel the same—about both of us—if he ever found out the truth?

Certainly not.

Could I be one hundred percent certain he never *would* find out?

No, not at all; not when it was his father's own secret, and when Jeremy himself had already remarked on Rose's red hair and noticed whatever else about her he wasn't telling me.

So I couldn't, in good faith, agree to form a legal family with him. Not with such a secret between us. If I ever signed a contract with a warlock, there would have to be complete honesty.

Therefore, I was destined to be alone. To raise this child alone—or as alone as my coven would let me, anyway.

I would be happy to let Jeremy get to know her, to be around as much as he wanted to. It was what Gregorio wanted: for Jeremy to continue to believe this was his child. That we could someday make "another" daughter together.

"Well," Jeremy said, after a long period where I thought these thoughts and he gazed at my baby, "I don't mean to stay long. I know you both need your rest."

I wanted to protest, to ask him to stay longer, but we both knew he was right. "Thank you for the gift, again."

He leaned forward and brushed a kiss on my cheek. "No, don't get up; I can see myself out. I'll call you soon."

I watched as he left the room, and then the house.

It was the dead of the night. I was sleeping, Rosemary in my arms, both of us curled in my bed.

And there was a presence in my room.

I came awake at once, on high alert yet not moving—I didn't want to startle the baby.

I didn't want to tip off whoever it was that I was aware of them.

How did they get past my wards? I wondered, even as I sent my senses around.

The essence was familiar—very familiar. I relaxed a little as my conscious brain came alert, found its sense.

"Gracie?"

She stepped from the shadows, somehow shy and proud and defiant all at once. She was barefoot and dressed in a simple black smock of a dress. "I didn't mean to scare you," she whispered.

"Gracie!" I sat up, pulling Rose to my breast with one arm as I threw the other out to pull the witchlet into an awkward embrace. She endured it stoically.

"I heard you had your baby," she said, after I finally released her.

For the second time today, tears were stinging my eyes. "Gracie!" Somehow, all I could manage was to stammer her name, again and again. "Where have you *been*?" I finally added.

She shrugged. "Around. It's not important. And I'm not staying long. I just wanted to see her." She sniffled a bit, maybe. "And you."

"Well, thanks for that," I tried teasing her, but it came out flat. I had too much emotion in my throat. I guess baby hormones weren't done with me yet. "Oh, Gracie, I'm so glad you're all right."

"Can I hold her?"

I started to say *she's sleeping*, but of course she wasn't. Rosemary was regarding Gracie with the same calm, solemn intensity she brought to everything. "Of course."

I was going to hand this baby to every member of witchkind in the greater Bay Area before this week was over, it looked like.

As I was quickly beginning to realize was her way, Rose accepted the new arms happily. She even deigned to drool on Gracie, which made the witchlet giggle.

Which, in turn, made her familiar, Minky, jump up onto the bed, followed in short order by Elnor.

As Gracie rocked Rose and made nonsense sounds at her, I said to Elnor, "Some watch cat you are. You didn't even let me know we had company."

Gracie looked up at me. "She let us in, actually."

I just gaped back at her. "What? What are you talking about?" Cats can't undo wards or open doors. Not even witches' cats.

"Through the portal," Gracie said, as though I was the one making no sense.

"*What* portal?" I asked. I was very calm, not shrieking or getting mad or anything. "I don't know anything about any portal."

"In the closet under the stairs. It's a cat portal." Now Gracie blinked at me and looked uncomfortable. "You don't know about the cat portal under the stairs?"

"No, Gracie," I said, still really calm. "Can you show me this 'cat portal' under the stairs?"

Gracie shrugged. "Sure."

I pulled on my bathrobe, reclaimed my baby, and followed the witchlet down to the first floor. Indeed, the closet door was sitting ajar. "In here," she said, pointing.

I bent down and started to crawl in before thinking better of taking a baby in there. "Here," I said, handing her to Gracie.

When I turned back, both Elnor and Minky darted in before me. They ran to the back wall of the closet, the place that Elnor had always been so interested in. The place where the channelers had left one of their stones during their investigation after Logan had died.

The blank wall that contained exactly zero portals, of any kind.

"Very funny," I said to Gracie, after I'd backed out of the small space.

She looked back at me, puzzled. "It was there earlier. I swear, that's how I came in."

I looked between her and the empty space before letting out a sigh. "I need tea."

One reason for never, ever having another baby was pennyroyal tea. Oh Blessed Mother, how I had missed it.

I would probably realize how much I'd missed other things too, like Witch's Mead, once I got around to it; but I'd lost my taste for all intoxicants. Pennyroyal, however, had never stopped sounding good.

Gracie sat at the kitchen table with me, sipping her own cup; Petrana held the baby, who as usual seemed perfectly happy with the arrangement. I took the opportunity to study the witchlet. She looked…calmer, somehow. All her teen angst had settled down. I could almost see the wise witch she was destined to become.

Which isn't to say there wasn't a sadness to her, as well.

"You really won't tell me where you've been?" I asked, at last.

Gracie looked over at me. Her cat nudged her hand; she scritched her absently, exactly as I always did with Elnor. "You can't let on that you know—or that you even saw me."

My heart sped up a bit. "I am good at keeping secrets." But even as I said the words, something inside me cried out in protest. *Too many secrets! No more secrets!*

But I had to know she was all right—and that she was going to *continue* being all right.

"Ma-ma-ma-ma-ma," Rose babbled, from across the room. Startled, both Gracie and I looked over at her. She was reaching for Petrana's wiry hair and kicking her tiny legs.

"She did *not* just say Mama," Gracie breathed, stunned.

"She's three days old," I said. "It's just noise."

I told myself I believed that and refocused on Gracie.

"I'm staying with some human friends," she blurted. "In the East Bay. You can't tell anyone—you *really* can't tell Leonora. I'm done with the coven school, done with that crap."

"We were looking for you in L.A.," I said.

Gracie gave a small smile. "I thought maybe you would. I wanted to throw you off the trail." She grinned wider. "It worked."

"So you don't really want to be an actor?"

"I might—I didn't lie about that part. Actually, I didn't really lie about anything. I just…let you get the wrong impression about things and didn't correct it."

It would be easier to get mad at her if she didn't remind me so much of myself. "Who are these human friends? What are you doing with them?" I shook my head. "Sorry, that didn't come out right. I just want to know what you're up to, and why."

She snorted. "You know why. I told you everything straight out, at least that part of it. It's dumb to hide our natures. Humans aren't the enemy." She narrowed her eyes and looked at me. "You of all witches know that."

"Hey, hey, wait a minute." I put my hands up in a warding-off gesture. "Just because I had a human boyfriend doesn't mean—" And that's when the enormity of what she had just said hit me. "Are you saying you've *told humans* that you're a *witch*?"

"Sure," she said, just a little too casually, watching me for my reaction.

I wouldn't give her the satisfaction. Even if it killed me. I forced myself to stay calm. I was getting good at this. "Gracie. Explain."

She shrugged again. "Just that. I told my friends I'm a witch."

"And...you told them what that means?" I had told Raymond I was a witch the night I'd met him. In a teasing, joking way that ensured that he would have no idea what I was actually talking about. He hadn't even blinked. In fact, that was when he'd told me that his sister was one too—a Wiccan, he'd meant.

"Yeah." Gracie sipped her tea, not meeting my eye.

I waited her out.

Finally, she looked back up at me. "I know we're not supposed to. That it goes against all the strictures of witchkind, blah blah blah. But Callie! Nobody cares. I promise you."

"What do you mean by that? Are you saying that they believed you?"

"Well, not at first."

"How did you convince them?" Though I could well imagine.

"I did some magic."

"And nobody was frightened or alarmed?"

She squirmed a little. "Not…a whole lot. Not after the first few minutes."

I shook my head, suddenly not wanting to hear any more.

"They're cool now," she hastened to add. "They think it's no big deal." She leaned forward, intent and serious again. "Callie, listen: witchkind is totally afraid of humans, and humans couldn't care less. They can do so much with their technology—what we can do is like just another flavor of the same thing."

"Gracie, you know that's not true," I said. "No human can teleport across town in the blink of an eye, or send thought-messages to one another, or cast zones of inattention on themselves, or—well, a thousand other things!" I glanced at Petrana, still tirelessly holding Rose. My baby seemed to be watching our conversation. I was probably projecting hard here. "Not to mention animating a golem!"

Gracie shrugged. "Well, sure, but humans can do plenty of stuff we can't. Like fly easily in airplanes, for just one example." She got that fierce, stubborn look on her face. The look I knew all too well. "My point is, they're not threatened by us. They think this is interesting, and different. My…um, my friends are wondering if maybe we can't work together. You know, join forces, be stronger if we both bring our own skills to—to whatever."

My brain was grasping at several different threads in what she was saying. What I seized on first was, "Your 'um friends'? Gracie, do you have a human boyfriend?"

Her face flamed up. "No." Before I could press her—because she was so totally lying, she totally was in love with someone—she added, "*Girl*friend."

"Oh." I caught my breath. This shouldn't have startled me—it was not long ago, and in this very room, that Sebastian Fallon had told me that he wasn't exactly following the Conservative Old Ways either when it came to his love life—but I hadn't seen any hints from Gracie along these lines. In fact, I seemed to remember her giggling with the other witchlets about young warlocks. "I mean, that's great, Gracie—" I started.

She laughed. "I know! It surprised me too. I guess I'm bi."

"I…" I stopped, shaking my head. "No, seriously, that's great, and it's also not what we need to talk about right now. I need to know you're safe—which I can see, and I'm very happy about that—and I really need to at least let Leonora, and your parents, know that you're all right." She was frowning, so I went on before she could interrupt me again. "Gracie, everyone has been really worried about you. Not because they want to control you, but because they *care* about you. *We* care about you. When you just vanished, after being so unhappy—can't you see how that made us all feel? Heck, you don't even like it when it feels like I spend too much time away from the coven house, and you know exactly where I am."

She looked down at her teacup again, which was empty. I stifled the impulse to wave a finger and fill it up for her. If she wanted to live as a human, she could darn well get up and put a kettle on the stove. "You knew I'd be all right," she finally said, her voice small. "You know I'm strong and capable, and that humans aren't a threat to us."

What was uncanny was that I'd said pretty much the same thing myself.

"It's still not okay to do this to the people who care about you," I insisted. "I am not telling you what to do. You can walk out of here at any moment and I won't try to follow or stop you. I won't even tell Leonora and your parents if you insist. But I will ask you, once more, to give me permission to let them know you were here, and that you're safe."

"I just wanted to see your baby," she said, sullenly. She got up and walked over to Petrana.

"It's all right," I said to them both. My golem handed Rose to Gracie, who took her and sniffed the top of her head. She paced the room with her, jiggling her gently, not meeting my eye. I gave her the time. Let her think. After a few minutes, she handed Rose back to Petrana.

"She's so cute," Gracie said, sitting back down at the table. "And she seems...smart. Wise. I don't know."

"I know what you mean," I said. "And, thank you."

After another minute, Gracie asked, "What was the birth like?"

"Awful."

She gaped at me, and then burst out laughing, and then closed her mouth a moment later, horrified with herself. "I'm sorry! I didn't—I didn't expect that."

I leaned back in my chair and rested a hand on my still weirdly diminished belly, smiling at her. "I promised not to lie to you. It was terrible. Long, and painful, and I don't even see why it has to be that way. With as much power as we have, as much magical control over our bodies—why did I have to endure endless hours of labor like that?"

"I don't know."

"I don't either!" I sighed. "Well, you asked."

"I did want to know. And I'm sorry it was so hard." She reached down and scratched Minky again. I could almost feel that she was getting ready to leave. "I wonder if it would be different if we could make babies with humans."

I practically bit my tongue bloody not reacting to that. "What do you mean?" I asked, wondering how she could have hit on such an idea only moments after I had reminded her of my promise not to lie to her. "Humans have at least as hard a time in labor as we do."

"Oh, that's true, I guess."

I couldn't get her to elaborate, and I certainly didn't want to press it. Within another minute, she'd stood up, gathered her cat, and left out the front door like a normal witch—after I'd eased the wards for her. I watched her through the æther. She walked down the front steps, looked up and down the dark street, and then vanished. She left no trace behind.

I sighed, returning my sight to the kitchen, feeling tired, and sad, and uncertain. Petrana asked, "Do you want to take the baby back?"

"No, not just yet, thank you."

The kitchen window showed the growing light of very early morning. It was too late to go back to bed, and I'd be napping later in the day anyway. I sat by my empty teacup and thought about our conversation. Gracie hadn't given me specific permission to tell the others she was safe, but she hadn't forbidden it either, when I'd asked the second time.

I would take that as tacit assent.

It was too early to call anyone, though; there was always the chance they'd be sleeping. Instead, I got up and headed to the front hall—specifically, the closet.

"Come on, Elnor," I called. "Show me what's going on back here."

My familiar dutifully followed me into the closet again, acting as innocent as could be. As if she'd never poked around in here herself, never showed undue interest in the place.

"Show me," I said again.

She sniffed everywhere—the entire back wall, the side walls, the floor. As far as she could reach. Then she turned her fuzzy gaze back to me, as if to say, *What?*

"Foolish cat," I muttered, and put my fingers on the back wall. A portal. Gracie said there was a cat portal here. Why hadn't I pressed her on this? I ran my fingers lightly over the plaster, back and forth, in a slow sweeping motion. I closed my eyes to better let my energetic vision see what was here.

Essence of cat, to be sure, and not just Elnor and Minky. "Willson," I whispered. Logan's cat had been here, and not all that long ago.

Beside me, Elnor held very still. Not helping. Not hindering.

What was *up* with this?

Then my fingers found an edge. It was just the tiniest seam, a little magical doorway, very well hidden, about cat-high.

I had just started to pull on it when Elnor bumped my elbow. The edge left my fingertips. "Cat!" I whispered. "You jerk."

She nudged my elbow again.

"I'm going to toss you out of here if you…" I started, and then sat back on my heels. "Okay, you're trying to tell me something." I wished she could just open her mouth and speak to me, dang it. Or even send me thoughts. But no, cats can't do that, even witches' familiars. "Am I not supposed to know about this?"

Listen to the cats echoed through my mind. Great, but what were they *saying*?

Elnor began to purr.

I petted her back, almost without consciously deciding to. Yep, she had me trained, all right. She purred louder, arching up into my touch. "Except if I wasn't supposed to know about it, you wouldn't have followed me in here and then just sat there. Right?"

More purring, but of course, that didn't tell me much.

I continued to think aloud, not pretending that Elnor was answering me, just working it through in my mind. "So I can know about it, but not how it works, or how to use it myself."

Purr.

"Except Gracie used it. How? How did she know about it? Minky is still a kitten. She shouldn't be anywhere near her full powers, much less know much about how the world works. She and her witch are supposed to grow together, melding their magic and their knowledge. Just as we did."

Still purring, Elnor now bit my elbow. Just a nip, but it got my attention.

"What is it?" I asked her. "What am I getting wrong?"

Elnor turned and left the closet.

"Kitty!" I called to her, but she ignored me.

I ran my fingers along the back wall once more, slowly and carefully, but I could no longer find the seam. Frustrated, I crawled back out into the foyer. I got to my feet, unbending rather creakily, still trying to find my way back into my body after pregnancy and childbirth. I brushed off dust and looked around.

Elnor was nowhere in the front rooms. "Here, kitty!" I called again, on my way back to the kitchen, where Petrana was still holding Rosemary. "I'll take her now," I said to my golem.

With my baby back in my arms, I went upstairs. I was even less sleepy now, so I took Rose to the front sitting room, where I rocked her back to sleep.

I sat holding her for several hours, pondering all that I'd learned. And hadn't learned.

— CHAPTER TWELVE —

In the morning—well, later in the morning, after it got light—I sent a message to Leonora through the æther, telling her that Gracie was alive and well, that she wasn't in Los Angeles, and that I had promised not to reveal her whereabouts—that I didn't even know them myself—but that I was going to continue to try to talk her into coming home. I asked her to please let Gracie's parents know.

Then I braced for her response. She would be sharp and bossy, she would demand to know why I hadn't let her know at once, why I hadn't detained the witchlet, why...

Thank you, Calendula, she said. *I am glad to hear that she is well, and I appreciate your letting me know. I will pass this along to her people. Please continue your efforts as you can.*

What? I sat in my chair, blinking, trying to parse this. It sounded...straightforwardly mild, supportive, grateful. Where were the hidden barbs? I couldn't find any. In my arms, Rose stirred, smacking her tiny lips together in what I was already learning meant she wanted to nurse soon. I opened my blouse for her.

I will do my best, I sent Leonora, as my baby began her breakfast.

Thank you. How are you feeling? How is your energy?

I smiled. Ah, there, at least, was my concerned coven mother. *I'm good. Nursing the baby now.*

I would like to have one of your sisters come by to see you, and her, and check on your food supplies. See if you need anything. It was not exactly couched as a request.

I started to protest but then realized that that might be helpful. *Okay. I'm having my birth parents over for brunch, so I could use a hand. Not Niad, though.*

Leonora sent a chuckle through the æther. *Will Sirianna do?*

Perfectly.

Very well. She cut the channel, and I leaned back in my chair, still rocking slightly as Rosemary nursed.

Life was certainly strange these days, wasn't it?

Siri helped me and Petrana get food together for a simple brunch. I worried I would think about cooking in this very kitchen with Logan, preparing a dinner party all those months ago... But Sirianna was so cheerful, and the new baby was such a delight, that it was easy to focus on happy thoughts.

I was also a bit nervous about my mom's state of mind. She'd checked in with me every day over the æther, but I hadn't seen her since before the birth.

When my folks arrived, though, they cooed and cuddled the baby just like everyone else. I watched Mom carefully; she seemed delighted, relaxed, and at ease. "She's so beautiful," she said, looking from the baby in her arms to me and back again. "And she so resembles you. I can see your chin and cheekbones, and definitely the brow line."

How anyone found cheekbones in that plump baby-face was beyond me, but I just grinned back at my mom. "Is that what I looked like as a newborn?"

"Pretty much. Not the red hair, though—yours was entirely black, before it all fell out and then grew in blond."

"Blond?" I put a hand to my dark brown tresses, held in a French braid.

"Yes, for the first year or two anyway." Mom smiled down at Rosemary. "So don't get too attached to any of it now, because it'll be something else before you know it."

Wise words.

"I still can't quite believe I'm a grandmother," she added, patting her own dark hair, tucked carefully behind her ears. She must have spelled it this morning, for it to be staying so still and smooth. Her face was also smooth, completely unlined; she could have passed for a human thirty. Or maybe thirty-five. I looked like a thirty-year-old, after all, and she had politely set her apparent age to be older than her daughter's.

"No one will believe it," I assured her.

After the meal, Mom pulled me into a strong hug at the doorway. "I'm so happy for you, my darling," she whispered into my ear.

"I am too." I hugged her back. I wanted to ask her more questions…and I also didn't. She seemed good now—she really did seem happy.

Maybe things were actually okay.

The next few weeks fell into a comfortable routine. Rosemary grew, and remained the mildest, happiest baby ever. I couldn't believe my luck…I mean, I really, truly had trouble believing it. Trouble believing that she was all right. But Nora, Manka, and Sebastian all examined her thoroughly and repeatedly.

"She's in perfect health," Nora said. "Growing just as she should, and already strengthening her magical channels."

"But she never, ever cries," I told her—I told them all. "You don't think that's weird?" Everyone just smiled and told me to be grateful.

And I was. But it was just too strange.

Jeremy visited nearly every day, briefly. He didn't press his suit, and he didn't bring any more emotionally laden presents. I was grateful for both of these things, and for the fact that we were relaxed together. Rosemary seemed to like him. She let him hold her as agreeably as she did everyone else. I knew I'd have to address the issue of the contract sooner or later, but for now, this worked just fine.

No more cats, or witchlets, came through the supposed portal in my closet. I went in there twice more, exploring—both with and without Elnor—and could never find the edge again. Finally, I gave it up. If it was truly a thing, then it was being kept from me. For some reason.

I was just beginning to wonder why Gregorio Andromedus had been so quiet when he sent me a message. *Calendula Isadora, my son informs me that the child is healthy and happy, and that you are recovering from your confinement.*

I had to smile at his old-fashioned notion, at the old-fashioned word. *Yes, thank you, we are both well,* I sent back.

I am glad to hear that. Then a pause. *I am also glad to hear that you are spending so much time in Jeremiah's company.*

But of course, I said, then couldn't resist adding, *my girl needs to get to know her father, after all.*

Just so. Good day, Calendula. Then he cut the channel.

What was that *about?* I wondered. Just checking on me? Reminding me, yet again, to be a good little witch and keep my story straight? How addled did he think I was?

What did he make of the removed ring? He knew, of course; he had to. I knew of no new leash he'd put on me. Was he letting me be, or was his current method of control just that much more subtle?

I fretted about all this for a while before shrugging and going back to enjoying my daughter.

I didn't hear from Gracie again. I sent her one message, letting her know that Leonora and her parents had been told that she was alive and safe. She didn't respond.

Foolish child, I thought, and ignored the part of me that felt envious of her—her what, exactly? Her freedom? Bravery? I wasn't sure what to call it, the thing in her that had just taken charge of her own life, at age fifteen.

Even if she was making a terrible mistake, she'd almost certainly recover from it. She'd be wiser for it, too, once she got over the pain.

I hadn't been anything like that bold when I was her age.

Christine and I finally had that lunch date. She took me out to an amazing Chinese restaurant near the medical center where she worked as a nurse-midwife. "My brother says you like Chinese food," she said, smiling at me over her plate of pot stickers.

"I love it," I said around a mouthful of Happy Family. "And this is incredible. Does this place do delivery?"

"Yep, anywhere in the city limits. Grab a menu when you leave."

Rosemary occupied the seat next to me. I'd finally gotten a clever little harness-chair thing that worked in both cars and stationary furniture, and could even be transformed into a front-pack, so I could wear her but leave both my hands free. She lay in it now, watching me eat, blowing her usual bubbles.

"That is the world's most adorable baby," Christine said. "And this isn't just redhead solidarity speaking."

"She is adorable, isn't she?" I asked, grinning at my child.

Christine laughed. "She'll have to learn humility somewhere else, though."

I snorted. "What am I supposed to do, pretend I don't think it's true?" I looked across the table at her. "Seriously, you work with moms and babies all the time. Who doesn't think their little one is the most precious perfect thing ever?"

"You'd be surprised, actually." Christine snagged a pot sticker with her chopsticks and bit off the end. "Some mothers get all worried about their babies. They think they're funny-looking, or they behave strange, or they aren't growing like they should."

Now that she mentioned it… "Is it normal for a baby to never cry?" I asked her.

She looked at me quizzically. "Literally never?"

I nodded.

"Really?" she insisted.

"Really never."

Christine shook her head. "I've heard of that, but… You had her tested for all the possible chromosomal abnormalities, right?"

"Sure," I bluffed. I'd have to go research what kinds of tests humans gave their babies. Maybe I could even run some of them in my lab at home, or at least modified ones to apply to us. "Everything came up normal."

"Huh." She looked across the table at Rosemary. My baby lolled her head about, looking back at Christine…or at the food…or the lights. Who could tell? "Well, babies only cry when they aren't getting their needs met. And every baby is different. They come ready-made with their own personalities and temperaments, to be sure. Maybe you're just really good at knowing when she's hungry or tired or needs changing."

"That's probably it," I said. "I guess I'm just lucky."

"Count your blessings," she said, taking another bite of the pot sticker. "I can see that you're getting enough sleep—you look great. Both of you."

"Thanks."

I steered the conversation away from my peculiar baby by asking Christine to tell me about her work, which she seemed more than delighted to do. It was fun to see her eyes light up as she told me about easing the birthing process, helping moms bond with their babies, seeing them months later as they grew and developed. The rest of the lunch hour flew by. "I gotta run—but thanks for coming all the way out to the avenues!" she said, getting up and grabbing the check.

"My pleasure. Anytime. And the next time's on me."

"Deal. And you don't have to leave—lunch rush is over, they won't need the table." She pulled her employee badge out from where she had tucked it into her blouse as she walked up to the register to pay.

I took her at her word and stayed, polishing off my own dish and then the few pot stickers Christine had left. Amazing food. I was going to throw away the menu from that other place. How come Raymond didn't know about this one? His own sister wouldn't have told him—

"Ba-ba-ba-ba," Rosemary babbled from her baby seat.

I looked at her, frozen. My mind was filled with memories of Raymond, and I could suddenly see his likeness all over her face. Did nobody else see this? Not even his own sister? It wasn't just the red hair; all her features were his.

I thought about what my mom had said, about her resembling me. Was that just the typical bullshit that people told all new moms? "Oh, she looks so much like you..."

Had anyone gone on about how much she looked like Jeremy? No, they hadn't, because she didn't.

"Ba-ba-ba." She waved her tiny, fat little hands in the air in front of her and smacked her lips.

I glanced around the restaurant. Only a few tables were still occupied; surely nobody would mind a nursing mother. I pulled

Rose out of her chair and got her latched on with only a minimum of indecent exposure.

While she had lunch, I thought about Raymond. I did miss him, and I was still unhappy with how we had left things, although they were better than they'd been for a while. He was probably really busy with his band, making their new album, doing cloud sound things or whatever. I had deliberately not asked Christine about him; I wanted to become friends with *her*, not with *Raymond's sister*. But now I wished I had.

Well, I could call him, of course.

And maybe I would.

But then he'd want to see the baby. Would *he* see the resemblance?

How could he not?

If he did, then what? Did I seriously imagine he was going to, what, call me on it? "Hey, you said that baby's not mine, but she clearly is!" Right, I didn't think so.

But it would be weird. He'd suspect, and he'd feel uncomfortable. Far more likely that it would go like that—that he'd want to ask, and not feel like he could, and we'd be right back in that awkward place where I was keeping secrets and he knew it and we couldn't talk about any of it.

I sighed and shifted the baby to my other breast. I missed him, and I wanted him to know his daughter, even if he couldn't know that she *was* his daughter; and I couldn't figure out how to make that happen in the actual universe that I lived in; so I decided to let it go, for now.

Maybe things would work themselves out…later. Maybe she'd lose this red hair and the resemblance would become less obvious. Maybe…

Maybe someday I wouldn't be such a freaking coward.

Sebastian visited me again. He'd been by with the healers a few times, but this time he came alone.

After the usual niceties of food and drink, and inspecting and then playing with the baby, and making sure that I was well and energetic and all that, he said, "So. I have an update on the missing research subjects."

My stomach sank. I hadn't *forgotten* about them, exactly, but…

He saw my face. "I wish I didn't have to bother you about it now, while you're still recovering—"

"No, no," I said, "I'm fine. Jeez. I'm going out to lunch with friends and feeling great. My baby doesn't even keep me up at night. I was just…"

"You were just getting over a difficult childbirth and getting adjusted to living with an infant," he said, his voice kind and gentle. "And there wasn't really anything to do, then—at least, not that I couldn't do myself. But now I need your help."

I nodded, swallowing hard. It was nice that he was trying to be cool with it, but there was no reason I should have been loafing at home, letting him deal with things. "Okay. So, what's going on?"

He sat back in his chair and looked at his hands, clearly gathering his thoughts. "First off, I have a confession."

I just looked at him.

Now he looked back up at me, bravely meeting my eye. "You told me not to try to use the gold ring, but…I couldn't help myself."

I sucked in a breath. "Sebastian!"

He put up his hands. "It's fine, nothing happened, but—"

"You don't *think* anything happened, but you don't understand—"

"Callie, listen to me, please," he said, more forcefully. "Hear me out. You can yell at me afterward if you want to, but at least just listen."

I nodded. "Okay."

He took a deep breath. "I didn't put the ring on. You were very clear about that, and I believed you. Still do. But I did some, well, experiments on it in my own home lab." At my expression, he went on, "I don't have anything like the setup that you do, but I do have the ability to run simple tests and stuff in my house. In the corner of my kitchen, actually."

I had to stifle a snort at this. I'd never have pegged Sebastian Fallon as a kitchen witch.

"Anyway, I was able to do a little probing about the magic embedded in the ring. And here's the thing. It's a very old artifact, yes, but it's been refilled with essence over the centuries. Even quite recently."

I leaned forward. "Was it…stealing my essence while I wore it?"

"No, it wasn't." I frowned, confused, as he said, "Just the opposite. Didn't you say it increased your power? It wasn't draining you…but it had to get that power from somewhere."

"Logan," I breathed. "And all the witches suffering draining essence…"

"Exactly. Dr. Andromedus is…I think he's been the one behind this."

"Behind what? Behind the *essence-stealing*?" He'd said just that, and of course I'd been suspecting it myself, but it was as though something shifted once it was spoken aloud. Now we would really have to face it.

It was too awful.

"Yes. Exactly that."

"Not Flavius Winterheart." Again, I'd had increasing doubts, but…

Sebastian shook his head. "It doesn't look that way."

I felt sick to my stomach all over again, thinking about what Jeremy and I had done to Flavius…burning his magic out of him, permanently, as punishment for a terrible crime…a crime that he probably hadn't even committed. "Oh, Blessed Mother." The old warlock had lied about so many things, fundamental, world-changing things. Of course he would assign a fall guy to be blamed for his own misdeeds. And make himself the hero for "discovering" it.

"I know." Sebastian looked very grim. On the verge of tears, in fact. Gregorio Andromedus was his mentor, his teacher. Yes, Sebastian had been suspicious of the old warlock for some time now, but he didn't know even the things I already knew...things I desperately wished I could share.

But I couldn't, I still couldn't. This confirmed what I'd not wanted to think...but I had to still keep pretending this was a terrible surprise.

Fortunately, I didn't have to pretend to be horrified. I reached across the table and took his hand. "This is just awful. I don't know what to think."

He looked up at me, blinking rapidly. "Callie, what do we do? If this is true—and I can't think of an innocent explanation, as much as I've tried—then he, I mean, he's—" He bit his lip, unable to even finish the sentence.

So I said it for him. "Dr. Gregorio Andromedus, the leader of our Elders and the oldest and most powerful warlock in our community, is preying on all of us, and lying about it. And he's probably been doing it for quite a long time."

We sat there with that for a minute. Well, I let him sit there with it; it of course wasn't the stunning, world-changing revelation for me that it was for him, just another brick in a really ugly wall.

Finally, he said, "We need more evidence. The other Elders and the rest of witchkind aren't going to understand the science."

"We need to find the missing subjects," I said. *And save them, if there's still time*, I didn't need to add.

Sebastian nodded. "We have to go to Berkeley."

I left a decoy of myself at my house, in case Gregorio was somehow still monitoring me. It wouldn't stand up to deep scrutiny—it was just a ball of substrate, spelled to give my energetic signature—but behind my wards, it should give the impression that I was there, and sleeping.

After I was reasonably confident that it would hold, I took Rosemary to the coven house. My sisters were thrilled to have the opportunity to babysit. "I shouldn't be very long," I told Maela, "but I've expressed some milk just in case she gets hungry."

She smiled and took the bottle, spelled to keep it body-warm and fresh. "Selfishly, I do hope you're gone for hours," she said, gazing down at Rose in her little carrier. "Even overnight."

Behind her, Leonora smiled indulgently. "Do hurry back, though, Calendula. We don't want to test your baby's remarkable temperament. This may be what she needs in order to learn to cry."

"Honestly, a little crying would be all right with me," I told them, leaning down to kiss my child. "Just a *little*, though, sweetie. Understood?"

She blew spit bubbles and punched at me with her tiny fists.

Maela handed the milk bottle to Leonora and bent down to pick up the baby. "Oh, who's the sweetest girl? So much fun we're going to have!"

Back out on the sidewalk, Sebastian said, "Everything all right?"

"A-okay," I told him, though it felt *really* weird to just walk away from her. Like I'd left an important limb behind, or something. "I just hope they let me have her back when we return."

He chuckled as we headed for the major ley line leading across the bay.

We emerged in Oakland. Usually, of course, we'd have taken the line straight to the junk shop at the edge of the Berkeley campus, but that was guarded, and would be far too obvious. We stood at the edge of Jack London Square while I showed Sebastian how to use my cell phone to call for a car.

"Neat trick," he said, as a nondescript beige sedan pulled up five minutes later.

"Humans have some uses," I said, smiling.

We had the car leave us at the north end of campus. It was a little less crowded than the south side, though if Gregorio was watching, he'd be looking in all directions. Still, it felt more prudent.

After we turned past the pelican, I paused on the path beside North Gate Hall, looking around. Nobody was in sight. "Here," I said, raising my hands. We built matching zones of inattention around each other—the thought being that the magical resonance would be stronger with our interlocking spells, rather than if we had each covered ourselves. Kind of the same theory behind Jeremy and me building house wards together.

"Well?" Sebastian said a moment later, stepping back. At least, I thought he stepped back, judging from the sound of his voice; my eyes couldn't find him at all. I had trouble even forcing them to look for him.

"Pretty good," I said. "What about me?"

"Not even a blip." He coughed. "Of course..."

"Yeah," I said. He didn't have to finish the thought. We both knew that this was basically a party trick, a cheap piece of misdirection. If Gregorio were looking for us, he'd find us in a heartbeat.

What we had to do was not attract his attention in the first place.

I took a moment to check on my illusion, back across the bay at my house. Yes, it was still in place, and giving me a weird, giddy feeling of dissociation as it insisted that I was *there*, not here.

I brought my attention back to campus. "All right, let's go."

Sebastian and I walked carefully along the path between Davis and O'Brien Halls, taking care not to step on any crunchy leaves or brush any tree branches. A few humans passed us, their eyes flitting past us as though we weren't there. One young woman glanced back over her shoulder, frowning, before turning back and walking on. I double-checked our spells. They were fully powered, covering us completely. Maybe the woman had been looking for something else.

As the Doe Library building came into view, I put a hand on where I thought Sebastian's arm must be, missed it, and had to push my focus to find it. "Wait here a second," I whispered.

I think he stopped. I took my hand away.

"Is he there right now?" I asked.

We both stared at the fourth floor of the building, where Gregorio's hidden laboratory was. It was warded so tightly, we almost couldn't aim our faces in that direction, but a little patience and persistence at least let us find the edges of the lab. More gentle probing revealed either no living beings inside…or someone so closely shielded that his presence wasn't leaking through at all.

"Wow," Sebastian whispered after a minute. "I gotta…" Then he went silent.

"Dude? You still there?"

"Callie," he said with sudden urgency. "Look down."

"What do you mean?" I wished I could see him. Was he pointing? Where was he looking?

"Down," he hissed. "There's a basement, under the library building. Look there—under where the first floor is."

I followed what I thought he must be talking about. I hadn't known the library had a basement, but it made sense. Decades earlier, the university had built underground stacks just below where we were standing to house its ever-growing collection of books without adding more tall buildings to the park-like campus. It would make sense that those stacks would be connected to the main building by a passageway of some kind.

But that's not what he was talking about. Because when I turned my attention to the area beneath the corner housing Gregorio's lab, I saw an ancient, abandoned warren of rooms and corridors. And not just that, but it was riddled with magical obscurations. "Oh…"

"There," Sebastian said. "We have to look there."

Now came the moment I'd been dreading. I had already known that Gregorio used storage rooms that weren't on the same floor as his lab. He'd never let me go there, and I thought now I knew why. "I want to go in alone."

"What?" I could tell from his voice that he'd turned to face me. "Callie, why?"

"A couple reasons. I need you out here keeping watch. If it's a trap, one of us needs to be free to go for help." These were both pathetic excuses, but I hoped he'd go for them.

"No way," he said. "That means *I* should go in and *you* should keep watch. You've got a newborn at home who needs you."

"I'm stronger than you," I argued. "I've been working with Gregorio longer than you have. I know much better what to look for. And I have a better chance of getting away with it."

He sighed.

I went on, before he could muster another objection. "Besides, having a baby at home is actually an advantage. Gregorio won't hurt or imprison a new mother, particularly not the mother of his own grandchild. Even if he's lost all his moral sense, he wouldn't do that to the community—he wouldn't be able to get away with it. He wouldn't take the chance." I shut my mouth, hoping this was true. Because how the heck did I know what Gregorio would or wouldn't dare to do at this point?

This was what I intended to find out. If I could just get into that basement.

"And finally," I added, "I'm familiar with Gregorio's door-wards and charms."

"Hey, I am too, I work with him at the clinic."

I shook my head, even if he couldn't see it. "He's just got something really basic at the clinic—he wants people to visit him there. Here, at the university? He's got layers of charms and spells that go back decades. And I've been working with them almost that long."

Finally Sebastian sighed again, this time in clear defeat. "All right. You go in. But let's make some ground rules."

"I need just a few minutes," I said. "Either the subjects are there or they aren't; I'll get out as soon as I see what's there."

"Of course, but I mean more specifically."

We retreated back behind Evans Hall to plan. By the time we returned to the library building a few minutes later, I felt as prepared as I was going to get.

— CHAPTER THIRTEEN —

Keeping the zone of inattention comfortably around me, I walked up the steps to the library's north entrance. I didn't pause to admire the lovely lobby, just marched straight ahead through it, jogged left, and made my way into a narrower hallway. Once there, I turned again, heading for the ladies' room.

As I put my hand on the bathroom door, I reached a toe to the very small ley line there and let myself drop down through to the basement floor. My nose tickled; I wondered if I was going to indulge in a fit of sneezing, as Elnor always did after ley line travel, but I managed to hold it together.

I stood there for a long moment, holding perfectly still, sending my senses carefully out to see if my arrival had been detected, by means magical or mundane. It seemed I was in luck: no alarms rang out, no hands fell upon me.

I wanted to send a ping out to Sebastian, to let him know I was in, but we'd agreed: no ætheric communication while I was inside, unless it was a call for help. We had no idea what Gregorio might be tracking. No sense taking unnecessary risks.

My eyes were adjusting to the dim space, lit only by the occasional dusty bulb. I looked around. It was a classic basement: a small room with low rafters, uneven concrete floor, piles of forgotten stored stuff…I almost expected to see half-empty paint cans stacked against the wall.

In any event, there was nothing suspicious here. None of this was Gregorio's, or had any magical residue around it; this was clearly human library storage. But this was only the first room. The warlock's space would be much better disguised.

I poked around anyway, to be absolutely sure, before making my way to the back of the room. There I found another door hidden in the gloom. With my hand on the knob, I sent my senses through but found nobody within. Then I tried to turn the handle. It was locked, but only physically; a simple spell undid it. The door creaked open, sending dust into the stale air.

I walked through into a narrow passageway with curved walls—an old steam tunnel, maybe?—one of the many we'd seen as we'd scanned the building from the lawn outside. It was similarly stacked with cartons and crates, heavy with dust and cobwebs, many not even labeled.

I opened each door I came to along the passageway, even after I noticed the glow of magical protection near the end of the corridor. Some rooms contained empty crucibles and bottles I recognized from the lab, and stacked cardboard boxes. It was clear he used this space.

Then I got to the last door. I stood there a moment an inch shy of touching it, mustering my courage and my strength before reaching out. The door tried to repel my hand, but I was ready for it. I drew on all my power, plus the power that Sebastian had loaned me, and I slowly, carefully unmade the spell on the door. I smiled as I worked. I'd been right about this, at least; this was the same charm that Gregorio had used a few years ago on the lab upstairs, with only a minor tweak to take advantage of the minerals in the walls around this room.

Once the spell unraveled and fell away, I opened the door…and gasped.

Bodies. Rows and rows of bodies, laid out neatly on little beds.

I shook my head and closed my eyes, but when I opened them, they were still there. The room was huge, cavernous—far larger than any of the other rooms had been. Impossibly large, to be under the building here; it occupied some fold of space, clearly, and I was focusing on the size of the space because the nature of it was still too horrible to contemplate…

It was kitted out as a creepy, dark mockery of a hospital or research facility. Peculiar lab equipment—stuff even I didn't recognize, couldn't identify—lined the walls, with some pieces hulking here and there in the middle of the floor.

I swallowed, bracing myself yet again, and stepped into the room. I barely gave the equipment a glance. Because…the bodies.

Dozens of sterile cot-like beds, containing dozens of lifeless bodies.

My heart pounding, I just stood in the room for a minute, trying to regain my equilibrium. Making sure I wasn't going to faint. Then I walked farther in, approaching the closest body. It was a young witch, someone I didn't know, entirely drained of essence. And yet, like Logan had been, she looked as though she had perished a moment ago.

Oh, Blessed Mother…

I walked slowly through the room, looking at them all, my brain refusing to take it in. I saw mostly witches, mostly young, but I also saw warlocks and a few older witches. Every one of them in this weird, undecayed state. More than dozens—nearly a hundred. Who *were* they all? Where had they come from?

How long had Gregorio been feasting on witchkind this way?

By the time I reached Logan's body, I was pretty much expecting it. What did surprise me was finding the bodies of her parents lying beside hers.

"Logan…" I moaned, sinking to the floor at her feet. I wept there a while, stunned, bewildered, and grief-stricken. She looked so much more dead here than she had in Leonora's office. So much more…victimized.

I forced myself to stop sobbing; my time here was limited. I'd found what I needed to find, and now I had to get out, back to Sebastian, to make a plan…

I got back to my feet and gazed down at Logan. My best friend. She still had that almost dewy blush of color in her cheeks, nearly a droplet of moisture at the corner of one eye.

Could she really be dead?

What did death mean, when something held the body in this bizarre stasis?

Magic could do so much, I knew that. But magic could not stop the progression of time, could not halt the flow of all things. Bodies died; spirits left them, and the dead meat decayed, returned to the earth, providing nourishment for the living. The cycle continued.

But her spirit had never entered the Beyond. Nor had those of her parents. And they looked as undecayed as she did.

Everyone did. It was a roomful of nightmare Sleeping Beauties.

Were all their spirits still here, somehow, somewhere, in these bodies?

Bending over Logan, I examined her again, though I had done this so many times before. Putting one hand on her forehead and the other over her heart, I probed and delved and scryed and insinuated my senses down through every cell in her body.

She was not there.

I withdrew my hands after a long time and just stood there. Then I moved to her mother—gone these many decades, yet looking ready to draw a breath. I put my hands on her as well and searched just as thoroughly, though I knew I would find nothing. And I did not. Lorenna was as empty as her daughter.

These vessels were all empty—a ghastly room full of them. Where were their souls?

I had to find them.

I walked slowly back toward the door, past the still, silent not-corpses. I glanced at the weird machinery as I passed. If I had more time, if I felt it was safe, I'd examine them, try to figure out their use, but—

Something caught my eye on one of the machines. It was a tall, narrow mechanism with a bell jar at the top, empty, at least apparently. The bell jar led to a funnel that pointed straight up. The device was near the door, and it wasn't nearly as dusty as a lot of the other machinery. I could almost taste the magical resonance it emitted; it had been used recently.

But it was the sign at its base that snagged my attention.

GRAND LAUREL MERENOC
ENCHIN ABERRA
ZCHELLENIN

Zchellenin. The town in the Old Country where Logan's parents were from.

Not only that, but half the words were in the language of spells. This machine…

I hurried around the room, now looking at the other unfamiliar devices, brushing dust and cobwebs off their signs and labels when I could find them. They all had the same first and third lines; only the middle line differed. *Enchin* was a borrowed word from the English "engine"; *aberra* was not a word I knew, but it modified *enchin* on the first machine. A few of the other devices also had *enchin* in their names, but there were at least four other nouns.

None of these devices made any sense to me. And I'd been doing complex biological research for decades.

"I have to go to the Old Country," I whispered.

It was all I could do not to rush outside. I forced myself to move as carefully as I'd come in, relocking the door behind me, resetting the spell, picking my way through the hallway, floating up the tiny ley line to the library's first floor, walking calmly out of the building. I held the zone of inattention tight as I walked across the lawn toward where Sebastian had promised to wait, though of course I couldn't see him there.

"Hey," I whispered, to what might be a shimmer in the air.

"Callie!" he whisper-shrieked. "Oh, Great Father, are you really there?!"

"Yes, jeez," I said. "And I'm fine. Come on."

I walked back toward the edge of campus, trusting him to follow. "You were in there forever," he muttered as we rounded O'Brien Hall.

"I know, and let's get out of here so I can tell you all about it."

We had a quiet, furious debate as we stood on the corner of Euclid and Hearst. "I can't get a car to come get us if we stay hidden," I hissed.

"Every minute we stay in the area is another minute when Dr. A. can find us."

"Just walk."

"Where?!"

I huffed out a frustrated breath. "West. Just head down Hearst toward the bay. I want to get farther away than this before we're uncloaked."

He stopped arguing and followed me, thank the Mother. Once we'd passed Sacramento Street, we were both out of breath, but I felt safe enough to let the illusion down a bit. At least we could see each other now, though it was easier through the corners of our eyes than straight ahead. But that meant we could keep walking as we talked.

"I found everything we've been looking for and more," I started. "It's far worse than we thought." I told him what I'd seen, and why I'd been so long. "I had to take a moment," I said, sadly. "She was my best friend..."

"I understand," Sebastian said, his voice gentle. "I had wondered where he had really taken her body, why he'd been so cagey about it."

"Further research indeed." I snorted in anger. "Anyway, I need to get to the Old Country. At once."

Sebastian barked out a surprised laugh. "Callie, what?" he added, when he realized I was serious. "We don't just...*go* to the Old Country. It takes preparation, days, even weeks—"

"I don't care," I snapped. "And I'm not even sure that's true."

He stopped on the sidewalk and stared at me. "Why wouldn't it be?"

I stopped, too, and looked at my friend. Of course I trusted him. But that didn't mean I could tell him what I knew...at least not right now. At least not all of it. "Let's just say that I've been learning that a few things we've 'always known to be true' aren't, exactly. Including what I just found in the library basement. But I *have* to follow this thread to the manufacturer of all those machines, and I have to do it *now,* before Dr. A. knows we've been here. Before he can stop me."

"Why the machines? Why now?"

"You're not listening," I said. "He used them to extract essence from witch and warlock bodies—and *souls*. We know where the essence is. He's using it, the greedy thieving bastard."

"You think he's sending the souls to the Old Country," Sebastian breathed.

"Where else? An entirely hidden country, protected by an entire witchkind population's worth of wards and shields. Impossible to get to, and in the throes of a terrible civil war." I stared at the young warlock. He was going paler with every word I said. "Sebastian, what if it's all a lie? What if it's a huge clearinghouse for stolen souls and essence harvesting and—oh, I don't even know what!" I drew a breath. "What if I can find *Logan* there?"

He swallowed, just staring back at me. Cars went by on the busy street, humans going about their safe, innocent lives. "Let me know what I can do to help you."

Of course he wanted to come with me. Of course he couldn't. "Same principle as going into the library," I told him, over drinks and a shot of my homemade strength potion back in my kitchen an hour later. I held a very happy Rosemary in my arms, having retrieved her from a very sad Sirianna. Even Niad had seemed a little wistful at letting the baby go. Would wonders never cease?

He snorted. "Oh, like I'm going to be able to cover for you as you travel *to the Old Country*. Callie, please."

I shook my head. "No, of course you can't do that. But you can deflect attention, you can give out misinformation, you can tell people I'm sick, or resting—you can do so many things to slow folks down, at least." To slow a certain very particular warlock down.

"What are you going to tell Jeremy?" he asked. "He's not going to buy a word I say."

I frowned, playing with Rosemary's red hair as I thought. "I don't know. Maybe I'll tell him…um…I need some time alone, to think, about his wanting a contract…"

Sebastian just gave me a look.

"I know, you're right," I sighed. "He'll know I'm not anywhere in the area, and he'll follow my trail." I rocked my baby, thinking furiously. I was starting to feel a little more like I could trust the warlock, emotionally; but that would all go out the window if I tried to tell him that his father was an awful lying criminal who was indiscriminately murdering our kind for his own gain. Or whatever he was doing…but it didn't look good.

I didn't see any way to bring Jeremy into this that would end up with him on my side.

"I don't know," I finally said, once more. "I mean, he actually offered to take me to the Old Country, after the baby was born…"

"I'm sure this isn't what he meant," Sebastian pointed out.

"No. He said like a year or two later. I have to go *now*." I sighed again, and got up and went to the fridge, still holding the baby on my hip. "Want some wine?" It was nice to be able to imbibe again, though while I was nursing, I still hadn't felt like going hog-wild. Oddly, Rosemary seemed to enjoy a glass or two of elderflower of an evening.

Surely I wasn't just projecting that. I mean, she was half-witch, at least.

"Sure," Sebastian said.

One-handed, I poured two glasses, then glanced over at the table.

Petrana, from her corner, said, "I can carry those over, Mistress Callie. You go sit down."

I startled a bit—I'd almost forgotten she was there. "Thanks, Petrana."

"In fact I could have poured them in the first place," she pointed out. Her voice still had very little affect, though I could almost believe I heard—humor? Affection?

"You take such good care of me," I said to my golem, as she brought the wine to the table.

"That's what I'm for," she said.

Sebastian and I clinked glasses and sipped. We sat silently for a few minutes, both of us worrying through the problem. Or at least I was; maybe he was pondering the nature of golems.

"You can't tell Jeremy where you're going, or why," he finally said.

Duh, I didn't say. I just nodded.

"But I don't think we should dismiss entirely your first idea—that you need a little space," he went on. He raised a hand to stop me from protesting. "Wait, hear me out. Set it up as a trust thing.

Of course he can find you if he really means to. But Callie, you're clever. Tell him you need to do this, and he needs to not try and follow you. Set a date when you'll be back, or at least when you'll be in contact. Make it emotionally important. If you can rely on him to honor your request for space and privacy...maybe you could promise to consider his suit. To give him an answer."

"But I can't sign a contract with him," I said.

"Why not?"

I shrugged. "Lots of reasons. I don't want to talk about it right now, but trust me, I have my reasons."

Sebastian just gazed back at me. "Callie, contracts are infinitely flexible. I know you still have feelings for Raymond—it's obvious that you do—but that doesn't mean you can't make some kind of a formal arrangement with Jeremy. You can put any conditions or terms in the contract you want—the sky's the limit. You can make it for a year; you can write in a dispensation for other lovers—for both of you, or just for you if you like; you can specify separate dwellings. Anything you want."

"How romantic."

He rolled his eyes. "Oh, you of all witches know that contracts aren't about romance."

I supposed I had to admit that.

"Just think about it," he went on. "Pack the deal with absolutely everything you might need to make it work, and set it to be as temporary as possible. Knowing Jeremy even the little that I do, he'll agree to anything, and imagine that his suave sexy lovely awesomeness will overcome your hesitation, and that he'll end up with everything he wanted all along."

I burst out laughing. "Oh, Blessed Mother," I said, after a minute, wiping my eyes and taking another sip of wine. "You sure have him pegged."

Sebastian smiled at me. "Give me some credit. I do know warlocks."

—☾●☽—

Time was of the essence. The longer I dawdled, the more chance I had of someone—Gregorio, Leonora, Jeremy, even my parents—clueing in to my intentions. I had to get moving, and fast.

Sebastian's advice, however cynical, proved spot-on. After he left, I invited Jeremy over for a serious talk. It went eerily like my friend had predicted; I could almost watch the gears moving in Jeremy's mind as he pretended to seriously consider the absurd demands I made. Once I kissed him goodbye, I felt quite confident that *he* felt quite confident that all his efforts at being a charming, stable, patient, attentive suitor to an impetuous, indecisive, immature witch were going to bear the fruit that he wanted.

"Thank you," I whispered to him at the doorway, still cradled in his arms. Behind us, in the front parlor, Rosemary snoozed in Petrana's capable grasp. "I really appreciate what you're doing for me."

"It is entirely my pleasure," he purred, looking down at me, his earnest green eyes radiating love and understanding. "And I do so look forward to resuming these productive talks when you return from your retreat."

"Two weeks," I said, giving what I hoped was a relaxed smile.

"I shall count the minutes." He leaned down and kissed me again, then released me, but not before he took my hand and kissed it as well—both back and front.

Oh, those Old Country manners.

I stifled the thought and hoped my smile wasn't freezing on my face.

At last, he turned and left.

"All right," I said, rushing into the front parlor. "Petrana, let's get a move on."

"Yes, Mistress Callie."

My golem had gotten a *lot* better at packing. Also, we were bringing a *lot* less stuff. I knew it was ley line travel, multiple ley lines at that, and uncertain ones. The longest underwater lines I'd ever taken were from San Francisco to Berkeley and back. Those were done in a moment; I could do it holding my breath.

The Atlantic Ocean was going to be another story.

But that was far ahead of us. We still had a continent to get across before we even reached the ocean. I'd been half-tempted to look into airline travel—what if that was a myth too?—but Sebastian had assured me that I could do permanent damage to the balance of my magical nature if I abruptly changed pressure and altitude that way, without weeks of preparation—spellwork and practice. And even then, it was no guarantee that I'd emerge unscathed.

"Who knew, when our forefathers and mothers were selecting for magical resonance, that they were selecting out so many useful traits?" he had mused.

"Like fertility?" I'd asked.

"That too."

"They made these decisions in the age of sea travel," I'd pointed out, though he knew the history as well as I did. "I'm sure nobody imagined humans would invent steel tubes that soared through the air."

Now I focused on getting the essentials together, mostly for Rose. Anything I needed, I could probably pick up while we were there.

And, with any luck, we'd be back sooner than I'd allowed for.

The very last thing I did was prepare a few near-identical messages to send through the æther as we were leaving. Following the lines of the story I'd told Jeremy, I spoke of the difficult birth, the emotionally laden process of adjusting to becoming a mother—enjoyable though that had been thus far—and my growing awareness of my need to examine everything I wanted from life, from my career and relationships and housing arrangements—and even my distress over Gracie's rebellion (and what that said about me as a teacher and, presumably, the most important adult presence in her life)—on top of the recent loss of my best friend—all of which had led to my need to step away from everything here in San Francisco for a little while. I needed to sit with all these dramatic changes in my life and process what they meant for me going forward. I hoped that everyone who loved and cared about me would understand my need for space and privacy during this time...and I assured them that I would be in touch within two weeks at the most, but please respect my request and not try to find me before then.

I sent versions of this message to everyone who could possibly have an interest in knowing my whereabouts. Then I gathered up my satchel, my golem, my familiar, and my baby, and we hopped the fattest ley line due east.

— CHAPTER FOURTEEN —

The initial travel was easy, almost boring. We took major lines and rode them for great distances, making it across California nearly to the Nevada border in less than two hours. Unfortunately, it was nearly dinnertime by now; I was hungry, and Rose was going to need to eat soon too.

I didn't know how lengthy ley travel would impact a newborn, and sadly, there was no one I could ask. But there was no way I was going to leave my child.

We emerged in a little town in the mountains just outside of Lake Tahoe, so small that it didn't even have a witchkind community—I could tell by the condition of the portal. It wasn't just unguarded; it had an unowned, unloved look about it. Like a gas station bathroom.

"Ugh," I said, taking a few steps down the quiet street. Rose shifted in my arms, murmuring quietly and rolling her eyes around, taking in the sudden brightness. Elnor sneezed; Petrana stood stolidly by. Somehow my golem was now carrying the satchel. I didn't remember handing it over, but ley line travel can be disorienting sometimes.

Elnor finished her sneezing fit and began sniffing around. The air was thin and bitterly cold. We were at a high elevation, and winter clearly came earlier here than it did in San Francisco. Recent snowfall dusted the ground. I'd seen snow before, of course. Mostly in pictures, but I understood the concept.

I shivered, wishing I'd worn a heavier jacket. The Old Country, nestled in high peaks in Eastern Europe, would be at least this cold. Maybe I could buy a coat here.

First stop, though, was a café I could see just down the street, its warm lights beckoning me. "Come on, gang," I said, and a few minutes later we were seated at a cozy table. They only had Lipton tea, but it was hot and the waitress brought it right away, so I was soon restored.

Petrana sat across from me. I'd laid a light glamour over her appearance, so that she looked even more convincingly human, and also—and more importantly—really, really uninteresting. It was a modification of the inattention spell: your eyes weren't exactly repelled, they just...slid away, looking for something catchier to focus on. Like the cracked linoleum floor, or the stained Formica table.

Elnor hid between my feet, and Rosemary was strapped to my chest in her little carrier. I'd modified it to be just the harness part, removing the seat elements; too bulky to travel with. The waitress had offered to bring a booster chair, but Rose was too tiny for that. "What a precious girl!" the waitress sang, grinning down at her.

I smiled back. "She's the sweetest."

I ordered a French dip with fries, a tuna sandwich, and a refill of the tea. When the food came, the waitress seemed confused for a moment before setting the hot sandwich in front of me and the tuna before Petrana. "Thanks!" I said, giving her another big smile and telling her everything looked great. Elnor was already poking at my legs, as if I was going to forget who the tuna was actually for.

The French dip was terrific—crisp bread, salty dip, succulent meat. Elnor poked me again. "Settle down, cat," I muttered at her. "If we get kicked out of here, you'll only have yourself to blame."

Eventually, with some mundane sleight-of-hand and another mild deflection spell, I managed to get a portion of the sandwich down onto the floor, quieting my cat down. If anyone in the bustling café noticed that the "woman" across from me never ate or drank anything, they didn't bother me about it.

I had the waitress box up the other half of the tuna sandwich as I paid the bill. "We're on the road, traveling east," I told her, "but we need a decent place to crash for the night. Can you recommend a good motel in town?"

"The Blue Bell just up the street is what you want," she said. "Better than any of those chains. Are you parked out front?"

"Pretty much," I fudged.

"Just turn right out of the parking lot and go two blocks. It'll be on the left. Sign might say No Vacancy but they always have something. I'll give Marybell a call and tell her you're comin'."

"Thank you," I said, feeling all warm and fuzzy and taken care of. "Marybell at the Blue Bell?"

The waitress chuckled. "That's why she bought the place—she couldn't resist the name. Said it was meant to be. Going on sixteen years she's run it, and you'll never find any place more welcoming."

She was right, too. Marybell showed us to a cozy, comfy room with two beds, a rocking chair, and a charming old-fashioned washstand complete with a steaming pitcher of water. Accustomed as I was to San Francisco prices, I was astonished at how cheap the place was. Dinner had been startlingly affordable, too, now that I thought about it.

I loved city life, but maybe I could begin to see the appeal of small towns.

Elnor claimed the bed closest to the door, jumping up and giving it a thorough sniffing before curling up to sleep. Petrana held Rose while I rummaged through the satchel for toiletries and then indulged in some of that hot water to wash my face.

Then we all tucked in. Witches, of course—ones who aren't pregnant—don't have to sleep every night, and certainly not eight hours every night...unless they're doing a lot of heavy magic. Like, oh, say, ley line travel, with dependents and gear. I slept from sundown till nearly eight the next morning, when we had a hearty breakfast at the same café (different waitress, alas, but she was just as friendly) and then hit the "road."

We made our steady way across the country this way, finding quiet towns with good food and shelter options, and little or no witchkind presence. It wasn't as though I was avoiding witches and warlocks, per se, but the more traditional way of traveling would have had me calling on every prominent coven mother and local Elder leader, and, well, I was in a hurry.

And trying to move covertly. That too, of course. So, okay, yeah, I suppose I was avoiding witchkind.

Messages filtered through the æther to me, along my way. Jeremy's was first, followed in due course by one from Leonora, and then a message from my mom. Nothing from Gregorio, which I tried really hard not to worry about. One from Sebastian surprised me; he of all people knew what I was up to, and that I wasn't likely to answer, but he sent me one all the same. *I hope it's going well. Everything's fine here.*

I tried to parse that, turning it around looking for hidden meanings, secret messages. If there was one there, it was hidden from me too. Eventually I decided he must just have been telling me that, well, everything was fine there.

I reached the east coast four days after I set out, exhausted and drained. I was already realizing that my "I'll be back in two weeks" thought was hopelessly optimistic. Naïve. Well, I'd never traveled before; what did I know? I'd known that I was unusually powerful, and young and healthy. I'd assumed the regular rules didn't apply to me.

Story of my life. Ha. Ha.

I sat in a little coffee shop in St. John's, a town at the tip of Newfoundland and as close to the European continent as I could get without actually getting wet. Sadly, it was time to get wet.

Not literally. But…now it was the time to choose my undersea ley line route.

I sipped my tea (oh Canadian tea was so much better than American tea, must be their English influence) and pondered it. From what I understood, the usual route was to make the biggest jump at first, crossing from here to the Azores, then resting up a day or two, then making the rest of the journey to mainland Portugal and on up the continent.

But what if I went north? Northern Canada to Greenland to Iceland (or maybe even Svalbard?), then a jump to Norway and through Finland and on down? Much shorter underwater distances that way. From where I sat to the Azores was almost 1,400 miles.

Terrifying.

The trouble was, it was November. Already the days were very short and *very* cold. The farther north I went, the worse that would get. I could save myself the stress and strain of undersea ley line travel only to perish from freezing to death. My pampered little California witch-body was not meant for these temperatures.

I sighed and ordered another cup of tea. There was clearly a reason everyone took the southern route. I just needed to buckle down and do it.

We ended up spending three nights in St. John's, resting and preparing and building up as much strength as possible. I relaxed my guard a tiny bit and sought out the local witches. It was the only way I'd get access to their botanical resources—or even learn where their community garden was.

A middle-aged witch named Elsie (it had to be a nickname for something, unless Canadian witches did things even more differently from us than I'd imagined) invited me to her coven's evening meal on my second night. They fed me well, cooed over my baby and my cat (I'd left Petrana in the motel room), and asked me many polite yet pointed questions, while keeping the information they gave me to a bare (yet equally polite) minimum.

When the meal was over, we lingered at the table, sipping a tea I didn't recognize. It was delicious, and I could feel its magical potency. I wondered what it was and whether it would be rude to ask. In fact, the whole house was a bit like this: familiar but different, with so much unspoken. Even the latent magic in the air had an unusual "scent" to it. Their cats kept their distance from both me and Elnor. Politely, of course.

"All right," said the coven mother, a gentle woman referred to only as Mother Witch, "we would be pleased to share with you our Helena cucumber."

"Cucumber?" I asked, startled. "I mean, I appreciate any help you can give me, but—"

Mother Witch smiled. "Yes, I know windrush is the more common approach, but it doesn't grow well here. Most practitioners find the Helena cucumber to be at least as potent. We have of course hybridized the local strain to meet our needs, along with some...additional tweaks." Her smile took on a quick note of mystery. "You should find it does the trick for you perfectly well."

"I'll get you some from the storage shed," one of the younger witches said, hopping up. She went by another nickname—Brick, I think. I'd been introduced very quickly to the whole table, and the unusual names were confusing. Also distracting were their varied appearances. Brick was something under five feet tall and perhaps of East Asian heritage, with copper skin and long dark hair that moved sinuously but subtly, staying neatly behind her back without any visible restraint. At least half the witches around the table were clearly non-white, non-European.

It made me realize how homogenous San Francisco's witchkind was—something I'd known intellectually, especially when compared with the city's human population—but I'd never given it much thought. We had older witches and younger witches, dark-haired witches and blond witches...but we were all white witches.

No wonder the magic felt different here.

As Brick left the room, I glanced at Mother Witch with a question in my eyes. She explained, "We keep a supply on hand. You hadn't imagined you were the only American witch to jump off from here to the Azores?" She chuckled. "We should probably just open a bed-and-breakfast."

"I'm happy to pay, of course," I assured her.

Which only made her laugh harder. "Nay, youngling. You know witchkind cannot go those human ways. Should a sister of our house ever find her way to San Francisco, we know you will return the hospitality, and be glad of it."

"Of course!"

Brick came back with several brown paper bags tied with a red cord. "This should be plenty, for both the journey over and for your return."

"How long will it stay fresh?" I asked, taking the bags and giving them a sniff. It was pleasant enough, bland and innocuous. Like, well, cucumber.

"How long are you planning to stay...overseas?" Mother Witch countered.

I shrugged, jiggling Rose slightly. "Not more than a few weeks, I hope." Of course, I really had no idea. But if I were delayed much longer than that, then finding herbs to help with my journey home would probably be among the smaller of my problems.

She nodded. "You should be fine, then. Keep it out of direct sunlight, and as dry as possible—once you're off the ley lines, of course."

"Right." I smiled at her. "Thank you so much for all your help—for everything. Dinner was delicious, and it was marvelous to meet you all."

Mother Witch rose to her feet. "I would offer to have you stay and observe our midnight Circle, but I do understand that you are hoping to keep a lower profile, so instead, I will bid you a deep rest this evening and a pleasant journey tomorrow."

I got up too, hearing what she didn't say: *Our Circle is private.* "Yes, it's probably best if no one in the Beyond knows I'm here. Besides, you're right. I should rest up as much as I can." I looked around their long table—so different from our own dining room at home, yet so welcoming. "Thank you all, sisters. Thank you for everything."

They bade me goodnight, and—after everyone had tickled, cuddled, and made funny faces and silly noises at the baby—let me go my way into the bitter, dark night.

Resting and building up one's strength is dull.

And I say this as someone who had just spent far too much time in *confinement*, to use Gregorio's obnoxious old-fashioned word. Weeks, anyway, lying around the coven house being pregnant, and then at home recovering.

I was ready to go.

But I wasn't so foolish as to attempt an under-ocean crossing without being fully prepared.

So, much as it pained me to make the decision, I decided to spend an extra night in St. John's, letting more of the Helena cucumber do its work in me (I could feel its strength and potency;

these Canadian witches weren't fooling around), and getting as much sleep as I could force my body to take.

Elnor thought this was a fine turn of events, of course. Sleep all night and then sleep all day? Sign her up! By the middle of the last afternoon, though, I was about ready to climb the walls. It was too cold to go outside for anything other than the essentials. Elsie's coven, friendly though they had been, had also rather pointedly sent me on my way; they had their own business to see to. They were not responsible for entertaining me. Rosemary had already nursed half a dozen times today. And there was nothing on TV, nothing, nothing.

I sat on my bed rummaging through my rucksack one more time, wishing I'd brought a trashy paperback novel.

Well, there were Logan's tarot cards.

I'd brought them along because I kept them with me always, as a way of keeping her with me. The feel of them in my hand brought her back to me, and made me feel sad and slightly spooked all at once. I didn't understand their power (if they had any power), I didn't believe in them (whatever that was even supposed to mean), I just...kept them with me.

I never used them—for all the same reasons I kept them close.

I almost tucked them away again, but the boredom made me open the box and dump the deck out onto the colorful quilt.

The pictures, all primary colors and broad lines, clashed with the fussy, intricate floral of the quilt, so I sat up and carried the cards to the desk under the window.

There, I spread them just as they fell, trying to let myself see the patterns that emerged. Logan sometimes did this, and when my mom was teaching me the cards, she made much of the wisdom of random chance.

Nothing leapt out at me. Every card was a story; and, as always, pretty much every card could be interpreted to mean either something marvelous or something awful, depending on how you looked at it; and this was just as bad as all the nothing that was on television.

I sighed, leaving the cards on the desk and returning to the bed. Maybe when I opened the room door to go get dinner, a gust of wind would blow in and arrange the cards in a meaningful pattern. Maybe they would spell out my name, or the name of the exact person in the Old Country who would answer *all* my questions and solve all the mysteries. I snickered as I told myself increasingly ridiculous stories of how I, a scientist, might get this wild magic to work for me: I would perform an assay on the cards and discover a previously unseen residue, which would lead to not only cracking open the mystery of the purposed "cat portal" in my closet at home, but would give me the definitive answer on what to do about my love life.

Or, a polar bear would break into the room. As I defended my baby, my cat, and my golem, my only weapon was the sharp-edged cards; I used the whole of the Swords suit and defeated the bear, and my fortune was thus laid before me, cleverly arranged in spots of bear-blood.

Or, Petrana suddenly developed divination powers, along with all her other recent accomplishments. These powers came straight from the Beyond, because it turned out that—utterly unbeknownst to me!—part of the soil from her making had come from the backyard grave of one of my long-departed coven sisters, and her soul resonated with the body of the golem, lending her extraordinary powers…

I sniffled, giving up the game. Thinking about the Beyond, and stray souls, just brought me back to what I was doing here, and why.

"Just *nap* already," I told myself.

Maybe I did.

I don't know if I was at my full strength or not, but by the next morning, I was so ready to go, I almost didn't care.

I packed up everything carefully, double-checking that I hadn't forgotten anything, not even strands of hair in the sink or on the bedding. I'd been keeping my hair bound back during the whole journey, of course, and this morning in particular I made sure that my French braids were tight and straight. Witch's hair has a mind of its own; it would be just like my hair to try and go leaving traces of itself everywhere I went.

Then I checked out of the room and took us all to my favorite local diner, where I ordered two complete breakfasts and ate them both. I hardly even had to pretend that Petrana was eating; nobody paid any attention to me.

Canadians are so polite.

At last, at last, it was time. I stood on the edge of the pier I'd chosen, the one closest to the first underwater ley line.

Ley lines are meridians of energy in the earth. When we talk about "ley line travel," we don't mean that we are literally flying through a tube in the ground or anything like that. It's far more metaphoric. We are opening our energetic channels and aligning ourselves with the earth's natural fluxes and flows, and following those pathways to where we want to go.

Ley lines rarely change position, though they can.

Ones under water can change much more readily than those on land.

During ley line travel, our bodies are in a state of…I don't want to say "suspended animation" because that gives a wrong (and far too science fictional) impression. It's more akin to deep meditation, if the travel is longer than a moment or two. We move to a quieter plane of being, while the physical matter of our bodies—and whatever we are bringing with us—flows to where we want to go.

It's a very convenient mode of transportation, and I suspect it's a large part of the reason why we haven't done more research into figuring out how to make airplane travel easier for ourselves.

Sadly, this is all much more challenging undersea. The lines exist in a network, and, as I mentioned, that network can shift. In San Francisco, if I'm traveling along a familiar line and come to an unexpected occlusion or dead end, I can just cast about and find another route. It's the magical equivalent of glancing around and spotting something a few steps away. Water dampens all that.

Despite what the humans of seventeenth-century Salem and the author of *The Wizard of Oz* may have believed, witches are not allergic to water and can't be hurt by being dunked or splashed. But water does interfere with our magical senses, and it takes a lot of energy to overcome that.

Standing on the edge of the dock, I felt at least as nervous as I was eager. "Just do it," I whispered to myself, trying to muster up my courage.

Petrana stood beside me, staring at the wide gray ocean. The wind whipped her thick hair about. Rosemary was strapped to my chest. She looked up at me with her big dark eyes. I could have sworn she was sending me encouragement, letting me know she believed in me, even though I still had received no actual mental communication from her.

Elnor, of course, stood between my ankles. She was ready too. I could see it in the arch of her back, the way her fur stood on her spine.

"Okay."

I took Petrana's hand and we stepped onto the ley line.

— CHAPTER FIFTEEN —

The world swirled around us, and my vision switched to witch-sight. Now everything was washes of colors and feelings, without formal shape, without a strong sense of time passing. Sound became muffled, more than it did in straight earth-lines; the water must be covering any noise beyond my own heartbeat, and that of my baby against my breast.

We flew, swam, floated—all and none of those things at once. The sensation was familiar and very strange. I took ley lines all the time at home, of course; and I'd just traveled across the country on them; but this was...well, it was about as different as I'd imagined, except now it was really happening, and it was nothing like my imagination.

I let myself be carried by the energy, the force. I held onto Petrana's mud hand and put my other hand on Rose in her carrier. Elnor still nestled between my ankles, because I wasn't using my feet. They were along for the ride as much as the rest of me.

Time passed. I'm sure it did.

Breathing is different on the ley lines too. It's a bit like being in a dream, the disembodied feeling that can come over you, even as you move and think and talk.

What you don't do on ley lines is eat or drink. Another reason why it's so challenging...and why I'd stuffed myself so much before we'd left, and made sure Rosemary was topped up. Yet I could feel the hunger—hers and mine both—as we traveled.

I twisted in the ley space, sending my energy forward as fast as I could. There was no way of knowing how far we'd come, or how long there was to go.

Surely it was rare to just vanish into a ley line and never re-emerge...

And then the sense changed. It felt a little bit like starting to wake up; when the dream is still fully in your mind, but you also realize you're in your bed, there's light coming in the window, and you have to pee. When you're in two places at once, illogically clinging to the dream-place even though you want to wake up, to rejoin the living world, the "real" world.

Whatever real means.

I twisted again, struggling, trying to open my mouth. To say something, to check on those who accompanied me. Was Petrana's hand still in mine? I couldn't feel my hands.

No, I did feel something...I felt my baby against my breast. She was moving against me, wriggling in her little harness. She was... was she punching me with her tiny fists?

I gasped, coughed, and dragged in a huge breath.

I heard the sound of sneezing—cat sneezing. It went on a long time.

At last, I dragged my eyes open.

We were in a small cave. It was raining, though not at all cold.

We had reached the Azores.

Hungry and thirsty as I was, I guess I must have fallen asleep, because suddenly I was blinking up into the face of a young warlock. He looked a little bit like Sebastian, though without the warm humor in his eyes.

"Welcome, traveler," he said, and gave a slight bow. There were traces of Jeremy's accent in his words. He must be from the Old Country.

"Thank you," I said, sitting up. Still strapped to my chest, Rosemary looked over at the warlock, then back at me.

"If you will come with me, we have sustenance and shelter just down the hill a ways."

"Right, of course." I looked around me. It was a natural cave, probably, though it had clearly been enlarged and smoothed out by both magical and human hands. I'd been slumped against a huge pillow; there were half a dozen like it in the room. Petrana, of course, was standing by the cave opening, unfazed.

The warlock followed my gaze to the pillows and gave the barest hint of a smile. "You are not the first traveler to require rest upon emerging from the line."

I nodded. "Yeah. I bet." Did anyone *not*? A nudge at my feet snagged my attention. As soon as she caught my eye, Elnor began informing me of the desperate, urgent, well-nigh fatal hunger that *she* was suffering. "I know, I know," I said, scritching her ears as I tried to get to my feet. But wow, I was drained.

"Would you like me to carry the child?" Petrana asked, stepping toward me.

The warlock startled a bit at this, though he tried hard to cover it up. Just as I tried to cover my own ongoing pride in the fancy, fancy golem I'd made. The golem with *initiative*. The golem who could be glamoured to pass for a *person*. "Yes, please, for now," I told her.

She even had to help me unbuckle the harness.

Through all this, the young warlock stood by, waiting patiently, not offering any more help than he already had. If he was this community's greeter, then the rules of hospitality were more different here than I'd even realized.

"My name is Callie," I said to him, once the baby weight had been transferred to Petrana and I could actually make my way all the way to my feet.

He raised an eyebrow. "I am known as Parson." Maybe it was just my imagination, but I could almost hear an undercurrent of *If you won't give me your real name, I certainly won't supply mine.*

Fine, whatever. He'd offered food and shelter. I put out my hand. "Shall we?"

Parson led me out of the cave and into bright—well, not sunlight; it was still overcast though it had stopped raining. But brighter light than my eyes were ready for.

And humid! "Wow," I said, wiping my brow. "It's damp here."

Parson smiled thinly. "Yes."

He led us down a trail. The cave had been in a rather steep-sided hill, which struck me as strange. Coming from underneath the ocean as I had done, I'd expected to emerge closer to sea level.

The landscape was green and lush. I saw no buildings. "It's beautiful though," I commented.

Parson nodded.

Five minutes later, we arrived at a small hut. He lifted his hand and performed a complicated spell with his fingers, muttering under his breath in what was probably the ancient language, though too quietly for me to make out. When he'd finished, I felt the tang of odd magic in the air, and the hut's door creaked open.

Show-off, I thought as I followed Parson into the hut—then immediately took the thought back.

The spell he'd worked had lifted the disguise off a palatial home, tropical style. It was built into the side of the green, gorgeous mountain we'd just climbed down. Layers and layers of rooms and stairs and gardens and waterfalls and—I turned my head, suddenly overwhelmed. Was I going to have to *climb* all those stairs, just to get to some food?

Parson probably couldn't read minds. No doubt he was just accustomed to weary travelers. "Here," he said, pointing to a low couch. "Wait here. Food will be brought, for..." He stopped, momentarily flustered as he glanced between me and my cat and my golem and my baby.

"Just a meal for me, and tuna for my familiar," I told him. "Thank you."

Another short bow, and he turned and left.

I sank down onto the couch. Petrana stood beside me, holding my bizarrely placid baby. Surely, if I was this hungry, she must be starving; I hadn't nursed her since Canada. "I'm not sure I even have any milk yet," I told my golem. Like she'd know any more than I did.

Petrana nodded anyway. "After you eat, you will replenish, no doubt."

"I expect so."

Rose just watched me, eyes big and calm.

It wasn't Parson who returned, but three witchlets, carrying platters full of fresh fruits, cured meats, aged cheeses, amazing pickles, a salad of tomatoes and basil and fresh mozzarella, pennyroyal tea, both elderflower and dandelion wines, hot buttered rolls that were the best things I'd ever tasted in my whole life—oh, on and on. I stuffed it all in my mouth faster than I can even describe it to you, and felt my energy plump up even as I chewed. Still exhausted, though; just...it was rare, and wonderful, to feel such a direct correlation between fuel and energy.

Beside me, Elnor gnawed on a whole tuna fish. No, it couldn't be; tuna were bigger than she was. Weren't they? "What is that?" I asked the witchlets, around a mouthful, as I pointed at the fish.

The youngest-looking one—maybe twelve, thirteen years old?—giggled and shrugged, looking to the others. They were nearly identical, and (now that I had begun to notice such things) as European-pale as a San Francisco witch.

"Anila," said the darkest-haired one, and also shrugged.

"Lantoon," said the third witchlet.

The first one added, "Meeg."

"Do you guys not speak English here?"

They all just looked at each other and giggled again.

Whatever. I wasn't staying here anyway; this was just a way station. And a very comfortable one, at that.

I returned my attention to my meal, and soon the witchlets were whispering amongst themselves, as witchlets do the world over.

I'd sat back, rubbing my belly, and begun nursing Rosemary when Parson returned. "All good?" he asked, looking at the demolished feast before me.

"Yes, thank you so much."

"All right, younglings, thank you," he said to the witchlets. They sprang up and began clearing the meal away. "They'll be back with dessert," he told me.

"You guys run a first-rate operation here."

Parson smiled. "It is our calling." He slipped out again, off on whatever mysterious errand took him away.

Dessert was even more spectacular and sumptuous than the meal had been. I was entirely stuffed, but I managed to squeeze in a bit of this and a bit of that, just so as not to hurt anyone's feelings.

I mean, hospitality was their *calling*.

After another while, Parson came back and asked if we were ready to sleep. "I think I'm halfway there already," I admitted. Rosemary had fallen asleep on my breast; Elnor snoozed across my ankles. I was dozy and overly full, but very happy about it.

He nodded. "Right this way." He showed us to a small, cozy sleeping room—essentially just a large bed, plus a shelf to put things on. No windows, no chair, no nothing. "Bathroom is shared, just down the hall here," he said. "Sometimes we get a big group through here, but you're the only travelers we have at the moment, so you'll have all the amenities to yourself. Yourselves."

"Thanks."

"How many days will you be staying?"

"Just overnight, I think," I told him. "I am in something of a hurry."

"Are you jumping to Ponta Delgada?" he asked, naming an island on the other end of the chain.

I shook my head. "No, straight to the mainland."

He frowned slightly. "Oh. All right. Just send a message to me when you want breakfast, and we can show you to the main line out of here."

"Is that weird?" I asked. He paused in the doorway. "I mean, staying only one night?"

"Most travelers spend a few nights in the Azores, even if they move from island to island. Two long stretches are a lot to ask of a body, without adequate time for recovery. Especially…" he glanced at Rosemary. "Especially for someone who has recently been through other taxing events."

"I'm pretty strong," I said.

"I was thinking more of the newborn." Then he gave a small, thin smile, and shrugged. "But we do not judge here—do not misinterpret my words! Every witch and every warlock is assumed capable of making their own assessments of their strength. We merely provide support."

"Right."

"I'm sure your baby will let you know if she is not up to the journey tomorrow." He nodded, his face softening as he looked at Rose again. "Well, goodnight, all of you. I will see you in the morning."

I lay on the comfy bed, holding Rose. "You would tell me, wouldn't you?" I asked her, rocking her gently. "Even though you're not talking to me yet. Or crying. Or anything."

"Ma-ma-ma-ma," she said, and stuck her fingers in her mouth.

I guessed that would have to do.

Somehow, I'd imagined the Azores to be closer to the European continent than they were. They were part of Portugal, after all; I knew they weren't *right* off the coast, like the Canary Islands are to Spain…or was that northern Africa? (Geography was never my strongest subject, nor was it focused on much in any San Francisco witch's education.) But I was dismayed to learn, the next morning, that I'd traversed only slightly more than half the Atlantic.

"You are sure you won't lay over one night in Ponta Delgada?" Parson asked again. "Our chapter has its headquarters there, and very comfortable accommodations."

"No, I really need to keep moving," I told him. I was already over a week into my two-week estimate, and I hadn't even gotten to where I was going.

"Very well." He paused a moment. "I will see to breakfast. Coffee, or tea?"

"Tea, please."

"Excellent. I'll be back in twenty minutes."

I used the time to explore the amenities, availing both Rosemary and myself of a delightful bath. Sadly, I didn't have a lot of clothes with me, so I had to change back into old travel-worn grubbies. Then I found my way back to the room where I'd had dinner.

"You will want to make landfall in Lisbon or Porto, to be sure," Parson told me as I munched on a plate of sliced tropical fruit. I didn't know what kind of fruit it was; it was pink, and sweet, with soft, tangy, edible seeds. "If you have a preference, I can send word along ahead of time."

"I thought I'd just follow the flow," I said. "Aren't these lines the most malleable?"

"They can be."

I ate another bite. "Which city has the best pathways to the Old Country?"

"Where are you trying to go, specifically?"

I paused. I had some very specific thoughts, but I was also trying to be discreet. "Balszt," I said, naming the capital.

"Either one will do, then. Porto's probably a bit easier; you should head there."

I nodded. I didn't imagine that Parson would blab my business to other travelers, but better safe than sorry. Zchellenin was near enough to Balszt. Once I got there, I could fine-tune it.

Besides, it's always easier to hide in a big city. I would need to lay low at first, get a feel for the country, and its inhabitants. Which reminded me: "Do they speak English in the Old Country? I mean, when they talk out loud at all?"

He looked up at this, clearly surprised. "Why, of course. What else would they speak?"

I blinked back at him. "I don't know, whatever it is you guys speak here, maybe? Or the old language, the...ritual language?" A lifetime of conditioning kept me from naming the language of spells.

Parson smiled as understanding dawned. "Were the witchlets pretending not to know English? My apologies, I will have to have a word with them."

"No, no," I assured him. "They were fine. They just used some words I didn't know, and I wondered—"

He laughed, but looked chagrined. "It's a phase they're going through. They've invented a whole new vocabulary so they can tell secrets among themselves, and imagine their elders are none the wiser."

"I teach witchlets myself," I assured him. "I understand perfectly." I took another bite of fruit. "It's good to know I'll be able to be understood in the Old Country, though. As long as I speak to adults."

Parson nodded. "Yes, it was decided early on that a common language needed to be established, so that immigrants and visitors from anywhere in our realms could function and communicate. English and French were in use over much of our world at that time, so you will see them both, though these days, more English."

"And then there's a lot of ætheric communication, too, right?"

He looked slightly puzzled. "Well, yes, of course. It is our home country, after all."

"Right." I thought again about how strange it must be, how silent. "Well, this has been very helpful," I told him. "Thank you."

"It is our pleasure."

After breakfast, I made short work of packing up, and then I was ready to hit the "road."

Parson showed me to the closest point for catching a ley line to Porto. Or, well, a ley line that would lead to a branch of lines that came closest to Porto...in the way of such things. It was across a wide lawn about two hundred yards from the building we'd slept in, next to a little stream which, he assured me, ran to the ocean.

"You all made it here in such good shape, I think you should be fine," he said, though he looked fretful. As if he wanted to check all my straps and peer into my gas tank, to mix about six metaphors. I decided he was the perfect person to have running a way station: fussy, detail-oriented, caring without being smothering, and entirely competent. It didn't even bother me much anymore, that he wasn't at all warm.

"Thank you again for everything," I told him. "If you're ever in San Francisco, do look me up."

"I will, of course," he said, sounding utterly sincere, even though I was quite convinced he'd never leave this island.

He stepped back a few yards, letting me find my own concentration, to feel for the energy of the ley line myself. Elnor leaned against my ankles, melding her feline energy with mine; Rose breathed against the skin of my chest. I clutched tightly to

Petrana's hand. I'd gotten so used to the feel of it, it almost didn't feel strange anymore.

"All right, ladies?" I said to my little gang.

"Miaow," Elnor replied.

"Yes, Mistress Callie," Petrana said.

Rosemary blew a bubble.

We stepped onto the ley line and resumed our undersea journey.

This stretch was somehow easier and harder. I knew something of what to expect, so I wasn't as nervous; but it seemed to take much longer than the first length, even though I knew it was shorter. Part of the problem was that the lines branched much more frequently here. It was a mess of rivulets and small streams, as opposed to the large river of the Canada-to-Azores segment. My way was always clear enough, but it took more concentration to focus on it. I couldn't just float along, lost in the mystery and weirdness of it.

And yet it was somehow more tedious, more boring. I suppose that had as much to do with the familiarity as anything else. But also the water surrounding the lines was warmer, which made everything less comfortable. My sense of urgency was greater, and I was starting to dread what I might find once I finally got to the Old Country.

All in all, I was very glad to make landfall.

I hadn't quite managed to hit Porto, but rather a small town a hundred or so miles down the coast. Fortunately, this was apparently a common enough occurrence that the way station workers had lookouts posted up and down the seaboard, and I was found and brought in quickly.

The Porto way station was similar enough to the last one that it was obvious that the same order ran them both. I will tell you, though, that Portuguese food is even more amazing than Azorean.

I was replete and thoroughly revitalized by the time we resumed our journey the next day, and Rosemary was as robust and content as ever—despite Parson's concerns.

"One more long push, gang," I told my little group. "And then we'll be in the Old Country."

The thought gave me a shiver.

You'd have thought that all this time on the road, much of it with nothing to do but float along on ley lines or rest up in between stints of floating along on ley lines, would have given me plenty of time to come up with a plan of action. It had all seemed so clear back in Berkeley: Gregorio was the mastermind behind the essence-stealing, and he'd victimized a number of witches and warlocks so badly that their very souls were missing. Furthermore, he was doing this with machines that had been manufactured by a particular company in Zchellenin, a village in the Old Country.

Even if I hadn't had that clue, Gregorio had strong ties to the Old Country. He was not simply born, raised, and spent many hundreds of years of his life there, but he'd fostered his son there, and he regularly ordered materials and supplies from there for his legitimate research. The old warlock was more Old Country than not, to the point where Sebastian and I had openly wondered why he even chose to live in San Francisco.

So, simple: I was just going to go to the Old Country and get to the bottom of…

That's where my bold ideas failed me.

I started to remember Jeremy's telling me about how he'd tried to find word of Logan's parents, also in Zchellenin, and how cold and unapproachable Old Country folk were…

Of course, we now knew where Logan's parents were. Their bodies, anyway. They were stockpiled in a basement underneath the UC Berkeley library building.

How much work would it be to transport soulless bodies that far?

Not that I needed to know the mechanics of it, just...it was another measure of just how *much* power Gregorio Andromedus wielded. How entirely outmatched I was.

And by now, surely he knew that I was onto him.

I rested in a small hotel room in southern Germany. It was my last night before making my entry into the Old Country, and that's as specific as I can get in disclosing its location. Tonight was the night I needed to figure out exactly where I was going, and what I was going to do when I got there.

Great.

When in doubt, I fall back on my scientific training. What I had was a problem with too many variables. So, the first thing to do should be to eliminate some.

Once I started thinking this way, things got a bit clearer.

I sat at the little desk in my room. It was too small for even me. So many things in Europe, I'd already found, were smaller than what I was accustomed to. Cars, café chairs, servings of food and beverages...except for steins of beer, here in Germany, at least. Those were absurdly large for some reason.

Notebook in front of me, I sketched out what I knew, and what I wanted to find out.

WHAT I KNOW ABOUT THE OLD COUNTRY:

-WHERE OUR LINES ARE ALL FROM

-TRADITIONAL, FORMAL

-HIDDEN, YET POWERFUL; UNWELCOMING TO HUMANS, NOT FRIENDLY TO TOURISTS

-TENSIONS BETWEEN THE IRON ROSE AND REGULAR OLD WITCHKIND. SOMETIMES OPEN WAR.

Useless, too basic. I put a line through the list and started another:

Iron Rose:

-*Uber-traditional witchkind fringe group, wanting 100% separatism between us and humans*

-*Not afraid to use deadly force to get their way*

-*Are they in power here? Or just a threat?*

Why hadn't I asked more questions before I'd just rushed off? Jeremy could have told me plenty...but then, of course, he'd have known where I was going. He wasn't stupid. By my second "casual" question about how the Old Country worked and what the Iron Rose was all about, he'd have sniffed out my intentions.

So, I just had to figure it out here.

Well, that made my initial destination easy: Balszt, the capital. Just as I'd told Parson. I'd find lodging and spend a few days getting a sense of things. Read the local newspapers, chat casually with people I met, if they were willing to talk. It made sense that folks would be cold and unapproachable, if you walked up and knocked on their doors and asked about neighbors who mysteriously disappeared decades ago. But surely a young witch with an adorable infant getting breakfast in a café would be able to strike up conversations.

I stared at my list a while. Then I tore off the sheet of paper and started another list on a blank page.

What I Need To Find:

-*Equipment company: Grand Laurel Merenoc*

-*Their method for extracting and collecting essence, and souls*

-*Incontrovertible evidence linking these crimes to Gregorio Andromedus*

-*All the lost souls*

Easy-peasy! I laughed at myself. But I had to start somewhere.

It's odd that no one mentioned to me that there is no way for a witch to just "slip in" to the Old Country, even off the most obscure ley line. Every entrance to the country is guarded and regimented, with the witchkind equivalent of Border Control.

Okay, maybe it's not odd, because of course nobody knew I was headed to the Old Country. But still. A little strange that it had never come up. I'd ventured into and out of Canada, not to mention the Azores, and several European countries, without running into any bureaucracy.

Now, I stepped into mundane existence in a small office, just behind a large sign that read "Wait Here To Be Called." Beyond the sign was a counter, with five or six windows, three of which were closed. Bored-looking functionaries toiled behind the open ones—all witches, I noticed.

Other than the fact of there being no line, it could almost have been a witchkind DMV.

The witch at the window closest to me scratched away at something with a quill pen for a minute, then raised her eyes to me. "You may approach," she said, out loud, in words.

I walked up to her window. Petrana walked with me; the clerk raised a hand, as if to stop her, but then lowered it and nodded.

"Name?"

"Is this…necessary?" I tried. "I'm traveling, um, quietly."

She stared back at me. "Name," she said again.

"Calendula Isadora," I said with a sigh.

"Country of origin?"

"Really?"

Again, the stare.

"America. San Francisco."

She made a note on a piece of paper, down below the counter where I couldn't see. "Reason for visiting?"

"Research," I said.

She eyed my baby, then my golem, very pointedly. "Research." Since she hadn't phrased it as a question, I just nodded. "What kind of research?"

"Ah, genealogical." I jiggled Rose, who sat adorably in her carrier, making sweet eyes at the clerk. "I've recently developed a greater interest in my origins, more than my birth parents have been able to tell me about. I had some time in my schedule, so I thought I'd pop on over. It's a secret, though. It's a, um, a surprise for my mother. So I hope word doesn't get back home." I gave her a brilliant smile.

The clerk gave no indication whether or not she was buying this line of bull. "Any reason you brought that...creature...with you?" She pointed at Petrana.

"She's my nanny," I said. "She cares for the baby when I'm busy. Busy researching."

"Busy researching." She stared at the baby, Petrana, and me again before making another note.

Well, I supposed she had to do *something* to liven up her day. Could she turn me away, deny me entry to the country? I noticed the other two clerks watching our interaction while pretending not to. No other visitors had come in. Maybe I was the only person to arrive at the Old Country today—at least at this station.

"Yep." I shuffled from foot to foot. "It's really convenient to have help with the baby. She helps around the house, too."

The clerk narrowed her eyes. "So you decided to build a golem rather than, say, *hire* someone?"

I kept the pleasant expression on my face as I asked, "Is it not legal to bring a golem into the Old Country?"

The clerk recoiled, just the tiniest bit. "It's not illegal, no. It's just unusual."

"Not sure I've ever seen such a thing before," the clerk at the next window put in, finally giving up the pretense that she was not following our every word.

I shrugged and smiled. This, at least, I was used to. "I guess I'm unusual, then!"

My clerk made another note. "Length of stay?"

"A week, maybe two," I said. Even though two weeks was supposed to have been the length of my entire trip...

"Maybe?"

"Depends on where my research takes me."

She looked back at me for a minute. "Local address?"

"Excuse me?"

She blinked and leaned forward. "Where will you be staying while you are in the Old Country? I need the address of that place."

"Ah. Right. I don't know that yet. I'll get a hotel, I thought." *The Old Country* has *hotels, doesn't it?* I thought in a sudden panic.

"A hotel."

"Yes."

"Not an inn? A hostel?"

I shrugged, wondering how long this bizarre cross-examination was going to go on. "Sure, or those—anything. A place to sleep, maybe near things, restaurants, shops. But, um, I did sort of leave on the spur of the moment, I don't have anything booked. Do you have any recommendations?"

She looked startled at this, shaking her head. "We don't recommend."

"Okay."

Now we were at a stalemate. We just stared at each other.

"I'll put The Majestic," she finally said, and made a note.

"The Majestic. Great."

"It's downtown."

"Wonderful."

"If you decide on a different place, you leave word at The Majestic, all right?"

"Sure," I agreed. "Sure thing." Would I be so hard to find, I wondered? How many American witches with infants and golems could there be, even in a big city like Balszt? I didn't ask this aloud, of course. "I'm sure The Majestic will be great, though," I added. In case it mattered to her. In case it would move this along at all.

Weirdly, that seemed to do the trick. She picked up a big metal stamp, thumped it onto an inkpad, and made a few stamps on the piece or pieces of paper I still could not see, below the counter. Then she looked up at me with a professional, artificial smile, and raised both hands. "Welcome to the Old Country, Calendula Isadora," she said, sending a tiny spell at me. It felt good, tingling and welcoming; I could tell that it coated my companions as well. Probably contained some sort of tracking capacity as well, but, so be it. "We hope you enjoy your stay."

"I…thank you?" I stammered. She hadn't handed me anything, or asked for Rosemary's name, or even Elnor's. Just that little spell. "I'm free to go now?"

The clerk's smile grew a little more genuine. "Of course," she said, waving a hand toward a door just beyond the counter. "Right that way."

"Okay. Um." I turned to Petrana. "Come on."

My little entourage made our way to the door, past all three clerks, who were just openly staring at us.

"Most exciting thing that happened to them all day," I muttered, as I opened the door and we all stepped out onto a bustling, cobblestoned street.

— CHAPTER SIXTEEN —

The Old Country. Here I was! At long last. I stood at the edge of the street for a while, taking it all in. Superficially, it was much as Jeremy described—a kind of old-fashioned European-looking city—but also completely *other.*

It took a while to pinpoint the exact nature of the *other*ness, even though it was something I already knew. Balszt was the capital city of a country in which magic did not have to be hidden. Everyone I saw was either a magic user, or—and these would be rare instances, very rare—mundane humans who nonetheless knew of magic and accepted it.

So the biggest thing was the gender balance. *Im*balance, rather; as there are far more witches than there are warlocks, the vast majority of the people I saw were female. It was like a witchkind party, or a night out at Rose's Bar. In the regular, public parts of San Francisco, the streets were of course filled with humans—men and women in roughly equal numbers. It was the same as I'd made my way across the United States, Canada, and Europe. Not so here.

But the differences didn't stop there. The buildings had all been built with magical assistance and decorated with magical embellishments.

I imagined every restaurant would feature food that was helped along by magical means, if the chef decided he or she wanted to do it that way. And they wouldn't have to hide this fact from their co-workers, because they'd be doing the same thing. Their customers would expect it. Even appreciate it.

The people I saw on the street—they might have been using glamours on their appearances. Or they might have gone further and performed magical adjustments to their very biology. I looked at a few passers-by with my witch-sight, just to see. Yes—that witch was wearing an illusion of long silver hair today, which was lying perfectly flat and straight down her back, as though spelled; her actual hair was cut short, and flitting about atop her scalp, in what might be angry protest or just reckless abandon. That warlock had added six inches to his height, though he'd put it all in his legs, which gave him a strangely scarecrow-ish aspect. A little witchlet, not more than seven or eight years old, had a long, striped tail reaching out from under her flouncy skirt, flicking back and forth like a cat's as she walked; her skin was striped as well, tiger-fur yellow and black.

Speaking of which: the cats! Of course every witch had a familiar—most of us did back at home, after all—but here, nobody had to leave them behind when they went out in public. Cats proudly strutted down the street with their mistresses, many of them embellished with the same levels of illusion and glamour that the witches and warlocks wore. I saw little lynxes, piglets, toy poodles, even a baby seal, but they were all cats. Astonishing.

I shook my head, bringing my sight back to the mundane. How did people do it here—how did they not keep trying to unpick the illusions?

Or maybe they didn't. Maybe it was rude.

Or, most likely, it was such a part of the landscape that they hardly noticed it.

I had so much to learn!

It took a while for the strangest thing of all to hit me, something that ran completely contrary to the story Jeremy had told me. Yes, the streets and sidewalks were jam-packed—and everyone was interacting with one another. Smiling, talking, and all *out loud*.

Why had he told me this was a gloomy, silent place? Yes, he'd been talking more about the small towns, rather than the capital, but this was striking. Had he been trying to discourage me from coming here, even as he'd promised to take me? He certainly hadn't made it sound like fun.

"Mistress Callie," Petrana murmured, at my side. "Mistress Elnor might be needing sustenance soon."

Startled, I looked down at my poor kitty. Elnor had indeed been meowing at me for some minutes, I realized. I hadn't even heard her over the bustle around me, and my distraction. "Sorry, kitten," I said. "Let's find..." I looked around. What had that hotel been called?

Perhaps I was hungry too.

And if *we* were hungry...

As if in answer, Rose wiggled on my chest, reaching out with her little hands. "Okay, gang," I said, more firmly this time. "The Majestic Hotel. We just need to—"

"One block down, turn right, go straight for two blocks, can't miss it," said a matronly witch passing by. She didn't slow down, but she did give me a warm smile.

"Thank you, Auntie," I called at her back. She nodded and waved in response.

I started off in the direction she'd sent me, still marveling at the buildings, at everything around me, like a small-town rube seeing downtown San Francisco for the first time. The sights continued to astonish me. Horse-drawn carriages shared the cobblestone streets with sleek luxury autos by makers I'd never heard of. A few witches even rode what could only be magic carpets, hovering through the air a few feet above street level. Businesses lined the streets, openly selling magical herbs and artifacts, scrying stones, and cauldrons of every size. Witches and warlocks were dressed every which way, from any era, to every level of formality—it was as though the whole city had raided Leonora's closet.

I even saw tourists. I could spot them because they looked like me—dressed in jeans, and gaping around like idiots, and wearing their own skins. I smiled at one group; they just stared at Petrana.

Oh, like *I* was the weird one here.

All this rubber-necking almost made me miss my first turn for the hotel. It didn't help that "block" was kind of an imprecise concept here; the city had obviously been laid out along different principles than right angles and regular distances. Eventually, though, I did find it. My growling stomach persuaded me to stop at its street-level restaurant first.

A young witch met me at the hostess stand. Her skin was black as midnight; she was extraordinarily tall and slender, and her hair was a marvel—tight braids that nonetheless shifted and curled around, slow and sinewy. I shifted briefly to witch-sight, surprised to see that she was actually of African descent. From what I'd been able to tell through their glamours, everyone else I'd seen on the street had been so very white—European white, I mean. I really wanted to know her story—Africa had its own magical history, distinct from ours—but I worried it would be intrusive to ask.

"Four for lunch?" she asked smoothly.

"Yes, please, though only two of us will be eating."

She led us to a table by the window. Impossibly, every table was by the window, though the restaurant was quite large…no, it wasn't large, it was intimately small…I couldn't pin down its nature, and I made myself stop trying. Maybe when I wasn't so hungry…

"I'll send your server by immediately," the hostess said, stepping away with a graceful smile.

The server was also a young witch, this time a redhead. Her exuberant long curls reminded me of Sirianna's, though they were much better behaved. "Would you like to see a menu, or shall I just go chef's choice?"

"Chef's choice?" I echoed.

She smiled. "Chef is a strong empath. She looks to see what you're hungry for, even if you don't know. It's our specialty here."

"That sounds amazing, I'll take that."

"Coming right up!"

Moments later, she was back with a big, thick drink. Like a smoothie, but…warm? "Chef said to start with this. You've just come off the Atlantic ley lines, haven't you?"

"Yes, but…" I took a sip, and the rest of my sentence fell away. The server didn't need to know that I'd been on the continent for a few days—indeed, she, and the chef, obviously knew far more about me than my babbling words would convey. The warm smoothie was astonishing. It had all the immediate satisfaction of a milkshake, plus all the soothing heat of a cup of thick cocoa on a cold night…plus something with a little zing in it, like Witch's Mead or aged frog brandy.

Yes, *just* what I needed.

The server had stepped away while I drank, so I didn't even embarrass myself. Or notice her leave. I gulped down the rest of the drink, feeling my very cells plump up with nourishment and energy.

"Ah," I sighed, leaning back.

Rosemary wriggled in Petrana's arms, turning to face me. Good thing some of the cells plumping up were milk ducts.

"Hand her over," I told my golem. I glanced around the restaurant, and though I still couldn't tell whether it was large or small, crowded or empty, I could see that I was seated perfectly to ensure privacy while I fed Rose. I unbuttoned my blouse, only then realizing that, along with everything else unexpected about the Old Country, it wasn't cold at all; the temperature was quite pleasant. I shrugged—I'd have to ask someone about this—and brought my daughter to my breast. She cooed with satisfaction as she drank.

I noticed that Elnor had been chowing down on something this whole time. The hostess had seated her on a special banquette by the wall, giving her a view of the room and raising her nearly to table-height, while keeping what she ate discreetly hidden from my view. How thoughtful, but also, of course. In a country where well over half the population had a familiar and brought them everywhere with them, there naturally wouldn't be any foolish laws barring animals from eating establishments. Even if we didn't want to watch them snarf down stinky tuna fish.

I can see why people might want to live here, I thought, and wondered if there were any way to make some of these changes at home. Rose's Bar, for example; the entire back room was for witchkind only. Why not cat seating in there? Granted, it was pretty small, but that was easy enough to work around. What if…

My thoughts were interrupted by the server returning to collect my empty glass. She replaced it with a small sparkly cocktail. "Drink this slowly, until you get more food in you," she advised.

"Thank you." I took a tentative sip. Wow. I had no idea what was in it, but it was *just* what I wanted. I decided not to even ask about it. I'd just enjoy the…well, the magic.

Anyway, the server was gone again by the time I looked back up. They moved whisper-quiet in here, that was for sure.

At my breast, Rose suckled on. The drink was flowing into my bloodstream but staying out of my milk, without my even directing it to.

My goodness, we could learn a thing or two back home from these Old Country witches.

When the food came, I wasn't even surprised that it smelled and tasted like General Tso's Chicken, even though it looked nothing like my favorite takeout dish. I tucked into it, eating every bite. It wasn't chicken; I'm not even a hundred percent sure it was meat. But it was, yet again, just what my body wanted.

I leaned back at the end of the meal, replete and satisfied. Rosemary had fallen asleep at my breast; she twitched a little, dreaming, no doubt. Elnor washed her whiskers; her dish had been removed. Petrana sat placidly in her chair across from me. "I wish you could eat," I told her. "You'd have loved this."

"I am certain that I would have, Mistress Callie," she said.

Okay, as a dinner companion, perhaps she left a little to be desired. But I was content in every other way.

The server returned. "Will there be anything else?"

I smiled at her. "You probably already know the answer to that, but no, thank you. Just the check."

"Are you staying in the hotel? I can charge it to your room."

"I'm hoping to," I told her, "but I haven't checked in—I don't even have a reservation. I came straight here."

She gave me a brilliant smile and glanced down at my sleeping infant on my breast. "Just wait here. I'll be right back."

Good as her word, she was back a few minutes later. "You're all set. Your room is on the seventh floor, number 719. Here's the key." She set a large, old-fashioned golden key on the table. "I can send a porter to help you with your things if you like."

I shrugged. "I don't have very many things—I think we can manage it. But, don't I need to see the front desk? And, like, pay or something?"

Her smile grew. "We know who you are, Calendula Isadora, and your coven's credit is good here. Nothing to worry about."

Oh. Well. Hmm. I wasn't sure how I felt about that…and then I wasn't sure whether I should be surprised or not. "Well, thank you," I said. "I'll make my way up as soon as I can untangle myself here."

"No rush at all," she said. "This table is yours as long as you'd like to stay."

A room, with privacy and a bed and all, not to mention a bathroom, was starting to sound pretty good, though. So I woke my baby, gathered my cat and golem and our few bags, and found my way to the hotel lobby.

It was as elegant as the rest of the building, and the witch behind the counter waved at me and smiled. "Greetings, Calendula Isadora. The lifts are right through there." She pointed toward a narrow passageway.

"Um, thanks," I said, trying not to stare at her. I couldn't discern her age at all; she was garbed like Leonora on a multi-century rampage, Elizabethan collar over an Edwardian dress with an extra petticoat or two on the *outside* and enough bangly jewelry to give Stevie Nicks a serious case of envy. There was an actual living spider in her powdered wig.

I didn't want to know what her familiar looked like.

In the lift (one of those old-fashioned numbers with a wire-cage doorway and elaborate scrollwork everywhere), I thought more about the situation. Should I have tried for a less conspicuous hotel? I hadn't been thinking strategically, or, really, at all; I'd been too hungry and too tired. Of course they would figure out who I was—heck, the border control folks had basically sent me here; the hotel owners wouldn't even have had to look into my identity magically.

But my coven had an account here? Just in this hotel, or in the Old Country generally?

See, this is what happens when you run off without telling anyone, without getting any help or advice, I told myself.

But what else was I supposed to do? "Hey, Leonora, I'm off to look into crimes committed by the head of our Elders. See you when I get back!" Or even, "Hey, Gregorio, I'm going straight to the source to reveal how you murdered my best friend and a whole bunch of other people for your own personal gain. Ta-ta!"

No, there was really no other way to go about it.

But I really ought to start being smarter.

The elevator gave a cheerful ding as it reached the seventh floor. I pulled the cage door open and found my room, opening it with the big shiny key.

The room itself was...well, let's call it cozy. It definitely looked comfortable, but in terms of size, it gave my coven house bedroom a run for its money.

Of course, Old Country—old world. Everything here was on a smaller scale than the vast expanses of America. I knew that, theoretically; I'd been noticing it since making landfall; this was just another example.

"Come on, gang," I said, as Petrana trundled in behind me. At least she didn't need much room. In fact, there was an unused corner just her size, I noticed.

As if people traveled with golems all the time.

She helped me unpack, such as it was. It took all of two minutes to stash my few changes of clothes in an antique armoire against the back wall. I sank down on the bed, not even unstrapping Rose from her sling, just letting her rest against my chest. She quickly fell asleep once more. The bed was a funny size and shape, something in between single and double, and not very long. Elnor jumped up and sniffed around, spending a lot of time on the quilts and pillows, before jumping back down and inspecting the entire room.

"Safe, kitty?" I asked her. I didn't doubt that it was—at least, safe from monsters and bogeymen and mice—but she needed to do her due diligence.

She responded by jumping back up on the bed and curling up by my side, purring, looking for a scritching.

I had big plans, but I took some time to help my familiar feel comfortable. Rose was snoring softly, and in a minute Elnor was too.

And then I must have been as well, because I opened my eyes and the room was dark.

Night had fallen; I'd slept the afternoon away. I felt momentarily chagrined—I had arrangements to make, a city to explore, crimes to expose—but apparently, I also had rest to get caught up on.

And I thought I'd never slept so much in my life when I was *pregnant*. Heck, undersea ley line travel put pregnancy to shame.

"Wow," I said, stretching and yawning, as Rosemary came awake with my movement. She blinked up at me and made a few of her nonsense sounds. "This is going to be the most boring secret research mission ever, because I'm afraid we all need another meal."

Before I headed out of the hotel, I stopped at the front desk. The same witch from earlier was there. I wondered how long her shift was, or if she had a series of identical siblings. But no; she was clearly unique. "Good evening, Calendula Isadora," she said politely. "I trust your room is to your liking? Everything is in order?"

"Oh, yeah, everything's great," I told her. "Very cute little room."

She smiled. "Wonderful. What can I help you with? Do you need transportation anywhere, or directions to popular ley lines or local attractions?"

"Yes, I probably do," I said, "but first I, well, was wondering something."

She raised a thin, painted eyebrow and waited.

"You know who I am—by my energetic signature, I'm guessing?"

"Of course. We are only sorry that we did not know in advance that you were coming. We would have had your room ready for you."

"Yeah, well, the thing is—I'm on kind of a quiet trip. I stumbled into this hotel by accident, really. I didn't know my coven had an account here?" I couldn't help making that last a question.

"Leonora Scanza is a great and longtime friend of The Majestic," she said, proudly. "Every member of your coven is a pre-registered guest."

"Right. Um. See, she doesn't exactly know I'm here..."

Understanding lit up her eyes, followed by worry.

"Is there—I mean, is it already too late? Does she get a message or something when anyone from the coven uses the account?"

"Oh." The witch paused, seemed to think a moment, then said, "Ordinarily, yes; though ordinarily, arrangements would have been made in advance, of course. Far in advance. In your case... well, there wouldn't have been any confirming message, so..." She thought further, looking slightly uncomfortable. "Of course, the thing to do would have been to send her an ætheric message upon your arrival, assuring her of your safe condition and satisfaction with the room. Since, er, nothing happened in the usual manner this time, no message has been sent." She frowned at me. "I am to understand that you would prefer that no message, er, continues to be sent?"

"Yes, please, if that's possible." I smiled at her. "Just for now, of course. Once I get back home, I will naturally tell her everything that has happened while I've been here, including what a marvelous hotel this is." My smile grew as I reached for the story I'd used on the border clerks. "It's kind of a surprise for everyone at home, what I'm doing here. I would hate to let the cat out of the bag before I'm ready to, if you know what I mean."

Actually, come to think of it, I wasn't even lying.

Her frown relaxed some, though I could tell she was still a bit concerned. "All right, I can hold off on the message. But Mother Scanza will receive her monthly statement of charges. I'm afraid there's nothing I can do about that."

"When do those go out?"

"First week of the month, covering the month prior. And they go by postal mail."

It was barely mid-November. I was golden. "That's not a problem at all. I'll be home long before the statement arrives, and Leonora will not be surprised by it."

"Ah, excellent."

She was so relieved, she spent the next twenty minutes giving me a thorough run-down of the central district of Balszt—restaurants, theatre options, the best places to shop, even good parks to take a child to, "though of course your little one is a bit young for that yet." We were all starving by the time I managed to extract us.

At last, we stepped out into the night. Our first night in the capital of the Old Country, and the weather was still comfortably warm. Petrana carried Rosemary in the harness, and Elnor walked proudly at my heels, clearly delighted by the presence of so many other cats out in public. Even if they were disguised as other creatures as often as not.

"You want me to do that for you, kitty?" I asked her. "Make you into a little weasel, or a baby goat?"

She just gave me a dark glance—well, as dark as her bright yellow eyes could manage, anyway.

I chuckled and led us on toward the central market square.

The night was bustling, the streets even busier than they had been in daylight. Of course, nighttime is when witches really come alive. It's when our magic is the strongest, when the sun's distracting forces are blunted, hidden on the other side of the planet. That's why we do our Circles at midnight, and why I did my best lab work by the light of the moon—or by no light at all.

Crowded though the streets were, I found the whole place increasingly welcoming. Passing witches still looked askance at Petrana, but they grinned at Rosemary, and as often as not complimented me on my adorable baby. Rosemary herself seemed to be enjoying the sights, especially after we'd grabbed a quick meal in a sidewalk café. I'd been tempted to find another fancy restaurant, but I was increasingly aware of my limited time here. We couldn't spend the *whole* trip dining out.

I couldn't get over what Jeremy had said about the folk being cold and reserved, not even speaking aloud to each other. Of course, Balszt was a tourist destination, a magnet for witchkind from everywhere. The capital catered to strangers, its economy was set up to welcome them.

But also…Jeremy was a warlock.

Once I'd had that thought, I started looking around with different eyes. Yes: witches were warm, open, and friendly to me and mine. Warlocks…they seemed to live on a different plane here. They greeted one another on the street, with glances or nods; they ignored the far greater numbers of witches surrounding them.

I wasn't sure a single warlock had spoken to me, not since I left the Azores.

Odd, but also not odd, when I thought about it. The power differential we suffered under at home—where warlocks ran the Elders and felt that they made the rules that governed all of witchkind—would be only more pronounced here, because of the very visible minority of the warlocks. They would have to project far more haughty unapproachability, just to protect their position. The political system was the same here as it was at home; we'd imported it wholesale. Even our local Elders nominally answered to bigger Elders here.

And yet…what I saw was a city full of witches basically ignoring the warlocks, cheerfully going about their lives.

Just like we did in our covens, except right out in the open.

I grinned right back at all these cheerful witches, dressed so dramatically and colorfully. It made my jeans and plain blouse feel like the drabbest, most boring choice ever, so I sought out one of the clothing stores the hotel clerk had recommended.

Yes, I knew I had to get busy with my research. I told myself I'd have better luck if I blended in a bit better.

An hour later, I emerged from the bazaar, dressed in snakeskin pants that clung to me like they'd been painted on (but that breathed and moved like I was wearing soft air), a shiny black top with cascades of black lace and pearl buttons down the front, and purple illusion-boots—they looked like they had six-inch heels, but they were as comfortable as sneakers. I'd been tempted by any number of gorgeous pull-over shirts and sweaters, but until Rose was weaned, I needed easier access in a garment.

And I would have to carry all this stuff home with me. Darn that ley line travel and its restrictions, or I would have bought out half the store.

As it was, Petrana was now carrying a small package as well as my daughter. I strode down the street, feeling far more comfortable, just enjoying the night.

But now it was time to get serious. I needed to find out as much as I could about the manufacturing company, Grand Laurel Merenoc, before I traveled to Zchellenin. So I headed to that bastion of information: the main library.

Balszt's library was not far from the central district, in a slightly quieter, slightly more elegant part of town. There was a river nearby; I could smell it, and the houses had taken on that air of old money that homes with picturesque water views tended to have.

The building was massive, and covered with spells and sigils. Not as witchkind buildings back home were, for protection and obscuration; here it was for more open access, even from afar—plus decoration, of course.

The access thing was interesting. Maybe I hadn't needed to come here in person? But it was a sight to see, and I was glad I had.

The building was nominally four stories, not unlike the main campus library back in Berkeley, and it resembled that building as well. (Interesting, I thought…coincidence, or not?) But a mere glance showed that it was far more complex and warren-like inside than even the Berkeley one. Corridors, additions, even entire floors sprang off in every direction, wrapped around each other, sharing magical and physical space in a way that made it clear this had been going on for centuries.

I stood on the library steps, admiring the intricacy. Many minds and many magics had gone into the place. A witch could learn a lot here.

It gave me ideas about my house.

Not that I needed to be focusing on my house right now, or even how marvelously arranged this building was. I tore my eyes away from the exterior and we headed for the doors.

The interior, once I was inside, did not disappoint. I had to school myself to stay on task. I would have much rather wandered about the building, trying to find the information I was looking for on my own, and enjoying the process of discovery—even if it had taken days. Instead, I stepped up to the information desk.

An incongruously plain witch sat behind the counter. She was neither old nor young; her hair was brown and coaxed into a long braid down her back; she was dressed in a navy-blue shirtdress. It was almost like she was in protest to the general tenor of the rest of Balszt. "Yes?" she said, looking up politely. At least she smiled at the baby, so I knew she was alive, and not some elaborate golem.

"I'm looking for any information you might have on a company called Grand Laurel Merenoc," I said. "It's in—"

"Zchellenin, yes, is their headquarters," she said, waving her fingers in the air as I spoke. Words appeared from her fingertips, as if she had consulted some sort of ætheric computer system. "They have a showroom here in the capital, but all their manufacturing and most of their sales efforts are in Zchellenin."

"Wow," I said, watching her fingers. I could almost-but-not-quite follow the magic she was using.

She smiled and coaxed the words around to face me more directly, though it didn't help; the lettering was in an unfamiliar language. "Proprietary spellwork," she said proudly.

"Did you write it yourself?"

Her smile grew. "I did."

"It's amazing."

"Thank you." She seemed to shake herself back into a more professional seriousness. "But I didn't give you anything you couldn't have found out from the local æthernet. What specifically did you need to know about Grand Laurel Merenoc?"

Local æthernet? I wondered, but set that aside for the moment. "I found a couple of machines labeled with their name back in the United States. Their function...confused me a bit, and there was no one I could ask. I need to know specifically what those machines do, and how they do it; and I need to be fairly quiet about finding this out."

Her fingers danced in the air; golden letters flashed into and out of view. She frowned as she worked—in concentration, or something more? Finally, she turned back to me, letting the spell vanish. "I'm finding an unusual number of blockages in the information path. Where in the United States? And can you tell me anything more specific about the machines?"

In for a penny... "Berkeley," I told her. "The University of California campus. One of them was tall and skinny and had what looked like a bell jar at its top."

"The Enchin Aberra?"

"Yes, that was it."

Her fingers moved again. Her frown deepened. No, this wasn't just concentration. "The blockages are active," she said, as the letters blinked out again. "Grand Laurel discourages virtual research and keeps shutting down my inquiries. I'm really sorry."

"What does that mean?" I asked, though I was afraid I knew.

"You're going to have to go to Zchellenin. It's not far—several well-established ley lines go there. I can give you a map."

"Thanks," I said. "I'd planned to go there anyway, but I wanted to know a little more before just showing up on their doorstep. It's…sensitive."

"Yes, so you mentioned."

"About Zchellenin…" I paused, trying to find the words. "Will I find it…as welcoming there as Balszt?"

The librarian shook her head. "Probably not. Though it's perfectly safe."

"Safe?"

"Yes. Visiting witches rarely get pulled into the struggles."

The Iron Rose. "What, exactly, are the struggles about?"

"Do you not have warlocks at home?"

I looked at her. Was that a hint of a smile? "So, it's just a warlock power struggle?"

She leaned forward and lowered her voice. "You did not hear this here, but that's exactly what it is. For all the useful things that warlocks do for us, they do ten things that are worthless at best and harmful at worst." She glanced at my baby and her smile grew. "Granted, the good things they give us are *very* good indeed."

Except that no warlock had given me this child… "What are they fighting about? Does anyone even know?"

"I think they sense the world changing and their relevance fading. It makes them grip harder, scream louder to preserve the old ways, to hang onto their control. How long have you been here?"

"Not even a day yet. But, it's not at all what I'd expected. It's even warm."

"See, that's just what I mean," she said, growing exasperated. "A witch did that, not a warlock."

"Did what?"

"The weather! It was a witch climatologist who figured out how to adjust the flow of the winds and keep the temperature stable."

"Wow."

"But do you ever hear about that in the new world? No, of course not! All the news that makes it overseas is about how *backward* we are here, how *dangerous* the Old Country is, how *traditional*. And it's just warlocks, warlocks, warlocks—as if well over half of the population didn't matter!" She rolled her eyes, and then gave me an apologetic smile. "Sorry, don't get me started. It's just, this stuff bugs me to pieces."

"I can see that," I said, "and I don't blame you a bit. Plenty of what goes on in San Francisco bugs me too." *And isn't* that *putting it mildly.* "Plenty of what *warlocks* get up to, specifically."

She reached a hand over the counter and made a fist. "Solidarity, sister."

I fist-bumped her back. "Solidarity."

"Well, that was fascinating, and not at all what I expected," I said to my little group, as we sat at a fancy restaurant table after all, waiting for our second dinner to arrive.

My infant and my cat did not answer me. My golem said, "Yes, Mistress Callie."

I sipped a cocktail that was entirely different from the one I'd had at the hotel this afternoon, yet just as delightful. What I really needed to do was steal an Old Country bartender and bring her home to work at Rose's Bar.

"Not yours," I said to my daughter, whose eyes found mine just as I thought the name. "Rose Elvinstone owns a lovely little bar back home, which I will take you to when you're of age." I thought about the witchlets at the coven house drinking Witch's Mead on Samhain, and amended that to, "or on special occasions. But not while you're still nursing. Blessed Mother."

I'm sure she hadn't read my mind, and I'm equally sure she didn't give me a sly or knowing smile in response. Anyway, she started blowing spit-bubbles again and lolling her eyes around.

She was just an infant.

The food came. Sadly, this chef was not an empath, so I'd had to make my own selections off the menu. I did a pretty good job, though.

I was going to have to steal a chef as well as a bartender.

— CHAPTER SEVENTEEN —

I was tempted to head for Zchellenin that very night, but despite all the feasting and napping, we were still not recovered from our lengthy journey. So, being the only one with both a brain *and* the power of speech, I made the executive decision that we would stay twenty-four more hours in lovely Balszt, and leave for the small town the following night.

Not that any of my companions seemed disappointed with my decision. It gave us more time to enjoy the city, and the very comfortable (if tiny) hotel room back at The Majestic. The witch behind the front desk had finally gone off shift; her replacement was equally charming, and even chattier. When she learned where I was from, she informed me that the hotel had a sister property in San Francisco.

"You're kidding!" I said.

"Not at all. It's on Sutter Street, at Gough."

I thought a moment. "I know that hotel! I had no idea it was witchkind."

She smiled. "Humans are allowed to stay there."

"I'll be sure to stop in and say hi when I get home," I told her. "And tell them what a nice time I've had here."

"Please do. Tell them Guinevere says hello."

The next day flew by. Even though I told myself I was not here on vacation, it was hard not to let myself forget, for a time, why I was here, and just explore the wonderful strangeness of the place.

But as I touristed around, I also thought about what the librarian had told me about the Iron Rose, and about warlocks in general. It sure seemed to be a witches' world here.

I wondered how long this situation would last. It didn't seem entirely…stable.

It seemed like the kind of thing that could lead a morally challenged, old, powerful warlock to lash out against witchkind. To steal power from witches…even while pretending to heal them, pretending to hunt down and punish whoever might be preying on them.

To be fair, there were a few warlocks in Gregorio's basement of horrors.

But not very many.

Near midnight on my second day there, we regretfully checked out of The Majestic and prepared to hit the road—or, rather, the ley line. The desk clerk from my first day, Magrit, was back on the job. "We will keep your room for you until you leave the country," she assured me, even though I told her I was unsure of my exact plans. She wouldn't hear of my protests. "We have plenty of space, and the capacity to squeeze more if we need it. But this is a slower time of year, so please don't give it another thought."

I couldn't dissuade her, so I stopped trying. "Thank you," I said, and took my leave.

We could have traveled straight to Zchellenin's main square in one uninterrupted jump, and it wouldn't have taken more than a half-hour, but I wanted to arrive far more quietly. So we took a few hours, emerging in a dark patch of woods a short walk from the outskirts of the town.

I stood there, baby strapped to my chest, golem and cat beside me, as I let my magic take the measure of the place.

It was dark here, certainly darker than the capital had been. And I don't just mean the absence of streetlights. There was a sad, ugly feeling to the very trees, the soil they grew in, the heavy, damp air around me that smelled of something stale and foul.

"Mistress Callie," Petrana said softly. "There is different magic here."

"I am feeling that," I told her, just as quietly. At my feet, I could sense Elnor's fur standing on end, even though I couldn't quite see it. "Does anyone have any ideas about the specifics?" I asked, because why not? Petrana had surprised me before.

Rosemary reached out her tiny hands and grabbed at my shirt, as if she wanted to nurse. "Not now, sweetie," I whispered to her. But she kept grabbing, and soon had hold of my braid, which had somehow migrated over my shoulder where she could reach it, though there was no wind.

I gently pulled the braid out of her hands. She didn't want to let go. "Ba-ba-ba," she said. If I didn't know better, I would swear she sounded cross.

"Now is *not* the time to decide to learn how to cry," I told her, patting her soft head, bouncing gently on the balls of my feet and rocking back and forth, trying to soothe her. "Come on, gang, let's walk."

I started through the trees in the direction of the village, picking my way slowly over the fallen leaves, trying to make as little noise as possible. Petrana followed; Elnor stuck close. We passed a darkened cottage. I didn't dare send out my senses to see if anyone was inside. It didn't matter. I wasn't looking for a cottage; I was headed for Grand Laurel Merenoc.

The librarian's directions had put the manufactory in the center of town, with offices adjacent to it, on a large piece of land with several outbuildings and storage sheds. It was clearly the village's main industry. What had Logan's parents done for jobs, when they lived here the first time? Had they worked for the company, or done something else?

It pained me to realize how little I knew of my best friend's family history. Of course, her parents had disappeared when we were barely teenagers. I'd only met them a few times, and they were as interesting as any parents are, to a teenager: not at all.

And then they had come back and settled here once more. In a cottage on the outskirts of town…perhaps one like the darkened one I'd just passed. Perhaps even that very one.

I shivered and told myself it didn't matter. I knew where their bodies were. It was their souls I was trying to track down now.

And everyone else's.

At last, I saw a soft glowing light through the trees, and then another. I slowed, making doubly sure I was not detected. I passed a corral for horses (uninhabited for the night, but the smell made its function clear), and a barn, then a few small houses. The deer trail I'd been following widened into a people-path, then something like a road. It was mostly dirt, with stray cobblestones here and there—more impediment than anything else, I thought.

I was in Zchellenin.

I followed the road past more houses and barns, then what might have been an inn in happier days. And then I reached the central square. It was as gloomy as Balszt's was vibrant; not a soul was out.

On the other side of the square was a large, squat building of dark stone. A small painted sign over its door read Grand Laurel Merenoc.

"Here we are," I whispered to my companions.

We walked across the square, my boots clicking on the flat paving stones. There were three steps leading up to a set of double doors. Just as I was wondering how to petition for entrance—I didn't see a door knocker or bell pull or anything—the left-hand door swung open.

A tall warlock stood there, wearing traditional dark robes—the kind our Elders wore when they were trying to be fancy or solemn or impressive. "Greetings, Calendula Isadora," he said. "We've been expecting you."

My heart beat fast in my chest. Rose pulled on my braid again, having somehow gotten her hand back around it. "You have me at a disadvantage," I managed.

He cracked the faintest of smiles; it was gone in an instant. "I am Dr. Mar. Please come in."

I wanted to go inside, I was here to go inside, I'd come all the way to the Old Country specifically so I could go inside, but... "You were expecting me? How?"

That smile flickered again, vanishing just as fast. "Dr. Andromedus sent word that you would be along."

I didn't fall over or pass out or anything. Rosemary yanked on my braid again; I untangled her hand once more, absently, as my mind raced. "I...I hadn't mentioned to him that I was coming here," I finally said.

Dr. Mar's smile hung around a little longer this time. "Just so. Do please come in, the night is cold."

Was it a trap? Well, if it was, it was already too late. I swallowed the anxious lump in my throat and took a step forward. Petrana took a step as well.

Dr. Mar put up an age-spotted hand. "Just you, Calendula Isadora."

"Wait, what? No, we're all together."

He shook his head. "Creatures of unnatural magic are not permitted within the walls of Grand Laurel Merenoc. Nor are witches' pets, nor minors. You may leave them all outside. I imagine the creature can take charge of the infant while we conduct our business."

What *business* did he think I had here, anyway? I was not looking forward to finding out. "I can leave the golem, but my familiar and my daughter stay with me." Why did warlocks have to be such assholes? He knew perfectly well what witches' cats were for. And he wanted to separate a mother from a newborn?

"Then I must bid you a good evening." He turned with a sweep of his ostentatious robes and started to close the door.

"Wait!" I cried.

He paused. "Yes?"

I thought fast. "I just have some questions. Can't we come in for a few minutes—do you have a lobby or something?" *A place where we won't sully your precious manufactory?*

"No."

The door closed, and we were alone in the night again.

I sat down heavily on the steps and removed Rose's fingers from my braid yet again. "Well," I said to my companions. "That went well."

Petrana walked down the steps, turned, and looked at me. "What are you going to do?"

"I don't know. I have to think."

"Dr. Mar knows we're all still here," she pointed out.

I nodded, the lump in my throat swelling, threatening to overwhelm me. "Yeah, and he knew I was coming—because somehow Gregorio figured it out and got word to him—and he's probably listening to our conversation right now, and you know what? I don't care!" I practically yelled, as if into an overhead speaker. "I'm tired of fighting so hard. I'm not some kind of international spy! I'm just a witch who wanted to make some actual decisions about her own actual life, and I'm tired of getting punished for it. I'm tired of trying so hard to get everything right, to be so careful, to keep all the secrets, to cover my tracks—only to find out it was all wasted effort anyway. I'm just tired!" I was on the verge of tears, frustrated and stymied, at the end of my rope.

"I don't even know what Gregorio wants from me," I went on, in a lower tone, to my golem. "Here I thought I was so clever, and he probably knew that, um, we'd found that, uh, stuff in Berkeley all along." But just in case he didn't know literally everything—or who I'd been with—it was probably smarter not to blurt it all out on the very doorstep of Grand Laurel Merenoc. "I don't know, I don't know, I just don't know," I wound down, and finally gave up trying to hold back the tears.

As I wept, Rose made little cooing sounds against my breast, and Elnor came and nudged her head against my legs, rubbing against me. Even Petrana stepped forward, somewhat stiffly, and patted my arm. It was really sweet, and not a little weird.

Eventually, my tears ran their course. I wiped my eyes with my sleeve, getting some snot on my nose.

"I still don't know what to do," I said.

And that was the moment when my daughter sent me her first coherent mind-communication. *Strong*, I received, as clear as if she'd spoken aloud.

I gasped and pulled back, staring at her. Her dark eyes gazed back at me, still slightly unfocused. "Did you just..."

Strong, I got again.

"Oh, sweetie," I said, leaning down to kiss the top of her head. "You smart, sweet, wonderful witchlet! You do speak!" I hadn't even realized how much I hadn't wanted to let myself worry about her lack of communication...I knew that not every witchlet or baby warlock communicated with their mother in the womb, but most of them did. And certainly, I'd never heard of one not "speaking" once she was born.

Of course, she was half-human, and Gregorio had made much of how weak she was going to be...but the relief poured through me all the same.

"Good girl!" I murmured, rocking her as we sat on the cold stone steps.

Petrana, bless her little mud-brain, didn't look curious or confused at all. "Rosemary just sent a mind-thought to me," I told her, anyway.

"That is good news, Mistress Callie."

"It is. It is indeed."

I still didn't really wish she'd start crying...but that would be another sign of normalcy. Well, one thing at a time.

I got to my feet and brushed off the back of my snake-pants. "Well, I guess we ought to—"

Behind me, the door opened again.

I whirled around, ready to give Dr. Mar a piece of my mind, but a young warlock stood there instead. He looked to be hardly into his twenties, though of course, it was impossible to know for sure. His robes were like a junior, starter-version of Dr. Mar's, and the power I could feel from him when I gave a reflexive, gentle probe was much less than that of the old warlock.

"Calendula Isadora?" he asked, almost timidly.

"Yes, that's me."

"I'm Dr. Spinnaker. I, um, Dr. Mar sent me to answer your questions."

"Did he now?" I stepped up to him; he took an involuntary step back. Afraid of me? Really? "Is he going to let us come in?"

"Ah, um, no, still just you. But we can all step into the garden if you like."

"Sure, fine." I mean, what were my options? "Lead on."

Dr. Spinnaker closed the door behind him and set a lock-charm before turning back to me. "This way."

I followed him down the stairs and around to the side of the building. A half-moon had risen, at last, sending its pale light into a small courtyard.

"In here," he said, leading us to a grouping of chairs. He stood until I was seated, then took a chair opposite me. "I am sorry for your, ah, reception here," he said. "If you let me know what your questions are, I will do my best to answer them."

His accent was a mix of Old Country and modern British English; my ear tried to parse it, until I reminded myself that it didn't matter. "Thank you, Dr. Spinnaker," I said.

He gave an embarrassed smile. "You can call me Helios if you like."

I nodded. "Then you should call me Callie."

"I will. So, Callie, what are your questions?"

I thought a moment. There were questions, and then there were things I might reasonably expect to get answers to. "I guess my first one is, um, when did Dr. Andromedus tell you-all that I was headed here?"

His smile eased, as he relaxed a tiny bit. "Perhaps a week ago? It was an ætheric message, of course, and you know how spotty those can be."

"I do." It was why Jeremy and I basically didn't communicate the whole time he was over here. Well, part of the reason, anyway. "So the timing isn't definite, but a week. Hmm." Gregorio had clearly known where I was headed, probably even as I sent those clever messages to everyone, about going on retreat.

Bastard.

"That's right. Though Dr. Mar didn't let me know until you'd arrived on the continent."

"I see." Dr. Spinnaker—Helios—sounded a little put out about this. Hurt, wounded? "Did you, ah, should you have been told sooner?"

He shrugged, not altogether convincingly. "I have worked with Dr. Andromedus many times in the past. He had even spoken of bringing me to San Francisco to work in his laboratory there. I suppose I might have expected that he would send word through me." He glanced away for a moment. "But of course, I'm just a junior scientist, nobody important at all. It was entirely appropriate that he should communicate with Dr. Mar."

Ah. "Is Dr. Mar the director here, or president, or…?"

"He is the owner of the company. Well, it's a family-owned business, has been for generations. He's the current senior member of the Mar family. I guess president would be the best equivalent; his actual title is just Senior."

"What does the company do, exactly?" I tried. "I know you make machinery. I saw a few in Berkeley, and I am curious about them." I saw no reason to hide this anymore. And maybe it would ease the flow of information if I didn't look like I was keeping secrets.

"We do make machinery, that's all that we do. For research." I just looked at him. *Vague much? You sound like me at the border control office.* He went on, "Well, lots of different kinds of things. The nexus between science and magic, and how the two forces work together."

"The two forces? Are you saying science is a force?"

He shook his head. "No, not like that. I mean—oh, it's hard to explain. Tell me what machines you saw and I'll see if I can be more specific."

I cast my mind back, making sure I got the unfamiliar words right. "The one I'm most curious about said Enchin Aberra on it, just under the company name."

"Ah." He frowned, nodding, and looking at his feet. "That's a complicated one. It does a number of different things." Before I could give him *the look* again, he went on. "You say you saw it in Berkeley. In Dr. Andromedus's lab?"

Kind of. "Yes."

"And you came all the way to the Old Country to ask about it, rather than asking Dr. Andromedus himself? Or even sending word to us?"

I stared back at this warlock. On my chest, Rose started patting at my breasts, with both hands. *Strong* she said again.

Thrilled as I was that she was talking to me now, this wasn't exactly helping. I patted her head and said to Helios, "Yes, I did. There were some very personal reasons why I didn't want to ask him about it. Why I wanted to come here myself." I swallowed, deciding to take it further. What the hell. "In fact, I very specifically didn't tell Dr. Andromedus I was even making this trip, yet somehow he knew. He's doing some things back home that I don't think are good news—for any of us. I'm trying to get to the bottom of it. Understanding what he's doing, very specifically, should help me figure this out." I held his eye. "If you can help me, that's great, I would appreciate it. I suspect all of witchkind would appreciate it. But if Dr. Andromedus is, I don't know, *invested* in this company in some way—if he has the power to turn me away or keep information from me, just let me know. I'll figure out some other way to get what I need."

There. Maybe I'd signed my own death warrant. Who knew? Maybe I could take my little household and move to Svalbard or something. Surely Gregorio wouldn't pursue me there.

Helios Spinnaker gave a small sigh, shifted the cross of his legs, gave a larger sigh, and finally got to his feet and paced across the small courtyard. Looking back at me, he said, "I'm sorry, Calendula Isadora, but that's the best I can do."

Almost concurrently, he sent me an ætheric message: *Meet me at noon in the Spanish Market.*

I blinked, also rising to my feet. "Um, well, thank you anyway. I guess I'll…head back to Balszt now."

"I regret that we could not be of more help. Please enjoy your stay in the Old Country." He held out his hand and I shook it. Then he turned and slipped into a side door, leaving us alone in the moonlit courtyard.

"I told you not to check out," the desk clerk at The Majestic said cheerfully, when I turned up an hour later. "See? Magrit knows best."

"Thanks, Magrit," I said, happy to be back.

She handed the golden key across the counter. "The room has been freshened up, and it's all ready for you and yours." She made goofy faces at Rose, who maybe smiled at her in return. Or maybe it was gas. Who can tell with babies?

"Where is the Spanish Market?" I asked her. "Is that here in the city?"

"Oh, indeed it is! Fun little district, I can't believe I didn't think to mention it earlier. Of course, it doesn't get the attention that the more major sites do. It's over on the other side of the river…here, I can show you on the map…"

Back in our room, I sat on the bed, opened my blouse to nurse Rosemary, and thought about what I had learned. Or, rather, what I *hadn't* learned.

Had I wasted everyone's time, and a colossal amount of energy, coming here?

No, that couldn't be true. I couldn't let myself believe that. What was Helios going to tell me tomorrow at noon? This reminded me all too poignantly of Sebastian getting a sudden hankering for coffee, then dragging me out to whisper his concerns about Gregorio in a crowded café.

Warlocks and their secrets. Honestly.

But I needed to know those secrets. To expose them. Those secrets were not just ruining my life; they were threatening us all.

Was I ever going to feel safe again?

— CHAPTER EIGHTEEN —

I hadn't thought I was tired enough to sleep, but the late-morning sunlight streaming through my window put the lie to that. "Oof," I said, rolling over in the oddly shaped bed, careful not to crush my baby. "And ugh," I added, catching a whiff of said baby. "Time for a change for you, missy—actually, probably a bath for all of us wouldn't go amiss."

"Surely not for me, too, Mistress Callie?" Petrana asked, from her corner.

I turned to look at her. "You aren't seriously trying to be witty, are you?"

I swear, my golem shrugged. "Do you want me to?"

"I want you to do whatever I ask you to—and beyond that, whatever you want to do." I thought back to an early conversation we'd had, not long after I'd made her. "Assuming you've developed enough to *have* wants, that is."

"You appear to enjoy conversations with people," she said. "In the absence of other people to have conversations with, you could have them with me."

I wasn't sure what to make of any of this. It wasn't like there was a handbook about golems, not about living with them, domestically. Or about having conversations with them. Witty or otherwise.

"Well, the thing I want to do now is bathe myself and this stinky child. You can help me with that."

"With pleasure, Mistress Callie."

We crowded my room's tiny bathroom horribly, even at Petrana's reduced size. But it was helpful to have four hands to control the slippery, squirmy infant, rather than just two. Rosemary clearly thought it was a great game. She giggled and shrieked as we tried to clean her up. It was a good thing I needed a bath as well, because I was soaked by the time we got her sorted.

Elnor watched the whole effort from a safe distance, in the bathroom doorway. Then she pointedly licked a paw and brushed it across her whiskers.

"Yes, yes, I know," I told her. "You are the far superior being in every way. No need to rub it in."

All told, it was a minor miracle that I got us all cleaned, dried, put into decent clothing, and to the Spanish Market by a few minutes before noon.

Helios hadn't been any more specific than just this market, so I was glad to see that it wasn't very large: not much more than a smallish city block. I wandered through the stalls, pretending to be a fascinated tourist—which wasn't hard to do, because I *was* a fascinated tourist, even as I looked around for the young warlock.

Given the name, I'd expected the wares to be, well, Spanish—colorful shawls, tile and pottery, Mediterranean spices, the like. But, no. This market was crammed with such a random assortment of offerings, I was hard pressed to find any underlying theme. A stall filled with used children's clothing sat beside one selling donuts; apothecary herbs were hawked next to an old witch offering tarot readings.

I hesitated in front of this last. Logan had run just such a stand, in San Francisco... I had paused just for a moment, but the old auntie noticed, and caught my eye with her steely old one. "Oh, young witch from the land of the new, with your babe in arms," she said, in a strong, lilting accent. "Tell your fortune, missy?"

"No, thank you," I said with a polite smile, starting to walk off.

The old witch lifted the first card off her face-down deck and thrust it at me. "See her and tell me that you don't want to know more."

It was the eight of Swords: a bound and blindfolded woman, surrounded by a fence of swords stuck into the ground. "I don't, thank you," I said, trying not to stammer. At my feet, Elnor gave a low hiss; I felt Petrana standing stock-still by my side, as though coiled, ready to spring to my defense.

This was a card about being trapped, but within your own illusions. In negative thoughts, the self-doubts that weigh us down in the dark hours of the night. Like so many of the individuals featured in the tarot deck, this woman only needed to step out of her own self-made situation, and she would see improvement. (Of course, someone would still have to untie her. But still.)

Or was that just the sort of thing tarot readers wanted you to think? After all, folks seeking wild-magic advice were looking to be told what to do. And if I was being cynical, I'd point out that it would never serve a tarot practitioner to deliver a message of hopelessness to her customers. "Step out from behind the swords, you will find that you are free." I could almost hear Logan or my mom saying such a thing.

I shook my head and tried again to step away, but the old auntie kept holding me with her gaze. She had never glanced at the face of the card herself, though it was magic of the simplest kind to perceive what was painted on it; probably Rosemary could already do that. Even so, it gave me a bit of the creeps. Had that card been on the top of the deck before I wandered by?

I glanced around again, still not seeing Dr. Spinnaker in the crowd.

The old witch dropped the card on the table and drew up a second one, again holding it to face me. "Oho," she chuckled.

This time it was The Sun.

"Very funny," I said. "Yes, I am looking for a sun, of sorts." And where *was* Helios, anyway? "Cute baby," I added. The Sun card has to be one of the most cheerful in the deck. An adorable baby rides a gentle white horse past a wall covered in cheerful sunflowers, all under the light—and gaze—of a brilliant, wise sun. Abundance, success, joy and happiness; it was all here.

"Methinks your infant is better adjusted than her mother," the old witch chortled. "So say the cards, anyway."

I'd had quite enough of this. *"Thank you,"* I said, more forcefully this time. "But I must go." I dropped a coin on her lace tablecloth and marched on, my golem and cat trailing behind me.

I walked through the market four times, up and down every aisle—even past the old tarot witch, who I steadfastly ignored—and still didn't see Helios Spinnaker. I was about to give up and go find a cup of tea somewhere when I felt a tug on my sleeve.

I turned to see a nondescript middle-aged witch I'd probably passed a few times, and barely noticed. "Psst," she whispered. "Walk with me."

Since I was already walking, I just kept on. Petrana stepped closer to me on my other side, but I didn't feel any threat from this witch. "All right," I said.

"It's me," she whispered, and only then did I look with my witch-sight.

It was Helios, in not only a literal, physical disguise, but also heavily spelled with illusion. My eye had slid right over her—him—without registering. Of course, so many folk here used appearance illusions, I'd almost stopped noticing.

It was kind of brilliant, in its way.

"Ah," I said. "Fascinating. I had no idea it was you."

"Good. I didn't want to make a big production of attracting your attention, especially after you stopped at Wenza's booth," Helios said. He kept his voice low, almost a hoarse whisper, likely both to cover its masculine tone and to keep us from being overheard.

"The tarot witch?" I asked.

"None other. Watch out for her. She's already been banished from most of the city's major markets."

"Really? Why?"

He shrugged, clearly uncomfortable. "Tarot isn't..."

"I know, I know," I put in. "It's not real magic. It's not even ancient, and it's a human thing."

"All that is true. But Wenza, she does something more with it." Helios shivered a little, or maybe that was just his baggy dress moving around on his slender body. "It doesn't matter. You didn't let her do a reading, so that's all to the good."

I didn't tell him she'd pulled two cards for me. I hadn't asked for them, hadn't wanted them; that was all on her.

"Anyway," he went on, "I have more answers to your questions. And you did not hear them from me."

"Yeah, I'm getting that," I said.

We turned another corner of the market, strolling together down a crowded aisle, pretending to consider the wares. "It wasn't always this way," he started, almost too quiet for me to hear. I leaned in closer, as if we were sharing delicious gossip. Petrana fell back a step, but kept up. "Grand Laurel Merenoc is an old, old company, and they've always been dedicated to solving the problems that witchkind faces."

"Like what?" I asked. "What problems, specifically?"

"Any problems. And that's where it went sour, I think. Mostly biological research, of course; tinkering with the witchkind genome is what made us a separate species from humans in the first place."

I nodded, trying not to show impatience. "Yes."

"Anything to do with strengthening our power, lengthening our lives, increasing our resistance to disease—all that kind of thing, that's what the company works on. We make biological devices that automate breakthrough discoveries. And, I can't stress this highly enough, our mission has *always* been to serve and support *all* of witchkind."

He was leading me there, so I saw no reason to be coy about it. "So, when someone like Dr. Gregorio Andromedus, the leader of the San Francisco Elders and an ancient, eminent biological researcher in his own right, who has always worked hard to benefit *all* of witchkind…"

Helios waved his hand in a *Yeah, yeah, get on with it* motion.

I smiled, though none of this was happy-making. "Someone like him could make a whole lot of breakthrough discoveries for you guys to build automation machines for—even if you didn't entirely understand what they were doing. He'd, what, send the specs, and you would construct what he asked for?"

"Pretty much. Of course, Dr. Mar and the other senior researchers would always be interested in what Dr. Andromedus was doing. They'd oversee the builds closely, at least as much because they wanted to figure out what clever new innovations he had come up with, as to, well, monitor whatever his intentions might be."

Well, that was a delicate way of putting it. Again, leave it to the American to be blunt. "So when he asked you guys to build a machine or two to harvest the essence from witches and maybe a few warlocks, and remove their spirits from their bodies, everyone just thought, *Oh, what a clever warlock, what will he think of next?*"

I could almost hear Helios swallowing. "Well. Of course, um. It was never exactly that, er, apparent."

"What did you think those machines were supposed to be doing?"

"I'm risking a lot to even come here, not to mention telling you any of this," he said, testily. He took a few quicker steps, moving ahead of me. I let him, and put a hand on Petrana's arm as she moved forward, as if to detain him.

"I understand," I said quietly. "I appreciate your doing this, and I'm not blaming you."

He walked on, but more slowly. Listening. Cooling down, too, no doubt. Finally, he slowed more, and I caught up with him.

"I haven't felt good about things for a while now," he murmured. "I haven't understood it all—I don't have the centuries of experience in the lab that he does, that any of them do. So at first, I figured I was misinterpreting things. I admired Dr. Andromedus so much..." He trailed off, looking away.

You and me both, honey, I wanted to say.

"I don't know what he said exactly—those conversations happened at higher levels than any I ever got to participate in—but I was given to understand that there is a new syndrome popping up in the Americas. That, because of excessive fraternization with humans, witchkind is in danger of becoming diluted."

My heart leapt in fear at this; it hit rather too close to the bone for me. "What are you talking about?"

"I'm not clear what exactly the mechanism was supposed to be, because of course witchkind and humans can't cross-breed, but that somehow, too much intimate proximity was draining our essence? I don't know, it sounds foolish to say it aloud, but there was a strong sense that we needed to develop the means to measure and isolate essence."

The big wallop of adrenaline was still dissipating through my system. On my chest, Rosemary woke up and started to wiggle around, reaching for me. At least she wasn't reaching for my hair this time. "That, um, does sound pretty foolish, you're right," I told Helios. "What, our essence is just supposed to leak out of our pores or something when we spend too much time with humans?"

He snorted softly. "I don't know. Like I said, I didn't get to sit in on the high-level meetings. But I did participate in building several *enchins* that were able to extract essence. Just for calibration purposes, of course; but it occurred to me that it would be easy to misuse the technology."

"To not put the essence back." I felt sick to my stomach. This very thing had happened to Logan…and in my house. How had Gregorio done it? He hadn't hauled a huge machine into my formal dining room.

Well, he'd done it somehow. And I was going to figure this out.

"Right." Helios sounded as ill as I felt. "And I…" He paused, shaking his head. "I fear that I contributed one of the most pernicious elements to an already pernicious design."

"What did you do?" We turned another corner and started down an aisle we'd been down too many times already; someone was going to notice. I grabbed his sleeve and added, "Let's go this way. Can we just walk down the street? By the river maybe?"

"I suppose," he said, distractedly, but he followed me. We left the Spanish Market and went down a narrow, cobblestoned street. It got quieter around us. He dropped his voice even lower. "It occurred to me that the spirit, the soul, might be in danger during the process of removing and measuring the essence. So I, I," he swallowed, "I designed a device to extract the soul and hold it safe. It looks a bit like a bell jar…"

I sucked in a breath. "The *enchin aberra*."

"Exactly." He shook his head, gazing straight ahead. Even in his nondescript-witch disguise, I could see the anguish on his face. "I was trying to *protect* witchkind. You must understand, you must believe me."

"I do." And I did, so help me.

"I never imagined it would be put to such, such wicked use, and that is on me. I was naïve, foolish," he said bitterly. "Dr. Andromedus was so impressed with my contribution! He heaped praise upon me, and it blinded my eyes to what he really wanted to happen. I didn't even see it."

"He fooled a lot of us," I said, patting his arm.

Helios pulled his arm away from me, almost recoiling. It felt like self-loathing, especially as he went on: "Dr. Andromedus even intimated that he might invite me to study with him in his laboratory in America. I've always wanted to go to America! The Old Country…" He waved his arms around, indicating the picturesque city street we were walking down, the ancient houses crowded together, the trees leaning over the river. "Witches here don't even pretend that warlocks are important anymore." He gulped and glanced nervously at me. "I mean, no offense, but—"

I had to laugh, but I tried to keep it gentle. "No, stop, I do understand. Warlocks have spent so much time thinking they're at the top of the heap…and I say this with all affection and kindness… it's going to be an adjustment, learning to share the world with witches."

He was silent.

I went on, "I mean, what did the warlocks think, letting witches have control of gender selection *and* letting conception become so darn hard? Of course we were always going to choose to have daughters."

"Ma-ma-ma-ma," Rose put in, tapping more insistently at my breasts.

"Do you mind?" I asked Helios, even as I was unbuttoning my blouse and shifting Rosemary so she could reach a nipple.

"No, of course not," he said, but he turned away, his cheeks reddening.

Well, I couldn't worry about his delicate sensitivities. I had a hungry baby here.

Once she was suckling, I tucked my blouse over her as best I could and said to Helios, "So, where are the souls?"

"What do you mean?"

I looked at him. "The souls that your machine extracted. I found a whole room full of spiritless bodies in Gregorio's laboratory building. Witches and warlocks who had gone missing." *And my best friend.* "Dead-but-not-dead, essence *and* spirit drained, bodies mysteriously still alive. Like suspended animation. I came here to get to the bottom of it—and to find the souls."

His eyes widened. "I don't know. To the best of my knowledge, that capability was never used."

"Well, I'm pretty sure it was," I said, trying not to pour too much sarcasm in my voice.

He nodded. "Yes. I see. Er, yes. That's terrible."

"It is."

We walked in silence for a minute while I let him digest the news. It couldn't have been a complete surprise to him, but it's one thing to suspect something awful, and quite another to learn that it actually came to pass.

Eventually, he gave a deep sigh. It was starting to weird me out a little, that he still looked like a middle-aged witch, but oh well. "There's an old building on the Grand Laurel Merenoc property that would be the first place I'd look, were I searching for a collection of lost souls," he said, as if casually.

I perked up. "Oh?"

"It's *very* old, actually; it was the first, the original. When we built the new manufactory, the one you visited last night, the operation moved, but we never tore down the old building. It's used mostly for storage now, but..." He glanced away, at the river. Clearly deciding how much to tell me. "Well, I'd look there."

"Can you get me in?" Before he could answer, I added, "No, Dr. Mar will have the whole property guarded, I'd trigger something the moment I set foot across the boundary line."

"I'm afraid so."

We strolled on. I shifted Rosemary to the other breast; she settled in contentedly. "I don't suppose you'd be willing to pop in and have a look around for me, would you?" I gave him a hopeful smile.

"Calendula, I'm taking enough of a risk already. And only because..." He shook his head.

"You really do want to leave here, don't you?" I asked.

"I don't know what I want anymore." His voice was full of dull despair. "I thought...I'd thought everything was different. But the world isn't at all as I'd been told, as I'd always understood it to be."

I knew that despair. Knew it very well. "I'm sorry," I told him, "I really, truly am—you have no idea. I'm at least as disillusioned as you are, about—well, a lot of things. But I'm doing something. That's why I'm here: I'm not giving up. I'm trying to solve this mystery and make a new life."

He gave a sad chuckle. "You've already made a new life," he said, nodding at my daughter at my breast. "And she gives you something to live for—something to fight for."

"You must have something too," I insisted. "You just, I don't know, haven't figured it out yet." An idea hit me. "So you don't want to stay here, and coming to work for Dr. Andromedus has lost its luster, but Zchellenin and San Francisco aren't the only two places in the world. I passed through a really interesting community in Canada on my way here. Just as an example."

"Canada?"

"Yeah, big country, north of the United States, lots of snow—"

He snickered. "I've heard of Canada, yes. I just never considered emigrating there."

"Well, of course not. That's my point. There's a whole world out there. You had one idea, and it's not working out. That's not the end of the story."

"I suppose."

Rosemary finished nursing. I gently extracted her and covered back up, then turned to Petrana, still ambling along behind us. "Do you mind carrying her for a while? I could use a little break."

"Of course, Mistress Callie." She stepped forward and took the baby in her arms. Rose, already half-asleep, nodded off.

Watching Helios Spinnaker, disguised as a witch, watch my golem, set wheels spinning in my head. I'd already laid glamour and illusion over Petrana before, many times, so she could walk in public without attracting attention. And we were magically connected, could already communicate silently: I could likely rig up a system where I could see through her eyes.

"I have an idea," I said.

Helios turned to me. "I don't even know you—I met you yesterday—but I already know I don't like that look on your face."

— CHAPTER NINETEEN —

It was tempting to try it in the light of day, for the unexpectedness of it, but in the end, I reluctantly admitted that midnight was best. I couldn't afford to lose the power of the night. This was going to be tricky enough as it was.

Fortunately, the remade Petrana was even easier to access and manipulate than she had been the first time around. And we'd been working with each other long enough, and intimately enough, that I found her magical channels a cinch to explore and set my senses in.

Since only warlocks worked at the manufactory, I dressed her in dark robes, bound her hair in a tail behind her, and laid the appearance of a dull, middle-aged, middle-powered warlock on her, then added a big ole deflection spell on top of that. If this worked, the eye would slide off her just like mine had off Helios in the Spanish Market.

If not...well, I'd figure that out when the time came.

"I'm not sure about this," Helios whispered to me. We stood in the woods about a half-mile from the old, original Grand Laurel Merenoc building, staring at my golem. Or trying to stare at her; the deflection spell was working really well.

"I'm not sure about anything," I told him, "except for the fact that if we do nothing, more witches—maybe even more warlocks—are going to die. Or whatever that is, that isn't even death."

He gave a shiver, nodding, biting his lip.

"Just do like we practiced," I told him, encouragingly. "You're taking some expired supplies to put in storage. You carry a pile of boxes out there, put them in the building, leave the door unlocked, walk away. Petrana comes in after you're gone, and looks around, with my guidance. If we find anything suspicious, she either carries it out herself, or she comes and gets us and we decide what to do from there."

"I know, I know." He paced back and forth in the dim, silvery moonlight. "I just…have a bad feeling about this."

"You don't have to help me any more," I told him, seriously. "You've already done plenty. I can…figure something out from here." I was already thinking about just having Petrana bust into the building. She was strong, she didn't feel pain…

"No, I'm in this," Helios said, standing a bit taller. Somehow, he'd reached in for his emotional bootstraps and given them a tug. "Can we check the lines of communication one last time?"

"Sure, but the less we use them, the less likely we are to be detected."

"I know."

But I'm happy to test them again, I sent him.

Thanks. He smiled at me. *And the golem?*

Petrana, please send us both a message, I said.

Yes, Mistress Callie, Dr. Spinnaker. What would you like me to send?

That will do.

I turned back to Helios. "Okay?"

He rolled his shoulders up and down, loosening some tension. "And you're sure the baby won't cry?"

"I'm not sure of anything in life, but she hasn't yet."

"Yeah, I haven't heard her cry all day. That's why I asked—she's bound to get fussy sooner or later."

"No, I mean she hasn't yet, ever, in her life."

Helios gave me a puzzled look. "That's…weird. Isn't it?"

"Extremely weird," I said lightly. "I'm trying not to worry about it, and I really don't want to get all focused on it right now, okay?"

"Okay, sorry!" He gave me a sheepish grin. "I'm just—nervous, is all."

"Yeah. Of course you are. I am too."

"You don't look nervous."

I shrugged. "I've been through a lot lately. Believe me, I'm all jumbled up inside."

"Oh, well, that's good then." We shared an awkward smile, and I patted him on the shoulder.

"Go on," I finally said. "It's chilly; I don't want to stand here all night. Get going."

"Yes, ma'am."

And my golem and a young Old Country warlock I'd met twenty-four hours ago slipped off into the night.

The first thing that happened was a bunch of waiting. I opened my vision to watch the channel through Petrana's eyes, though I didn't want to ride her too much. It took energy, and there was a slim chance my presence would be detectable through her. So I just peeked through to make sure it was working. She walked toward the unused building and stayed hidden in some trees a few dozen yards away from the back door.

Any passive protection wards or spells would have triggered if a warlock, witch, or even human walked across the boundary, but Petrana was not alive, so she didn't register as much as even a deer would have.

At least, that was what I was counting on. If a warlock were actively guarding the building for some obscure reason, he would see with his plain old eyes that something was not as it should be.

So here was hoping that didn't happen.

Mostly, I paced quietly around the little patch of the woods Helios and I had decided was a safe (or safe-ish) place to wait: outside the Grand Laurel Merenoc property, not under open sky, not near any significant ley lines. It was indeed chilly, and I was indeed nervous. If I kept moving, I kept Rosemary entertained and myself warmer, and burned off some anxious energy in the process.

Elnor hated it, though. She wanted more than anything for me to sit down and make a lap. I could tell this by the way she swiped a claw-laden paw every time I passed the rock she was sitting on.

"Sorry, kitty," I said to her, dodging so she wouldn't scratch me again. She was going to ruin my new snaky pants if she kept this up. "I guess I should have left you in the hotel."

She gave a low hiss and turned to look into the dark woods, as if suddenly detecting an approaching bear.

"You could have snoozed on the bed this whole time. But no, you wanted to come along." At least, I was presuming that she'd wanted to, by the way she was not letting me step more than two feet away from her. "Life is full of hardships, and we all have to live with the consequences of our decisions."

And now I'm lecturing to my cat, I thought. *Great life choices.*

I did send my witch-sight to following her gaze, though. I mean, I was pretty sure there was no bear there.

But wouldn't it be inconvenient if there was?

I am heading out to the building now, Helios sent me.

I sprang to alertness. *Good. Keep me posted when you can.*

He didn't answer, which was fine—we were keeping communication to a minimum, after all; I shouldn't even have answered him.

I never said I was perfect.

I see the warlock, Petrana sent me, a few minutes later.

Good. I opened my visual channel to her again, briefly, just to take a peek. Yes, there was Helios, carrying an armload of boxes. He walked up to the front door of the building, shifted the boxes to one hip, and did something with his hands—probably the spell to unlock it—before opening the door and going inside. I left the visual channel, though I *so* wanted to keep watching.

Then, more waiting. A little breeze came up, making me realize how nice it had been when the wind wasn't blowing. Ha, I'd thought it was cold before. I was dressed warmly, but it felt like I was wearing gauze; the icy breeze wasn't strong, but it chilled me to the core.

Apparently that smart witch who'd solved the climate in Balszt hadn't seen fit to bestow the same favor on the 'burbs.

I paced around faster and considered using some power to heat up my core, but I didn't want to waste any in case I needed it later. But I would if Rose needed it. I put a hand on the top of her head, under the little cap I'd bought for her in one of the markets near my hotel. Nope, she was still toasty-warm.

Lucky witchlet.

Mistress Callie, more warlocks approach, came Petrana's terse warning.

What? I opened the channel again.

Four robed figures approached the building's front door.

Who are they? I sent to Petrana.

I do not know.

Stay hidden.

Yes, Mistress Callie.

I watched as they tested the door—finding it unspelled, unlocked?—opened it, and went inside.

Helios, I sent, hoping this wasn't a terrible idea. But he would need the warning. *Four warlocks just walked in. Watch out.*

He didn't answer.

Did he not answer because he was trying to keep a low profile, or because he was in trouble?

I couldn't stand it. I had to stand it. The worst thing I could do right now would be to rush in there and screw everything up. I had to trust that Helios could handle himself, that he knew what he was doing. He worked here; he almost certainly knew those dudes. We had planned for this. He was taking boxes to the storehouse, and storing them there, no big whoop. We'd even discussed his taking stuff that was random and unrelated, so that he'd have an excuse to spend more time in the storehouse, to poke around in several different rooms. He could talk his way out of this.

I paced, and fretted. I just wished Helios wasn't so *young*, so *nervous*. If they confronted him, his guilt would be written all over his face.

Out of my hands. Nothing I could do. I rocked my baby and hummed under my breath. Why didn't I know more lullabies? What was I thinking, having a baby and not knowing more lullabies?

As a distraction, fretting about lullabies lasted roughly four point seven seconds.

I opened my visual channel to Petrana again. *What's going on?* I asked her, as we stared at a dark building in the middle of the night.

Nothing, she replied. *No one has emerged. I have heard no sounds. Would you like me to go inside?*

I hissed out a frustrated, anxious breath. *Not yet.*

Should I send another message to Helios?

Whose stupid idea was this anyway?

Without my consciously having decided to do so, I realized I'd walked a little closer to the property boundary. I couldn't see it visually, but I could feel the energy of the spells guarding the place. I'd searched for them before, and set my attention to remain aware of them.

I stopped, well shy of the border line.

Well, I didn't know for a *fact* that it would alert someone to my presence if I stepped over it…

Yes, yes I did. I mean, not a fact per se, but a more-than-reasonable assumption. Dr. Mar had met me upon my arrival at the company last night, hadn't he? I hadn't even had to knock on the door. Clearly, they knew when intruders stepped onto the property.

It's what any magical company harboring deadly secret crimes would do.

More minutes had dragged by. *Still nothing?* I asked Petrana.

Still nothing.

Helios was in trouble. I just knew he was. I had to get in there and…what? Save him? What could I do against four Old Country warlocks? For all I knew, they were as powerful as Gregorio Andromedus, or even more so. What was I going to do, march in there with my baby strapped to my chest and smite them down with my mighty maternal mojo?

Elnor bumped against my heel. *Right,* I thought. *My mighty maternal mojo* and *my fearsomely ferocious familiar.*

Helios, I sent, before I could talk myself out of it. *What's going on?*

No response.

I took a few steps back, and sent my magic very tentatively out, opening my witch-sight to its fullest, taking the measure of every single magical thread in the vicinity. The boundary spell glowed a dim blue, passive and quiet. It didn't contain a lot of power. I looked more closely at it. Did it repel, or only detect-and-report? I couldn't tell for certain, but it looked just like detection.

I tested it, sending a tiny flicker of magic at it. A thread thrummed, then went still. Nothing sparked, nothing bounced back on me.

Okay, detection; and I'd committed myself, so that's how I forced myself to walk in there, behind my own back.

"Come on, Elnor," I said, marching forward across the boundary spell. I felt its inquisitive magic brush over my skin, and I told myself that by the time anyone came out to deal with me, I'd have found what I was looking for anyway and it wouldn't matter. And that I could brazen my way through—whatever.

As I walked past where Petrana was lurking, she said, "Mistress Callie, what are you doing?"

"I'm going in there," I told her, though it must have been obvious. "He's in trouble and he's not answering." Before she could ask me the same questions I'd asked myself about just what I was planning to do about it, I added, "Stay out here and—guard the entrance."

"Yes, of course, but I believe the danger is within."

Uppity golem.

"If I'm not out in five minutes, then come in."

"Yes, Mistress Callie."

"And if you're challenged—go for help."

"I will."

I walked up to the building, where I spent several precious seconds debating whether to try the back door that Helios was supposed to leave unlocked for me, or just go in the front. *Might as well try,* I told myself, and headed around back.

Locked, and spelled.

"Well, crap," I whispered. Front door it was.

I went the other way around the building, in case there was any other entrance I'd missed, but no luck. Then I was back at the front door. It was much less prepossessing than the current headquarters, more like a smallish warehouse.

I put my hand right over the doorknob, seeing whether I could sense any spells or traps. Nothing. So I opened it and stepped inside, closing it softly behind me.

I stood in a vast, empty space; it looked to be roughly half the size of the building. It was indeed used for storage—I saw old, decommissioned equipment, parts, and stacks of cardboard boxes nearly to the ceiling. Bits of trash littered the floor, and the space was pretty dark, lit only by candles in sconces set irregularly around the huge room.

What I did not see were any people—not Helios, not the four warlocks in dark robes.

I held my breath, listening as hard as I could, but I heard nothing. At my feet, Elnor's nose twitched. "Check around," I told her, and she started sniffing in a near corner. Even in the dim light, I could see her tail sticking straight up in the air and her back arched, her fur fluffed up so that she appeared almost twice her size. Full alert.

I took a few tentative steps forward, keeping my footfalls as silent as I could. When this didn't produce any response, I opened my magical senses, seeking for signs of life in the building.

There: near the back, but it was blurry. I couldn't get a count. They were hiding their natures, and their numbers.

This didn't surprise me; what I found hardest to understand was why they weren't *more* protected. They were obviously up to no good, and Helios was clearly in trouble. But it smacked of typical warlock arrogance for the four to have come in here, not locked the door, and put the barest of shields over themselves.

Kind of like not really warding the property.

Elnor had reached the right-hand wall, or as near as she could come to it, around all the boxes and parts and dead machines. She remained on high alert. "Come on, kitten," I whispered to her. "They're in the back."

She followed me as I walked across the gloomy, dusty room toward a small doorway at the far end. I rested a hand on my daughter's head. She was looking around with wide eyes, keeping utterly silent. As (almost) always.

A faint light showed through the doorway, growing a little brighter as I approached. My eyes adjusted, but I still walked slowly, not knowing what I was going to see through that doorway. I knew I was coming closer to the living beings in here—whoever they were, however many of them there were.

I got to just this side of the doorway and stopped. Elnor took another step, peering around the corner, and went even more rigid than she had been before.

This was not good.

I took a deep breath, swallowed some sudden spit in my mouth, and stepped forward.

The door opened into a much smaller room than the first one, but still fairly large. It was almost entirely empty—no boxes, no old equipment.

In the center of the room lay a very dead man.

I knew he was dead, because of the ten tall swords piercing his back. Pinning him to the floor. Blood pooled around the motionless body. The resemblance to the Ten of Swords tarot card could not be accidental: this was a message. A ritual murder, a most gruesome one.

I knew who he was. It was Helios, it had to be. He was wearing the same clothes Helios had been dressed in. His body was the same size. Who else would it be?

All this tumbled over me in an instant. I stifled a gasp and just stood there, heart pounding, stomach sick. I didn't realize I'd put my hand to my mouth and nose until I started missing breathing. I pulled my trembling hand down and dragged in a breath, and made myself walk up to the body.

Now I could see the side of his head, part of his face; and yes, it was poor Helios Spinnaker, an expression of surprise and dismay forever frozen on his face. "Oh, Blessed Mother," I whispered, bending down to look more closely. "I am so, so sorry."

"Not as sorry as you're going to be, witch," came a cold voice from the far end of the room.

I shot back to standing, nearly wrenching my back in the process (having forgotten the baby weight strapped to my chest) and throwing a protection spell around me, Rosemary, and Elnor with my left hand.

The four warlocks who stood across the room from me lifted their left hands in unison. The one on the end closest to me—the one who had spoken—sneered and said, "You dare to challenge the Iron Rose?"

Then they flung a blast of power at me so hard, it blasted my protection spell apart and knocked me to the floor.

I landed hard on my back, all the wind knocked out of me. Rosemary gave a little surprised *whoop,* but she still did not cry. Instead, she sent me *Strong* again, and then *Bad*.

Yeah, hon, these are very bad guys, I thought to her, almost too surprised to be terrified. Also I was struggling for breath. I guessed adrenaline would come in a minute; right now, all my thoughts were moving in eerily calm slow motion.

The warlocks—the Iron Rose warlocks!—walked over to me. The one who had spoken, yes, it was Dr. Mar, just as I'd begun to suspect. He peered down at me as I gasped like a fish out of water, a look of bored disdain on his face. Then he turned to one of his companions. "Put her in the cellar."

The second warlock reached out with his right hand, and consciousness left me.

I came back to awareness in a dark, nasty, cold, stinky little room. I had a moment of panic before my hands found Rosemary, still strapped to me, and still breathing. A second check told me Elnor was beside me. She was out cold, but also still breathing.

"Whoo," I exhaled, and pulled myself to a seated position. There wasn't much room to move around down here—the ceiling was low, it was a cellar indeed—but I scooted over to the wall and leaned against it, so I could take stock.

Helios Spinnaker was dead, clearly killed because he meddled in the business of the Iron Rose. Because he was searching for the souls that Gregorio Andromedus—and who knew how many others—had extracted from unsuspecting witches and warlocks, after draining them of their essence.

Or killed because he was simply asking questions, raising doubts. Surely they knew. Surely, if the Iron Rose was involved in this essence-stealing scheme, it was far larger and more organized than I'd suspected.

Poor Helios.

So why hadn't they killed me too?

Because they know who you are, my brain told me. Helios was just a young warlock studying to be a scientist. I was…

Who was I?

I was the daughter of a middlingly accomplished new world researcher and a young witch in her first union. I was the *inamorata* (maybe) of the son of Gregorio Andromedus. I was well-known enough in my own community, and a thorn in the side of my coven, but not especially famous or important or anything, even in San Francisco.

I was the mother of a half-breed daughter, but then, did they know that?

I was the witch who'd built her own freaking *golem*…and then *re*built her, stronger and more supple than ever.

With this thought, I realized that far more than five minutes had to have gone by since I'd told Petrana to come in after me—or to go for help. We'd spent at least five minutes sniffing around the first room; something must have kept her from coming in.

Petrana will save us, I thought, sending the words to both myself and to Rosemary. She gave a little giggle—oh thank the Blessed Mother, she was awake.

"Oh, sweetie," I whispered to her, rocking her gently. "You're okay, tell me you're okay?"

Strong, she sent again.

What did she mean by that, exactly? "You're strong? Is that what you're telling me? Of course you are. Or do you want me to be strong? I'm working on it." I knew her words would be limited. I was just glad she had any at all.

And I was so glad she didn't seem to be harmed.

Now to get in touch with my golem. I began by trying to reopen the channel between us, to see out of her eyes once more. But that line was blocked.

I was only a little surprised; Petrana would have severed it prior to going for help, and she might even have been clever enough to cut it before sneaking—or bursting—into the building. Any magical connection leaves a trace of itself, which was how I'd managed to see the boundary spells here (not that that had done me any good).

Ætheric communication, however, was something else entirely. *Petrana,* I sent. *Where are you?*

There was a pause. I almost tried again, but then got an answer: *I have gone back to the city for help. When you did not emerge in five minutes, I tried to enter, but the way was blocked.*

Wow, the city; enterprising. *Okay, that's great. Listen, I'm being held captive, and Helios…met with a bad end. These are warlocks of the Iron Rose, so I don't know how much help is going to, um, help right now.*

What do you want me to do?

I thought about it a minute. I sure wished I knew more about the Iron Rose, about who was involved and what their true aims were. I didn't know who I could trust. Everyone back in Balszt had been really friendly, but… *Can you come back here for now? I don't know who you should go to, is the issue.*

Another pause. *I had thought to start with the helpful desk clerk at The Majestic,* she said. *Magrit.*

She is very helpful, I allowed, *but what if she's a supporter of the Iron Rose? A collaborator?* Stranger things had happened in the world.

That is a good point. I will come back to Zchellenin, and let you know when I arrive.

Good. A noise overhead pulled my attention back to the room I was in. *I'm going to go now—when you get here, don't send me a message; I'll contact you when it's safe.*

Then I cut the connection.

Footsteps, that's what I heard—footsteps on stairs, most likely. I hoped they hadn't noticed the ætheric communication going back and forth. But if they did, would it matter?

I told myself it wouldn't. That in fact they would assume I would seek outside the building for help; it would be weird not to.

That's as far as I got when Dr. Mar entered the room, followed by his three cronies or whatever they were. They had their hoods pulled so low over their faces, they looked like extras in a cheesy 1970s horror movie.

Naturally, I did not speak this thought aloud. I just met Dr. Mar's eyes as he stepped in, and did not get to my feet.

"My apologies for detaining you," he started.

I raised an eyebrow. Beside me, Elnor stirred awake, and moved to sit right next to my thigh, glaring at them.

"My colleagues and I have been discussing the matter," Dr. Mar went on, when I didn't give a verbal answer. "You will be pleased to know that we have decided not to kill you."

"Oh, that's very kind of you."

His eyes narrowed at my sarcasm. "Yes, as a matter of fact, it is. We would be well within our rights to do so."

"You were out of swords?" *Oh, stop it, Callie,* I told myself. *No one likes a smartass.*

Smart, Rosemary sent me.

Trying to cover my surprise, I jiggled her a little, then did my best to smile up at the looming warlocks. "Sorry," I added. "I tend to babble when I'm nervous."

"You are forgiven. But please do keep a civil tongue. Several of my colleagues were in favor of eliminating you, as we were forced to do with the unfortunate Dr. Spinnaker."

I just nodded, making a big effort to keep quiet. But that only made it more frightening. Mouthing off had been a way of venting the absolute panic I felt. *If they wanted to kill you, they'd have done so,* I reminded myself. I petted Elnor's back, trying to let the softness of her fur calm me.

"But I argued for compassion. After all, you are a young witch with a new child, and healthy younglings are rare enough in our society that we cannot afford to be dispatching them every time they stray into our business."

I shook my head. *Nope, you sure can't afford that, nope.*

"However, the question remains: what to do with you?

What, indeed? I wondered.

"You have come here, to our country, to our enterprise, asking questions which do not concern you, showing very little comprehension of our culture and our ways. Despite being a witch, you are behaving as though you were human." He gave a little shake of his head, and was his lip curling up just the tiniest bit? Oh, how dreadful to be acting like a human.

Asshole, I thought.

He couldn't read my mind, but he was surely seeing the expression on my face. "What you will do, Calendula Isadora, is walk out of this building. You will return to Balszt and begin preparations to go home immediately, and you will never speak of what you have seen here to anyone, ever."

Holy Blessed Mother, what? I got to my feet, only swaying a little, grabbing Elnor on the way up. She didn't even squawk. "Yes, absolutely, I will do that. No worries. Thanks."

"And what *we* will do," he went on, as though I hadn't spoken, "is ensure that you will hold up your end of the bargain." Now his ugly old face cracked a small smile. I didn't like that smile. Not one bit.

"What…how?" I asked, my head filling with examples of the dreadful magic that Jeremy and I had performed on Flavius Winterheart. The *innocent* Flavius Winterheart. We'd cauterized his very magic out of him. Had these monsters perfected some sort of…silencing procedure?

Dr. Mar's smile grew. "Oh, nothing that you need to worry about. In fact, soon it will be as though all this never happened." He turned to his cronies. "Come, let us take her upstairs."

Two of the robed warlocks stepped forward, as if to bodily haul me along. "I'm coming, no need to manhandle me," I said, stepping out of their reach.

Dr. Mar shrugged. "Fine. Do not step out of line. You *will* stay with us."

Petrana's voice came into my head, faint but real: *Here.*

I didn't even get mad at her for disobeying my orders. I just sent her an immediate message back: *Stand by. Don't answer.*

She didn't.

We returned to the first floor of the building, continuing down the passageway leading off from the room where Helios's body still lay, pinned to the floor by those dreadful swords. Not much time had passed; his blood still looked fresh, and it hadn't spread much. I swallowed and looked away.

Dr. Mar led me to a small room. In it was a chair, with straps on the arms and a silver helmet-like device at the top. It looked for all the world like an electric chair, except without the electricity.

"What's that?" I blurted out.

The old warlock smiled proudly. "It will not hurt a bit, as the old saying goes. It merely...sorts through your memories and removes particular ones. Particular *inconvenient* ones."

"Wait, what? You guys need a machine for that?" I was so bemused, I almost forgot to be afraid for a moment. Why, I'd fogged a whole evening out of Raymond's mind not all that long ago. Of course, he was just a human, but still.

"We do if we want calibration. Measurability. Precision." He waved a hand dismissively. "This is much more effective, and much more permanent, than just a 'forget-this' charm."

And much more damaging, obviously. Fog could be cleared; a burnt-away memory was gone forever. Now my dread returned. I couldn't let them do this to me. *They're going to suck my memories out of my head with a machine!* I sent to Petrana.

Shall I break in?

I thought wildly. Even a golem was no match for four powerful warlocks. They would just break her, and then return to breaking me.

No! Stay outside. But...here.

In a mad mental rush, I sent her everything I knew of everything that had gone on here. Helios's murder. What this awful device looked like. As much as I could glean from the other warlocks. "How does it do that?" I asked Dr. Mar, both stalling for time and genuinely curious, baffled even. "Does it read minds?"

"Not in the sense that you are undoubtedly thinking," he said, looking proud. "But particular thoughts and emotions make specific patterns in the brain. With much laborious research, and much trial and error, we have found a way to remove particular... subjects, shall we say, from the brain. Particular *concerns*. Then, it is a simple matter to apply spells to cover the gaps convincingly. To write a new story, as it were." He smiled. It was not a pretty smile.

"Why didn't you just do that to Helios?" I kept my ætheric channel to Petrana open, thinking my words at her too, sending her everything I could. "Why did you have to kill him?"

Dr. Mar sighed. "Of course, we did try this route. More than once. But he just kept wondering...kept returning to his questions. Questions which were no business of his. We could not disable his underlying inquisitiveness without destroying his mind entirely—and then he would have been useless as a researcher." The warlock shook his head sadly. "He was just too curious. And you know what they say about curiosity."

I clutched Elnor closer. "Yes, I do."

Behind Dr. Mar, two of the silent warlocks shifted, clearly growing impatient. Wanting, no doubt, to haul me onto that machine and strap me in.

I needed to get more information out to Petrana. "Do you keep the souls in this building here?" I blurted out.

The old warlock looked at me with a hint of surprise on his face. "Souls?"

"The ones that Dr. Gregorio Andromedus stole from dozens of witches and warlocks, when he was also stealing their essence—for whatever nefarious reasons he had for doing that. With one of *your* devices."

"I am sure I have no idea what you are talking about."

"But you do." I glanced back at the robed figures behind him. I didn't have much longer. "I saw the bodies, back in Berkeley. He's stashed them in the basement of the library building, right next to the extracting machine. The one that Helios Spinnaker told me he'd help build. He told me everything."

I knew that was too much even as I said it. Dr. Mar's face hardened. "That is enough," he said, turning to his confederates. "Put her in the chair." Then he looked at me with a grim smile. "But thank you for laying out your concerns so specifically. It will make the process easier."

The two warlocks who had been fidgeting sprang forward and grabbed my arms, one on each side. Elnor hissed and swiped at the one she could reach. He cursed and dropped my arm, then reached back to strike her. I let go of her and she sprang to the floor and darted into the far corner, still hissing. "Elnor! Don't," I cautioned her.

The warlock she'd scratched looked undecided for a moment about whether to go after her or take hold of me. He settled on grabbing me again and glaring at her. Fine. I'd rather lose my memory than my familiar.

Both warlocks started hauling me toward the chair. I resisted, but not hard; I had no idea how I could overpower or outwit them all. All I could do was keep feeding Petrana everything I knew, everything that was happening. *Close down the link when they start,* I told her. I didn't want anything of what they were doing to me to make its way to her.

We were in front of the chair now. They yanked me around and pushed me down into it. I landed hard, jarring my tailbone. "You didn't have to do that," I said.

On my chest, Rosemary gave a sudden shriek. "BA!" It was the loudest sound I'd ever heard out of her. All four warlocks jumped; I wanted to rub my ears, but my two captors were already strapping my arms down. "BAAA!" she yelled again.

"Shut that child up," Dr. Mar said. The *or else* was strongly implied.

"I don't control her!" I wailed. "She's an infant!" If I didn't want to lose my familiar, you can probably guess how I felt about my *daughter.*

"You can speak to her mind," he said, dismissively. "All witch mothers can."

Sweetie don't antagonize them! I sent to her, near panic. *We're going to be okay. Just bear with me.* I couldn't even rock her or cuddle her or pat her head; I was now immobilized in the chair. The warlock goons pulled the headpiece down.

Remember, I swear she said back, but that couldn't have been; she hadn't articulated such a complex notion to me yet, and it was quite unlikely that she would start now. Then she added, *Strong,* which at least she'd said before.

Be strong, I thought, to her and to Petrana and to myself. And even to Elnor, backed in the corner across the room, looking at me—and my captors—with such fierce intensity. If looks could kill, we'd be waltzing out of here right now, stepping over four dead bodies.

But they couldn't, and we didn't. Instead, Dr. Mar went to a panel on the wall and pushed a few buttons.

Then he turned and gave me that ugly smile again. "As I said before, this will not hurt a bit."

— CHAPTER TWENTY —

I had had such an amazing time in the Old Country, I was almost sad to go home. Though I did miss San Francisco, and my house, and my work, and everyone I loved there.

I still wasn't entirely sure why I had decided to come all this way—at such expense and trouble—for my much-needed post-partum retreat. I only knew that it had been just the right thing to do. I had learned *so much*. I would never be the same again.

Balszt is nothing like how they describe. I mean, it's a whole city full of magic users! So freeing; nobody has to hide.

I wished we could live so openly everywhere. Of course, that was impossible, every witch knows that. But I could certainly see why witchkind had established its own country, with its own capital city. Honestly, every witch and warlock should make a pilgrimage at least once in their lifetime.

I'd been told that the natives here were stuffy and closed-off, unwelcoming to visitors. That couldn't be further from the truth. Everyone I met, from the front desk clerk at my gorgeous hotel, to waitresses and shopkeepers all over the city, to the friends I met in cafés and bars and on the street—even this cool old auntie who read my tarot cards in one of the markets—*everyone* was just so friendly! I would definitely be coming back here again.

Maybe even with Jeremy. I smiled as I packed my satchel, bulging now with all the mementos and souvenirs I'd bought, and all the new clothes. I'd tried to keep the shopping to a minimum, but oh, it was hard to resist such fun things.

I was going to have a heck of a time bringing all this back on the ley lines.

Oh well. I'd manage somehow. I always did.

I'd spent the last few days of my vacation getting beefed up for the journey home, taking my special Canadian herbs, resting up. Ley line travel undersea was incredibly taxing. I didn't have a lot of memory of the trip over, except that I'd needed to eat and sleep a lot, before and after. So I did the same now. Not that I needed much encouragement to do that! Seemed like every day, I was discovering an amazing new restaurant within walking distance of The Majestic Hotel.

Though I ate at least half my meals in the hotel's own restaurant. Their empath chef always knew what I wanted. I finally got to meet her in person, three days before I left. "I will be cooking for you strengths foods," she said, patting Rosemary's head and grinning at her. "You and the bébé will need the strengths for your travelings!"

Strong, Rosemary agreed. It was her favorite word. She was as cheerful as ever, and still didn't cry, though I wasn't terribly worried about that. Now that she could communicate with me, there was really no need to. Yes, it was odd, but then, who isn't a little odd?

I couldn't believe it was time to go home. "I could just totally live here," I told Magrit at the front desk, as I signed the invoice. It would all be charged to our coven house, but I had to approve the bill.

She looked at me with a sad smile. "I do hope you return to see us soon, Callie."

"Oh, believe me. I'll be back."

After our business was done, she came around the desk so she could give me a strong hug. Petrana was holding Rosemary, so I could actually hug. "You take care, okay?" Was she wiping away a tear? Gosh, they were friendly here.

"I will, and you too!" I said, feeling maybe even a little choked-up myself.

The journey home was as long as the journey over, but at least this time I knew what to expect. There were the long spans of boredom, the periods of exhausted recovery, the times when my mind sort of drifted away and let the journey happen.

I saw some of my same pals from the trip over: Parson from the Azores, the friendly coven in Canada. But mostly I was just antsy to get home. I didn't linger anywhere, just long enough to recharge for the next leg of the journey.

And then...at long last...I emerged from a ley line and was back in San Francisco.

We were a few blocks from my house; it was the most direct line heading west. I stood on the sidewalk, just breathing in the damp clean air, while Elnor sneezed. In Petrana's arms, Rosemary gave a happy giggle, then said, "Ma-ma-ma!"

"That's right," I said, taking her and rocking her a bit. "This is Mama's city, and your city too. We're home!"

Tired as I was, it still felt good to walk to the house. I barely had enough energy to put a little shroud of indirection-spell around Petrana so she wouldn't freak out the humans. Gosh, it had been nice not to have to do that in the Old Country. Not that everyone had golems or anything—she was still a uniquely weird thing, as far as I could tell—but at least there everyone knew what she *was*.

I climbed the steps to my front porch and paused, testing to see if my wards were still intact. They were; I unmade them and let us in.

"Are you hungry, Mistress Callie?" Petrana asked, as I set my bags down in the front hall.

"Always, these days. I don't know what we have in the house, though—just cook anything."

"I will see what I can find." She headed down to the kitchen.

I went into the front parlor with Rosemary and flopped down on the couch. She grabbed at my blouse, of course. "You're welcome to try," I told her. "But until I've eaten, I'm not sure how much luck you're gonna have."

It didn't dissuade her; she was soon suckling happily.

Petrana returned after about ten minutes with a plate of toasted cheese sandwiches, cut into triangles. "Oh Blessed Mother," I moaned. "How did you *know*?"

My golem smiled, I think (she was still not quite as expressive as I'd have liked). "I know a lot more than you realize, Mistress Callie."

"Do you now," I said absently, around a mouthful. I was *so* going to bed after this.

"I do, yes. And I look forward to sharing all my knowledge with you, when the time comes."

I chewed and swallowed, then grinned at her. "Okay, well, you just let me know."

It was fascinating, how she was developing such a personality. I ought to write a research paper about golems, I thought—not how to make them, there was plenty of lore about that, but about how to *grow* them. To tend them, teach them, live with them. Who ever followed up, after the initial creation?

Something in the back of my mind pinged. Had I read something about this before?

Had I had this thought before?

I shook my head and grabbed another sandwich triangle. "Ugh, travel is so disorienting."

"Yes, Mistress Callie," she said, and went back to the kitchen.

Meanwhile, Elnor was working her way around the house. It had been so long since we'd been here, she had to explore every nook and cranny all over again. "Can you let her into the closet under the stairs?" I called out to Petrana. "I don't think I can get up."

"Of course," she called from the kitchen. "You just rest."

"You betcha."

I must have fallen asleep right there on the couch, once my belly was full of toasted cheese. When I woke up, night had fallen. Rose slept on my chest, her mouth hanging open around my nipple. Her little breath on it was chilling me; I supposed that was what had awakened me.

"Brr," I said, shifting around a bit to pull us up to sitting, and buttoning my blouse. Rose murmured in her sleep as I laid her down on a couch cushion, pulling her tiny fist to her face.

Elnor must have finished her inspection and deemed the house safe. She slept on the far end of the sofa, next to Rose.

Ah, it was good to be home.

I did need to check in with my parents and with the coven, let everyone know I was home and safe, but first, I wanted to unpack. Maybe take a shower. Reacquaint myself with my house, my life.

I got up, gathered my bags from the front hall, and peered back into the front parlor. Rosemary was sacked out on her cushion, but I couldn't leave her there. If she rolled over, she'd fall on the floor. But she looked so peaceful. I didn't want to carry her up to her crib, and I wasn't ready to go back to bed myself.

"Petrana?" I called. "Can you come in here and watch the baby? I'm going to put all this crap away."

"Of course, Mistress Callie."

Upstairs, I poked my head in all the rooms, even though I knew Elnor had been through here. The air was a little musty, but everything was in order.

The shower felt great. My bathroom at the hotel in the Old Country was...minimalist, let's say. And the facilities on the road were, for the most part, even worse.

After I was clean and dressed in clothes I hadn't seen in weeks, I headed up to the third floor, just to look in on my lab—I wasn't ready to start working just yet.

I stood in front of my lab bench, trying to even remember the last time I'd done anything up here. I kept meaning to start an experiment after Rosemary was born, but I just...hadn't. I didn't think. And what had I been working on before my "confinement," as Dr. Andromedus had so charmingly put it?

Oh, right, strengthening our fertility. How ironic, that I should have conceived, and so easily, right in the middle of that research! I laughed at myself a little as I grabbed a rag and dusted off the bench, and some of the bottles of potions and reagents.

One of the vials gave me pause. I pulled it down, and there was another one just like it.

What was I doing with all this blood?

Shifting to my witch-sight, I looked inside the first vial. Huh. Witch blood, and it looked perfectly ordinary, perfectly healthy. The vial was labeled with a sample number.

I set it down and picked up the second one. Different number, different witch; same healthy blood.

Jeez, what *had* I been doing? I couldn't remember this at *all*. I'd have to dig through my lab notebooks—and hope I'd even written down what I was up to (not always my greatest strength as a researcher, I am embarrassed to admit).

Blessed Mother, pregnancy brain much? I thought, setting the vials back on the shelf. Then I went back and opened one of the windows a crack to let some air in here. Dusting had just made the room seem more stuffy and stale.

Then I locked the door and headed back downstairs where I checked on Rosemary. Petrana was still watching her; my baby snoozed on. "I guess ley line travel is hard on baby witchlets too," I said.

"I expect so," Petrana agreed.

I went to the kitchen and poured myself a glass of elderflower wine, bringing it back to the front room and sitting in the easy chair. "You don't have to keep watching her if you don't want to," I told my golem.

She just looked back at me.

I laughed. "Right, you want to do what I want you to do. I'll get used to that eventually."

"Yes, Mistress Callie."

I took a sip of my wine, set the glass on the table, and sent a message through the æther to Jeremy. *I am home.*

I had been wondering! I'm happy to hear that. You must be exhausted?

I am, I told him, *but I just had a long nap and a marvelous shower. Are you busy right now?*

Never too busy for you, he answered at once.

I smiled. *Rosemary and I would be pleased if you would come for a short visit.*

I will be there in five minutes.

I was looking forward to seeing him again. I knew he hadn't understood, not completely, my need to get away with the baby, to go away from everything for a little while. Even so, he had not given me any trouble at all about it. He was trying so hard, I knew that.

He was giving me all the space I needed, even as it must have pained him.

That, unlike anything else he could have done, was softening my heart.

Punctual as ever, I felt his presence approach my front door in just under five minutes. I gave a *don't worry about it* wave to Petrana and headed over to answer it.

"Hi," I said, grinning at him. "Please come in."

He stepped inside and opened his arms, but waited for me to step into them. I did, and hugged him hard, appreciating how his body felt against mine.

"I've missed you," he breathed into my hair. It moved a little, responding to his proximity. He brushed a strand out of my face.

It felt natural enough to lean up and kiss him. It wasn't a passionate kiss, but it wasn't rushed either. Sort of a tentative reaching-out kind of kiss.

He let me go, and I led him into the front parlor. Rosemary was just waking up, rolling her eyes around the room. I picked her up and handed her to Jeremy.

He took her with a gentle, awed smile. "Oh, she's grown so much!"

"Has she? She looks the same to me."

"Well, you see her every day. For me it's been…a while."

"I guess so." I smiled, watching him with her. So natural, they looked. It was too bad…

My thought trailed off. What was too bad? Something was too bad, but everything was all right here. Wasn't it?

Of course it was.

"Do you want something to drink?" I asked.

Jeremy wrested his reluctant gaze from the baby and looked up at me. Love was all over his face. "Er, yes, please. Anything is fine. May I keep holding her?"

"Of course." It melted my heart even more, watching them together. And then I knew why I'd invited him here, what I needed to do. "And sit down, if you like." I indicated the sofa, and took a seat next to him, close enough to feel his warmth.

"Bulgarian frog brandy?" Petrana asked him.

He looked up in surprise, probably at her taking initiative. *My smart golem.* "Yes, please, that would be delightful."

"Coming right up."

She went to the kitchen. Jeremy looked at me and shook his head, smiling. "Truly remarkable, that."

I felt myself blushing. "Thank you. She was a great help on the trip."

"I want to hear all about your trip, actually."

I leaned forward, reaching out to take his hand. He shifted Rosemary so he could hold her one-handed, and looked back at me, a question in his eyes.

"I'll tell you everything," I said. "It was amazing—but there's something I wanted to talk to you about first."

"Yes?"

Petrana walked back in with a snifter of greenish-amber liquid and set it on the coffee table, then withdrew to the front hall.

I looked into Jeremy's emerald eyes, shining with happiness, with love. "I've thought about everything we've talked about, and everything you've said to me over the past—well, almost a year now, I suppose. I care about you tremendously. I may even love you. I think we've been really good together; I love how you look at the baby; I appreciate more than you can possibly know how patiently you've given me space, to figure out how I feel."

His eyes grew more serious and he squeezed my hand. "Calendula, it has been my greatest pleasure to come to know you over the past year. I have never met anyone like you, and I am honored to be in your life in any way you choose to let me."

I took a deep breath, held his gaze, and said, "I've decided I do want to sign a contract with you."

He broke into a relieved, delighted smile and squeezed my hand again, so hard I could almost feel the bones moving around. "You do? Calendula, that's wonderful!"

I smiled painfully back at him, trying to extract my hand before he broke something. "Yes, I think it will be. Of course, I have a few conditions."

Now his smile grew knowing, and even more charming. "I never doubted it. Lay them on me."

I shook my head at his colloquialism; goodness, he was becoming practically American. "Some of them are rather…unusual."

"I would expect no less from you."

I grinned. This was going to be fun.

Has any witch *ever* been so lucky, in the whole history of witchkind?

ABOUT THE AUTHOR

Shannon Page was born on Halloween night and spent her early years on a back-to-the-land commune in northern California. A childhood without television gave her a great love of the written word. At seven, she wrote her first book, an illustrated adventure starring her cat Cleo. Sadly, that story is out of print, but her work has appeared in *Clarkesworld, Interzone, Fantasy, Black Static,* Tor.com, the Proceedings of the 2002 International Oral History Association Congress, and many anthologies, including the Australian Shadows Award-winning *Grants Pass,* and *The Mammoth Book of Dieselpunk.* She also regularly publishes articles and personal essays on Medium.com, including the widely read "I Was a Trophy Wife."

Books include *The Queen and The Tower* and *A Sword in The Sun,* the first two books in The Nightcraft Quartet; *Eel River;* the collection *Eastlick and Other Stories; Orcas Intrigue, Orcas Intruder,* and *Orcas Investigation,* the first three books in the cozy mystery series The Chameleon Chronicles, in collaboration with Karen G. Berry under the pen name Laura Gayle; and *Our Lady of the Islands,* co-written with the late Jay Lake. *Our Lady* received starred reviews from *Publishers Weekly* and *Library Journal,* was named one of *Publishers Weekly*'s Best Books of 2014, and was a finalist for the Endeavour Award. Forthcoming books include Nightcraft books three and four; a sequel to *Our Lady*; and more Orcas mysteries. Edited books include the anthology *Witches, Stitches & Bitches* and the essay collection *The Usual Path to Publication.*

Shannon is a longtime yoga practitioner, has no tattoos (but she did recently get a television), and lives on lovely, remote Orcas Island, Washington, with her husband, author and illustrator Mark Ferrari. Visit her at www.shannonpage.net.

ALSO BY SHANNON PAGE

Novels

Eel River
Our Lady of the Islands (with Jay Lake)

The Nightcraft Quartet:
The Queen and The Tower
A Sword in The Sun
The Lovers Three (forthcoming)
The Empress and The Moon (forthcoming)

The Chameleon Chronicles (with Karen G. Berry, writing as Laura Gayle)
Orcas Intrigue
Orcas Intruder
Orcas Investigation
Orcas Illusion (forthcoming)

Collections

Eastlick and Other Stories
I Was a Trophy Wife and Other Essays (forthcoming)

Edited Books

Witches, Bitches & Stitches (anthology)
The Usual Path to Publication (collection)